MIAMI NOIR

MIAMI NOIR

EDITED BY LES STANDIFORD

Published by Akashic Books
©2007 Akashic Books

Series concept by Tim McLoughlin and Johnny Temple
Miami map by Sohrab Habibion

ISBN-13: 978-1-933354-13-2
Library of Congress Control Number: 2006923116

Second printing

Akashic Books
PO Box 1456
New York, NY 10009
info@akashicbooks.com
www.akashicbooks.com

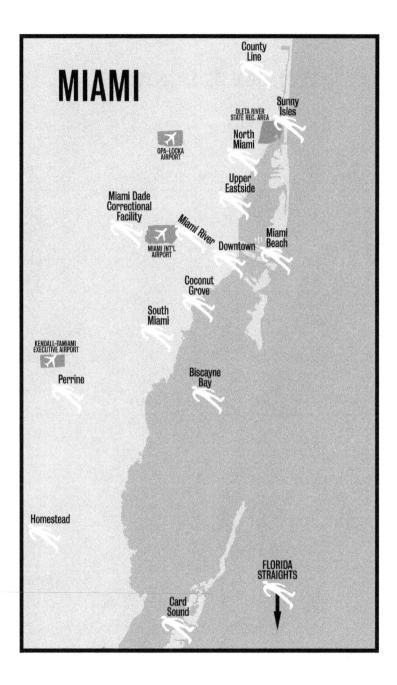

TABLE OF CONTENTS

PART III: VICES OF MIAMI

PART IV: CHASING THE CITY

For the good that I would, I do not:
but the evil which I would not, that I do.

—Romans (Ch. VII, v. 19)

INTRODUCTION
TROUBLE & PARADISE

As both a teacher and a writer, I have often been asked to explain why Miami is such fertile territory for writers who write well and truly of crime and violence and of the dark side of the human condition. Sometimes the question is put out of honest curiosity. Other times, it seems as if there is a challenge there. As if the questioner might have continued, given half a chance: *Why aren't you writing novels of manners down there? Drawing room comedies? Something literary, for God's sake?*

The former types are fine—honest curiosity is a good thing; as for the latter interrogators, they tend to become the models for the victims in our upcoming work. But let there be an attempt at an explanation:

The truth is that Miami, though naturally lovely, is a frontier town, perched on the border between the known and the rarely before experienced. The poet Richard Hugo once said that the natural place for the writer was on the edge, and "edge" might well be the definitive word when it comes to this city.

We are not only on the edge of the continent, we are to this country what New York was in Ellis Island's heyday, what the West Coast was in the middle of the twentieth century. This is where the new arrivals debark these days, and it is no mistake that during the last decade of the last century, commentators as diverse as Joan Didion, David Rieff, and T.D. Allman devoted entire volumes to Miami's role as the harbinger for America's future.

All the flux of a beautiful city where everyone is on the make and almost nothing has quite been settled creates an exceptional place for writers to live and work—and to put it simply, we write what we observe. Once this part of the world has settled down a bit—the tide of newcomers calmed, all the hustlers gentrified, the gators chased away—perhaps our literary output will morph into something a bit more "civilized." But for now, the novel of crime and punishment is the perfect vehicle to convey the spirit and the timbre of this brawling place to a wider world.

Nor is this exclusively a late–twentieth century development: In 1936, Francis Wallace published *Kid Galahad*, a novel of mob-influenced boxing set in Miami. In the 1940s, Leslie Charteris set an episode or two of *The Saint* series here. After Charteris came Davis Dresser, a.k.a., Brett Halliday, and his Mike Shayne series of the '40s and '50s, with such understated titles as *Die Like a Dog*, *The Homicidal Virgin*, and *Blood on Biscayne Bay*. In the 1960s, John D. MacDonald cranked the quality of the proceedings up several notches with the debut of his long-running Travis McGee series, set in the slightly less menacing environs of nearby Fort Lauderdale.

But the true founders of the so-called "Miami School" are Douglas Fairbairn, author of the quintessential Miami noir, *Street 8* (1977), the story of a hustling car dealer up against Cuban zealots, and his contemporary Charles Willeford, creator of the Hoke Moseley novels, which include *Miami Blues, New Hope for the Dead*, and—perhaps my favorite title of them all—*Kiss Your Ass Goodbye*. What Nietzsche wondered about, Fairbairn and Willeford nailed flat out. These two pioneered a kind of writing that so many of us pay homage to: captivating stories rich in character and sense of place, carefully wrought, complex in theme. And what was the question about *literature* again, please?

Veterans of Miami mayhem will find many of their favorite

authors in the lineup that follows. And they will also savor the appearance of several new perpetrators whose dark endeavors will fill the pages of many a novel to come. I was tempted to join in the fun myself, but given the plethora of talent, there seems no need to swell the rout. On the subject of Miami, I'll give my last words to Vernon Driscoll, ex–Miami police detective and erstwhile sidekick of that endlessly put-upon South Florida building contractor Johnny Deal: "Do your worst," Driscoll muses, while searching for his kidnapped pal in my novel *Presidential Deal*, "set off your explosions, spread your gases, litter the landscape with bodies, and when you tire of it all, in a few thousand years, the sawgrass will come creeping back, the roots will split the seams of the concrete, the heat and the moisture and the rot will do the necessary work, and all will be as it was before anybody got any big ideas. Big ideas. Miami. Yeah!"

Until *Miami Noir 2*, then.

Les Standiford
Miami, Florida
September 2006

PART I

EDGE OF THE COUNTRY

RIDE ALONG

BY JAMES W. HALL

Coconut Grove

J umpy was reaching for the door handle to get out when Guy took hold of his arm, saying, "Nothing weird this time. Promise me."

Jumpy took a few seconds to turn his head and look at Guy. "Define weird."

He had a point. It was more than weird already, an oddball pair like them out on a Sunday morning, 4 a.m., parked in a gravel lane next to a boarded-up house, with the orange sulfur lights from Douglas Road flickering like sky-fire through the big banyans. Three blocks north was the rubble and peeling paint of the Coconut Grove ghetto, three blocks the other way the mansions rose like giant concrete hibiscus blooms, pink and yellow, surrounded by high fortress walls, video cams, and coconut palms. The have-nots getting the exhaust fumes from Dixie Highway, the haves taking nice sweet hits on the ocean breezes.

Thirty feet in front of where Guy was parked, standing next to a battered Oldsmobile, two black dudes were fidgeting while Guy and Jumpy stayed inside the white Chevy with the head-lights off. Been there two, three minutes already. Doing deals with fidgety folks wasn't Guy's idea of good business practice.

"The soul train must have a station around here," Jumpy said.

"You're jacking yourself up, man. I told you. You freak out this time, it's over, I walk."

"I don't like dreadlocks," Jumpy said.

"It's a hairstyle is all," Guy told him. "A Rastafarian thing from Jamaica. Same as a crew cut is to you."

"I never did like dreadlocks. It's a gut reaction."

"Okay, so you don't like dreadlocks. But a little fashion incompatibility, that isn't going to keep us from doing our business, right?"

"It looks dirty," Jumpy said. "Unkempt."

"Yeah, well, then let's forget it. Start the car, get the hell out of here."

"You losing your nerve, teach? Get right up close to the devil, feel his warm breath on your face, then you back away?"

"Nothing weird, okay? That's all I'm asking."

Jumpy was 6'4", skinny as a greyhound, pasty-skinned, all knuckles and Adam's apple. Kind of muscles that were easy to miss in that string bean body, like the braided steel cables holding a suspension bridge together. From what Guy had been able to learn, Jumpy had a couple of years of college, then he'd shipped out as a Marine for two hitches, then a lone-wolf mercenary for a while, off in Rwanda and Venezuela, spent a few years in a federal pen in Kansas, now he was on the prowl in Miami. Whatever unspeakable shit he'd been into never came up directly in conversation. Guy didn't ask, Jumpy didn't say. But it was there like a bad smell leaking from a locked room. The man was dangerous, and Guy loved it. Got a little tipsy from the proximity. So much to learn, so much to bring back to his own safe world. Riding the knife blade of violence, ever so careful not to get cut.

Jumpy didn't pump up his past. Very understated, even flip. Guy considered that a form of extreme cool, like those muscle-bound bodybuilders who only wore loose clothes. Tight shirts were for showboat assholes.

Jumpy didn't have to flaunt. There was a halo around him nobody could miss, a haze of androgen and pheromones that could turn a barroom edgy in a blink. Guy had seen nights when the bad boys lined up for a chance at Jumpy, pool cue in one hand, switchblade in the other, one by one coming at him like twigs into a wood chipper. Going in solid, coming out a spew of sawdust.

Trouble was, in Jumpy's line of work, nuance might be a better strategy than overwhelming force. But try to tell that to Jumpy. Dialing back that guy's throttle, even for Guy, a silver-tongued specialist, a man Jumpy respected, it could present a challenge. Not that Guy was morally opposed to violence. In the abstract, inflicting pain and drawing blood was fine. He'd written about it for years, described it in excruciating detail. But putting it into flesh-and-blood action, no, that wasn't his instinctive first choice like it was with Jumpy.

"So we cool on this?" Guy said. "Do your deal and walk. No crazy-ass banter, no stare-downs. Right?"

Jumpy kept his lasers fixed on the two dreadlocks.

"I need some signal of agreement, Jumpy. A grunt is enough."

Jumpy turned his head and blinked. That was all Guy was getting.

They got out and Guy tried to match Jumpy's casual saunter over to the Olds.

The two gangstas insisted on patting Guy down, then after a moment's indecision, they did a hurry-up job frisking Jumpy and stepped away like they'd burned their hands. The tall one went around to the trunk of the Olds and popped the lid.

Guy stayed a couple of steps behind Jumpy while the tall dude, wearing a black T-top and baggy shorts, showed off the Squad. His dreadlock buddy stood by the driver's door watching. His right hand fiddling around his shirttail, ready to quick-draw if things went bad.

Dreadlock One was extolling the merits of the Squad Automatic Weapon, otherwise known as SAW. Eight hundred–meter range, lightweight, just over twenty pounds with the two hundred–round magazine. Talking straight English with a little Bahamian singsong, none of the hip-hop, we-badass bullshit.

When Dreadlock One paused, Guy said, "You want to hold it, Jumpy? Inspect it?"

Jumpy was silent.

"One of you should check that shit, man, we don't want no pissing and moaning later on."

"Let me know when the sales pitch is over," Jumpy said. "I'll get the cash."

Dreadlock One shifted his angle, moving for a better view of Guy.

"What're you looking at?"

"That's what I'm asking myself," he said.

"Do that again?" Guy said.

"Who'm I doing business with," Dreadlock One asked, "man or woman? From across the way, you look like a dude; up close like this, you could be a bull-dyke bitch."

Guy felt Jumpy shift closer to him.

"Happens all the time," Guy said. "It's the haircut."

Guy had blond shoulder-length Jesus hair, slender hips, and sleek Scandinavian features. A man of long smooth planes. Not feminine so much as asexual. A floater. Hovering between the sexes. Some women found him sexy, and just about as many men.

"More than the freaking haircut. It's your whole entire weird-ass self."

Jumpy stepped between Guy and Dreadlock One and said, "Why don't you reach down my partner's pants and find out?"

The second dreadlock cackled, then grinned a big gold smile. "Yeah, Willie, do it, man, reach your hand in there and squeeze."

"I was just curious," Willie said. "It don't matter. Forget it."

"Don't be shy," said Jumpy. "Reach in, take a handful, make yourself happy. Guy's cool with that, aren't you, Guy?"

Willie stared at Guy's face for a few ticks, then shook his dreads.

Jumpy took two quick steps and grabbed Willie's hand, took a grip on Guy's belt buckle, pulled it out, and jammed the dude's spidery fingers down the front of Guy's pants.

The other dread had his pistol out and was aiming at Jumpy, ordering him to step the fuck away from his partner, let him go, stop that shit.

Jumpy released Willie's hand and the man yanked it out of Guy's pants.

"So what am I?" Guy said.

Willie didn't say anything. He turned and saw his partner with the pistol out.

"Put that shit away, man. Put it away."

"So what I am?" Guy said. "Did your field trip enlighten you?"

"Two thousand for the SAW. Five hundred for the loaded magazine. Take it or leave it, no negotiating."

"Two for the whole caboodle or I'm outta here. Starting now. Ten, nine, eight, seven . . ."

"Two'll do," Willie said.

"Hard bargainer," Jumpy said. "Tough nut."

Jumpy and Guy walked back over to the stolen Chevy, Jumpy getting into the passenger seat. Staying there for a minute, another minute with Guy standing back by the trunk waiting, watching, recording.

Jumpy's door was swung wide open, the overhead light on.

The two dreadlocks were talking near their Olds Ciera, but after a while they started shooting looks over. Willie held the SAW in one hand.

Jumpy sat there and sat there and sat some more until finally the head dread came strolling. Dumbass carrying the SAW one-handed.

"You got the bread or you fucking with me?"

"It's stuck," Jumpy said. "Fucking glove box is stuck."

"Stuck?"

Jumpy leaned back in the seat, gestured toward the glove compartment.

Willie leaned in the door, peered through the darkness.

"You got a screwdriver," Jumpy said, "something that can pry it open?"

Willie craned another inch forward and Jumpy took a grip on the padded handle and slammed the door closed on the dreadlock's neck. Opened it and slammed it again and then a third time. Then one more for good luck and pushed the dread out of the way and reached down to the gravel and took hold of the SAW and aimed it out the crook of the open door at Dreadlock Two, who was trotting over with a big-ass chrome .45 in his right hand.

Guy was frozen. It was a freaking movie streaming around him. Every outrageous, amazing second of it. Hand down the pants and all.

The SAW kicked against Jumpy's shoulder. Jumpy fired again over Dreadlock Two's head, yelling at him to drop his weapon. Which he did. Not giving it a second thought, just tossing it into the gravel.

The downed dread struggled to his feet. Jumpy aimed the SAW at his chest.

"So what're we going to have here? Two dead assholes?"

"No, man. Don't be doing that. Ain't no need. We just get the fuck up and be gone."

"Sounds like a plan," Jumpy said. He fired the SAW into the air and the two men sprinted off toward the neighborhood where lights were coming on in bedrooms.

Jumpy got out of the Chevy and walked over to the Oldsmobile. "We got about ten seconds. You coming? Or you want to stay here and get the police point of view on things?"

Guy trotted over to the Oldsmobile and got in.

Jumpy pitched the SAW onto the backseat. Guy could smell its oily warmth. Jumpy must've used nearly forty rounds. Which left one-sixty still in the magazine.

Guy started the car. Put the shifter into drive and made a U-turn.

"Can you use any of that?" Jumpy said when they were five blocks away, cruising down Douglas Road into the ritzy jungle shadows of Coconut Grove.

"Think I can," Guy said. "Yes sir. I think I most certainly can."

Guy dug the little Sony from his front pocket and found the record button and he started to speak into the miniature device. Jumpy smiled and took them south toward the condo parking lot where he'd left his old Civic.

Sirens filled the night like the wails of predatory beasts circling their night's meal.

"What's this mean?" Jumpy held up a sheaf of papers.

He was standing in the doorway of Dr. Guy Carmichael's tiny windowless cubicle. Guy's office hours were from 4 till 6. At 6:15 his evening graduate fiction workshop started and ran till 9:40. At the moment it was 5:30, so at worst he'd have to deal with Jumpy for fifteen minutes before he could claim he had to rush off to class.

"Could you be more precise? What does *what* mean?"

"Okay," Jumpy said. "What the fuck is this? A fucking C minus on my story."

"Did you read my comments? Is there something you're confused about?"

Jumpy looked down the hall, then checked the other direction. He was wearing a white button-down shirt and blue jeans and loafers without socks. Trying to fit in with some preppie image of a college student still surviving from his first fling at higher education back in the early '70s.

"I wrote what happened. You were there. You saw it. This is what happened. And that's all it's worth? Not even a fucking C? What've I got to do, kill somebody to get an A?"

"It's the writing," Guy said. "Not the events you describe."

"On my paper you said—shit, where is it?" Jumpy started fumbling through the typed pages, looking for Guy's tiny scrawl.

Jumpy used a battered Royal typewriter and he whited out his mistakes with big glops smeared across paragraph-sized portions of his paper. Guy admired his stamina, hunched over the tiny machine, those enormous fingers drilling letter after letter onto the white page. Stamina was one thing. Talent was another. Guy had tried hard with Jumpy, made him a special project, devoted hours and hours to one-on-one's in his office and in a bar on Biscayne. But after a minute or two of anything short of unadulterated praise, Jumpy glazed over and slid back into the murky grotto inside his bulletproof skull.

Jumpy found the comment he'd been searching for and put a finger on Guy's words as he read.

"*It's not credible that two such dissimilar men would pair up for such an effort.* That's what I mean. *Not credible.* But we did. We paired up. So why in fuck's name is that a C minus?"

"You have to convince the reader it's credible."

"You're the reader, Guy. You were fucking there. You were fucking standing right there pissing your fucking Dockers. And you don't believe what happened right in front of your fucking eyes? I'm missing something here."

One of Guy's grad students, Mindy Johnston, stuck her head in the doorway and said, "Ooops. Didn't mean to interrupt."

Mindy was a poet, aggressively ethereal. Wispy red hair, enormous breasts that defeated her every attempt to conceal them.

"I just came by to drop off my assignment. I can't be in class tonight. Migraine's acting up."

Guy accepted the paper and told Mindy he hoped she felt better soon.

"Try a pop of heroin," Jumpy said. "Blow that migraine right away."

Jumpy's gaze was fixed on Mindy's bosom. A smile slathered on his lips.

"Heroin?" Mindy said.

"Say the word, and I'll drop a couple of hits off at your apartment. Special delivery. First two are free."

She squinched up her face into something between a smile and a scream.

"That's a joke, right?" Mindy backed out of the office and floated quickly down the hallway.

"Inappropriate," Guy muttered.

Jumpy said, "You got anything going Saturday night?"

Guy drummed the nub of his red ink pen against his desktop.

"Not more gun dealing," Guy said. "I've had my fill of that."

"I got so much shit going on I gotta get a bigger appointment book," Jumpy said. "Name your poison. Something that'll get me an A this time."

"I remember one time you mentioned organized crime. That caught my attention. There's a place in the book I'm working on, I could use some details."

"The mob," Jumpy said. Then he looked around Guy's office at the framed diplomas, the photographs of his kids and wife and two little dogs.

"Might could arrange something," Jumpy said. "I'll give you a call."

"And about that C minus," Guy said.

"Yeah?"

"I'll read it again. Maybe I missed something the first time."

"That's cool," said Jumpy. "Maybe you did."

Jumpy picked Guy up in the Pink Pussycat parking lot at 1 a.m. on Saturday. He was driving a green Jaguar convertible, top down. Chrome wraparound sunglasses and a black aloha shirt with red martini glasses printed on it.

Guy got in, and without a word or look in his direction, Jumpy peeled out, slashed into traffic on Biscayne. Once they'd settled down into the flow of vehicles, Guy smoothed his hand across the leather seat. His long blond hair tangling in the wind.

"Car yours?"

"It is tonight."

"A loaner," Guy said, smiling, trying to get with the lingo.

Jumpy looked over. His expression was dead tonight, maybe he was working himself up, or he was nervous, Guy couldn't tell. That had been his biggest challenge, trying to capture the interior life of a man like Jumpy. Was he constantly on drugs and so blitzed there was no coherent thought rolling through his head? Or was he dumb, just incapable of nuanced feelings or thought? Based on the writing Guy had seen, he was tilting toward the dumb option. Jumpy couldn't string two sentences together without making half a dozen errors of grammar, syntax, or logic. By the end of a paragraph, Jumpy's ideas were so insufferably scrambled, making sense of his story was impossible.

Guy was getting good detail from these ride-alongs, some nice asshole-puckering moments of violence, but overall, Jumpy wasn't giving away a lot about his psychodynamics. What pushed the man's buttons? Who the hell could tell?

After tonight, Guy figured he'd bail on this whole enterprise. He'd had enough of the street for a while. A night or two like the gun-buy last week could keep Guy satiated for a good long time. His wife, Shelly, had no idea what he was up to. But she could smell the fear on him when he returned, the stink of sweat and cigarette smoke and the prickly tang of danger. And she was beginning to make irritable noises.

So after tonight Guy was done. Cash out, walk away with his winnings. Spend the rest of the semester using this brief immersion in the back-alley world of Jumpy Swanson to fuel his imagination for one more crime novel.

He didn't know how Jumpy would take it, him making his exit. Or what quid pro quo Jumpy was expecting. C minus was already a mercy grade. And Guy wasn't about to fudge on his own academic values as payback for a half dozen adventures on the South Florida streets. There would come a day, Guy was pretty sure, when Jumpy would stomp out of his office disgusted with Guy's failure to give him the secret key to the kingdom Jumpy so passionately and unaccountably wanted. Jumpy Swanson, an author? Oh, get serious.

Jumpy headed north off Biscayne into neighborhoods Guy didn't recognize. Residential, middle-class, or maybe edging down to lower-middle. The cars in the driveways were mostly midsize, newer models. The houses were dark, probably retirees or working-class folks who'd had their fill of TV movies for the evening and had headed off to the sack.

It wasn't the sort of neighborhood Guy had been expecting. Though Jumpy had revealed only that his mob friends were eager to meet Guy, a professional writer. Guy assumed the gangsters had the customary overinflated sense of their own glamour and the resulting ambition to have their lives portrayed on the screen, or on the pages of some runaway bestseller.

Guy was always ambivalent about being introduced as a writer. On the one hand, it embarrassed him to be the object of admiration to people who had no inkling what the artistic endeavor was all about. It felt silly to get the little bows of courtesy from illiterates. On the other hand, in an instance like tonight, meeting men for whom crime was a way of life, having some professional connection with the larger world was, to Guy's way of thinking, like wearing Kevlar. Sure, he was a snitch. But it was all in the open, and for commercial, not legal gains. He'd make sure these guys got a copy of the next book, maybe even put their nicknames on the acknowledgment page.

Johnny "The Nose." Frank "Hatchet Breath" Condilini.

Jumpy wheeled into a yard that was crowded with cars. They were parked in every direction: beaten-up compacts, a brand-new white Cadillac, a couple of BMWs, a pickup truck from the '60s. Hard to decipher the demographics, but the haphazard parking jobs suggested the occupants had arrived in haste and under the influence of dangerous substances.

There was a peephole in the front door. A cliché that Guy saw instantly he would be unable to use. The man whose face appeared was fat and his greasy skin danced with colored lights. Guy could feel the throb of bass music rising up from the sidewalk, a beat that was as hypnotically slow and primitive as the heartbeat of a dying man.

"Who's the pussy?"

"I told Philly I was bringing him. He's the guy, the writer."

"What's he write?" the thug said. "Parking tickets?"

"Open the fucking door, Moon."

The door opened and the wall of music rushed like dark wind from the house. Guy waded past Moon. The man was at least four hundred pounds and he moved with a sluggish wobble like a deep-sea diver running low on air.

"What is this place?" Guy spoke an inch from Jumpy's ear but wasn't sure he heard. Jumpy made no response, just led the way across the room.

The living room stretched half the length of the house and through sliding doors looked out on an empty swimming pool and a dark canal. The strobes were covered with colored lenses and Guy was almost instantly seasick. No furniture, no rugs on the terrazzo. Half a dozen mattresses sprawled around the room, where knots of naked people squirmed in the flickering light.

"You brought me to a freaking sex party, Jump?"

The music cut off halfway through his question and Guy's voice echoed through the room. Someone tittered and there was a muffled groan. A second later, as Guy was still processing his embarrassment, the music restarted, something faster and even louder, and the strobes picked up their pace as well. The air was tainted with chemical smells, booze and weed and other compounds he could only guess at.

Guy followed Jumpy over to a makeshift bar, a long picnic table laid out with iced buckets full of longnecks and pints of gin and bourbon. Jumpy mixed a gin and tonic in a clear plastic cup and handed it to Guy.

"Relax you, put you in the mood."

He made his own drink, then held up the plastic cup for a clink.

"To improving my grade," Jumpy said.

"To creating credible characters." Guy wasn't backing down on his values for some quick tour of a sleazy hashish den.

Jumpy gulped his drink and Guy followed suit, *mano a mano*.

Jumpy led Guy deeper into the house, down a long narrow corridor. This was architecture Guy had seen in dozens of Florida tract homes built in the '60s. Three bedrooms down that tight corridor, a single bath. Sliding doors on the closets and hard surfaces in every direction. He had never considered such spaces forbidding, but given the present circumstance Guy held back a few paces behind Jumpy, and started to consider his options for escape.

At the end of the hall, the music had softened to a thudding growl. Jumpy halted before a closed door and tapped four times and a voice answered from within.

Jumpy opened the door, then looked at Guy hanging back. "You wanted to meet my people, right? Get down and dirty. Isn't that the idea?"

Guy felt his fear collapsing into something more extreme. A dark knot of dread. He was not up to this. He felt suddenly trapped, cornered by Jumpy. Conned into deeper water than he'd bargained for. A wave of paranoia rolled and crashed in his gut.

"Philly, meet Guy. Guy, Philly."

The man was bald and short and his stomach was as tight and perfectly round as a bowling ball. He wore striped under-shorts or perhaps pajama bottoms, but was otherwise naked. The room was lit with a vague blue light as though rare mushrooms might be growing in long trays somewhere nearby. It was the master bedroom and was probably half the size of the living room. Its sliding glass door had a view across the canal, looking into the patio of a house where an elderly couple were slow-dancing under paper lanterns.

Philly shook Guy's limp hand and stepped back to size him up.

"This is Mr. High and Mighty? Pardon me, Jump, but he looks like a fucking twit."

Guy was turning to leave, to run back the way he'd come, jog all the way home if it came to that, when a hand touched his bare ankle, the fingers sliding around the knobby bone and tak-ing a strong grip.

Down in the blue haze on the bedroom floor he saw the girl, naked, with enormous breasts. Her wispy red hair was tangled and dirty, and there was a sloppy grin on her face as if Mindy Johnston had finally entered the gossamer stratosphere she was always writing about.

Guy staggered away from her touch and lost his balance. He shot out a hand to steady himself, but the wall beside him moved away. As Guy lurched toward it, the wall moved again. He flapped his arms like a clumsy tightrope walker, and after another moment found his equilibrium.

The gin and tonic was spinning inside his skull.

"You son of a bitch." Guy turned and stepped into Jumpy's face. "What the fuck have you done?"

"Hey, professor, come on in, the water's fine." It was a woman's voice he vaguely recognized.

He turned back to the mattress and saw beside Mindy was Paula Rhodes, a new grad student who'd been struggling to find her place in the program. A bit more mature than the others, a woman who'd written for New York travel magazines and already had a Master's degree. She, like Mindy, wanted, for some ungodly reason, to write poetry. To sing the body electric.

She had risen up to her knees and was reaching out to Guy with her unloosened breasts wobbling and her eyes on fire with some chemical enthusiasm. Around the room, he made out at least four other students from the program, all of them tangling and untangling like a nest of snakes.

"Hey, I want to thank you, professor," Philly said. "You got us hooked up with a better class of consumer than we been seeing lately. I owe you, man."

Moon, the bull-necked gatekeeper, appeared in the doorway. He too was now wearing only his underwear. Saggy white briefs with dark hair coiling out around the edges. In one hand he was holding a silver tray with syringes and rubber straps, and an array of other nefarious equipment that Guy didn't recognize. In the other he gripped the barrel of the SAW. Eight hundred–meter range, lightweight, just over twenty pounds with the two hundred–round magazine.

Moon presented the hors d'oeuvre tray to Guy, poking him in the sternum with its corner.

"A little hit of research, Guy?" Jumpy said.

The walls of the bedroom were breathing in and out and the lights had invaded the interior of Guy's chest.

"You used me. You son of a bitch, you used me to take advantage of these kids."

"I used *you*, Guy? I fucking used *you*?"

Mindy Johnston's hand snaked inside the leg of Guy's trousers, her fingers trickling up his calf. Her voice a swoon.

"Come on, professor. Come on, it's fun. It's so wild."

Guy looked across the canal and saw the old couple still fox-trotting to some melody that didn't pass beyond their walls. He thought of Shelly, his wife of ten years, the way they used to dance in their own living room. Languorous steps, drifting around their barren house for hours at a time.

Jumpy edged to the door, slipping past Moon into the hallway. Moon slid sideways like the bars of a cell locking into place between Guy and the world he'd known.

"Hey, Guy, enjoy yourself, man. Moon'll show you the ropes, won't you, big fellow?"

Moon had stashed the tray and gun somewhere and now had a grip on Guy's right biceps and was injecting some clear solution into a bulging vein in the crook of Guy's arm. The room was bigger than Guy had originally thought. The ceiling was no ceiling. Where the roof should have been, there were stars, whole galaxies exposed, comets shooting from left and right. A cool solar wind swirling down from the heavens.

"This is what you wanted, right?" Jumpy said from the hall. "Up close and personal."

There were bare hands on his ankles drawing him down to the quicksand mattress, down into a pit of flesh and crazy-colored lights, a world he'd written about before. But he'd gotten it all wrong. All completely wrong.

DEAD STORAGE

BY CHRISTINE KLING

County Line

Mama loved to watch those old movies on TV and she used to tell me that since I was born in Hollywood, she'd named me Kate and I was gonna grow up to be a movie star. Like the dumbshit I was, I believed her. But kids are like that and after she left, when I told Daddy what she'd said, he smacked me upside of the head, called me an idiot, and told me that the movie stars lived out in California, not here in Hollywood, Florida.

So I figured that's where she went. I'm not stupid and I knew she'd been hitting the crack pipe, but I figured they got drugs out in California same's here. Sometimes now, I have a hard time remembering what Mama looked like. The last time I saw her she'd got so skinny her elbows looked like broomsticks and her hair had gone all patchy, but I try to push those pictures out of my head. She was gone for some long spells before she finally took off for good. That was when I was ten. Six years ago. And still being a dumbass kid back then, I believed for the longest time that she was gonna come back for me.

Daddy and me been living in this trailer at Pattie's Ravenswood Marina and Trailer Park on a canal by the airport ever since she left. I knew even if she did come back she'd never find me in this shithole. That's how Daddy wanted it. Besides, she was probably out in California getting high with movie stars. Daddy said we were better off without her, and I thought, yeah, sure, you'd think that.

I knew my daddy got some kind of disability check from the government, and when Mama was still with us, he spent most of his days either outside lifting his weights, the sweat pouring off him, or inside sitting in his chair watching HSN or QVC on a little TV he had connected to the cable on the pole. And he'd drink beer. I still went to school back then, and I had some friends and could go over to their houses, so I wasn't home all that much 'cept to eat and sleep.

I used to tell my friends my mama was a movie star, that she was gone lots 'cuz she had to fly to places where they was filming, and then finally 'bout how she'd gone out to California to act in a TV show. We moved before any of her movies come out.

Now, Daddy's got me working in the office at Pattie's here, though there ain't a whole lot to do and he gets my paychecks before I do. Says I owe it to him for rent. Not like he buys us much food around here. We pretty much live off Corn Flakes, powdered milk, mac 'n' cheese, and the occasional catfish I catch in the canal. He's got an old Chevy pickup that he drives down to Flossie's Bar sometimes. That's when I like it here. Nights when he's gone and it's quiet and I can pretend he ain't never coming back. I pretend I'm going to take a taxi to the airport, get on an airplane for Hollywood, California, go find Mama, and become a movie star. But he always comes back. And if he ain't too drunk, he always comes to me.

The first time, I was missing Mama so much and I cried happy tears when he come in and hugged me and touched me and told me he loved me. It seemed like the first time in my life he wasn't calling me stupid. And then all of a sudden it was like, what the hell, and he shoved his finger up inside me. I was only ten and just this dumbass kid who didn't know what the fuck was going on, but he was my daddy and he was telling me he loved me and I would like it, so what was I supposed to do? We was already living at Pattie's then, and outside the trailer window there's these tall poles in the distance with red flashing lights for the airport, and I just watched them, trying not to smell his breath, and counted how many times they flashed until he climbed off me. One hundred ninety-seven flashes.

We'd moved to Pattie's when Daddy got the job managing the dead storage yard. If you wanted to use your boat pretty much, you put it up in the stacks and Fred over on the other side of the basin drove the forklift and slid your boat out of its parking slot in that four-story beehive. But some people had boats and they just never used them. They had broken motors, holed hulls, peeling paint, and all kinds of palmetto bugs crawling all over them. They ended up with Daddy in the dead storage yard. The rent was cheaper. Daddy showed them where to park their crappy old boats and then they paid him their rent and they never come back for months and months. Some of them never come back at all, seemed to me. I saw boats go into that yard, but I hardly ever seen any come out.

The boats in the marina, most of them didn't look much better than the ones in dead storage. Some had people living on them and they had so much crap piled on their decks, it was like Pattie's was some kind of big shit machine. You'd get up in the morning, and it seemed like there were more old tires and rusty boat parts and broken beer bottles than there had been the day before. Shit just came out of nowhere.

About half the trailers in the park were boarded up and abandoned. On one side of us there was this old guy. Daddy called him Bud and he just sat out on his concrete slab and drank beer every day till he passed out. He was deaf and he'd never wear his hearing aids, so even if you did try to talk to him, he couldn't ever hear a goddamn thing you were saying.

On the other side, the trailer had sat empty for a couple of months ever since old Mrs. Jackson died. I noticed her cat was squalling one day and it didn't smell too good over there, but I could hear the TV was on inside. She give Daddy a key to her place one time so's I could feed the cat when she went to see her daughter. I got the key and called out her name, but she didn't answer so's I went into her trailer to see what was wrong. She'd died on the crapper in her nightgown with her big cotton panties down around her knees. She'd pitched forward and I found her with her neck bent sidewise on the floor, her eyes open, and her huge fat naked ass sticking up in the air in the doorway of the trailer's little head compartment. I didn't even like to look at her trailer no more and Daddy was talking 'bout moving it into dead storage. What was the point? The whole fuckin' place had become dead storage.

That's why I was surprised when I got up Saturday morning and saw a truck in front of old Mrs. Jackson's place and some men was carrying out all the old crap and taking some nice new furniture inside. That's when I seen Daddy out there wearing jeans and a wife beater, leaning against his pickup and talking to this short redheaded lady who was holding old Mrs. Jackson's cat, which I ain't seen since the morning I found the old lady dead. Somebody said it was Mrs. Jackson's daughter what took the cat, and I wondered if that was her outside talking to my daddy.

When I went out there, I guess the short lady didn't hear me walk up 'cuz she flinched like she'd been snake bit. The cat jumped to the ground and run off.

"Oh! Child," she said. "Don't go sneaking up on people that way. You gave me a fright." Her voice sounded squeaky as a cartoon character on the TV.

Standing next to her like that, I got the full effect of just how short she was. I could look down on the top of her head and see a line of pink scalp and about an inch of gray hair at her roots.

"You Mrs. Jackson's daughter?" I asked.

Daddy shook his head and said, "Sorry, ma'am. She's got no manners. I try to teach her but it just don't stick. This here's my daughter Kate. Kate, this is Mrs. Murphy."

The redheaded lady put out a hand the size of a little kid's.

She was old, though, lots older than Daddy, and heavy makeup was caked on her face, but she probably didn't weigh no more'n a hundred pounds. When I reached out to shake her hand, she looked scared, like she thought she might catch something.

"Hello," I said. Her palm was squishy with sweat and she yanked her hand back after one pump. She wore these fake eyelashes like you buy at Walgreens for $6.99. They fluttered at me when she tried to smile.

Daddy said, "Mrs. Murphy's gonna move into her mama's trailer. She'll be our new neighbor."

For such a little lady, Mrs. Murphy had a good-sized rack on her, and with her low-cut blouse Daddy couldn't take his eyes off her titties. He kept on talking to her and she kept on backing up, her hands messing with the buttons at the top of her blouse. When her ass hit the side of her trailer, she scooted inside and disappeared.

Daddy sat down at his weight bench and told me to go in and fix him some cereal.

Over the next few weeks I barely ever saw Mrs. Murphy. She mostly stayed inside her trailer, only coming out a few times to drive her little Ford Taurus to the Winn-Dixie to get her some groceries, and even when she done that, she nearly run out to her car like she thought somebody outside was gonna jump out and grab her. One time when she come home in her car, Daddy went over and offered to help carry her groceries but she shook her head no, and she carried those bags up high so's to cover her chest and her face and she run into her trailer. Daddy laughed out loud.

I seen it all from the windows in Pattie's Marina office where I went to answer the phones and take folks' rent checks and mostly just watch TV or jaw with Fred and Pattie. Sometimes I read books. Pattie had a whole bunch of paperback books that folks had left in the office and most of them were pretty good.

They were stories about detectives and spies and shit like that. Beat the crap out of watching *Days of Our Lives* with Pattie.

After she'd been living there about a month, Mrs. Murphy come into the office one day to pay her rent. Pattie'd gone out to her boat to sleep off last night's Jack and Coke and Fred was over running the forklift for some Miami hotshot. It was just me and her.

"Hey," I said when she walked in. She didn't say nothin' but just pulled her checkbook out of her little handbag and started writing out the check.

"How d'ya like living here at Pattie's, Mrs. Murphy?"

"Okay, uh, Kate, was it?"

"Yeah. Like the movie star, Kate Hepburn."

"I'm surprised someone your age would know about her."

"I'm not stupid, you know."

"Oh dear, I didn't mean to say that you were."

"Mama used to say I have a active imagination."

"I'm sure you do, Kate," she said, but she turned away when I looked up at her from the receipt book where I was writing in the number of her check. She had a look on her face like she just tasted milk that had turned.

"You sure do stay in your trailer lots. You don't work?"

"Well, I did. I'm an administrative assistant," she said, like I knew what that was, "but I'm currently between positions."

"What's that mean?"

She blinked her eyes real fast and those fake lashes looked like moths that just been hit with bug spray. "It means," she said, and her voice sounded funny, even for her. "It means that I got laid off." She was stuffing her checkbook back into that little purse of hers and then she zipped the pocket closed like she thought I was gonna reach across the counter and snatch it away from her. "I still have trouble believing it. Four years short of earning a pension. They said I wasn't quick enough, but that really means they think I'm too old." She started crying for real and dragged out that word "old" like it had about sixteen letters.

"I'm sorry, ma'am." I wished I knew what to say. I hated her crying like that. It was goddamn irritating.

"And I keep sending out resumes and the unemployment is going to run out soon. I sold my condo and I'm reduced to living alone in this place." She looked up at the ceiling like she thought it was gonna just cave in on her that minute, then she snorted up the snot that had started to drip out her nose. I handed her a paper towel from the roll Pattie kept behind the desk.

"Well, Mrs. Murphy," I said, "living here sure must be lots different from a fancy condo."

She rolled her eyes. "Don't I know."

"Pattie's Trailer Park's not exactly what you'd call a good neighborhood. I hope you got plenty of locks on that trailer of yours, 'cuz a pretty little lady like you—"

"What are you talking about?"

"Must make you pretty scared living in a place like this all alone with no one to protect you."

"Yes, yes, it does. But it sounds like you know something. Has something happened?"

"You haven't heard?"

"Heard what? What are you talking about?"

"You ain't heard about the rapist?"

Her eyes grew big and those lashes quit twitching. "Rapist?"

"Yes'm. I figure I better warn you."

"Around here? Close by?"

"Yes'm. They're calling him the Trailer Park Stalker in the papers."

"Oh my Lord."

I looked down at the greasy countertop, leaned in closer to her, and spoke quiet. "Happened to me. Daddy was down at Flossie's. He come into the trailer late at night and climbed on top of me and, well, you know. There weren't a thing I could do. He's too strong."

"Oh, you poor child."

"I wished I'd a had a gun or something. I would'a killed him," I said, and I meant it.

"Yes," she said. "I've been thinking about that. Getting something for protection."

I shrugged.

"It must have been so terrible for you. It's no wonder you dress like that now."

"Like what?"

"Those clothes—they're men's clothes. Those big T-shirts and jeans, and that hair of yours. You know, if you got it cut in a stylish way instead of that mop of snarls, and got your teeth fixed to close up that gap, why, you'd be pretty."

"Mrs. Murphy, I don't give a shit about pretty."

It was about two weeks later, when I was walking over to the office on my day off to get another book to read, that Mrs. Murphy's door opened a crack and she whispered, "Kate, pssst. Kate."

When I got to her door, she opened it and pulled me in, slammed the door, and locked it. The inside of the trailer was different now. It was all clean and neat and the furniture looked like it was new and bought all at the same time. There was curtains on the windows with bright yellow sunflowers on them. Against one wall, she had these shelves that looked like miniature boat stacks, but inside each little box was an old-timey doll in a pretty dress.

"Nice place," I said.

Mrs. Murphy sat down on a couch cushion that was wrapped up in some kinda plastic and patted the seat. "Sit down, Kate, and talk with me for a while. I could use a little company."

I sat and kept my hands to myself. There was too much stuff in that trailer. I was afraid I'd break something.

"How have you been, dear?"

"All right, I guess."

"You don't go to school?"

"Not since I turned sixteen. My daddy says I had enough school."

"I see. Your daddy says, huh." She crossed her arms over her chest.

"My daddy likes you," I said.

"Oh," she replied, and she wiggled her butt on the plastic and it made crackling noises.

"He hasn't been with a woman since Mama left. He was all broke up about that."

"What happened to your mother, Kate?"

"She went out to California to work in the movies. She sent for me and I was gonna go out there too, but then we heard she was dead."

"Oh dear, what happened?"

"She was murdered. Stabbed sixteen times in her own bed."

Mrs. Murphy sucked in her breath so hard she started coughing. I got up and got her a glass of water.

"Thank you," she said, and she drank the whole glass. When she put it down, her hands started fussing with the buttons on her blouse and the whites of her eyes looked extra bright.

"Remember what I told you last time, you know, about what's been happening around here?"

She nodded.

"I heard he attacked another woman over in the Shady Palms Trailer Court. This one almost died. Daddy said he hoped you could protect yourself 'cuz he sure wouldn't want to see anything like that happen to you."

That night after dinner when he was about a six-pack and a half down, he brought it up. Daddy come to the door of my room and said he seen me go into Mrs. Murphy's trailer.

"I want you to stay away from that woman," he said. "You got no business going over there."

I was lying on my bed reading one of Pattie's books. It was about a private detective named Elvis out in Hollywood, California. "She was only being nice to me, Daddy. We just talked. She don't have no friends."

"She sure as hell don't need a dumbass kid like you hanging around bothering her, probably telling her all kind of lies."

"I'm not stupid, Daddy. Wish you'd quit calling me that. Leastwise I don't sit around all the time drinking beer and slobbering over stuff I can't even buy on the Home Shopping Network."

It only took him two steps to cross my room and backhand me across the mouth. "Shut up. You think you're so smart reading your books now. But that don't change nothing. Your mama was a crackhead whore and you ain't gonna be no different."

He left to go to Flossie's after that and I turned off the TV and sat in the quiet night reading my book under the lamp, pretending it was me in the book, out in Hollywood, California, hoping he wouldn't never come back, but knowing he would. I was in bed when he come in and, one more time, I watched the red blinking lights at the end of the runway and held my breath as I floated up out of my body and counted. One hundred thirty-six flashes.

After that, I done my best to listen to Daddy and stay away from her. Shit, it weren't no fun getting hit. Avoiding her wasn't no big deal because she started going out and staying out for hours in the afternoons. Daddy said he wondered if she found herself another job because when she went in and out, she was carrying a black zipped case hugged to her chest.

One afternoon a couple of old boys come into the office and said they wanted to store their broke-down airboat in the dead storage yard till they could order a new engine for it. They both had shaved heads and yellow teeth but one of 'em had a gut on him that stuck out and hung low over the front of his belt. The other one wore cutoff jeans and a T-shirt about two sizes too small stretched tight cross his chest muscles with the sleeves cut out to show off his guns. They both smelled like beer and the one in the cutoffs leaned over the counter and told me that he knew of something he'd like to stick in that gap in my teeth. I went out the back door of the office and hollered for Daddy. When he come into the office, he hit it off with these two and invited them to go back to our trailer for a cold one before he opened the gate to the yard.

They'd been at it most of the afternoon, all three of them drinking beers and leaning on the old boy's boat trailer, when Mrs. Murphy come driving up in her little Taurus. The sky had turned light blue and the last rays of sun was slanting across the boat basin. I'd stayed in the office way past quittin' time when Pattie and Fred had all left. I told them that I had some stuff to finish and I wanted to pick out another book, but in fact I knew better than to show my face anywhere near what was going on out there in the yard. Mrs. Murphy didn't have no choice, though, since she couldn't get her car past their truck and trailer that was parked in front of the gate to the dead storage yard.

She stopped her car in front of Bud's trailer and got out, holding that black case so tight she was squishing her own boobs. Them boys was on her before she took two steps.

"Yeeuuii," the muscled one said. "Looky here, Franky. We seem to be blocking this lady's way."

"Shit, Jimmy, would you look at the tits on her?" the fat one said. He moved up close like he was gonna touch one.

Daddy just leaned there against the trailer watching 'em, his eyes half closed and a smile on his face.

The muscled one was trying to stand in her way like a foot-ball player ready to tackle, and she was pulling at the zipper on that bag of hers. Even in that low light I could see those eye-lashes outlined against her white skin—not moving. Then she got her hand into the bag and she faked right, then ran left. The old boy got his legs tangled and fell and Mrs. Murphy run into her trailer and slammed the door before his fat buddy could help him up off the ground.

They was still laughin' and jokin' when the three of them backed the airboat trailer into the dead storage yard and then took off for Flossie's.

I never did turn on any lights. I just sat by the window and watched her trailer. Every few minutes the sunflower curtains moved aside and even though I couldn't make it out in the dark, I imagined those lashes blinking at the night, her hand inside that black bag, and I knew where she'd been all these afternoons she'd been away.

I went to bed when her last light went out and I lay there waiting for Daddy. He come in just past 2:00, and as usual I heard him whispering curses and bumping into things in the front room of the trailer. He couldn't come home quiet when he was drunk. Didn't matter if it was the first time or the last time, though, I always felt the same when I heard him coming. Every muscle in my body tightened up and it seemed like somebody'd sucked all the air out of the room and the saliva in my mouth started to taste real sour. I heard the noise of his zipper, then he yanked off my covers, rolled me onto my belly, pulled off my panties, spread my legs, and kneeled back there lifting my butt up and jamming himself inside me, over and over.

It hurt. It always hurt, but this time I couldn't see my red lights, I couldn't leave my body, I couldn't do nothin' but scream into my pillow.

I waited till I heard the snoring start in the other room, then I got up and washed myself and put on a clean nightie and pair of panties. I didn't have to turn on the light in the kitchen to find the key. I stopped for a minute in the doorway to his room and watched him sleep. He had passed out on his bed, one shoe on, the other'd fallen on the floor. His jeans was still unzipped, and since he never wore no underwear, I could see the dark shadow at his crotch.

I thought about Mama and the movie stars out in Hollywood, California. I couldn't find any picture of her in my head no more. I tried to remember what it felt like when she touched me, and I couldn't find that neither.

He caught his breath and coughed on a snore when I grabbed his shoulder and shook him.

"Daddy! Daddy, wake up. I heard something, Daddy."

He groaned and tried to push me away.

"Daddy, wake up. There's a man out there. He broke into Mrs. Murphy's trailer."

I helped him to his feet and buttoned his pants for him.

"Kate, what you saying? You seen what?"

"Daddy," I said as I helped him to the door to our trailer. "I seen a man nosing around Mrs. Murphy's place. You better go see if she's okay." I pressed the key into his hand and he started across the dirt toward her trailer.

It was only a few steps from my bed to the front door. The trailer wasn't big, not like the movie star mansions out in California, but it was home. I wondered, as I crawled under the covers, if Pattie'd give me his job. Then I tipped my head so's I could see the lights on the tower, and I started counting. Fifty-nine flashes. Six shots.

SILENCE OF THE STONE AGE

BY GEORGE TUCKER

North Miami

T he moment he saw Eustace Green, Dr. Vernon Lemaistre knew his job interview wasn't going to work out as planned. Green, dressed in his trademark sleeveless flannel shirt and battered jeans, stood next to a man with a leonine halo of hair and academic loafers. Was it too late to walk away?

The crowd pushed past Vernon, heading for craft booths lined up like boxcars in the thin shade of the Australian pines. A breath of air fluttered the white vinyl banner:

WELCOME TO THE BISCAYNE BAY UNIVERSITY

PALEOLITHIC POWWOW

Vernon wiped beads of sweat from his forehead. Why Green, why here, in Out of the Way University, Miami? Last he'd heard, Green had a cushy endowed chair somewhere in Massachusetts.

You simply didn't see him, Vernon told himself. Like many academics, Vernon was familiar with the application of tactical ignorance. He turned away to search for Dr. Wallace Mackenzie. The interview wasn't officially till tomorrow, but he wanted to make a good impression today. I have the best years of my career before me, Vernon told himself. I have a lot to offer this university. He had a page with several other affirmations folded in the breast pocket of his jacket—and with Eustace Green around, he felt pretty sure he'd need them.

"Vernon!" That familiar gravelly boom.

Too late. Vernon groaned, turned, tried to rearrange his face into something like a greeting.

"The woods are just full of old friends and acquaintances today," Green said. He offered his hand, which, after a moment's hesitation, Vernon took. Eustace's knuckles felt like steel ball bearings wrapped in leather.

"Quite a surprise," Vernon said. He smiled at the loafered man and then asked Eustace, "How are you?"

"Full of piss and vinegar as ever," Eustace said. "Wall, meet Vernon Lemaistre."

"Dr. Lemaistre?"

To Vernon's dismay, Eustace and Dr. Wallace Mackenzie, he learned, went way back. Grad school at Cornell. Shovel-bummed around the continent together. Vernon waved at a swarm of gnats that seemed to be attracted to either his sweaty face or his rigid smile.

"So, you here for the festivities? Going up against the world atlatl champ this afternoon?" Green said.

"Yes—uh, I always try to . . ." Vernon said.

"Dr. Lemaistre's applying for our opening," Wallace said. "The interview's scheduled for tomorrow. Right after yours, Eustace."

Vernon froze. Eustace grinned at him. "Reckon I'll see you in the lobby, then."

Vernon excused himself and wandered away through the crowd. What the hell was Eustace doing here? Applying for the opening—was that a joke? Eustace Green was the reason Vernon needed this job. They'd both been struggling post-docs interested in lithic tech, Stone Age weaponry. Vernon had dis-covered the true nature of the atlatl, an ancient spear-throwing device that was little more than a stick with a notch on the end. Eustace helped him refine his theories and offered encourage-ment, an occasional insight. And then Eustace published everything under his own name and never returned another of Vernon's phone calls.

Now Eustace had an endowed chair at Blueblood U somewhere in Massachusetts, while Vernon held a sufferance post at Lake Okechobee Community College where he taught five introductory classes each semester. He lectured to students who thought evolution was a leftist conspiracy. He worked far too hard to do the kind of research that'd lead to a better job—banished for eternity to the fringes of academia and archaeology.

He watched Eustace saunter through the crowd carrying his atlatl. The forearm-long piece of wood had been used by ancient mankind for millennia to launch slender arrow-like darts at their prey. Archaeologists had discovered hundreds of atlatls with odd stones—"banner stones"—attached to them, presumably as good-luck charms. Vernon had proven that the banner stone kept the atlatl from vibrating from the force of a throw, acting as a Stone Age silencer. Archaeologists theorized that only a heavy, rigid spear would have sufficient momentum to bring down an animal. Vernon and Eustace put the lie to that theory by proving that a slender, flexible dart was much more efficient.

Go on, Vernon told himself, talk to him, ask him to put in a good word for you—why would he want this job anyway?

Not far from the booths and the milling crowd, a long strip of lawn had been set up with hay bales and tacked-on paper targets fluttering in the faint breeze. Along the side, propped-up white signs ticked off the distance from the target: 50, 100, 150.

Eustace nodded to him. "Need to warm up for this afternoon," he said.

Vernon's own atlatl—a fine Nanticoke he'd made himself—and two four-foot-long darts lay in the trunk of his dusty gray car. He'd thought of participating in the atlatl throw himself—thought it'd be worth a few brownie points with Mackenzie, show off his skills with the tools of his trade—but if Eustace planned to join the contest, there wasn't much chance of winning.

Vernon watched Eustace settle his dart along the atlatl. "You really here for this job?"

Eustace glanced at him. "I miss the Everglades," he said. "Nothing like 'em up north."

"But it's only an assistant professorship." Vernon tried to keep from whining. "Wouldn't that be a big step down?"

A shrug. Eustace turned to the distant target and flung the dart downrange with barely a hiss. Despite everything else, Vernon still felt vaguely amazed when he remembered he'd been right about the banner stone's function.

"Why'd you do it? Why'd you take all our work and publish it as your own?" Vernon asked. A question he'd wanted to put to Eustace for so long—but the words just fell out of his mouth. Not at all the delivery he'd imagined.

Eustace looked at him. "The fact that you're asking that question should be answer enough."

In that moment, all Vernon's disappointment and outrage blazed like a lightbulb filament in his brain—he hated Eustace Green more than he'd ever hated anyone, would've gouged those narrow black eyes out with his thumbs and . . . Eustace raised a bushy eyebrow at him. Then deliberately turned his back on Vernon and strolled toward the target.

Vernon followed him, his mind white-hot and completely empty. He watched Eustace put a filthy sneaker against the hay bale and tug the dart. The wooden shaft slid free but the stone point remained stuck.

"Goddamnit," Eustace said.

"Can you at least give me a good recommendation?" Vernon said, and hated himself for asking.

Eustace walked away laughing. Vernon stood beside the target, fists clenched, took long deep breaths until his heartbeat eased. He turned to the hay bale and used the blade of his Swiss Army knife to work Eustace's arrowhead free. The onyx point gleamed black in the bright sun. Vernon remembered how particular Eustace was about his tools—perhaps it would make a good peace offering.

Vernon stepped up to the white chalk line drawn across the clipped grass. Even with his glasses on, the paper targets 150 yards downrange seemed pitifully small. An Ice Age tree sloth, he thought, or a cave bear—those would be proper targets. This was a bad joke.

The crowd, clustered off to his left, rustled and coughed its impatience. Hurry up. All his back-and-forth mental debate about whether or not to deliberately lose the competition to Eustace seemed ludicrous. He hoped he didn't look like a silly stoop-shouldered academic to the crowd.

He balanced his dart on the atlatl, stepped, and threw. At the top of his arm's arc he felt a muscle, something small and vital, let go in his shoulder and he shouted—the sound halfway between a karate battle cry and a yelp.

Vernon tucked the atlatl under his arm and rubbed his shoulder to scattered applause. He squinted downrange and saw his dart sticking out of the extreme upper-right corner of the stacked hay bales. No less than six feet from the edge of the paper bull's-eye. He felt his face burn and turned away, headed for the crowd. He used to be good, back when he practiced weekly in an empty field along Harp Creek, back when he and Eustace e-mailed one another every day with new thoughts, ideas, theories.

He saw Mackenzie at the edge of the crowd and turned toward him. A self-deprecating comment, *academics and sports just don't mix*, or something along those lines, might answer perfectly. Then he noticed Green beside Mackenzie. He kept walking anyway.

"Good shot, Dr. Lemaistre," Mackenzie said.

"Not really," Vernon replied. He tried to smile.

"Those things are tough to aim. The first time I ever shot a dart I accidentally killed a steel garbage can," Mackenzie said. "I haven't touched one since."

Eustace snorted. "That's because you didn't know what you were doing. This guy," Eustace jerked a thumb at Vernon, "he used to be pretty good. Not as good as me, but pretty good. What happened?"

Vernon felt his body heat rise and his heart swell as if it was about to explode. While he spoke, a separate part of his mind attended to the strange feeling and took notes. What a strange sensation. Am I having a stroke?

"Did you know Eustace and I used to work together?" he said to Mackenzie. But somehow his voice wasn't quite in control. "We worked on atlatls together, everyone used to think they were made to throw a rigid spear and the banner stone was just a decoration, but I thought they were wrong and Eustace and I worked on it together and I trusted him—" Words tumbled out, fast and shrill. "And then he stole my research!" he added, his spare dart pointing at Eustace like a sword.

Vernon's search for further accusations faltered when he noticed the amused expression on Eustace's face, Mackenzie's wide eyes and open mouth.

"Come on, Mac," Eustace said. "Let this guy simmer down for a little while." He turned to walk away.

"Admit it! You stole my research." Vernon noticed the crowd staring. Even the next contestant in the atlatl throw had turned to watch.

Eustace paused and shook his head. "You are uniformly the worst researcher I have ever known. I would be embarrassed to put my name on anything, and I mean *anything*, you worked on." He turned to Mackenzie. "Goddamn shame," he said.

"Yeah? Well, you weren't embarrassed when you slept with my wife!" Vernon shouted at Eustace's back.

The two men left Vernon standing there sweating in the middle of the crowd. His clenched fists trembled. Then, out on the fringes, someone clapped their hands. The applause gathered slowly until everyone, even the people closest to Vernon, took it up. A clatter like rain on tropical leaves.

Vernon slurped at his fifth beer. In the dim cool bar, his prospects seemed much better. No reason to get in his car and drive back to Orlando tonight. He'd go to the interview tomorrow, tell Mackenzie about the bad blood between him and Eustace. Maybe he'd even imply that he'd deliberately missed the target because he didn't want to compete against his former research partner.

This trip could still be salvaged. Vernon crunched a stale pretzel. Unless, of course, Eustace was serious about applying for the job. But who knows? Maybe Mackenzie's department didn't have enough of a salary budget to attract Eustace. Vernon grinned when he thought about how much he made—heck, it'd be the first time his mediocre tax bracket had ever been an advantage.

Vernon pulled the powwow schedule out of his back pocket and smoothed it on the bar. A little spilled beer left a dark spot on the paper. If he left now, he could get back in time for the bonfire. He waved a hand at the bartender for the bill. He'd show them. He was a good sport—he wasn't beaten. Not by a long shot. Vernon drained the last of his beer.

The next morning, Vernon sat in an uncomfortable chair and watched across the desk as Mackenzie blinked at a piece of paper. Purple hollows sagged under Mackenzie's eyes and Vernon wondered if he too was hung over.

After a long moment, Mackenzie lowered the page. "Eustace Green died last night."

"What?" Vernon stared.

Mackenzie shook his big head. Tropical light filtering through the high narrow windows gilded his hair. "The police seem to think it's suicide."

"I . . . I don't understand." Vernon glanced out the office window, saw the tops of palms and blue sky. "I just . . . Did he seem depressed to you?"

"No. Did you see him last night, surrounded by those groupies?" Mackenzie shuffled through some papers on his handsome walnut desk, but when he stopped his hands were still empty. "I don't understand it either, but they say he impaled himself with an atlatl dart."

"Christ almighty. That just . . . that just doesn't make any sense."

"God—what happened to him? Eustace was a good friend. Not as close as I could've wished, not for a long time, but . . . I just didn't see that coming."

Vernon watched Mackenzie put a wide hand over his eyes for a moment and then saw glistening trails of tears work their way down the creased pink cheeks. Vernon tugged at the decorative handkerchief in his breast pocket. He'd always assumed it was just a decoy, stitched into place, but to his relief the fabric pulled free. He offered it to Mackenzie, who took it with a nod. Vernon looked away while Mackenzie wiped his eyes and resettled his glasses on his nose.

"My apologies," Mackenzie said. "Now." He shuffled the papers on his desk again. "Let's try to get back on track."

"I mean this respectfully, Dr. Mackenzie, but I don't think now's the right time for this conversation. You're very upset." Vernon tried to keep his voice upbeat and confident.

Mackenzie shook his head. "He's gone. I don't think there's anything else we can do."

"I could—let me ask some questions." Vernon nodded. "I'd really like to help."

Vernon was so distracted by thoughts of exactly what questions he was going to ask that he almost bumped into a student at the department's exit.

"Excuse me," Vernon said.

"Are you Dr. Mackenzie?" the boy asked. When Vernon straightened out his identity, the guy introduced himself: "I'm Detective Sheldon. Assigned to the Green case." A brassy flash of badge from a brown leather wallet. "I'd like to ask you a few questions."

"So you would say that you and Dr. Green had disagreements?" Sheldon asked.

"Well, I, uh, pretty much hated him, actually," Vernon said.

The two stood together in the shade of the Australian pines, near the flattened and litter-strewn park that had hosted the powwow. Long sagging filaments of yellow tape bounded an irregular square where Eustace's body had been found that morning by a Guatemalan groundskeeper.

"Hated him?" Sheldon squinted. "Why?"

"We had a disagreement about some research. He took a lot of collaborative material and published it under his own name. Then he slept with my wife. Does that about sum it up?"

"Your wife, huh? Listen, you saw him last night." Sheldon pointed to the flattened patch of grass with his chin. "Did he seem depressed to you? Any irrational behavior, that kind of thing?"

"He was acting rather cranky," Vernon said. "And he drank a lot last night." As he said it he wondered if the ghost of last night's beers lingered on his own breath.

Sheldon nodded, hands behind his back. He wasn't even writing anything down.

Vernon waited a long moment. "So, what do you think happened?"

Sheldon rubbed his chin. Vernon noticed a small cut from the morning's hasty shaving. "He came down here because he didn't like his job up north. Acted cranky. Had a fight with a former colleague," a nod to Vernon, "in public. Spent the evening drinking cheap beer." Sheldon walked toward the police tape and Vernon followed. "Wandered out here, saw the futility of his life." Sheldon turned to Vernon and lowered his voice. "You'd be surprised how many people kill themselves on moonless nights. I don't know what it is, something about the stars. The immensity of the universe."

"He killed himself?"

"Without a doubt," Sheldon said.

Vernon shook his head at the absurdity of the scene—two men in full suits sweating in the subtropical sun. And the world atlatl champion impaling himself on one of his own darts.

"I want to help you, detective. When you recover the tip of the dart, the stone point, bring it to me. An expert can look at it and tell you who the craftsman was."

Sheldon nodded. "I'll make a note of it," he said. But he didn't. "How exactly do these things work, anyway?"

Vernon arranged to meet Sheldon that evening for an atlatl demonstration—enough time for Sheldon to get the stone point from the pathologist. Maybe enough time for Vernon to figure out a plausible theory for what happened to Eustace Green. Sheldon didn't seem to be working on one.

Vernon sat at the plastic table in his underwear, surrounded by charts of the crime scene he'd drawn. His motel room smelled vaguely of mildew and sweat. Thin blades of burning sunlight pierced the drawn curtain and illuminated the unmade bed, the rumpled clothing, the pages he pored over.

Several hours after their morning meeting, Sheldon had knocked on the door and showed him an onyx point in a plastic bag.

Vernon examined it, rubbed the stone through the thin plastic. "That is definitely Eustace's work," he said. "He liked to serrate the edges of his stone points like that. Don't know why, it's really tough to do."

Sheldon nodded. "That's what Dr. Mackenzie says. Do you

think somebody could take one of these darts and just," he mimed an overhand toss, "throw it?"

Vernon shook his head. "Not enough mass. It'd be like hitting someone with a wadded-up piece of paper covering a pebble—nothing but a nasty cut. You really need an atlatl to throw it with enough force to hurt anything."

Sheldon gave a brief shrug, barely more than a hitch of his shoulders.

"You still think it's suicide?" Vernon said.

Sheldon crossed his arms. "For a minute there I was starting to think *you* did it."

Vernon's heart stopped.

Sheldon said, "But you couldn't kill him with his own dart. Mackenzie said he treated his tools like they were his children."

Vernon nodded.

"The other competitors couldn't. It's just Oscar's Razor—he must've killed himself. But why not use his flint knife, cut his wrists? He still had it on him when we found the body."

"And he had a gun somewhere, right?" Vernon asked

"A Charter Arms Undercover," Sheldon said. "Loaded. How'd you know that?"

"He waved it at me once, when he came to pick up my wife's clothes. But stabbing himself with a dart?" Vernon shook his head. "You'd have to be an anatomist to get that right. Who would take that chance? He could've just lay there bleeding."

Sheldon held up the stone point again. "Look at this thing. Three inches long, sharp as broken glass. The pathologist cut himself on it. It's more than enough to kill someone." He tucked the arrowhead into his breast pocket. "Anyway, according to the blood tests, he was seriously drunk. Alcohol thins the blood, you know. He wouldn't have just laid there bleeding for long."

Vernon had watched Green consume at least a dozen cans of beer and pitch the empties into the bonfire. "I'm sorry, but that just doesn't make any sense. He had women all around him, he'd just won the contest, coming to Florida for a new job—then he kills himself in suicidal despair? I mean, despite the moonless night . . ."

"There's something else you need to understand, doc," Sheldon said. He hitched his jacket back with one hand and Vernon caught a glimpse of the holster on his belt. "This isn't exactly the crime of the century. You read the paper? Two nights ago a guy tried to rob a Burger King, shot three people. Still at large. Understand, doc? We've got to prioritize."

"You can't just close the case because you're busy," Vernon said.

"Be realistic. A guy from out of town gets drunk and depressed and kills himself. People do stupid things all the time, even when they're not playing cowboys and Indians. A closed case is a good case."

But there are no closed cases in archaeology. How tidy detective work must be, with its filing cabinets full of closed cases. Vernon felt a momentary pang of jealousy.

"Give me till 6 o'clock to come up with something. We're still on for 6, right?" Vernon asked.

Sheldon held out his hands, palms up. "What's the point?"

"If Mackenzie sees me demonstrating the atlatl to you, it might put his mind at ease," Vernon said. "He'll be there too."

After a moment, Sheldon nodded. "All right. But keep it quick."

Only a few wisps of hay clinging to the grass indicated there'd ever been a target range here. Vernon found a scrap of the bright police tape. He found a suitable branch and forced it into the ground, took the wooden clothes hanger from the hotel and arranged his suit coat into a makeshift scarecrow. He examined his own Nanticoke atlatl and two four-foot darts, one aluminum and one of fine-grained ash.

He stood about where Eustace Green had, his back to the

targets, and waited for Mackenzie and Detective Sheldon. Fifty feet away, a shadowed line of cabbage palms and twisted sea grape had born mute witness to the death. At this range, in daylight, Eustace would've been able to knock a squirrel off a branch. But he'd been drunk.

Vernon walked to where Green's atlatl had lay. According to Sheldon, drunk, depressed, lonely Green had walked out into perfect nighttime solitude, dropped his spear-thrower here, then walked over here. Turned around. Faced—what? The moonless sky? And then Green had yanked his dart with its glittering obsidian point through his sternum and into his heart, fell backward. Vernon sprawled on the grass, acting out the scene. His arms instinctively spread. But Green's hands had been on the dart's shaft. Was he trying to press it in further? Or pull it out? The pain must've been punishing. Everything he deserved. How long had he lived? Four minutes until brain death, his heart trying to beat around the black razor edges while he attempted to tug the barbs of the dart from his sternum.

"You'll catch cold, rolling on the ground like that," Sheldon said from the shadows.

Vernon jumped, even though he'd been expecting him. He managed to modulate his scream into a mere howl of greeting.

"Yeeargh yourself," Sheldon said. "What'd you want to show me?"

"Dr. Lemaistre? Is that you?" a voice called.

Mackenzie emerged from the brush and walked over. Gloom had settled into the clearing much faster than Vernon anticipated.

Sheldon sighed and tried to read his watch. "Let's get this over with," he said.

Vernon said to the detective, "Eustace lay about here. His atlatl wasn't beside him—where was it?"

"Great props, by the way." Sheldon walked to a patch of ground forty feet from the scarecrow and pointed with his sneaker. "Here. We have pictures of it all."

"Right," Vernon said. "You ever wonder why he threw his atlatl twenty feet away before he killed himself?"

Sheldon shrugged. "Suicides do weird things. Once I saw a guy who took all his clothes off, even his shoes, folded them up and left them on the beach. He waded out into the ocean and shot himself in the head."

Vernon held up his atlatl. "Ever seen anybody use one of these, detective?"

Sheldon shook his head and stuck his hands in his pockets.

"It's not like a gun. You can't turn it on yourself." Vernon set the aluminum dart on the atlatl's hook. "It's like a bow and arrow—it shoots the dart away from you. Watch close." He reared his arm straight back and brought it down hard as he could, and the dart snapped forward and disappeared into the gathering shadows. The pulled muscle in his shoulder throbbed.

Sheldon whistled.

Mackenzie said, "Stone Age man used it to bring down mammoths. Cave bears. Sabre-toothed cats—all the megafauna. Wiped it out ten thousand years ago."

"Mammoths, huh?"

"When Cortez invaded the Aztec empire, their warriors still used atlatls," Mackenzie said.

Vernon added, "Their darts went right through the Spanish armor. They could shoot farther and straighter than a musket." He glanced at Mackenzie, who was just another unreadable silhouette.

"This is a fascinating lecture, docs, but can we speed it up a little? I have work to do."

Vernon resisted the urge to roll his eyes. He offered Sheldon the atlatl and the wooden dart. "Here, you try it."

After a moment's hesitation, Sheldon walked over and took the weapon.

While Sheldon fiddled with the two pieces of wood, Vernon said, "Two steps back. Right there." He pointed to his suit-jacket scarecrow. "Eustace was standing right about there."

"I don't see your point," Sheldon said.

"Ah," Mackenzie said. That single syllable full of under-standing and remorse.

Vernon waved Mackenzie back, behind Sheldon. "Throw the dart."

Sheldon swung the atlatl back and faced the scarecrow.

"No," Vernon said. He pointed. "Aim down there. Where the targets were, remember? Nothing but trees."

Vernon watched the detective peer into the shadows, then give a little shrug. He cocked his arm and swung forward and down.

The dart flipped off to the left. The three men watched it pierce the suit-jacket without even slowing down and plow into the ground some forty feet beyond.

"I'll be goddamned," Sheldon said. He let the atlatl fall from his hand.

Vernon couldn't have asked for a better demonstration. "See what you just did?"

Sheldon looked around, his eyes wide. "But I was aiming . . ." he said, then noticed the atlatl at his feet. His mouth hung open.

"The same thing happened to me first time I shot one," Mackenzie said. "Put a dart right through a steel garbage can. What a waste. What a terrible waste."

Sheldon stared at the dart's path. Maybe he was envisioning Green transfixed, the look of surprise on his face, the backward fall.

"I think that happens because the dart's not settled just right on the hook," Vernon said. "The idea of the atlatl's easy, but actually getting the dart to go where you want, that's hard."

"I'll be goddamned," Sheldon said again.

"Mackenzie and I both saw him with women last night. And what would groupies of the atlatl world champion want more than anything? A quick lesson."

Sheldon nodded, but his eyes were still on the scarecrow. "Sure. A quick lesson."

Vernon walked over to Sheldon's side. "She stood here, with his atlatl. Had no idea what she was doing. Aiming downrange, toward the target. He stood right over there," Vernon nodded at the jacket, "probably rooted her on."

"He just wasn't far enough out of the way," Mackenzie said.

Sheldon turned to them. "But she hit him square in the heart."

Vernon shrugged. "Luck. You'd have to be a doctor to be able to do that on purpose." He knelt and touched the fallen atlatl. "Then she dropped the evidence, just like you did." There must've been no sound at all except Green's body hitting the ground. "Then she ran."

"God, it was all just an accident," Mackenzie whispered. Then he cleared his throat. "We still have the list of registrants." He put a hand on Sheldon's shoulder. "You could track them down, right?"

"No fingerprints—the handle was wrapped with leather. But we can check the list," Sheldon said.

Vernon looked at the young detective. You aren't going to check anything, he thought, because a closed case is a good case.

Vernon walked behind the scarecrow and plucked the dart out of the ground. Rolled it between his fingers to insure it was still straight.

"Thanks for the demonstration, Dr. Lemaistre," the detective said, but he didn't sound like he meant it. Sheldon stuck his hands in his pockets and slouched, as if in thought. "I better go check on that list." After a moment, he turned and plodded away through the dark.

Mackenzie walked over and rested a heavy hand on his shoulder. "Hard to believe it was just a ridiculous accident. Eustace deserved better than that." He cleared his throat. "Good work, Vernon," he said. "Come to my office tomorrow morning. We'll finish up that interview." He shook his head. "Such a waste."

Alone in the clearing, Vernon stared east at the acrylic lights of Miami Beach blazing on the horizon. He hadn't deliberately planned anything. He'd taken Eustace's onyx point and set it into one of his own darts, for good luck, he thought. Nothing but luck put Eustace on the range when Vernon had been trying for one more bull's-eye, despite the dark, despite the beer. He wasn't sure if he'd aimed or not.

Vernon tapped his atlatl against his palm. Eustace hadn't even heard it coming. The dart hit him, he fell down and died without even knowing what happened. Vernon was right, though—the banner stone really did quiet the throw. Technology had reached forward from the Stone Age to silence Eustace Green.

Vernon pulled his coat off the makeshift scarecrow and stuck his finger through the hole in the cloth. He'd need to get that mended. He walked downrange, into the trees. His first dart should be here somewhere and he didn't like the idea of leaving it out overnight.

No witnesses, a dead man already rotting on a mortician's table. A detective who was happy to forget anything had happened. A new boss, a new job. A new life. Vernon searched the trees for his dart until he heard something moving through the underbrush. He backed away, into the clearing. Maybe he'd come back in the morning and look for the dart. Or maybe he'd just leave it, stuck in a tree, until the aluminum shaft eventually oxidized. That might take a hundred years. The stone point, he knew, would outlast him. Would outlast even his bones.

SAWYERS

BY KEVIN ALLEN

Perrine

T he boy, Speck, and his father, the sawyer, were wrestling
a log onto the sawmill carriage and didn't see the two
strangers when they first appeared at the edge of the
clearing. Nor had they heard them calling because of the thump-
ing engine of the Fordson tractor that powered the mill and its
screaming saw blade. The boy looked up through the swirling
sawdust to idly scan the yard and down the dirt road, and that's
when he saw the man and girl.

"Look there," he said.

The two strangers stood at the head of the log wagon path
that led to the road to Perrine, eight miles to the east. The young
girl, carrying a suitcase strapped up with a piece of baling twine,
stood alongside a much older man with a canvas bag like a sail-
or's duffel slung over his shoulder. Both were chalked with dust.
The man was lean, sharp-boned, dark, and bristled with a
growth of whiskers. The girl was rounder, but a bit frail too, her
brown hair tied up under a man's brimmed hat, in spite of which
her nose and cheeks were red and freckled from the sun. She
wore a shapeless dress that came down below her knees but
clung to her body under her arms and along her chest where she
was wet with sweat.

John Talley beat the sawdust from his bib overalls with a
stained handkerchief, pointed to the tractor, and told his son,
"Cut that off." He wiped his hands, sizing up the two, and left a
trail in the sawdust and wood scraps as he shuffled across the

mill yard toward the strangers. His big voice echoed from the board sides of the two box-house shacks and the slash pine beyond them. He said, "If you folks're lost, then you done a good job of it."

Speck slid down from the tractor and moved over to the empty shack where there was a double-bitted ax resting against the wall. He reached into his pocket for a whetstone, spat on it, and began working the blade.

"Mr. Talley?" the man said. "My name's Calvin Hallaway." He untangled his hand from the girl's and offered it to shake, but the sawyer turned his attention to the boy and the ax even while telling the stranger that, yes, John Talley was his name.

Calvin's narrow, hooded eyes darted while he surveyed the contents of the yard: the two shacks, the portable mill, the tractor, the beat-up Ford truck. He took a long drag on the cigarette clinched in his tight lips and then pinched the butt and flicked it away.

"What brings you here?" the sawyer said.

"Well, sir, it's a long story," Calvin said. "We come from up around the lake. Been working our way south, you might say. We stayed a time in Miami, but that was a regular hell-hole. I'm an out-of-doors man, sir, like yourself, I suspect."

They had been on the road for weeks, Calvin said, riding when they could but mostly on foot. "It's unusual to see a man and his daughter out on the road, I'll grant you. But there's nothing usual about these times. Them last few miles liked to done this little girl in," he said. "I felt just terrible about it. Thought I'd have to carry her sometimes. But she made it. This here's Marcy. Say hello, honey."

The girl nodded.

"My daughter," Calvin said.

They had heard in Perrine of the sawyer and his tractor-run sawmill from a man at the collection yard on the Florida East Coast Railroad.

"Fella there said you maybe need some help," Calvin added. "I been logging and sawmilling all over, up in Georgia and Carolina, mostly, but up and down the coast in Florida too. All I know is timber. And Marcy can cook real good. She'd be a big help to your wife. We're not looking for a handout. We want to work."

"There's no wife. Just me and him." The sawyer pointed to his son. "We manage. This is Speck. He usually knows better than to gawk, but we don't get many visitors. Come on over here, boy. These people are looking for work."

"Pleased to make your acquaintance," Speck said.

"Ain't we mannerable," Calvin said. He grinned like he'd heard a secret. "Pleased to acquaint you too, young chap."

"I can't give you an answer now," the sawyer told the visitors. "But you can stay the night in the empty house here. It's not much, but it'll beat sleeping in the swamp. We'll see if we can't get you something to eat. I'll let you know in the morning about staying on."

"That's much appreciated," Calvin said. "They told us you was fair."

Inside the helper's shack, Marcy had pushed the suitcase under the bed, taken her shoes off, and was examining her blisters. Calvin was stripped down to his dingy undershorts and sprawled on the mattress.

Speck watched them through the window of the shack, then listened just outside the door.

"You think they'll let us stay here for a while?" Marcy asked.

"Depends," Calvin said, lying back with eyes closed and blowing cigarette smoke toward the roof slats. "You saw the way that boy looked at you. Wouldn't hurt our chances if you was to show him some attention. Must be a lonely thing, strong young fella like that one, working out here on this ridge, nothing but gators and toads for company day after day."

"What are you saying?"

"Nothing bad, baby girl. You're a charmer. Just be nice to him. Maybe get him to put in a word with his sourpuss of an old man. We need some time here. Maybe after they get to know us better we might even be partners. Or something like that. They got a nice truck out there, did you notice that?"

Speck paused a moment at the open door to the hired-hand's shack to make his presence known before he walked in. Calvin remained where he was on the bed. Marcy jumped up and hurried over to the door, and when she took the canned goods Speck had brought over she brushed her hand across his. She was a couple of inches shorter than the boy, and she looked up to speak.

"Thank you, Speck," she said.

"You're a regular little gentleman," Calvin said, lifting up from the bed. "Your daddy must of raised you right. But you don't favor him." He turned to Marcy. "He must take after his mama. Maybe he's his mama's boy."

"You should stop," Marcy said.

"He knows I'm just fooling," Calvin said. "You didn't take offense, did you, son?"

In reply, Speck shook his head and walked quickly out the door. Marcy followed him.

"You shouldn't let my daddy bother you," she said. "He didn't mean no harm. He was just saying how much he admires you and your father for working so hard up here all alone."

They were standing in the middle of the clearing between the two shacks, near a rough-hewn table with stumps for chairs.

"Do you mind if we sit here awhile? My feet ache from walking." The girl's palms were rubbed raw from carrying the battered suitcase, and the broken-down brogans had rasped blisters on the heels of each foot.

She said they had walked all morning from Perrine before turning off onto the log road and heading up the ridge into the woods. Some cars passed. Two or three slowed before speeding on, and one pulled to the side of the road, but it too hastened away when the driver apparently got a closer look at the two.

"People just aren't too trusting," she said. "But just listen to me complain. It sure was nice of your daddy to let us stay."

Speck spat in the dirt and sat. "What do you want?" he said.

"Just talk," Marcy said. "How old are you? How long you been out here? How much longer you going to be working here?"

The boy said he was sixteen. He and his father had hauled the tractor mill up Cutler Ridge more than a year before and had been working this stand of scratch pine ever since. But no matter how hard they worked something was always breaking down, and then the sawyer would say it was God's will. They were on a contract with the owner of the land, a farmer who himself barely scratched out enough of a living to make his mortgage payments to the land company. If they didn't finish here in the next two weeks and move the mill they'd forfeit the contract, and the lumber already cut would go to the farmer.

"Where's your mama?" Marcy asked.

"She died in a hurricane three years ago," Speck said. "That's why we came out here. My dad was a minister in Miami, but he said he was through with preaching. He was through with people, I guess. We come out here and went to work for ourselves."

"Looks like you could use some help." She reached over and put her hand on the boy's. But Speck stood up.

"We're managing," he said.

"I was just observing," she said. "And I was thinking that if you did need a helping hand then maybe you'd put in a good word for us with your daddy." She smiled sweetly. "I sure could use some rest."

The boy backed away a few steps and then turned toward the main shack. "We'll see," he muttered.

Back inside the main shack, he watched the girl rubbing her

feet in the middle of the clearing. He knew his father would let her and Calvin stay on. The sawyer wouldn't ask where they'd been, what they were running from. He'd never bothered to ask any of the hired hands. All that mattered was the work. In their time on the ridge a half dozen men had come and gone. Black, white, young, old, every one had something or someone trailing them, pushing them south and then, when there was almost no farther south to go, west toward the swamps. This ridge was the edge of the solid world, and no one who thought he had any other choice would put up with the heat and bugs and toil for more than a few days. The sawyer would let the strangers stay for as long as they were help. He would overlook their trouble because he had no choice. He'd make use of them, the same way he'd made do with the cranky tractor and balky sawmill. The boy would put aside his suspicions too, because the girl would be close for a while. But it wouldn't be for long. This was not a place where strangers took comfort or refuge.

Speck was up early the next morning, and as he stood at the edge of the woods, he watched Marcy shuffle out of the helper's shack and make her way to a little creek just beyond the clearing. She was carrying clean clothes, which she hung on a branch, and then leaned from the waist to pull off the dingy dress she was wearing when she arrived. The boy saw the gray hem rise like a curtain revealing pale shins and thighs, the dark triangle between her legs, the slight swell of her belly, and the circles of her breasts. She waded into the green water up to her waist and bathed, and as she climbed back onto the bank she turned and looked up into the woods where Speck stood still, trying to make himself invisible. If she saw him, she pretended not to notice. She pulled on the clean dress quickly, washed her dirty clothes, and hung them on tree branches to dry. Then she slowly made her way back up toward the mill yard. The boy moved over to the sawmill and pretended to study the machinery.

Calvin appeared in the doorway of the helper's shack, barefoot and shirtless, and when he stretched his arms mightily high over his head, he revealed a red scar that curved along his pale flank. When the boy looked over, Calvin balled his hand into a fist and made a pumping motion toward his groin. The boy glared at the man.

John Talley came out of the main shack eating a biscuit. He walked on over to Calvin. "Well, sir, I guess we might see how it works out with the two of you here awhile," the sawyer told Calvin. "I don't know you from Adam, and I don't need to know. But the fact of the matter is, I have to get this lumber cut and delivered to the collection yard. Truth is, it's hard, hot work, and I've had men come and go that wasn't up to it. But you're saying you can, so I am offering you a chance." Together, they worked out the wages. They agreed Calvin would be paid after the sawyer delivered the last load of lumber to the collection yard.

"I'd like to get to work," the sawyer said. "So soon as you're ready, come on out to the mill. I'll have Speck show your girl to the supplies so she can get started on dinner. You be quick about it," he then told Speck. "We got work to do."

For a week, Calvin worked shoulder to shoulder with the sawyer and the boy, cutting the pine, dragging it back to the clearing, and bucking the timber at the tractor mill. And then one morning when Calvin didn't show up for breakfast, the girl said that he had left the night before to take care of some business.

He still hadn't returned the next day, and that night there was light in the window of the helper's shack, and the girl was moving about inside alone. Speck stole closer in the darkness to the window.

Marcy wore a clean white dress, and arranged around her on the bed were women's things, brushes and tins and powder. She sat with her back to the window and picked up the brush and began to stroke her brown hair. But then she heard the boy at the window and turned with a start. "You scared me," she said.

Speck moved closer and looked around inside.

"It's all right," Marcy said. "I'm all alone."

"I'm sorry," Speck said.

"Sorry I'm alone, or sorry I caught you peeping in my window?"

"I saw the light and wanted to make sure everything was all right."

"Why wouldn't it be?"

"I just wanted . . . Sorry," he said, and he turned to leave.

"Wait a minute," Marcy said. "Go around by the door. I'll be out."

When she met him at the door, the boy reached to touch her cheek. He wanted to do something, to kiss her, maybe, but he didn't know where to start.

Marcy reached up and took his hand before he touched her face. "Be careful," she said.

"I was just—"

"You was just maybe figuring we're alone out here and you'd take advantage of the situation. If my daddy knew, he'd—"

"I'm sorry." The boy turned his head to check the edges of the clearing. "Where is he?"

"He went looking for something to drink," Marcy said.

"He won't find much around here."

"He's got his ways. He says he's got a sixth sense."

"A what?"

"Sometimes he sees things before they happen. Not always, and not that he can control it, but I seen it work. Like coming here."

"Visions, like?"

"I don't pretend to understand it." The girl's face darkened for a second and she shivered. "I shouldn't be talking to you. If he knew I was alone with you . . ."

"He won't know if you don't tell him. We're just talking. So why are the two of you out on the road?"

"There was trouble."

"With your mama?"

She looked up at the boy. "My mama's dead. This trouble was with the law up in Duval County. They said Cal, my daddy, they said he stole. Said I was in on it. It was a lie, but we had to go anyway. I didn't have no one else, so I went with him. I didn't have a choice."

"You could leave him."

"He needs me, and I need him. You understand that, don't you? Ain't that why you're out here in nowhere?"

"I could leave. I will someday."

"But you haven't yet."

"It don't seem right, though. You, a girl, out on the road."

"Well, we're not on the road now, are we? Come on inside. There's something I want to show you."

Marcy took Speck's hand and led him inside over to the bed. She reached down and slid the battered suitcase from underneath. "This is my hope chest." She untied the twine and lifted the lid. She took a carefully folded white cotton dress from the case and then a patchwork quilt, a pair of polished black leather shoes with hard buckles, something made of lace that she quickly hid beneath the quilt, the brush and mirror, and finally a photograph—Marcy when she was a fair-haired child wearing a long white dress—in a gold frame.

"This ain't the hope chest itself, naturally. It's what goes in one." She arranged the few pieces on the bed. "These are my pretty things. I'd hate worse than anything to part with these." She lifted from the suitcase a wad of newspaper and unwrapped a small glass globe.

"I thought it'd be broke," she said. "It's so delicate."

She showed Speck. Beneath the little roof of glass there was a tiny city of white with steeples and onion-shaped domes, castles, and palaces. Blue lagoons and arched bridges connected the white streets. On the bottom of the globe there was gold printing: *Enter herein ye sons of men.*

"What is it?" Speck said.

"It's the World's Fair. In St. Louis a long time ago. This came from there. It was a keepsake. It's for looking and dreaming. Watch." She turned the globe upside down and hundreds of silvery flakes floated above the miniature city before settling silently back to the bottom. "Don't they look just like stars?" Marcy said. "Don't you wish you could be somewhere so pretty? It was handed down in my family from my mother's side. Her daddy helped build it—the fair."

"You saw it?"

"It was a long time ago. It ain't there no more. They built up this great white city and people came from all over the world, and then when it was over they tore it all down like it never happened, like it was kind of a dream. Still, I want to see where it was someday."

"I could take you there."

"That would be nice. Maybe someday you'll be there, and you'll look up and I'll be getting off a trolley car, just like that. It's nice to think so." She carefully rewrapped the globe and put it back in the suitcase in the folds of the quilts and dresses.

"Why can't you just go back to where you came from?" Speck asked. "Back to your people. There must be someone."

"I told you, they wouldn't want me," she said. "Not now."

"But why? You deserve better than . . . than this."

"Oh, it's not so bad." She cupped her hand on Speck's smooth cheek. "Now you better go." From within the woods came the sound of movement, and Marcy told Speck, "Go. Now."

The boy ran for the door as Marcy hurried to put out the light.

Calvin made his way unsteadily toward the door and then stopped and pissed on the ground before going inside. Speck creeped around to the back of the shack and watched through the widow.

"What's all this?" Calvin said. He grabbed the girl and threw her onto the bed. Marcy tried to scramble for the door, but Calvin caught her by the leg and dragged her back. He pulled his belt off in one quick motion and began to lash her legs. Marcy curled into a ball and covered herself with her hands, but then Calvin whipped the belt across her face. She whimpered and begged for him to stop. And then she lay still while he climbed on top of her.

The boy felt powerless to stop it. He told himself it was for the girl that he hesitated. That it would be worse for her if he interfered. But he knew he was afraid for himself. So he waited while the man's grunts and moans subsided, watched as the girl turned her face into the mattress and waited for the whole thing to be over.

The next morning, Marcy moved like an awkward, tentative bird. She wore the old floppy men's hat pulled down over her forehead. Calvin, meanwhile, emerged from the shack smiling his thin, menacing smile. "Breakfast ready?" he said as he passed by Speck on his way to the sawmill.

Marcy's eyes were raw and the red edges beneath her right eye darkened to almost purple above her cheek. Before Speck could speak, she said, "I fell. Don't ask no more."

"He did this to you," the boy replied.

"I just fell," she said, looking over the boy's shoulder. "Leave it alone. You'll be better off. I have to get the cooking started."

"This ain't right. You can't . . . Your own daddy . . . Something's got to be done."

"Not now, and not by you," she said. And she pulled the broad brim of the hat lower over her eyes and started off for the main shack.

Speck hurried to catch up with her. "I want to help you," he said.

She stopped abruptly. "Then leave me alone. I appreciate

you wanting to help. But this here, this little mark on my eye, it's a pimple, a scratch. If you want to help, leave it alone."

Speck reached his arm as if he meant to wrap it around her, but she backed away. "What are doing? Didn't you hear a word I said?"

"I'm not afraid."

"You should be," she said. "Go on. I'll find what I need."

Calvin sat at the table in the middle of the yard smoking and gazing absently into the clear blue morning sky. He turned abruptly and grinned slowly at the boy until Speck turned away.

"Where you been?" John Talley asked, coming out of the sawyer's shack. "If you're running off like that without any notice, I got no use for you. You'd be better off gone."

"I'm here to apologize," Calvin said. "I know it was sudden. But it couldn't be helped. I had business, a personal matter. I hope you can appreciate that."

"What I'd appreciate is if we could cut some lumber," the sawyer said.

That morning they hauled and cut more timber than Speck and his father had for the previous two days. The boy had to race to keep up with the older men. The two of them winched the pine logs onto the sawmill carriage, and then while John Talley kept an eye on the big blade Speck and Calvin would move around to the other end to buck the cut timber as it came off the saw.

"We keep this up, we'll strip these woods bare in no time," John Talley said to Calvin. "Glad you come back."

"Ask and ye shall receive," Calvin said. "I do believe in that."

Calvin and Speck hustled another log down onto the carriage. "How 'bout you, boy, what do you ask for when you say your prayers at night?" Calvin said.

"Nothing," Speck said.

"I don't believe that," Calvin said. "Young, healthy boy like you must want a lot of things. I know I did when I was your age. Still do." He stopped to wipe the sweat from his face with his shirtsleeve, watching Speck from behind the crook of his elbow.

"I doubt I want what you want," Speck said.

The saw screamed and sent up a cloud of sawdust that settled down on Speck and Calvin, who had moved to the opposite end of the mill to catch the ripped lumber.

"How 'bout it, boy," Calvin said, effortlessly swinging a ten-foot pine plank down off the mill. "You think the man above sent us here?"

The boy was sweating, trying to keep pace with the older man. "I thought it was the fella from the collection yard," Speck said, and he loaded the plank onto the wagon bed.

"Maybe you get that smart mouth from your mama too," Calvin said.

Just then the saw made a terrible screech as its teeth bit deep into the hard heart of the log. The blade stopped, but the tractor engine kept growling. Speck grabbed a piece of scrap board and reached in to push it against the log.

John Talley came running from around the far end of the saw, waving his arms. "Cut it off!" he screamed.

Calvin ran to the tractor and pushed in the throttle.

The sawyer grabbed Speck by both shoulders. "Don't ever reach in to that machinery," he said. "You know better. That old mill's touchy. Any trouble, that's it. You shut it down. You hear?"

Speck tossed the scrap aside, and the sawyer and Calvin rocked the log until they inched it away from the blade. Across the yard, Marcy called from the doorway of the main shack.

"Dinner's ready," John Talley said.

The men and Speck sat outside at the rough table and waited for the girl to carry the plates to them. She was flushed when she finally sat down. Calvin attacked his food while John Talley said grace. The girl wiped her forehead with the back of her arm. A strand of brown hair stuck out from under her hat and was matted across her pale brow.

"This is real good," the sawyer told Marcy, his mouth full of cornbread. "You ain't eating?"

"Not hungry," Marcy said. "I just need to sit awhile."

"And I need some pepper," Calvin said.

She stood and began to make her way back to the shack, but halfway across the yard she slumped to her knees. Speck stood, but he didn't move when he saw how Calvin looked at him.

John Talley waited for the hired man too, but Calvin continued to eat. "You think you might better see to your daughter?" the sawyer said.

"She's all right," Calvin answered, and he leaned over his plate and spooned in another mound of beans.

"She's hurt," Speck said. "You did this."

Calvin's fist, still holding the spoon, pounded the table as sudden and sharp as a thunderclap. "What do you know about it? If I say she's fine, she's fine. You can just stay the hell out of it."

"I won't," the boy said. "This ain't right. You're a goddamn criminal."

The sawyer straightened his spine. "That's enough," he said. "You, boy, hold your tongue." He turned on Calvin. "And you had best remember why it is you're here. I need help with this timber, but you can just keep on going down the line if you mean trouble." And he went to help the girl back to the table.

Speck could see the storm pass from Calvin, at least for the time being. His smile showed his stained teeth and pieces of his dinner.

"She's overcome by the heat," the sawyer said. Then he looked at Calvin. "What happened to that eye?"

"She fell out of the bed," Calvin said. "She ain't used to sleeping in a bed. She was turning in her sleep and fell out. Them things happen." And then he continued to eat beans like he didn't have a care in the world.

"You're a goddamn liar," Speck muttered.

"I told you, that's enough," John Talley said. "We've got

work to do. But she's got to get that eye seen to. Speck, I want you to take Marcy to the doctor."

"She don't need no doctor," Calvin said.

"I don't understand you, mister," the sawyer said. "Your girl is hurt. If you don't care no more for her than that, then maybe you should be on your way. Maybe we'd all be better off. Right now, though, she's going to the doctor."

"Go on, then," Calvin said, and waved them off.

Marcy said she didn't want to go to town. She was feeling better. But the sawyer made her get in the truck with the boy.

As they pulled onto the main road toward Perrine, Marcy told the boy again not to take her the doctor. "I'm fine," she said. "Really."

"If you don't go," the boy said, "I'm taking you to the sheriff. I may go myself anyway."

"You can't do that, Speck. You don't understand."

"What I don't understand is why you put up with him."

"I tried to tell you, I'm his daughter," she said. "I don't have anyplace else to go. And he ain't a bad man, really. He's just rough."

"Only an evil man could do such a thing. Especially if he's your father. Where did you come from? Don't you have people who could help?"

"The kind of trouble I was in, they wouldn't want no part of. I can't tell you, Speck, what it was. Can you just not ask me to tell?"

"But you're not in trouble now. You don't owe him. You could tell him to leave. You could stay here."

"With you? How would your daddy like that? You think he'd welcome me just moving in with you?"

"You heard what he said. He wouldn't turn you out."

"And I'm supposed to just tell my own daddy that he's going and I'm staying? He's not the type that'd just leave. And say you and I did go away—it ain't that easy. He wouldn't rest till he found me. And nothing and no one would stand in his way."

"Maybe I could, I don't know . . . do something."

"Speck."

"He hurts you."

"He'll hurt you worse."

"We could run him off, my dad and me."

"Your daddy'd have done that long ago if he cared about such things."

"There must be something."

Marcy touched the boy's face. "Don't say no more," she said. They were nearing the town. Marcy leaned over and almost in a whisper said to the boy, "If you could find us something to drink, maybe we could find us a peaceful spot and just talk like friends."

It didn't take much liquor for the boy to get drunk. Marcy didn't try to stop him when he kissed her, and she helped him when he fumbled with his pants. It took him only a couple of seconds, and even then he didn't know at first when it was finished.

"That was real nice," Marcy told him.

It was getting late, and they still had to go to the grocer's to pick up supplies. The boy was too far gone, so Marcy drove to the store and parked the truck on the street a few buildings away. They both got out, and Marcy went on into the store with the sawyer's list while Speck lingered outside. On the window of the grocer's someone had pasted a single piece of white paper. The black type said:

Missing Girl—Mary Whitt, 14
If you have seen or know of a young girl with brown hair
and green eyes unfamiliar in these parts, please contact Mr.
C.W. Whitt R.R. #1, Big Fork, Ark.
Or your Sheriff
Reward Offered

Identical handbills had been pasted on the windows of

nearly every shop and office she passed on the street. Speck rested his head against the glass of the front door. Suddenly, he doubled over and vomited into the street. He stood up and wiped his mouth with his sleeve.

Speck went to wait in the truck, but before he opened the door a man in a white shirt and bib overalls came walking over from across the street. He held a stack of papers and handed one to a passerby.

"I hate to trouble you, son," the man said to Speck. He had the leathery neck and hands of a farmer. "My name's Whitt," he continued, handing Speck a flyer. "I wonder if you've seen a strange girl around. Her name's Mary. We heard she may have come this way."

"What?" Speck said.

"I'm her father," the man said. "I'm afraid she's mixed up with some bad sorts. I've been looking for her. I want her safe, I guess you might say."

Speck nodded, took the handbill, and backed away.

"Don't forget," C.W. Whitt said. "She's dear to us."

Speck folded the handbill and put it in his pocket and sat and waited for the girl. He knew that C.W. Whitt was Marcy's father, and whatever it was that she or Calvin had done he had already forgiven. He could tell her, and she'd be safe, free to go back to wherever she'd come from. But then he'd be left to go back to the mill where Calvin was waiting. He knew Marcy was right, that Calvin wouldn't just allow her to walk away. He was afraid of Calvin. But he was even more afraid of losing Marcy. The two of them could find a way so that they could be together.

The boy was quiet on the drive back to the mill, and so was Marcy. Finally, he took the handbill from his pocket and studied it. Marcy pretended not to notice the paper.

"This changes things," the boy said.

"Changes what?"

"That farmer back there in town gave me this. This is you.

He was your daddy. Whatever you did to him, whatever made you think you couldn't go back, you were wrong about him. Otherwise, he wouldn't be out searching the country for you."

Marcy pulled the truck to the side of the road and took the paper from the boy. She read it several times before she spoke.

"I stole his truck and twenty dollars," she said. "It was Calvin's idea. He told me if I went back they'd throw me in jail."

"Now you know better. We could just turn around."

"There's still Calvin. You seen him. You think he'd just let me go? You think he'd not bother you or your daddy?"

"Nobody's looking for Calvin," the boy said.

"What's that supposed to mean?"

"It means that if he vanished from the face of the earth, no one would miss him. If he was to fall and hit his head on a rock stumbling through the woods, no one would mourn his passing. It'd be better than he deserved. I could make him just disappear."

Before, when he talked about her leaving Calvin, it was just ignorance and fear, and he gave her no reason to trust him. She knew not to listen, for her sake as well as his own protection. Now, things were different. He knew full well what kind of man Calvin was, knew what danger he could be. He knew the truth about her. Killing was a sin, no matter what. But was it worse than keeping her from her tormented father? Was it worse than keeping him from Marcy?

"You can't do it, Speck," the girl said. "You'd be doing it for me, and I ain't worth it."

"To me you are."

"But I wouldn't be if I let you do this. I'm no older than you are, but I've seen enough to know that no one just disappears. The past don't give up easy, no matter how far away you get from it. You think your daddy'd just let you walk away?"

"You could stay here. Without him here, you could stay."

"I have to go back, Speck. And you have to stay."

* * *

There was no sign of the sawyer or Calvin when Marcy and Speck pulled into the clearing.

"Quick," Marcy said. "I'll get my things, and then you can drive me back to town."

Speck had grabbed the ax from the side of the building and was standing watch outside the shack when he heard the tractor engine start up and looked over to see Calvin move in place to hoist a pine log onto the carriage. When he glanced up and saw the truck, Calvin dropped the timber and headed directly for the shack. Before Marcy could get the suitcase back under the bed and hide the handbill, Calvin was at the door.

"Where's my father?" Speck said.

"Mr. Talley is up in the woods cutting timber. But my question is where the two of you have been, and what's that you've got there, darling?"

Calvin ripped the paper from her hands, read the handbill carefully, and smiled. "Well, well, now. This is quite a little bit of news, ain't it?"

Speck could see the wheels spinning in Calvin's head.

"Looks like the cat's out of the bag," Calvin said. "Looks like somebody needs you more than I do. Reward and everything. Hoo haw. Well, sweetheart, I tell you what, I've never been one to stand in the way of family harmony. I think what this means is our time together is come to an end. It'll pain me to part with you, it really will, but you're worth more in leaving me than in staying. I think I'll just borrow this young man's truck here and the two of us can go and find Mr. C.W. Whitt and see about that reward."

"I'll not go another step with you," Marcy said.

"Oh, I think you will. I don't see how you or anyone else's going to stop me." He grabbed Marcy by the arm and pulled her outside.

Speck followed them. He raised the ax, and Calvin released Marcy, but he advanced toward the boy.

"Get inside," Speck told Marcy. But Marcy followed as Speck began backing toward the saw.

"So this is how it is!" Calvin said. He had to shout over the roar of the tractor. "You think you can take what's mine, boy?"

He careened around the saw and had to lean on the carriage frame for balance, but Speck stood his ground, and when Calvin came close the boy swung the ax wildly. Calvin leaned away, and the blade stuck deep into the log on the saw carriage. While Speck struggled to pull the ax free, Calvin steadied himself and pounced. He grabbed a handful of the boy's yellow hair.

"You'll pay now," he growled. He let loose of the boy's hair and stood catching his breath as if he was plotting just how to resolve things. The boy crouched by the side of the saw.

Speck looked up just in time to see Calvin's arm come swinging around at his head. He didn't try to duck away; instead, he lowered his head and threw his weight against Calvin. Calvin's feet gave way and he reached out blindly for something to catch him from falling.

The sound of the man's hand crushed in the mill's flywheel was no more violent than the snap of a pine bough. The sound Calvin made, though, was long and loud and anguished. After a moment of struggle to withdraw his hand, he dropped to his knees and then slumped against the carriage frame. Blood ran back down his wrist and arm and then into the sawdust.

His arm was drawn up into the machinery of the saw well past his wrist. He was moaning in pain. The boy went over and shut off the tractor. Marcy had reached the saw, where she watched blankly as Calvin's eyes rolled back and his head dropped. His face had been red with rage a few seconds earlier. Now it was the color of weathered lumber.

"Do something," Marcy said.

"He deserves it," Speck said.

"He'll die, bleeding like that."

"What do you want me to do? He's caught in the gears. I

don't think I can take it apart. There's no time to go get help. We'll have to take him into town. But he's going to have to go without that hand. You decide. I'll do whatever you say, but you tell me what to do."

Marcy looked at Calvin, still slumped against the machine. "You can't ask me to decide," she said.

"You can leave him and we can go for help, or we can get him loose and take him into town. I'll do whichever you say."

"How're going to get him loose?"

Speck pulled the ax from the log and showed it to the girl.

She breathed slowly, watching the blood run down Calvin's arm and drip off his elbow into a pool beneath him. She held her head up. "Cut it off," she said.

Speck didn't hesitate. He raised the ax and brought it down. The first blow struck just above the man's wrist and produced a dull sound followed by Calvin's piercing shriek. The second one sounded only of metal and bone. Calvin made not a whimper.

They wrapped the ragged wrist in one of Calvin's white shirts, and Speck tied a piece of twine high up on the wounded man's arm to keep him from losing any more blood. He and the girl dragged Calvin to the truck and loaded him onto the bed.

"Get in," Speck told the girl.

She shook her head.

"Why not? He can't hurt you now."

"You go on. I did what I had to. Now I'm through. You go on and when they ask, tell it all just like it happened."

Speck backed the truck in front of the log wagon. "Marcy, go on and get your things. There's no time to argue."

"My name's not Marcy," she said.

"I know it. But it doesn't matter now," Speck said. "Get your things."

"I can't go with you," she said.

"If you don't, I'll dump him in the swamp where nobody will ever find him."

"No you won't. It's all over, Speck. You go on."

"You wait for me here. I'll be back and we'll tell my daddy. We'll go to St. Louis to the fair."

"That's all over with, Speck. You go on now."

She wore the white dress and carried the battered suitcase. She had cleaned up the main shack and then packed everything of hers and gathered Calvin's things from the helper's shack. She went outside and built a fire and fed the man's clothes and finally his sailor's bag into the flames.

Alone by the firelight, Marcy took the glass dome from the suitcase and held it out. At first it seemed empty, a void above the dark outline of the miniature city. But then she shook the thing in her fist and held it out again, and the tiny silver flecks caught the light from the fire and glowed there in the night, brief sparks, like stars you glimpse through wind-blown boughs of pine.

She set the globe on the table between the two shacks. She picked up her belongings and walked off down the log road, toward the place—she didn't know where yet—someone was waiting for her.

PART II

WIND, WATER, AND GRIME

BLOWN AWAY

BY ANTHONY DALE GAGLIANO

Homestead

The roof was halfway peeled off the house; the Volkswagen was in the swimming pool; and for the past two nights I had fallen asleep watching the stars fade away into my dreams. Now, two days after the storm, I had taken to sleeping with my rifle because the looters were out, and night was their favorite time. The only good thing was that it was my wife's car at the bottom of the pool and not mine. She had left me a few weeks before the storm, and I was still feeling a little bitter about it. The bad thing was that she had driven away with my car because it could hold more stuff, so it wasn't exactly a total victory on my part.

The day after the hurricane, the sky was clear but the world I saw was broken, right down to the streets. I got lost every time I took a walk. Finally, I got my flashlight and dug out an old compass I had kept from the army. I took a bearing on the emptiness of the front door and started rambling around the neighborhood, looking to see what was left. People were creeping around like zombies and digging through the ruins of their houses. I passed an old man bent over like a prospector on a nameless street. He straightened up and looked at me.

"You got a cigarette?" he asked.

"I'm trying to scout some out," I told him. "There a store around here somewheres?"

He pointed to the north. "I think over that way. See that flagpole? It used to be right by there. Maybe it still is."

I looked out across the damage and the distance. The flag-pole looked a long way off. In Miami you drive every place, and I wasn't used to walking.

"What brand you smoke?" I asked.

He looked bewildered by the question. "I don't know. I don't smoke." I noticed then that he was wearing underwear—a pair of polka dot boxers and a white tank top that was never going to be white again.

"I know what you mean," I said. "I'm not much of a smoker myself."

I started walking, sometimes right through people's houses, not to be mean or anything but because the houses were all in pieces spread out like a puzzle. It was hard to tell where a thing began or ended. I could see that my place had done better than most. At least my furniture was still inside. I just hoped it was still there when I got back.

I smelled a barbecue and came up on a group of people sitting in a ring of sofas like they were inside a living room. Some people were laughing. They looked like a big family, except that some of them were black and some of them were white and some of them were speaking in Spanish. A black man was standing over a barbecue made out of a pair of steel drums with a grate over them. He held a pair of tongs and was turning pieces of meat and chicken over with them. He looked at me, and I looked at him. Then he waved me over. The fire and the heat made him look like a Vulcan. It was the best food I ever had.

I finally found the store. Where, I don't know. It was a 7-Eleven. The windows were shattered and people were climbing in and out of the place, carrying armloads of cans and boxes of cereal and cases of beer. I had never done anything like this before and for a moment I just stood there looking. Finally, I stepped over the jagged sill and into the store, feeling like I was crossing some kind of line, which I was, except it was a little hard to see exactly what kind of line it was. At least I wasn't a cannibal, I told myself. So far, I had only made it down to shoplifting.

I was behind the counter looking for smokes when the squad car pulled up, lights blazing like wild Indians. Everybody started to run like roaches. The cop came in through the window with his hand on his gun. I stood up. I put my hands up. He was a black kid—not much more than a rookie, I thought—and everything about him said *soldier*. He pointed his eyes and his gun at me at the same time, shook his head, and holstered the automatic.

"Turn around and put your hands behind your back," he said calmly. His voice was edgeless, as though he had said, *Give me a cup of coffee.*

"Officer—" I started to say.

"I know," he said. "Don't tell me. I got no choice. This shit has been going on all day and the captain wants to make a statement. Sorry, man."

I rotated and he bound my hands with a plastic tie. It was like an episode of *Cops*.

"I've never been arrested before," I said, more to myself than to the officer.

"Don't worry about it. You'll be out in the morning, maybe even later today."

The cop seemed tired, though not physically; his movements were crisp and professional. He was tired in another way. I could feel it coming off him. He reminded me of a teacher who had made it to the end of a long day at a bad school. He walked beside me without holding my arm, as though we were a couple of buddies heading to the bar for a beer or two. Sometimes he even walked a little bit ahead of me, as though he had forgotten that he had a prisoner. I guess I didn't seem that dangerous.

Right before we got to the cop car, he bent over and picked up a photograph that had blown in from another life. He stared at it for a moment, then held it up so I could see. It was the picture of a young woman, very pretty in a Nebraska sort of way: big smile, corn hair, gray eyes—innocent. I looked at the picture of the girl for a moment and nodded. Then, very gently, almost reverently, he placed the picture back on the ground on the exact spot where he had found it, as though it belonged there. Neither of us said anything. I felt a strange, indefinite sadness rise in me all the way up to my neck until I felt as though I were wearing a heavy curtain over my shoulders.

"You find stuff like that everywhere," the cop said. To me he sounded like a tour guide in a ruined temple who knew the tale of ancient disaster so well that he had learned to tell it without words.

"I wonder where it came from," I said.

"Somewhere," the cop replied aimlessly.

He opened the door of the patrol car and gently pushed my head down as I crouched. I was glad there were no cameras around. We drove slowly, both of us looking from side to side.

"You live around here?" the cop asked.

I told him my address. He said he knew where it was. Then he asked me what I did for a living.

"I'm an English teacher," I told him. "Edgewater High. Richard McManus."

He looked at me through the rearview mirror. "That's where I went," he said. "I thought you looked familiar."

"Were you one of my students?"

"No, my sister was though. Maybe you remember her? Her name was Taisha Duncan."

The rolodex that is every teacher's brain rolled, and a face appeared from a few years back.

"Sure, I remember her," I said. "Nice kid. Very good writer. Said she wanted to be a reporter someday. I wrote some letters of recommendation for her. Last I heard, she had gotten a scholarship to Georgetown, I think it was."

"That's right; that was her. Hey, you know, I think she kind of had a crush on you."

"That's because I'm so debonair. Where we going, officer? I

think the station's on the other side of the canal we just passed."

"You in a hurry to get to jail, Mr. McManus?"

"Not really," I said. "But these plastic cuffs are cutting into my hands."

He was silent for a few moments, then stopped the car suddenly and got out. I didn't know what to expect, and it seemed to me, judging from the landscape, that I wasn't going to know what to expect for a long time. I had a morbid vision of being thrown to the ground and kicked repeatedly in the stomach. There was fear and a weird kind of excitement that I didn't understand.

The cop came around and opened the door. "Come on out," he said. "This is bullshit."

I got my legs over, stuck them through the door, and stood up. He told me to turn around and then, much to my surprise, he undid the plastic ties and threw them over his shoulder. He smiled at me as I rubbed my wrists.

"What's up?" I asked.

"What were you doing in that 7-Eleven?"

"I wanted to buy some cigarettes."

"This might be the omen to quit you been waiting for," he said. "You want to take a ride with me? You know, just drive around, check things out, look for adventure."

I must have appeared dumbfounded. He laughed.

"Sure," I said lamely. "Why not?"

"You want to drive?" he asked.

"I think that might be against regulations," I offered.

"The whole fucking world is against regulations. Look at this place. He spread his arms and peered around. I looked with him. He had a point. God had poured the city of Homestead into a blender and dumped the contents onto what was left of the street, and in that world nothing was impossible. In that world English teachers could be shoplifters and shoplifters could drive police cars.

"Okay," I said. "What the hell."

We drove around for about an hour, talking about everything and nothing. The young cop's name was Robert Paulson, and he told me he had been in the Gulf War over in Iraq. I asked him what it was like.

"Not much," he said. "We sat in the desert, doing squat for six months. Then we rolled. There was a lot of smoke and fire, but it was all over quick. I never even fired my gun. We were lucky; nobody I knew got killed or anything. You had to be careful of mines though."

"You been out long?" I asked.

"It's, *Have you been out long?* You're not forgetting your stuff, are you, Mr. McManus?"

"Well?"

"A few months. Not long. It seems long though. It's funny: You come back from a war and something like this hurricane happens. Shit," he said. "This place looks worse than Iraq."

"Maybe I should be getting back now," I said. "It's getting late."

"Okay, but we got to make a stop first."

"Where to?"

"My old place. I'll tell you how to get there. Are you cool with that? It won't take long."

"What happens if another cop sees me driving you around?" I asked.

"Man, don't you know? You're undercover." He laughed and slapped me on the shoulder.

We drove west for a few miles. The sun that had seemed so high earlier in the day was plummeting now, dragging the day down with it behind a row of broken trees. With all the lights in the neighborhood out, the coming darkness affected me in some primeval part of myself, and for a moment something akin to panic began to overtake me. I wanted to go home. Even my house with its gone wife, its ripped-off roof, and its drowned car was better than the sprawling mess the world had become. I began to talk to dispel my nervousness.

"How's Taisha doing? She must be in college now."

For a moment the cop said nothing, and I wondered if he had heard me.

"Taisha's dead, man. Didn't you know?"

"Dead? What are you talking about?" I couldn't turn to look at him. I had to keep my eyes on the darkened road.

"Drunk driver. You know how it is. About a year after she graduated from Edgewater. It was up near Gainesville, near her aunt's house. Maybe that's why you didn't hear about it."

"Jesus," I said. "A young kid like that. I can't believe it."

"Maybe you heard about it but forgot. You must have had a lot of kids in your class over the years."

He was right. They came and they went. Some students you would remember for better or worse for the rest of your life, while others left barely a trace of memory behind them when the semester was over.

"No, I remember Taisha," I said, wishing in a way that I was lying. I didn't want that sweet young face floating around in my head with night coming on, not in this shattered world.

"Turn here," the cop said. "I recognize that tree." He pointed to an uprooted banyan tree lying on its side.

"Where are we?" I asked. "What is this place?"

"My old crib. Go on down this way. I'll tell you where to stop."

I soon saw that we had entered a cul-de-sac. The houses were small wrecks of wood and lopsided roofs. At the end of the street I saw the silhouettes of a man and a woman sitting on the front steps of their house. I drove slowly. When my beams from the headlights hit them, they stood up and went into the house, shutting the door behind them. They had moved so quickly, I thought they might be looters. I glanced at the cop. He was looking straight ahead.

"Stop in front of the house," the cop said. "That's where I used to live."

"You know those people?" I asked.

"That's my wife, or rather she used to be my wife."

"Who's the guy?" I asked.

"A friend of mine, used to be. Since I got back, everything is *used to be*, seems like. I asked him to keep an eye on Doris when I was over in Kuwait. Sources say he got a little bit too dedicated to the mission. You know what I'm saying?"

I looked at him. He was still staring straight ahead. He was locked in position. There was a sphinxlike quality to his profile that I didn't like.

"We had better leave," I said. I put the car in reverse and turned around to see where I was going. That's when I saw the pump action shotgun lying on the backseat, or rather, I saw its shadow. I didn't like the look of it. Without warning the cop reached over, grabbed the steering wheel, and with his other hand shifted the car back into park. We jerked to a stop. We stared at each other. The next thing I knew, I was looking at his gun, its small triangular sight lined up quite nicely with the middle of my nose.

"That's my house," he said.

I got as close to the driver's side door as a person could get without actually merging my atoms with the metal and pulled my hands way back behind my head like an extra set of ears.

"I can walk home from here," I said. "I could use the exercise."

"Not yet, professor. I want you to do me a favor."

"Look," I said. "Just put the gun down so we can talk for a minute, okay?"

He set the gun on his lap with the barrel still pointed in my general direction and his finger still on the trigger. I think he was afraid I might try to take it away from him. Little did he know how much like distant Pluto that thought was from my mind.

"I like you," he said seriously. "But don't try and do anything stupid."

"If you take a look at where I am, I think you'll see that it's a little too late for that particular bit of advice, but thanks anyway."

He smiled, but the gun stayed where it was. "You're all right," he said. "I wish you had been my teacher. I had some bitch named Ms. Duncan."

"Listen to me," I said. "You need to get the hell out of here. We both do. There's nothing here for you. I know it's easy for me to say, and I know how I would feel if I were in your place, but I'm telling you, I can read your mind like a fucking book and it's crazy. This too shall pass, but if you go in there tonight, I'm telling you, you will regret it. Let her go. She isn't worth it and neither is he. You know I'm right."

"I know you're right, but that's my house; that's my wife."

"Let the lawyers handle it. Fuck them both. Let's get out of here."

"I bet you were a pretty good teacher," he said.

"Maybe I was—once. I don't know anymore. I don't know anything anymore. I just know we need to get the hell out of here before I have a heart attack."

"I've been driving around all day, looking at everything," he said in a voice that was half anguish, half wonderment. "Everything's gone, teach. It's all gone. I can't do it no more. Go to work, act normal, do my job knowin' that they're in there together in my house. Where's the respect in that?"

I didn't know what to say, so I said: "You're a cop. Think about that. Respect that, Officer Paulson."

"I tried, but it's not enough. Stay here. I'll be right back. Got to get a few of my things. Don't go driving off now."

"Why don't you leave the gun with me?" I said.

"You think that's a good idea?"

"I know it's a good idea," I told him.

"All right." He handed me the automatic. I set it down on the floor between my feet. Officer Paulson got out of the car, straightened himself, and stared at the house for a long moment. Then leaned down, looked at me through the passenger's side window, and smiled.

"I appreciate you driving around with me. It's been a real crazy day, hasn't it?"

"I think so. Go ahead and hurry up. Don't be in there too long, you understand me? I don't want to have to come in there and drag you out."

"You sound like my pops."

"Stay cool." I gave him the peace sign, wondering if it still meant the same thing.

He smiled and began walking toward the house. When he got to the porch with its roof hanging down like a half-closed eye, he turned and waved at me. I waved back. I watched him knock politely on the door, and I watched the door open slowly. I could see the muted glow of a lit candle through the broken window. The tail end of a white curtain licked out at the breeze.

For about two minutes it was all quiet, and then the shouting started. Before I knew it, I was out of the car. I was halfway to the house when I remembered the gun on the floorboard and ran back to get it—why, I don't know, since I've never shot one in my life.

I was running toward the house when the front door opened and a man came dashing out, a young guy not much older than the cop. He was wearing a black Miami Heat T-shirt and a pair of camouflage pants. I recognized him immediately. His named was Roger Starks. He had played point guard for the basketball team at the high school where I taught. He stopped when he saw me and his eyes focused on the gun. I reached back and stuck it in my pants. Starks turned to glance back at the house.

"Roger . . ." I started to say.

He began running back toward the house, but I caught up

to him before he could pick up speed, grabbed him by the shoulders, and spun him around. He swung his right arm at me and pulled free.

"What the hell is going on?" I asked.

"He told me to go outside," Roger said. "Said he wanted to talk to her."

"It's his wife; he's got a right. Why don't you get out of here? If it's over, then it's over. Don't worry; I've got his gun."

"No, man. No you don't."

We both jumped when we heard the gunshot. Then, stupidly, we were both running toward the house. The second shot came a few seconds later, like an afterthought to a bad idea. Roger and I slowed down and looked at one another. Roger ran ahead of me, but I knew there was no need to hurry. I stopped and looked around. Shadows had begun to come out of their houses.

"Somebody call the cops!" I shouted.

"Looks like they're already here, bro!" someone shouted back.

A moment later I heard Roger wailing from inside the house. I walked up and sat down on the steps of the slanted porch and peered up at the stars in the night sky while the boy cried in the darkened house behind me. It came to me that as a boy I could name all the constellations, but now, as I looked up, it seemed to me I could barely remember a single one.

After a while, I went into the house and tried not to look at what I saw. Roger was kneeling on the floor, holding the limp body of the young woman in his arms. The cop was in a leather lounge chair with his feet up, his head over to one side, and there was a splash of blood on the wall across from him. A small silver-plated automatic lay on the floor beneath his outstretched hand. One of his pant legs was hiked up enough for me to see the empty leather ankle holster.

I went over to where Roger was and put my middle and

index fingers on the girl's carotid artery, but it was only a formality. There was no way she could have lived. Together, Roger and I put her on a waterlogged sofa, and I covered her with a comforter I took from one of the bedrooms. I walked over to the body of Officer Paulson and for some reason lay the palm of my hand across his forehead, as though he were a child with a high fever from which he would soon recover, who was napping now and would soon wake up.

I left Roger inside and went back out to the patrol car. It was country-dark and the gondola-shaped moon was the only light. Somehow, after many tries, I got the squad car's radio working and told the story to a dispatcher. She asked me who I was and where the house was located, and I told her to hold on while I went back and asked Roger for the address.

It took a long time for the police to get there. I left out the part about me driving the patrol car, and instead told them that I had just happened by. They seemed to believe me, but even so, it was nearly dawn before they let me duck under the yellow tape surrounding the house and go on my way. I was more than a bit lost when I remembered the compass in my pocket. I took it out, lined up the needle with the North Pole, and started back toward Homestead.

ONE MAN'S CEILING

BY TOM CORCORAN

Card Sound

I never knew why my stepmother called it the piano room. I never saw the piano or a picture of one and I never asked, so her explanation went with her when she died. The old pine floor measured ten-by-twelve between the front room and kitchen—fine for an upright but too tight for a baby grand. It could have been a dining room except for no table and no real upkeep for thirty years until this morning I'm talking about. Two days earlier I'd cleared it of old booze boxes full of crap like *Saturday Evening Post* magazines and mildewed utility bills from the '80s. I knew the mound of trash would piss off the city's garbage associates, so the next morning I stashed a twelve of malt liquor under the top layer and it all went away, no problem. Now, into my first renovation project, I was harmonizing with Garth Brooks, pouring Parisian Taupe flat interior enamel into a plastic paint tray, when someone double-knocked on the front screen door. At that moment the piano room dimmed—a cloud crossed the sun. I knew only two people who might show before 8:00 on a Saturday. I felt a balls-deep fear that both women had arrived at the same time. I hoped for the best and yelled out for my company to come on in.

"I ain't one of your homies, Clance. You best come see who it is."

This can't be good, I thought. The last time I heard the voice of Detective Sergeant James Task he was the county prosecutor's puppet. A starched white shirt and a ten-year-old's haircut, dealing law jargon to a jury of my non-peers, knowing full-on that his technical words connoted expertise and truth. I was guilty as hell, but that didn't mean he had to be so proficient, writing my upstate ticket to puff his tin-badge image. Four years later, I needed to kick myself for bad ears, for a lazy warning system. Not that my mental alarm could've ejected him from the porch, but his knock had been all cop and staccato and I might have offered a less jubilant invitation. I finished the pour and used a two-inch polyester brush to dab rim drips and squish paint out from behind the can label. I took my time, gathered a few yard smarts as I stood, muted my CD player, and ambled out to face the fucker.

Half the foyer back from the door, I waited for Task's opener. He was shorter than I remembered, maybe 5'6" or 5'7", but built thick like a lifter. His forehead was an inch taller than it had been that day in court. His remaining hair was slicked back as if he had just showered and was a perfect shoe-brown, a screaming admission of a dye job.

"Clancy Whidden, smack in front of me," he said. "'Sup, dawg? Same ol' same?"

"You jump off by strokin' me, take your salesman dance down the road."

"I thought I was coming in clean."

"I can do without that dumb-ass inside lingo the rest of my life."

Task gave me a loser's shrug. "I took a cram course last winter."

"Selling door-to-door?"

"Being inside."

"Start over," I said.

"A few months earlier, I could've been your cellie."

"I won't buy that shit either."

"Straight up," he said. "I had an ugly accident on 836. You must've heard about it."

I hadn't heard and I wasn't interested. My paint was drying in the pan and I hadn't even dipped the roller. "I broke my newspaper habit while I was reading ceilings," I said.

"My brake foot slipped, the lady ahead of me spun and got upside down in her Saturn. I bolted and made it about four miles, then they wedged me to the shoulder. I didn't think I was toasted but I blew a 1.8. They smeared me all over the TV. Perp-walkin' with hat-hair and blood streaming out my ears."

"I broke that television habit too," I said. "I couldn't buy a chair in the prison rec room and now I can't afford cable."

"Anyway, four months," he said, "I did it holding my breath."

"So that means you went . . ."

He looked away and shook his head. "They offered, but I couldn't go that low. Rob a bank, do your time, you stop being a bank robber. But protective custody . . ."

"Right," I said. "You're a weasel forever."

"So I opted to mingle with the population. It was known that I'd nixed PC, so I got slack, but I kept that grommet tight as a lug nut. I still walk like a duck."

"No slash scars on your belly?"

He stared cold for a flash, then shook his head.

"And you're here because . . ."

Task stuck an index finger into his ear, gave it a twist, pulled it out, and inspected for goo. "I need help on a wash job."

"Not my expertise. Never was, never will be."

"Money's money," he said. "You went up on a money crime, that sales-tax beef."

"Because you never proved what I sold was stolen."

"We had a semi-trailer full of Korean DVD players and a storage shed—two hundred toasters with Washington Mutual logos. The state attorney opted to streamline and go the tax route. His decision, believe me—I had no input. What were those toasters, for people who opened new accounts?"

I shrugged, shook my head. I didn't know, never thought of

it. "None of that means I can launder a damn thing, Task. Cars are cars, you don't get a brake mechanic to replace your headliner."

He peered through the screen, toward the room to my right. "That living room suite, you're doing something."

"Nothing that'll pull me away from blue sky."

"Can we at least talk?"

He'd parked a dark red four-door at the curb, a Town Car with its own long history. I weighed the chance that the state would put a badge in the joint for four months to build his undercover cred. It might, I decided, but not a small man like Task. Still, the dude had seriously screwed my life, kept me from attending my stepmother's funeral.

"Some other year," I said. "These days I'm on a problem-avoidance kick."

"No way I'm here to create—"

"You just standing there is shit I didn't have ten minutes ago."

He tried to look righteous, like I should take him at his word. "No peril to your renovated moral code, you follow me? Nothing illegal on your end."

I looked up the wall, decided the foyer would be my next project. "So, I like make your coffee?"

"Be my introduction."

"And if you go south, I take your strain?"

"That direction isn't built into this trip."

The foyer ceiling would get priority attention. Maybe a crown molding. Not too fancy but a class touch. "I got work to do, Task. My paint's drying in the pan."

"I smell that fresh latex," he said. "How long you got left on probation?"

"Fuckhead keeps bumping me. No reasons, no end in sight."

He said, "They got a name for it, those lame-duck POs. They laugh and talk about Perpetual Pro. After I tell you how come, you're two-thirds the way to getting off."

"This is just wonderful."

"More judges are sentencing full boogie, going stingy on probation," said Task. "Even with overcrowding, it's the wave of the future. Maybe the prisons-for-profit have judges in their pockets, I don't know. Anyway, the caseload's dropping, and Miami-Dade is cutting back. The longer a PO keeps your case active, the better his job security. You, my man, are the key to that asshole's free checking and health insurance. He keeps the ring in your nose, his kids see the orthodontist. We live in a great country, don't we?"

"I'm not feeling that two-thirds vibe."

Task looked away. "They scarfed my badge but I still got numbers to call."

"I'm into gaming it my way."

"You got a point." He peered again through the screening. "This furniture showroom paradise . . ."

"Triple paradise compared to thirty-eight—"

"—months, one week, and two days," said Task. "Surrounded by tender loving curly-cues of razor wire which day and night makes for a sparkly view."

"You did your research. You want to know how many hours that last day?"

"You didn't take a full sentence to the door. Who'd you rat?"

I shook my head. "Reduced. I fixed and maintained the central air handler."

Again, into his ear and out, and the finger's close inspection. "My numbers to call, I got more than just one."

"I don't hold a grudge, Task, especially since you told the court I was nonviolent and cooperative. But you slap a PV on me, you best be looking for another side."

"If you had to sit the rest of your—what, thirty-four more— sentence plus twelve months on the violation—"

"Eighteen."

"Still, it wouldn't be any more than . . . You'd hit the door in four years. Sell all this furniture, you might cover your property taxes, still have a roof when you walk free."

I thought about the question with no answer: *Why me?*

My curiosity took over. I let myself look convinced of his goodwill, and my face gave me away.

"You've never been a stupid man," he said.

"There's only one thing I need to know. What ballpark we playing in?"

"We're talking five-seventy-five."

"Shit," I said, "in this town? You could stash that roll under the mattress. Why stick out your neck for bird feed?"

"The people I'm working with, they don't want to jump with both feet, you know what I mean?"

"They're testing you."

"That's good logic but it ain't the case. What we need to flip is no fat fortune, but one man's floor is another man's ceiling. Isn't that how it goes?"

No, I thought. "Close enough," I said. "Hand me your shirt and pants."

Task froze. "I wouldn't bring a weapon into your home, Clancy."

"You tell that one lie, Task, I go to prison."

He didn't turn to check for neighborhood onlookers. Without hesitation he peeled down to a pair of boxers. Not the least bit self-conscious. That's when I knew he'd done time. At least that part wasn't bullshit.

"You can watch and talk," I said. "When I'm done painting, you're done talking."

You learn the ropes by bouncing off. So I set myself up as the fall guy knowing he'd knock me down and curious how he'd do it. I would hear him out and keep clean; nobody ever said that being polite was a conspiracy. If his chatter gave me the heebie-jeebies, I'd boot him. Meanwhile, I showed him his choice of chairs. Task picked the one farthest from me.

"This living room," he said, "reminds me of the house I grew up in."

"Where was that?"

"Over the bridge in South Beach," he said. "After the days of high deco fashion and before all this tits-and-bling showed up."

"The in-between was a geriatric skid row," I said.

"But growing up, you didn't know the whole world didn't wear purple wigs and play canasta. You got a bunch of fresh furniture in here, Clancy. Where you working, Rooms To Go Out The Door?"

Bastard had done his research.

My mother died a month before I got out. I inherited her house with the living room done up in 1975 porch furniture, so I decided to hit my problem head-on. I found a gig in a Dixie Highway furniture store owned by an old Miami family. I refurbished repos and returns and I repaired broken stuff. I explained to Task that the family loved the volume of ciggie-burned and butt-busted pieces I pushed back to the sales floor, even if a few had to go out as scratch-and-dent specials. What didn't pass boss lady's inspection went to trash. If I wanted to take home rejects, they were mine to carry. At first I didn't go for it, but Mrs. Minton saw through my reluctance. She printed out a release form with blank spots for me to describe the furniture, write the date, and a place for her to sign off. That way, nobody could come back later and say I stole anything. So far I had toted home four chairs, an end table, and a fancy-ass coffee table—none of which matched—and a VHS tape rack to hold paperback books.

Inside, marking time and living without a toilet seat, you learn to stifle emotions, look oblivious while your mind strips gears and spins dirt. Task rattled off opinions: Hispanics, profitable opportunities, cops he knew who were worse than the criminals they caught. I couldn't tell if cunning or fake enthusiasm or rookie hots were driving his pitch.

I didn't push him to explain his money-laundering scam. I just listened and rolled paint. Home Depot's brochure said to start with a W-shaped pattern each time you wet the roller. Then you filled in bare spots and distributed color evenly in one area before moving along the wall. It worked, but I wondered if it didn't use up more paint than necessary. Clever, those brochures.

"Best part of living in South Beach was Biscayne Bay," said Task.

"You had a motorboat?"

"How'd you know?"

"My cousin had a little skiff we ran out of the Grove," I said. "Over to Cape Florida, sometimes down to Soldier's Key. Every decent weekend for years, even during high school when we couldn't get jobs. Some days I'd go in with my mask and snorkel, and he'd tow me for miles. My private under-water cinema."

"My buddy and me, we did the same exact thing. We had to run under causeways to reach the bay, keep away from rich dudes' yachts and wakes, then weave through all those exiles hooking sponges from their ten-foot boats."

I dipped my paint roller, let the excess drip away. "They came over from Havana in those small sailboats."

"You didn't get tired of being towed around, watching the bay-bottom movie?"

"Oh, we grew up," I said. "We got to crashing parties in Stiltsville. Topless college girls wouldn't care if we stared, and the boys would sell us beer. We'd get tanked on two or three Pabst Blue Ribbons."

"Shit," said Task, "one time we took extra gas and went all the way to the bottom of the bay. We had to duck a squall up a tidal creek down below Turkey Point, and stupid me, during the rainstorm I stole a fifteen-horse Johnson off a piece-of-crap rowboat. I wrapped it in a foul-weather slicker and all the way back north, sunburned and stinking of raw gas, I waited for the

Marine Patrol to bust us. I pictured them scouring marinas all over Dade, finding that damned motor, and hauling me off to jail. I scared myself so bad, I finally pushed it overboard by Virginia Key. That was my only crime until, you know . . ."

"Not even a candy bar into your shirt pocket?"

"Not even that, until the accident. I was what they called a good little boy."

I knew where I wanted to take Task to hook up his deal. It was such a good idea, I got antsy, couldn't even finish my first wall. I wrapped the brush in a plastic grocery bag, did the same with the roller, and capped the paint gallon.

"Your car but I'm driving," I said.

"Now it's time for me to pat *you* down."

I tried to keep pity out of my voice. "Have at it, rookie."

When I was playing Mister Bad Guy, a few old Miami racketeers—the retired elders of Dade action with no desire to die in prison—hung out at a low-rent country club for a while, then a hotel lounge on LeJeune. Their presence drew the wannabes, and each place gradually filled with snoopers, thug groupies, and dipsticks staging self-important sit-downs. To escape the idiots, the elders pooled loose cash and bought a two-bedroom in Kendall, decorated it with whatever anyone in the inner circle cared to donate. They called it "The Boys Club" and that's about when I got to know them. Their days quickly fell into a sloth routine: Honduran cigars, *Law & Order* reruns, Kahlua in snifters, and getting tired of looking at each other. So they sold out and shifted their scene to Alabama Jack's, a floating restaurant ten miles south of Florida City. I ran errands for them, got a few free meals, and endured their endless bullshit sessions.

While I was doing my gray-bar penance, two thoughts buoyed my mind. The first was skin-specific. Depending on a given day's toss between nostalgia and resentment, any one of four women could've provided elevation. The second was culinary. I promised myself a fat fish sandwich and a bowl of lima bean soup at Alabama Jack's. Sure as hell, my first time back I reconnected with the crusty crew. Once they knew I was ninety-percent clean and totally clammed up, they let me sit in, even fixed me up to buy a motorboat which I keep in Key Largo. I knew I could take James Task to the master dock jockeys and they would decide how to handle him. I could play spectator and try to guess the ending.

A three-vehicle convoy passed us, blew dust into our grille. A Cadillac SUV, whatever they're called, an S-series Benz sedan, and a Lincoln Navigator. High-cotton members of the Ocean Reef Club in a hurry for their midday toddies.

"First pedal on the right," said Task. "Step on the fuck, why don't you?"

What did he expect? I was doing sixty-five in a fifty-five. The washboard road made it feel like ninety. "These are the Everglades, the real-life boonies, Task. This is your chance to commune with the quiet pace of undisturbed nature. You come down here to speed up your life, you're wasting resources."

"Middle of fuckin' nowhere," he said. "This two-lane got a name?"

"Card Sound Road."

"You're lugging it. You'll clog my plugs."

"Not until after your heart attack for worrying about your ignition. I hope you brought a package of cash."

"If I didn't, it's less than an hour away—by the way most people drive."

"Where we're going, Task, I can't float a balloon so you can say maybe. Do we need to go back a few miles?"

"Keep going. On second thought, pull over along here, let me drain the barracuda."

"You don't want to do that. Swamp skeeters are drawn to pecker temperature. We got all of six minutes to a flush toilet."

"I wish to hell you'd goose the throttle."

"Maybe not." I lifted the gas pedal as we passed a ramshackle camp with BUY BLUE CRABS and JESUS SAVES signs tacked to spindly roadside posts. I tapped the brake pedal, slowed for a left bend in the road. Before our eyes was a scene you could sell to all-night TV. Two black and gold Florida Highway Patrol Camaros with their roof racks flashing had all three speeders pulled to the shoulder. I didn't say a fucking word.

A half mile later Task said, "That's either a bad sign or I'm glad I'm with you."

"Both because I know the turf?"

"You're not as dumb as you look, Whidden."

A server near the door recognized me. She feigned exhaustion, teased her sweat-damp hair, and pointed to a round table near the waterside railing. Rigoberto and Duane. A third-generation Cuban-American and a fifth-generation peckerwood. Rigo was the old-timer; he was wearing a NASCAR T-shirt. Duane, in a fatigued guayabera sports shirt, was closer to my age. He'd started as an errand boy just like me.

We did the introduction, got invited to sit. Task said, "Pleased to meet you," and Rigo and Duane sized him for a cop, trusted that I'd brought him for a reason. We were invited to share their brunch of conch fritters and the sliced pineapple that Rigo brought from his home garden in Coral Gables. I ordered a Bloody Mary and Task got a Captain Morgan on the rocks and Rigo joked to lighten things up. The gang had razzed me about getting rid of my stepmother's doilies and trivets. Rigo asked if I'd had my yard sale yet, marked down the afghans and tea sets, held out for high dollar on her five-foot silk palm tree. Duane changed the subject, which I appreciated, and mentioned that a bonefish guide friend of his—he pointed to a large man at the bar—had released four tarpon that morning. The angler had tipped him a day's pay.

Task gazed down to the southwest. "This is Card Sound?"

"Barnes Sound," said Duane.

"We came down a road called . . ."

Rigo jacked his thumb to the northeast. "Card's up there."

Task looked in that direction. "Okay, then where's the Gulf of Mexico?"

Rigo pointed back the other way. "Down past Blackwater Sound and Florida Bay."

"A boy could get lost around here," said Task.

"Plenty have," drawled Duane.

Uh-oh, I thought.

Rigo focused the conversation. He pointed at a lumpy scar on Task's forearm. "The chief make you lose that tattoo?"

"Family thing," said Task. He tried to mask his disappointment in having been spotted as a cop.

"Your mother told you she'd die on purpose if you didn't take it off?"

"Almost her exact words."

"Just like mine," said Rigo, "bless her soul."

"But it's good that it's gone." Task rubbed his scar. "It was a fuckin' skull, dumb to start with."

"Where you stay now? Whatcha into?" said Rigo.

"West Palm. Fab, Tide, and borax."

"Ah, yes, the laundry. Into that long?"

"For a while it was a storefront, payday loans and check advances. We'd loan against car titles, that kind of crap."

"You quit that? Sounds like cash flow to me."

"We got asked nicely to close up shop. One of the polite requests you don't ignore."

"Let me guess," said Rigo. "Not the mob."

"Right you are," said Task. "A legit company, branches all over the southeast. But they had muscle on their team, that's for sure."

"So now you're into what, cleaning counterfeits, washing profits for importers?"

"No counterfeits, but everything else," said Task. "As long as they print C-notes, somebody'll build a stash of dirty ones."

Rigo cut a slice of pineapple into one-inch sections, then used the knife to stick a piece into his mouth. "Discounting's a growing industry."

"Numbskulls coming in, their rookie mistakes, makes it tight at the top."

"I hear they got a joint-ops group all over that shit."

Task faked a chuckle. "That group is turning up five-year-old rocks. They 'bout as tuned-in as polka dot pants."

"You know that for a fact?"

"We keep an eye out," said Task. "That's how it is."

"So we need to get down to the gritty," said Rigo. He looked at Duane and me. "You two wanted to sit at the next table, correct?"

The two of us left behind our near-empties, took new seats. Duane ordered fresh drinks for both tables and two more baskets of fritters.

"You're a lot calmer since you went away."

"I know. I'm four years older," I said. "I didn't think I'd changed so you'd notice."

"You were so wired up, we called you the electric fence. How's that Wellcraft you bought?"

"I don't know. It sits lopsided, heavy to starboard. The gas gauge tells lies, so when you see it's half-full you know it's full empty. And with that seventy-five Mercury, if you go for optimum cruising tilt, the turbulence kills your water pressure."

"Cavitation," said Duane.

"So I change the tilt, ride ass high, the bow thumps. If I ride ass low, the water pressure lifts, but I get less RPM for more throttle."

"Using ninety-three octane for your mix?"

"Always."

"Mount that motor an inch lower on the transom."

"I will do that."

"He's got you in a twist."

"Do tell," I said.

"Ex-cops don't know how to cut pie. He'd rather shoot his knee than give you a percentage, so you didn't get pushed here by money. Where's he coming from?"

"Claims he's got juice in the probation system. He can make it either better or worse for me. I don't need to fucking go backward."

"That's a good one. Be better if you could hold him to it. Telling lies, he's had years of training."

"What if his deal takes a shit?"

Duane looked down the canal as if the resident cormorant was an essential factor in his dockside existence. "If it goes good, you get a snack from Rigoberto."

I waited for the rest.

"Something goes sideways . . ." He turned to look me in the eye. "You'll be glad your mother died first."

Change the subject. "How did The Club happen to migrate to Alabama Jack's?"

"My doing. I've always come here. I grew up a half mile up the road."

I asked tactfully, "In a stilt home?"

Duane shook his head. "A lopsided shack that started as a house trailer which became a houseboat which survived I can't count how many storms and got attached to the canal's edge. We were scroungy-ass poor but never hungry except one summer when I didn't have a boat motor. I had to troll out of a fucking canoe. That was the summer me and my sisters almost starved."

"Mister James Task over there bragged to me two hours ago about coming down Biscayne Bay from Miami Beach in the 1970s and boosting a fifteen-horse Johnson off what he called a piece-of-crap rowboat."

"Boys will be boys," said Duane. "You come in your pickup?"

"I drove his Town Car."

"What color is it?" He turned, gave a slight wave, caught the attention of our server.

"Dark maroon," I said.

Duane's cell phone rang. He unclipped it from his belt, raised his bifocals to read the caller ID, scowled, stood, and walked fifteen feet from the table. His conversation lasted no more than ten seconds.

I wondered what had happened to our server. I watched her take a walk-around phone from the fishing guide at the bar and hang it back on the wall.

Across the table, Rigo and Task looked up when Duane took his seat.

"Kids," said Duane.

Rigo nodded and asked us to rejoin him and Task.

"I've been explaining the new realities of yacht restoration," said Rigo. "How someone finds a stripped and abandoned boat, reports it to the Marine Patrol, then tries to claim salvage rights. When that fails, which is no surprise, the finder buys it from the insurance company and hires an outfitter to make the yacht presentable again."

"It's a great concept," said Task. "You got the original claim, the stripped stuff in a storage locker, the cost of the lawyers, and the hull. Then the resale including finder's fees and brokerage fees, you got cash flow at every stage."

Duane looked up at a twirling fan. "The rebuilder has to reapply for a boat title, so every time it gets stolen, rebuilt, and resold, it's officially a different boat. The state of Florida will catch on someday, but they haven't done it yet."

Task picked his ear and did a wax check. "I love it," he said, "and so will my people."

The fishing guide from the bar appeared at our table. "Who wants to go sightseeing?" he said. "A pickup truck just sailed into Elliott Key."

"A refugee raft?" I said.

"Eighteen Cubans running a bus diesel with a prop on the driveshaft. God knows how they made it across. You want to ride up with me to look?"

"Shit yes, Bear," said Rigo. "This is current-day history in action. We'll all go along if there's room."

Captain Bear shook his head. "Room for three but not four."

Duane said, "I'll stay behind."

"I want you along," said Rigo. "We got something in motion. We need to talk with Mr. Task."

"I'll sit at the bar," I said. "I can watch golf and daydream about painting walls."

They left and I took Captain Bear's vacated stool, a mere ten feet from the TV, and nursed my third Bloody Mary. Ten minutes into my wait, the server I knew handed me a folded-up bar napkin. The note read: *NO PASSENGER SIDE AIR BAG. 75 BIGS AND TASER IN CAVITY. PIG STICKER IN DRIVER'S SIDE VISOR.*

Forty minutes later, I heard Bear's skiff maneuver to the dock. Rigo and Captain Bear returned to our table by the railing, and Duane motioned for me to follow him outside. We walked down the dock toward the Hewes that Bear chartered. Over the railing the dredged canal bottom reflected early-afternoon sun. It looked like a painter's dreamscape of aquatic pastels, except it was real and just the ditch.

"Strange sky this afternoon," I said.

"You're in South Florida, Clancy Whidden. After enough time ain't nothing strange here."

"Where's our man Task?"

"He got side-tracted," said Duane. "Stupid asshole was running solo. He had the *cojones* to ask for security cash."

"Not too damned smart," I said.

"True, and you should be offended. He didn't think much of your smarts, either. He volunteered to . . . What'd he say? Remove you from the equation."

"Not a surprise," I said.

"Rigo thinks you should be compensated for Task's rudeness." Duane reached into the Hewes skiff, grabbed two cans of Budweiser, and handed me one. "Don't pop it open just yet," he said. "There's ten grand in there. Where are you going to leave that Town Car, and don't tell me the airport?"

"I'll park it behind a bar in South Miami. They'll think for a week that some drunk forgot where he left it."

"That's plenty of time. You didn't drive the Turnpike, right?"

"Don't worry," I said. "No toll booth photos."

"That's a healthy chunk of change, Clancy. How will you spend yours?"

"A Yamaha piano. I can't decide between baby grand or upright. I'll stash the rest and trickle-spend. You?"

"That's a coincidence—Yamaha. I'm going to order a 225 four-stroke for my workboat. Replace that Johnson someone stole a lifetime ago."

"You think he did it?"

"I figure a five-year gap between our ages, maybe six." Duane popped open his beer. "I'd sure like to know who it was, but it wasn't him."

SOLOMON & LORD DROP ANCHOR

BY PAUL LEVINE

Florida Straits

W hat aren't you telling me?" Victoria Lord demanded.
Jeez. Her grand jury tone.

"Nothing to tell," Steve Solomon said. "I'm going deep-sea fishing."

"You? The guy who got seasick in a paddle boat at Disney World?"

"That boat was defective. I'm gonna sue." Steve hauled an Igloo cooler onto the kitchen counter. "You may not know it, but I come from a long line of anglers."

"A long line of liars, you mean."

The partners of Solomon & Lord, Attorneys-at-Law, stood in the kitchen of Steve's bungalow on Kumquat Avenue in Coconut Grove. The place was a square stucco pillbox the color of a rotting avocado, but it had withstood hurricanes, termites, and countless keg parties.

Unshaven and hair mussed, wearing cargo shorts and a T-shirt, Steve looked like a beach bum. Lips glossed and cheekbones highlighted, wearing a glen-plaid suit with an ivory silk blouse, Victoria looked sexy, smart, and successful.

"C'mon, Steve. What are you really up to?" Her voice drizzled with suspicion like mango glaze over sautéed snapper.

Steve wanted to tell his lover and law partner the truth. Or at least, the partial truth. But he knew how Ms. Propriety would react: "You can't do that. It's unethical."

And if he told her the truth, the whole truth, and nothing but the truth? "You'll be disbarred! Jailed. Maybe even killed."

No, he'd have to fly solo. Or swim solo, as the case may be.

Steve pulled two six-packs of Heineken out of the refrigerator and tossed them into the cooler. "Okay, it's really a business meeting."

Victoria cocked her head and pursed her lips in cross-exam mode. "Which is it, Pinocchio? Fishing or business? Were you lying then or are you lying now?"

For a tall, lanky blonde with a dazzling smile, she could fire accusations the way Dan Marino once threw the football.

"I'm going fishing with Manuel Cruz."

"What? I thought you were going to sue him."

"Which is what makes it business. Cruz wants to make an offer before we file suit. I suggested we go fishing, keep it relaxed. He loved the idea and invited me on his boat."

So far, Steve hadn't told an outright fib and it was almost 8 a.m. Not quite a personal best, but still, he was proud of himself.

For the last five years, Manuel Cruz worked as controller of Toraño Chevrolet in Hialeah, where he managed to steal three million dollars before anyone noticed. Teresa Toraño, a Cuban *exiliada* in her seventies, was nearly bankrupt, and Steve was determined to get her money back, but it wouldn't be easy. All the computer records had been erased, leaving no electronic trail. Cruz had no visible assets other than his sportfishing boat. The guy didn't even own a house. And the juiciest piece of evidence—Cruz fled Cuba years ago after embezzling money from a government food program—wasn't even admissible.

"Just you and Cruz, alone at sea," she said. "Sounds dangerous."

"I'm not afraid of him."

"It's not you I'm worried about."

Victoria punched the *record* button on her pocket Dictaphone.

"Memo to the Toraño file. Make certain our malpractice premiums are paid."

"You and your damned Dictaphone," Steve complained. "Drives me nuts."

"Why?"

"I don't know. It's so . . ."

"Organized?"

"Anal."

Victoria pulled her Mini Cooper into the Matheson Hammock Marina, swerving to avoid a land crab clip-clopping across the asphalt. The sun was already baking the pavement, the air sponge-thick with humidity. Just above a stand of sea lavender trees, a pair of turkey buzzards flew surveillance.

Victoria sneaked a look at Steve as he hauled the cooler out of the car's tiny trunk. Dark, unruly hair, a slight, sly grin as if he were one joke ahead of the rest of the world. The deep brown eyes, usually filled with mischief, were hidden behind dark Ray-Bans.

Damnit, why won't he level with me?

Why did he always take the serpentine path instead of the expressway? Why did he always treat laws and rules, cases and precedents, as mere suggestions?

Because he has more fun making it up as he goes along.

Steve drove her crazy with his courtroom antics and his high-wire ethics. If he believed in a client, there was nothing he wouldn't do to win. Which was exactly what frightened her now.

Just what would Steve do for Teresa Toraño?

They headed toward the dock, the morning sun beating down so ferociously Victoria felt her blouse sticking to her shoulder blades. The only sounds were the groans of boats in their moorings and the caws of gulls overhead. The air smelled of the marshy hammock, salt and iodine and fermenting seaweed. The fronds of thatch palms hung limp in the still air.

"Gimme a kiss. I gotta go," Steve said, as they stepped onto the concrete dock. In front of them were expensive toys, gleaming white in the morning sun. Rows of powerful sportfishermen, large as houses. Dozens of sleek sailing craft, ketches and sloops and schooners.

"Sure, Mr. Romance." She kissed him lightly on the lips. Something seemed off-kilter, but what? And what was that pressing against her through his shorts? Hadn't last night been enough? Twice before *SportsCenter*, once after *Letterman*.

She sneaked a hand into his pocket and came out with a pair of handcuffs. "What's this, the latest in fishing tackle?"

"Ah. Well. Er . . ." Gasping like a beached grouper. "You know that store, Only Sexy Things?" He grabbed the handcuffs and slipped them back into his pocket. "Thought I'd spice up the bedroom."

"Stick to cinnamon incense. Last chance, loverboy. What's going on?"

"You're fucking late, *hombre!*" Manuel Cruz yelled from the fly bridge of a power boat tied up at the dock. He was a muscular man in his late thirties, wearing canvas shorts and a white shirt with epaulets. A Marlins cap was pulled low over his eyes, and his sunglasses hung on a chain.

The boat was a sportfisherman in the sixty-foot range, all polished teak and gleaming chrome. A fly bridge, a glass-enclosed salon, and a pair of fighting chairs in the cockpit for serious deep-sea fishing. The name on the stern read: *Wet Dream*.

Men, Victoria thought. Men were so one-dimensional.

"*Buenos días*, Ms. Lord."

She gave him a nod and a tight smile.

"Let's go, Solomon," Cruz urged. "Fish are hungry."

Steve hoisted the cooler onto the deck. "Toss the lines for us, hon?"

She leveled a gaze at him. "Sure, hon."

Victoria untied the bow line from its cleat and threw it up

on the boat. She moved quickly to the stern, untied the line, propped a hand on a piling crusted with bird dung, and leapt aboard.

"Vic! Whadaya think you're you doing?"

"Going fishing."

"Get back on the dock."

She smiled and pointed toward the growing body of water that separated them from land.

"You're not dressed for fishing," Steve told her.

"I'm dressed for your bail hearing." She kicked off her velvet-toed pumps and peeled off her panty hose, distracting Steve with her muscular calves, honed on the tennis courts of La Gorce Country Club. "Now, what's with the handcuffs?"

Steve lowered his voice so she could barely hear him above the roaring diesels. "You remember Solomon's Law number one?"

Oh, that. Steve's personal code for rule breaking.

"How could I forget? *If the law doesn't work . . . work the law.*"

"In the matter of Manuel Cruz, the law isn't working."

"What's that?" Cruz asked, eying the cooler on the deck.

"Brought beer and bait," Steve said.

"What for? I got a case of La Tropical and a hundred pounds of shiners and wiggles."

All three of them stood on the fly bridge. Twin diesels throbbing, the *Wet Dream* cruised down Hawk Channel inside the barrier reefs. The water was green felt, smooth as a billiard table, the boat riding on a plane at thirty knots.

Cruz ran a hand over the polished-teak steering wheel. "I come to this country with nothing but the clothes on my back and look at me now."

"Very impressive," Steve said, thinking it would be even more impressive if Cruz hadn't stolen the money to buy the damn boat.

Cruz winked at Victoria, his smile more of a leer. "You two want to fool around, I got clean sheets in the master stateroom."

"Sounds lovely," Victoria cooed. "Want to fool around, Steve?" Her smile was as sweet as fresh-squeezed *guarapo*, but Steve caught the sarcastic tone.

"Maybe after we catch something," he said pointedly.

"Heads and A/C work, faucets don't," Cruz said. "Water tank's fouled."

Steve studied the man, standing legs spread at the wheel, a macho pose. A green tattoo of a scorpion crawled up one ankle. On the other ankle, in a leather sheaf, was a foot-long Marine combat knife. It looked like the weapon Sylvester Stallone used in those *Rambo* movies. Out here, it could be used to cut lines or clean fish.

Or gut a lawyer planning to do him harm.

They had just passed Sombrero Light when Cruz said, "So here's my offer, *hombre*. The Toraño bitch gives me a release with a promise never to sue. And vice versa. I won't sue her ass."

"I don't like the way you talk about my client," Steve said.

"Tough shit. I don't like Fidel Castro, but what am I gonna do about it?"

"Your offer stinks like week-old snapper."

"You sue me, what do you get? A piece of paper you can wipe your ass with. I got nothing in my own name, including the boat."

Steve looked right and left to get his bearings. Off to port, in the direction of the reef, he spotted the fins of two sharks heading toward strands of yellow sargasso weed, home to countless fish. Red coral just below the surface cast a rusty glow on the shallow water. To the starboard was the archipelago of the Florida Keys. From here, the island chain was strung out like an emerald necklace.

"Let Vic take the wheel a minute," Steve said. "I want you to see something."

Cruz allowed as how even a woman lawyer could keep a boat on 180 degrees, due south, and followed Steve down the ladder to the cockpit. Just off the stern, the props dug at the water like a plow digging at a field. Steve opened the cooler, reached underneath the ice, and pulled out a two-foot-long greenish-blue fish, frozen solid. A horse-eyed jack.

"Great bait, huh?" Steve held the fish by its tail and let it swing free. It had a fine heft, like a small sledgehammer.

"Already told you, I got shiners and wiggles."

"Then I better use this for something else." Steve swung the frozen fish at Cruz's head. The man stutter-stepped sideways and the blow glanced off his shoulder and sideswiped an ear. Steve swung again and Cruz ducked, the fish flying free and shattering the glass door of the salon. Cruz reached for his knife in the ankle sheath and Steve barreled into him, knocking them both to the deck.

On the fly bridge, Victoria screamed, "Stop! Both of you!"

The two men rolled over each other, scraping elbows and knees on the planked deck. Cruz was heavier, and his breath smelled of tobacco. Steve was wiry and quicker, but ended up underneath when they skidded to a stop. Cruz grabbed Steve's T-shirt at the neck and slammed his head into the deck. Once, twice, three times. *Thwomp, thwomp, thwomp.*

Steve balled a fist and landed a short right that caught Cruz squarely on the Adam's apple. The man gagged, clutched his throat, and fell backward. Steve squirmed out from under, but Cruz tripped him. Steve tumbled into the gunwale, smacking his head, sparks flashing behind his eyes. He had the sensation of being dragged across a hard floor. On his back, he opened his eyes and saw something glistening in the sun.

The knife blade!

Cruz was on his knees, knife in hand. "*Pendejo!* I oughta make chum out of you."

"No!" Victoria's voice, closer than it should have been.

Steve heard the clunk, saw Cruz topple over, felt him bounce off his own chest. Straddling both of them was Victoria, a three-foot steel tarpon gaff in her right hand.

"Omigod," she said. "I didn't kill him, did I?"

"Not unless a dead man grunts and farts at the same time," Steve said, listening to sounds coming from both ends of the semiconscious man.

He shoved Cruz off and stood up, wrapping his arms around Victoria, who was trembling. "You were terrific, Vic. We work great together."

"Really? What did *you* do?"

"Come on. Help me get him up the ladder." Steve pulled the handcuffs from his pocket. "I want him on the bridge."

"What now? What insanity now?"

"Relax, Vic. In a few hours, Cruz will be dying to give back Teresa's money."

Steve had played fast and loose with the rules before, Victoria thought, but nothing like this.

This is scary. And in the eyes of the law, she was dirty too.

This could mean trading the couture outfits and Italian footwear for orange jumpsuits and shower shoes.

With one wrist handcuffed to the rail at the rear of the bridge, Cruz had been berating Steve for the past twenty minutes.

"Know what, Solomon? She hits harder than you do."

"Mr. Cruz," Victoria said, "if you begin to feel dizzy or nauseous, let me know. Head trauma can be very dangerous."

"What about *my* head?" Steve demanded.

"It's impervious to trauma. Or reason."

The *Wet Dream* was planing across the tops of small whitecaps when Steve said: "Take the wheel, Vic. Keep it on two-zero-two."

"Please," she said, irritated.

"What?"

"'Keep it on two-zero-two, *please*.'"

"A captain doesn't say 'please.'"

"Maybe not Captain Bligh." Victoria slid behind the wheel, thinking perhaps she'd hit the wrong man with the gaff. She still didn't know where they were headed, and Steve's behavior was becoming increasingly bizarre. He had the beginning of a lump on his head, and blood trickled from his skinned elbows and knees.

"Kidnapping," Cruz said. "Assault. Boat theft. You two are gonna be busy little shysters."

"Shut up," Steve said. "Under the law of the sea, I'm master of this craft."

"What law? You stole my fucking boat."

Once past Key West, they entered the Florida Straits, the water growing deeper, the color turning from light green to aquamarine to cobalt blue. No reefs here, and a five-foot chop slapped at the hull of the boat. The wavecaps sparkled, as if studded with diamonds in the late-afternoon sun.

"Gonna tell you a story, Cruz," Steve said, "and when I'm done, you're gonna cry and beg forgiveness and give back all the money you stole."

"Yeah, right."

"Story starts forty-some years ago in Havana. A beautiful lady named Teresa Toraño lost her husband who was brave enough to oppose Fidel Castro."

"Tough shit," Cruz said. "Happened to a lot of people."

"Teresa came to Miami with nothing. Worked minimum wage, mopped floors in a car dealership, ended up owning Toraño Chevrolet."

"My *papi* always told me hard work pays off," Cruz said,

smirking. "Too bad he never got out of the cane fields."

"A few years ago, she hires a new controller. A fellow *exiliado.* This guy's got a fancy computer system that will revolutionize their books. It also lets him steal three million bucks before anybody knows what hit them. Now the banks have pulled Teresa's line of credit, and she could go under."

"I'm not crying, Solomon."

"Not done yet. See, this lady is damn important to me. If it hadn't been for Teresa giving me work my first year out of school, I'd have gone broke."

"*Lo único que logró fue posponer lo inevitable,*" Cruz said. "She only postponed the inevitable."

Victoria knew there was more to it than just a financial relationship. Teresa had virtually adopted Steve and his nephew Bobby, and the Solomon boys loved her in return. After Victoria entered the picture, she was added to the extended Toraño family. Each year at Christmas, they all gathered at Teresa's estate in Coral Gables for her homemade *crema de vie,* an anise drink so rich it made eggnog seem like diet soda. All of which meant that Steve would do anything for Teresa. One of Steve's self-proclaimed laws expressed the principle: "I won't break the law, breach legal ethics, or risk jail time . . . unless it's for someone I love."

Now that Victoria thought about it, the question wasn't: Just what would Steve do for Teresa Toraño? It was: What *wouldn't* he do?

"That sleazy accountant," Steve said. "In Cuba, he kept the books for the student worker program, the students who cut sugar cane. Ran the whole food services division. But he had a nasty habit of cutting the pineapple juice with water and selling the meat off the back of trucks. The kids went hungry and he got fat. When the authorities found out, he stole a boat and got the hell out of the worker's paradise."

"Old news, *hombre.*"

"Vic, still on two-zero-two?" Steve asked.

"I know how to read a compass," she said sharply.

"Where you taking me?" Cruz demanded.

"Jeez, how'd you ever get from Havana to Key West?" Steve said.

"Everybody in Havana knows the heading to the States. You want Key West, you keep it at twenty-two degrees."

"A bit east of due north. So what's two-zero-two?" said Steve.

"A little west of due south."

"Keep going, Cruz. I think you're catching the drift, no pun intended."

Steve waited a moment for the bulb to pop on. When it didn't, he continued, "202 minus 22 is 180. What happens when you make a 180-degree turn, philosophically or geographically speaking?"

"Fuck!" Cruz jerked the handcuff so hard the rail shuddered. "We're going to Havana!"

"Bingo. We're repatriating you."

"You crazy? Cuban patrol boats will sink us. You remember that tugboat, *Trece de Marzo*? Forty people dead."

"The *Marzo* was trying to leave the island. We're coming in, and we're bringing a fugitive to justice. They should give us a reward, or at least a bottle of Club Havana rum."

"They'll kill me."

"Not without a trial. A speedy trial. Of course, if you tell us where you've stashed Teresa's money, we'll turn this tub around."

"Damnit, Steve," Victoria said. "We have to talk."

Steve put the boat on auto—202 degrees—and took Victoria down to the salon.

"We could be jailed," she said. "Or killed. Right now, the best case scenario would be disbarment."

"That's why I didn't want you along."

Steve walked to the galley sink and turned on the faucet, intending to rinse the dried blood from a scraped elbow. The plumbing rattled and thumped, but nothing came out. He opened the ice maker. Empty too.

"Cruz is a lousy host," Steve said.

"Are you listening to me? Let's go back to Miami. I'll see if we can talk Cruz out of filing charges."

They both heard the sound, but it took a second to identify it. A scream from the bridge. "Sol-o-mon!"

Followed a second later by machine-gun fire.

Steve and Victoria ran back up the ladder to the bridge. Cruz was tugging against the rail, his wrist bleeding where the handcuff sawed into his skin. Three hundred yards off their starboard, a Cuban patrol boat fired a short burst from a machine gun mounted on its bow. Dead ahead, the silhouette of the Cuban island rose from the sea, misty in the late-afternoon light.

"Warning shots," Steve said. "Everybody relax."

Steve eased back on the throttles, tooted the horn, and waved both arms at the approaching boat. "C'mon Cruz. It's now or never. When they pull alongside, I'm handing you over."

"Do what you got to do, asshole."

"Steve, turn the boat around," Victoria ordered. "Now!"

The patrol boat slowed. Two men in uniform at the machine gun, a third man holding a bullhorn.

"I'm not fucking with you, Cruz," Steve said. "You've got thirty seconds. Where's Teresa's money?"

"*Chingate!*" Cruz snarled.

"*Señores del barco de pesca!*" The tinny sound of the bullhorn carried across the water.

"Last chance," Steve said.

"*Se han adentrado en las aguas territoriales de la República de Cuba.*"

"Steve, we're in Cuban waters," Victoria said.

"I know. I passed Spanish 101."

"*Den la vuelta y salgan inmediatamente de aquí, o los vamos a abordar.*"

"They're going to board us if we don't turn around," she said.

"I kind of figured that out too." Steve turned to Cruz. "Absolutely, positively last chance, pal. I'm handing you over."

"I'm betting you don't," Cruz said.

The patrol boat was fifty yards away. One of the men in uniform pointed an AK-47 their way.

"Steve . . . ?" Victoria's voice was a plea.

This wasn't the way he'd planned it. By this time, Cruz should have been spouting numbers and accounts from banks in the Caymans or Switzerland or the Isle of Man. But the bastard was toughing it out. Calling Steve's bluff.

Is that what it was? An empty threat?

Steve wanted to hand Cruz over, wanted him to rot in a Cuban prison.

But damnit, I'm a lawyer, not a vigilante.

He wished he could turn his conscience on and off with the flick of a switch. He wished he could end a man's life with cold calculations and no remorse. But the rats gnawing on Cruz at Isla de Pinos would also visit the house on Kumquat Avenue in Steve's nightmares.

"Take the wheel, Vic." Filled with self-loathing, wishing he could be someone he was not. "Twenty-two degrees. Key West."

"Say 'please,'" Cruz laughed, mocking him.

Just before midnight, the lights of Key West off the port, the *Wet Dream* cruised north through Hawk Channel, headed toward Miami. The sky was clear and sparkled with stars. The wind whipped across the bridge, bringing a night chill. Victoria slipped into her glen-plaid jacket. Hair messed, clothes rumpled, emotionally drained, she was trying to figure out how to salvage the situation.

I came aboard to save Steve from himself and I'm doing a lousy job.

Steve stood at the wheel, draining a La Tropical beer, maybe listening, maybe not, as Cruz berated him.

"You fucking loser," Cruz said. "Every minute I'm tied up is gonna cost you." Cruz rubbed his arm where the cuff was biting into his wrist. "I got nerve damage. Gonna add that to my lawsuit. When this is over, you'll wish the Cubans had taken *you* prisoner."

"Steve, I need a moment with you," Victoria said.

Steve put the boat on auto—Cruz complaining that it was a damn reckless way to cruise at night—then headed down the ladder, joining Victoria in the salon.

"You can't keep him locked up," she said.

"I need more time."

"For what?"

"To think." He walked to the galley sink and turned the faucet, intending to splash cold water on his face. Same rattle, same thump. "Damn, I forgot. Cruz put all that money into his boat and still can't get the water to work."

"What?"

"A fancy boat like this and you can't wash your hands."

"No. What you said before. 'Cruz put all that money into his boat.'"

"It's just a figure of speech."

"Think about it, Steve. He doesn't own a house. He leases a car. No brokerage accounts, no bank accounts. Everything he has, he puts into his boat. If he ever has to leave town quickly . . ."

"Like he left Cuba," Steve said, picking up the beat. "With nothing but the clothes on his back."

"This time it would be different because . . ."

"The money's here! On the boat."

In sync now, she thought. A man and a woman running stride for stride.

"Vic, why don't you go back up to the bridge and make sure we don't crash into any cruise ships?"

"And what are you doing?"

"I'm gonna fix the plumbing."

Steve opened the hatch in the salon floor and climbed down a ladder to the engine compartment, wincing at the noise from the twin diesels. He found the black water tank first, tucked up under the bow. Sewage and waste water. Nothing unusual about it, and Cruz wouldn't want to dirty his hands with that, anyway. Then Steve found the freshwater tank, a custom job built into one of the bulkheads. Made of fiberglass, it looked capable of holding five hundred gallons or more. The boat had desalinization equipment, so why did Cruz need such a big tank?

A big tank that wasn't working.

Steve grabbed a flashlight mounted on a pole and took a closer look. He peered into an inspection port and could see the tank was three-quarters full. On top of the tank was a metal plate with a built-in handle. He turned the plate counterclockwise and removed it. Then he aimed the flashlight into the opening.

Water. Well, what did you expect?

He grabbed a mop that was attached by velcro to a stringer and poked the handle into the tank. The end of the handle clanked off the walls.

Clank. Clank. Clank. Thud.

Thud? What the hell?

Steve pushed the mop handle around the bottom of the tank as if he were stirring a giant vat of *paella*. It snagged on something soft. He worked the handle under the object and lifted.

Something as long as a man's body but much thinner.

Thin enough to fit into the opening of the custom-built tank. The object was a transparent plasticized pouch, and when the end peeked out of the opening, Steve saw Ben Franklin's tight-lipped face. A hundred-dollar bill. Stacked on others. Dozens of stacks. As he pulled the pouch out of the tank, he saw even more. Hundreds of stacks, thousands of bills.

Damn heavy, Steve thought, lugging the pouch up the ladder from the engine compartment. Then he dragged the load out the salon door and into the cockpit.

"Now you've done it." Cruz sounded almost mournful. He stood on the bridge, aiming a double-barrel shotgun at Steve. The rail where he had been cuffed hung loose. "I didn't want this. But it's your own damn fault."

"I'm sorry, Steve," Victoria said. "When I came up here, he'd gotten out."

"It's okay," Steve said. He dragged the pouch to the starboard gunwale.

"Stop right there!" Cruz ordered. "Step away from the money."

"Nope. Don't think so."

Cruz pumped the shotgun, an unmistakable *click-clack* that Steve felt in the pit of his stomach. "I'll blow your head off."

"And leave blood and bone and tissue embedded in the planking? Nah. You may kill us, but you won't do it on your boat." Steve hoisted the pouch onto the rail. "If I can't take this to Teresa, I'm sure as hell not gonna let you have it. Your treasure, pal, is strictly Sierra Madre."

The shotgun blast roared over Steve's head, and he flinched. The pouch balanced on the rail, halfway between the deck and the deep blue sea.

"Put the money down, asshole."

"Okay, okay." Steve shoved the pouch over the rail and it splashed into the water. "It's down."

"Asshole!" Cruz grabbed both throttles, slowed the boat, and swung her around. He turned a spotlight on the water.

Nothing but a black sea and foamy whitecaps.

He swung the spotlight left and right. Still nothing, until . . . the beam picked up the pouch floating with the current. Cruz eased the boat close to the pouch at idle speed, slipped the engine out of gear, then dashed down the ladder. Grabbing a tarpon gaff, he moved quickly to the gunwale. Shotgun in one hand, gaff in the other, he motioned toward Steve. "Back up. All the way to the chair."

"Do what he says, Steve!" Victoria called from the bridge.

"Only because you say so." Steve moved toward one of the fighting chairs.

Cruz leaned over the side and snagged the pouch with the gaff. He struggled to lift it with one arm, still aiming the shotgun at Steve.

Suddenly, the boat shot forward, and Cruz tumbled into the water, the shotgun blasting into space as it fell onto the deck. On the bridge, Victoria had one hand on the throttles, the other on the wheel.

"*Coño!*" Cruz shouted from the darkness.

"Do sharks feed at night?" Steve leaned over the side. "Or should I just drop some wiggles on your head and find out?"

"Get me out of here!" His voice more fearful than demanding.

"Nah."

"*No me jodas!*"

"I'm not fucking with you. Just don't feel like giving you a lift."

Victoria raced down the ladder and joined Steve in the cockpit. "Testing, testing," she said, punching a button on her pocket Dictaphone.

"What are you doing?" Steve said.

"Mr. Cruz!" Victoria called out. "We'll bring you on board once you answer a few questions."

Cruz was splashing just off the starboard side. "What fucking questions!"

"Do you admit stealing three million dollars from Teresa Toraño?" Victoria said.

Pink slivers of sky lit up the horizon and seabirds squawked overhead as Steve steered the boat into the channel at Matheson Hammock. He had one hand on the wheel and one draped on Victoria's shoulder. A shivering Cruz, his arms and legs bound with quarter-inch line, was laced into a fighting chair in the cockpit. His taped confession would be in the hands of the state attorney by noon. The pouch of money lay at his feet, taunting him.

"What are you thinking about?" Victoria asked.

"I was just imagining the look on Teresa's face when we give her the money."

"She'll be delighted. But it was never about the money, Steve."

"Whadaya mean?"

"When you were a baby lawyer, Teresa believed in you and nobody else did. You needed to prove to her that she was right. And maybe you needed to prove it to yourself too."

Steve shrugged. "If you say so."

She wrapped both arms around his neck. "But remember this, Steve. You never have to prove anything to me." They kissed, at first softly, and then deeper and slower. The kiss lasted a long time, and when they opened their eyes, the sun was peeking above the horizon in the eastern sky.

Victoria folded the contours of her body against him. "What's that?"

"What?" he asked.

"Pressing against me. You have another pair of handcuffs in your pocket?"

"Nope."

"Then what . . . ?" She jammed a hand into one of his pockets. "Oh. That."

Steve smiled. "Like I said, no cuffs."

"It's okay, sailor." She brushed her lips against his cheek. "You won't need them."

THE LAST OF LORD JITTERS

BY DAVID BEATY

South Miami

The hurricane brought Woody and Isolde Trimble home on the last flight from San Francisco before the authorities closed the Miami airport.

A Miami neighbor had phoned them at Woody's mother's house in Bolinas, north of San Francisco. They'd just pulled into her driveway after ten days of camping in the Trinities. Woody's mother had recently died, and the camping trip was a vacation after all the sad cleaning and sorting they'd done at her house, preparing it for sale.

From the driveway, they heard telephones ringing in the empty rooms. Isolde ran into the house and answered in the kitchen. It was just after 9 p.m. A woman's voice, hoarse and dramatic, said, "It's coming." Isolde, suspecting a joke, said, "Tell me about it." Hurricane Ernestine, the woman said. One huge—pardon her French—fucking monster, *coño*, and what are you going to do about your hurricane shutters? It was their neighbor in Miami. She and her husband, the woman said, were leaving tonight, driving up to Disney World. Oh—and that fucking alligator had come back again.

The next morning at the San Francisco airport, the ticket agent warned the Trimbles that the Miami airport would be closing down soon. Their flight might be diverted. Woody told her they'd chance it. The agent asked if they'd ever experienced a hurricane.

Woody glanced at Isolde, who said that she hadn't. Woody said that he had.

Isolde had a bad feeling about Hurricane Ernestine. Her marriage to Woody was new, but their house in Miami was old. They'd lived in it for five months. They had metal hurricane shutters for only the front and back porch windows. In June, Woody had stored water, hurricane supplies, and plywood sheets in the garage. Now they had to get back in time to cut the plywood sheets to size and bolt them over all the other windows.

Woody remembered his last hurricane, when he was a kid living in Coconut Grove. He remembered their shuttered house, the humidity, the god-awful noise outside; and, next day, the high water mark on the walls downstairs, the thin layer of stinking mud on the floor, and his twelve-year-old younger brother Chip hosing out the television set, singing "I'm All Shook Up." Aha, umm, ooohhh yeah. Chip said he loved hurricanes.

Woody and Isolde first met at an exhibition of Brazilian art at the Bass Museum on Miami Beach. He was peering at a drawing by Mira Schendel when he noticed a tall, tanned, athletic-looking blond woman with gray eyes leaning toward the same drawing.

Woody knew as soon as he saw her that she was his woman, he was her man. Call it *coupe de foudre*, flash of lightning, pure insanity, Woody didn't care. He wanted Isolde with a fierceness he'd never felt with any other woman. He looked around for rivals, thinking, Why not throw her over my shoulder and scamper into the night?

Isolde looked at him and saw a man with thinning blond hair, not tall, wearing gold-rimmed spectacles. He radiated confidence, a sense of fun. She heard something in his voice that disarmed her, and she trusted him. He's an honest man, she thought.

By the time she began to focus on the meaning of Woody's words, they were drinking Chardonnay in the museum courtyard, and she was wondering, Why is he talking about Byron and *Don Juan?* Is he an English professor?

But before she had a chance to verify this, she'd agreed to join him for sushi at a nearby restaurant. They were walking away from the museum, and he was describing a Thai restaurant in Coconut Grove, where—he mimed pulling something like string out of his mouth—he found the elastic waistband from a pair of women's underpants in his Pad Thai. "Fruit of the Loom," he told her. "Size ten."

Over sushi and warm saki, she learned that Woody had been a graduate student of English, but now was regional manager for Cardiotron, a company that made cardiac CT scanners—very, very expensive machines. He sold them to hospitals and doctors' groups in Brazil, Argentina, and other countries in South America. He spoke fluent Spanish and Portuguese. He said, "Our scanner gives you a real-time, beating, 3-D rendering of the human heart. Amazing! I love it." Woody laughed and clinked his glass against Isolde's. "Can you see it? My business is the human heart."

Isolde told Woody that she was studying Early Childhood Education at Florida International University. She'd just moved to Miami. Before that, she'd spent seven years, the years since high school, working as crew on big, ocean-going sailing yachts, spending her summers in the Mediterranean, her winters in the Caribbean.

She'd grown up in Colorado, an only child. Both parents were dead. She'd always wanted to be a sailor. She asked Woody, You know that Mediterranean blue? Her favorite color since she was five. She'd wanted to live in that color.

Her favorite song was an oldie version of "Somewhere Beyond the Sea," sung in French by Charles Trenet, who made love sound dreamy and poetic, but also sexy, in a genial way. When she heard it, she imagined love on a clear day, with no memories.

"So now," Isolde said, touching the rim of her wine glass to Woody's, "I've told you everything important there is to know about me."

There was something important Woody didn't tell Isolde until they were living together in a rented apartment in Coral Gables and were talking about marriage. He'd been married and divorced when he was a graduate student in English at the University of Georgia. Isolde, after a stunned silence, asked if they'd had children. Woody said no.

Isolde packed a suitcase and drove away in her white Volkswagen Jetta. Woody thought he'd lost her for good. She left a message on his office voice mail the next day. She said she felt confused and needed to be alone, so she'd driven to Key West.

She returned in two days. She'd cut her lovely blond hair and wore a Jenny Holzer T-shirt that said: *When someone beats you with a flashlight you make the light shine in all directions.* Woody kissed her, told her how worried he'd been, how he'd missed her.

He said, "Don't you have anything you regret, too?"

Her face took on a complex, haunted look that frightened Woody. He thought, She wasn't angry at *me.* For the first time, he tried to imagine Isolde's seven years as a sailor.

The house was on a half-acre of unincorporated Dade County, west of Red Road, between Coral Gables and South Miami. It was a one-story, two-bedroom, two-bathroom bungalow with a tiled roof. The pool lay just beyond the back porch. A botanist who worked at Fairchild Gardens built the house in the 1930s. He planted gardenia bushes near the house, and lychee, orange, grapefruit, key lime, avocado, and mango trees in the yard. He also planted a calamondin tree from the Philippines, and, from Brazil, a jacaranda tree and a jaboticaba bush, which bore purplish-red, thick-skinned fruit the size of a cherry directly on its trunk and branches.

"I love this," Isolde said to Woody. They were strolling around the yard. They'd been together a year and were getting married. It was April, the sun was shining, the jacaranda tree was a purple cloud of blossoms, and the real estate agent, who sensed that the house was selling itself, drifted away.

Isolde placed a hand on Woody's shoulder in a beseeching gesture that startled and moved them both. She looked as if she were going to cry. "Oh, Woody. This is paradise. Can't I have this? Please?"

Woody had never seen Isolde so unguarded, and he told her of course she could have it, he wanted her to have it. When they embraced, he felt Isolde's hand move up to the back of his head, support a woman only offers a baby or a lover. Over her shoulder, Woody too had a vision of paradise, with green grass, flowering shrubs, fruit trees, birds arriving and departing, and their real estate agent furtively field-stripping a cigarette.

Everything fell into place. When they visited Woody's mother in Bolinas, she and Isolde got on right away. "Such a beautiful girl," Woody's mother told him. "*What* an interesting life she's had." She smiled at Woody. "You're going to learn a lot from Isolde." Woody's mother helped them buy their house. Knowing she didn't have much time to live, she gave Woody a loan against his inheritance. Isolde came up with some money too, quite a lot of it, money she said her grandmother had left her. So they married and put a hefty down payment on the house.

Isolde loved their house, but the pool gave her the creeps. She'd refused to swim in it long before the alligator arrived. Woody insisted that they couldn't have afforded the house if not for the corpse that had been found in the pool. News of the corpse had made the house a hard sell, even after the price was slashed. Maybe it wasn't a coincidence that Isolde was inspecting the kitchen when the real estate agent told Woody the story in the garage.

The house had been owned by a gay couple. One of them, Howard, wound up dead and floating. The police suspected murder, but nothing could be proved. Isolde didn't hear about Howard until after she moved in. A retired pediatrician from down the street told her. A pool's a perfect place for murder, he said. If you're going to do it, do it in a pool.

Isolde was furious. "You knew about this?" she said to Woody.

"You wanted the house so badly."

"You never would have told me, would you?"

Woody apologized, saying that he'd been waiting for the right moment.

Soon after they married and moved into their house, Isolde's mother, Thais McCracken, arrived. She was tall, bulky, gray-haired, silent. She wore bright muumuus and took over the back porch. She spent mornings on a rattan lounge chair studying the *Miami Herald*, drinking coffee, and chain smoking Marlboro Lights, and afternoons watching soap operas, chain smoking Marlboro Lights, and sipping from a tall, never-empty glass of gin and tonic. To Woody, she represented another secret chamber in Isolde's heart. Mrs. McCracken seemed to regard him with grim amusement. He was delighted to drive her out to the airport to catch her flight back to Boulder.

On the way home, he said to Isolde, "Didn't you tell me your mother was dead?"

Isolde said that she must have been talking about her stepmother.

In the late afternoon, their flight from San Francisco landed, nearly as scheduled, in Miami. The airport shops and restaurants had closed, and travelers clustered around television sets in the terminal waiting areas, watching an orange circle spin northwest over a map of the Bahamas and the Florida Straits.

Isolde and Woody retrieved their luggage and found a taxi. While they rode south through sunstruck, emptying streets, they held hands and made plans. Woody would put up the hurricane shutters; Isolde would drive to the supermarket and the gas station. When the taxi turned into their driveway, Isolde gasped. "Oh my God." Woody saw the doors of his house and garage wide open and his junkie brother Chip and another man putting metal shutters on the front porch windows.

The taxi stopped near the open garage. Woody apologized for his brother, saying that the last he'd heard, Chip was living in a halfway house over on Miami Beach. Isolde said, "He can go back there right now," but Woody explained that Miami Beach had probably been evacuated.

"I can't leave my little brother out in a hurricane."

Isolde said, "Let them go to a public shelter. Please, Woody, tell Chip and his friend to go away. I hate junkies. I've told you that before. Send them away. They'll be all right."

Woody replied that Chip was his little brother and needed his help.

Isolde said that Woody just didn't get it. Chip didn't care about anyone. He cared about drugs. He'd send Woody naked into the hurricane in two seconds if he had to do that to get his hands on drugs. Chip was a junkie, not a brother.

By this time Chip had put down the metal shutter he'd been carrying and was ambling toward the taxi. He was skinny, sallow, balding, twenty-eight, with acne scars on his cheeks. Woody thought he looked like the actor who played Salieri in the film *Amadeus*. Chip wore dark prescription glasses and talked with a lighted cigarette stuck in the right corner of his mouth. In the past, he'd survived on menial jobs and handouts from their mother. Now he walked around to Woody's side of the taxi and tapped on the window. Woody lowered it.

"Hey, bro," Chip said, his cigarette bobbing. "Hey, Isolde."

Woody let the silence hang on them. Finally, he told Chip, "I persuaded them to drop the lawsuit. It's all coming out of your part of Mom's estate, that and the value of the other things you sold, so you were only stealing from yourself."

Right after their mother died, Chip insisted on flying out to Bolinas to "do his part" preparing her house for sale, while Woody went to Brazil on business. Chip sold her Leica cameras, her good rugs, and her silverware for cash to buy drugs. He also sold her sickroom medical equipment—oxygen tanks, hospital bed and bedside table, special toilet seat, even her walker—not knowing that it had been rented. Woody was their mother's executor, so the medical equipment company had been hounding him for restitution.

"Thanks, bro," Chip said. "I really mean it. I'm sorry for the trouble."

Woody asked Chip who the other guy was.

Chip said, "A guy from the shelter. Would you believe he's an English lord?"

Woody looked more closely at the man. "What are those scars?"

Chip glanced over his shoulder and said they were bullet wounds. Those were just entrance scars. "Wait till you see where they came out. He used to own a bar in Jamaica, shipped a lot of ganja, until some bad guys came into the bar and let loose with a couple of Mac-10s."

Isolde and Woody stood blinking in the heavy sunshine as the taxi reversed down the drive. Woody asked Chip how he'd gotten into the house; the alarm was on.

Chip said, "I cut the phone wires at the main box and disabled the alarm."

"You cut my phone wires?"

Chip said the first thing a hurricane did was blow down phone wires, everybody knew that. "And I was in a real sweat to put up your hurricane shutters." Chip added, "Got your cell phone?"

Without thinking, Woody handed it over. Chip slipped the cell phone into his shirt pocket.

Woody waited, then said, "I thought you were going to use the phone."

"Yeah." Chip nodded, his eyes sliding around the yard.

"Don't let me stop you."

Chip laughed. "Like, half a mo, bro."

"Make the call."

"I'm taking it for a walk in the yard, okay? Gotta speak to this guy."

"I want it back."

"In just a minute, okay?" Chip, looking amazed and a little hurt, spread his hands and, turning to Isolde for support, said, "I hope you can find something in the medicine cabinet to calm him down." Isolde looked steadily back at Chip and said nothing.

Woody asked how Chip had gotten over here. Chip said, "We found a bike."

Woody laughed, said, "The two of you on a bicycle?"

"No, no," Chip replied. "We, you know, found a bike."

Woody said, "You stole a motorcycle?"

Chip grinned boyishly, then said, "Did you know you've got an alligator in your pool?"

"Karma," Isolde said. The English lord with the bullet scars had come around the corner of the house and was moving, slightly bent over, toward them. He was a slim, good-looking man in his early thirties, with curly brown hair and the bluest eyes Woody had ever seen in man or woman. Woody thought he looked remarkably like the Byron of Count D'Orsay's 1823 Genoa sketch, which made the poet appear thin, almost convalescent. In another life Woody had written his Master's thesis on *Don Juan.*

This lord was shirtless, wore dirty khaki shorts and orange flip-flops, and had a thin gold ring in his left earlobe. His four bullet scars formed an irregular diagonal from right shoulder down to left waistline. He moved with a tentative air, and, smiling as he came up, he told Woody that it was awfully kind of them to take him in at such short notice.

Chip introduced Isolde and Woody to Peregrine Balfe, Lord Balfe.

"Please call me Perry," the Englishman said. He nodded, friendly, but didn't offer to shake hands. Perry said that he hoped Woody didn't mind that they'd begun putting up the shutters. It seemed the right thing to do.

Woody said he was glad they'd begun.

Isolde, without a word, turned and walked into the house.

"Long flight?" Chip asked, watching Isolde.

"Bumpy landing," Woody said. Chip glanced at Perry, then wandered into the yard, opened the cell phone, dialed, and began to talk. Perry was immediately at Woody's side, obliging, cheery, picking up their suitcases with a grunt. Perry looked much too weak to carry both, but he insisted. Woody led the way indoors.

Isolde passed them, saying that she had to get to the supermarket before it closed.

The house, partially shuttered now, was dark and humid. The television muttered in the living room. They paused to check on Hurricane Ernestine. A weatherman pointed at the bright orange circle and said it would intensify and come ashore in the middle of the night. Woody led Perry into the master bedroom, where he put the suitcases down and then, turning away, leaned a hand against the wall for support.

"Those suitcases were monsters," Woody said, fascinated by the bullet scars on Perry's back. They were bigger than on the front: like smooth, fleshy flowers, almost.

"Light as a feather." Straightening up, Perry looked around the bedroom with an expression of unbelief. "Right," he said. Woody assumed he was speaking to himself.

In the living room, they paused again at the television as a man dressed in yellow foul-weather gear, standing under a torrential downpour, shouted, "It's raining in the Bahamas!" Woody led Perry out the back door and onto the pool deck.

Perry said, "Chip told me you keep the alligator as a pet." It was about ten feet long and lay motionless on the bottom of the pool. They stared at it. Perry asked how long it could stay down there. Woody shrugged and said he didn't know, exactly.

Perry said, "So it isn't a pet?"

"God, no," Woody said. "It's a pest. We think it's male, because in May and June, mating season, it came and went and upset the neighborhood. Every time the Fish and Game wardens arrived to pick it up, it disappeared. They swore that somebody was tipping it off. It went away for a long while, and we thought, phew. But it came back last week."

Perry said, "Does it have a name?"

"Mrs. McCracken."

Perry's laugh turned into a fit of coughing. Woody stared at him and said, "You know her?" Perry, smiling, said the name had a good, bone-crunching sound to it.

Woody said, "Tell me about your bar in Jamaica."

Perry said, "In Negril. Perry's, it was called. Not very original. Maybe I should have called it The Green Parrot."

Woody said, "Everyone came to Perry's?"

"That's it," Perry said. "Everyone came to Perry's."

Woody said, "I wonder if my wife ever went there."

Perry frowned, thinking hard. He said, "You're referring to Isolde?"

Woody thought, Who else would I be referring to? He said, "She used to spend winters sailing in the Caribbean. Maybe she came to Perry's too."

"Might have," Perry said. "She very well might have. So many people did."

Woody said, "My brother says you're a lord. Is that true?"

Perry said that it was.

Ancestral acres? Woody asked. Marble halls?

Perry said, "Sadly, none of that. My grandfather was given—some say purchased—a peerage. He was a surgeon, rather famous in his day. He pioneered the use of rubber gloves during surgery, and said such memorable things as, 'Every surgical incision is an adventure in bacteriology.'"

"That's food for thought," Woody said.

"I remember it," Perry said, "every time I cut my thumb."

Woody said, "You ever been married?"

Perry nodded. "I was, some time ago. Actually, I think I still am, in a way."

Isolde was in shock from seeing her house wide open and Chip and Perry wandering around. Now, pushing an empty cart into the supermarket, she felt grateful for the cool air that soothed her sweating skin. She saw the coiling checkout lines, the aisles dense with shoppers, and she sensed their fear. Dizzy, thinking, This is all too much for me, she fought down the urge to turn and run. Where could she go? She'd worked so hard to create a new life with Woody. She ordered herself to concentrate on the task at hand.

The supermarket was about to close. The aisles were full, the shelves empty. The ululations of the disappointed rose into the fluorescent light. Isolde saw how fragile and transitory her life was. Her carefully constructed happiness was toppling. She hurried around, crossing unobtainable items off her list: water, Sprite, Coca-Cola, ginger ale, canned soup, canned tuna, sardines, salmon, Spam, baked beans, bread, crackers, Oreo cookies, nuts, potato chips, canned milk, long-life milk, powdered milk, peanut butter, jelly, batteries, toilet paper, paper towels, Chlorox, ice. Her cart was empty. Still, she had the stockpile of water and supplies at home. But with four people that wouldn't last long.

Then she had an idea. Their stove was fueled from a propane tank. She'd cook pasta and vegetables. That might last until stores reopened. She found lots of pasta. She tossed boxes of it into her cart, then hurried into the fresh produce section. The fruit was gone, but Isolde filled her cart with onions, peppers, garlic, tomatoes, mushrooms, carrots, celery, fresh herbs.

Near her, the double doors leading to the back of the supermarket swung open and twelve policemen in riot gear, lace-up black boots, black bulletproof vests, carrying shotguns and batons, filed into the produce section and spread out across the back of the store. They took up positions at the ends of the aisles against the back wall and muttered into microphones on their left shoulders.

A voice blared over the public address system: "*Attention all shoppers, this store is shutting down NOW. All shoppers must report to the CASHIERS. I repeat, all shoppers must report to the CASHIERS. This store is shutting down NOW.*"

The policemen yelled, "Let's GO! Let's MOVE it!"

Isolde froze. The supermarket, she'd often thought, was her last refuge. Now she thought, There's no place safe for me. The nearest policeman, a giant block of a man with a thick black mustache, swiveled his body toward her, shotgun held ready across his chest. He yelled, "C'mon! MOVE it!" He stepped closer.

Isolde was shaking. Her voice came out in a bleat. "I need food."

"Whatever's in your cart," the policeman said, "that's it. Take it to the cashier."

Isolde pushed her shopping cart to the front of the supermarket. She was weeping. The policeman, shotgun at the ready, kept pace behind her. Policemen with guns herded shoppers toward the cashiers. Isolde wept as the startled checkout girl rang up her pasta and vegetables, she wept as an old man pushed her cart of groceries out to the parking lot. He loaded the grocery bags into her car, and Isolde blindly pressed money into his hand and got behind the wheel. Leave, she told herself. Drive north. Outrun the storm.

She knew Perry Balfe's crooked heart well. She saw how he'd deteriorated, how junk had taken over. And now Woody, the man she loved and wanted to build a life with, to have children with, a man who truly loved her, Woody would learn she'd been married to, had probably loved, Perry Balfe, con man, dope runner, junkie, *child murderer.*

In her heart, Isolde had known this day would come. She'd always expected Perry to reappear. The deeper her love for Woody, the sunnier her new life, the more certain Isolde became that it couldn't last. She didn't deserve it. She'd forfeited the right to happiness. She'd sent up clouds of prayers, and now they were falling like dead letters around her feet. Soon she'd have to explain herself.

By "explaining herself," Isolde imagined telling Woody something like, "Woody, my love, it's this: I met Perry and we got married and had a baby girl, Fiona, and one day when Fiona was almost two years old, she was playing with, of all things, a pair of rabbit-ear television antennae, and her daddy, who was supposed to be watching her *for just five minutes while Mommy takes a shower,* decided to shoot up. While Daddy's nodding off in a chair, Fiona sticks the broken end of one of the antennae into an electric outlet, so when Mommy comes back and sees . . . what she sees, she goes clean off her rocker."

She'd practiced telling Woody this every day since she fell in love with him. When she ran away to Key West, it wasn't because she was shocked to learn he'd been married. It was because she saw that either she told him the truth about herself, or she was lost. But she worried that if she told Woody the truth, she might, probably would, lose him. How could Woody love her, once he found out about Fiona? How could Isolde find words to explain, to make acceptable, her desolation and her nervous breakdown? How could Woody believe she would ever be a fit mother again?

She felt that by not telling Woody, she was continually denying Fiona, who had the right to a public place in Isolde's heart. But no amount of practice made it easier for her to say to him, My baby died. After she got married, she thought, I'll wait until I get my degree in Early Childhood Education. It might help convince Woody that I'll make a good mother. Every day brought a moment when Isolde yearned to tell Woody. And every day, for fear of losing him, she decided to wait for a better moment.

Now, in the Publix parking lot, Isolde dried her eyes and turned the ignition. She checked the fuel gauge. Half a tank. Not enough. She needed a full tank of gas. A Texaco station was just around the corner. That would be her final stop.

Woody, Chip, and Perry began putting up the remainder of the metal shutters on the front and back porches. These faced south and north, respectively, and had tall jalousie windows on three sides. The three men set to work exchanging hearty remarks such as, "That's it! Great! Okay. We'll soon get this sucker done," but the afternoon was hot and windless, the sun oppressive. Chip and Perry soon tired. They paused, smoked cigarettes, scratched themselves, wandered into the yard to stare at the road.

Woody finished the metal shutters by himself, while the others set up the wooden saw horses and carried out the plywood from the garage. Woody had five big sheets, which, cut in half, would cover ten windows.

"Men," he said, "here's the plan. We cut the plywood with this electric saw. With this," he held up an electric drill, "we drill holes in the four corners of each sheet. We hold the plywood sheet up over the window and mark the holes on the wall. Then we drill half-inch holes in the masonry and insert expansion anchors. We bolt the plywood over the windows with these three-eighth-inch lag bolts and then we tighten them with this—" Woody held up a wrench and saw that neither Chip nor Perry was paying attention.

Woody tested the electric saw and the other two flinched. They laid the first plywood sheet onto the wooden horses and Woody began to saw it in half.

When Isolde came back, everybody helped her unload the supplies and carry them into the kitchen. Chip and Perry drifted into the yard and exercised the cell phone.

A little while later, Woody went into the kitchen to drink water. Isolde was filling every container she could find at the tap. She embraced him, saying, "You don't know how much I love you."

"As much as I love you, I hope."

"More. Much more."

Woody pointed toward the yard. "Our junkies be waiting for The Man."

Isolde said, "Not in my house." Then, realizing that she wanted Perry happy, not strung out, for the next few days, she said, "Maybe we'd better let them."

"We don't want them freaking out during the hurricane."

Isolde said, "They can smoke and whatever in the guest room." Woody nodded and drank three glasses of tap water.

On his way outside, Woody paused at his desk in the living room and stared at a partially opened drawer. He'd shut it three weeks before. He pulled the drawer out farther. Inside were four unused checkbooks. Woody picked them up, telling himself, Think like Chip. He opened the fourth checkbook. The last check was missing.

Woody put back the checkbooks, closed the drawer, and went outside, calling for Chip and Perry. They came running around the corner like little boys and halted in front of him, winded and laughing. He asked them what was so funny.

Chip said, "We just made sure that Mrs. McCracken's still alive."

"Oh shit," Woody said. "The alligator's out of the pool?" Chip and Perry looked at Woody and broke into fresh fits of laughter and coughing and shook their heads, and then lit fresh cigarettes. "You bozos," Woody said. "That alligator's no fucking joke." He reminded them that they had a lot of hurricane shutters to put up.

But the three of them lacked coordination. They messed up the first two windows, drilling extra holes in the plywood and in the stucco before they managed to bolt the plywood to the wall. Chip and Perry were weak, clumsy, unfocused, and they stank. They gave off a sharp, sweet, rotten odor, a mixture of stale sweat, tobacco, and God only knows what else that startled Woody every time he got close.

What Chip and Perry did best was watch Woody work. This allowed them time to talk in their jittery way, chain smoke, scratch themselves, dial the cell phone, wander out to stare at the road, or fade inside the house. Woody finally suggested that only one of them at a time help him. Chip and Perry could trade off. They liked this idea.

Isolde was at the kitchen table, listening to the weather channel on the radio and filling their hurricane lamps with kerosene, when Perry came in. His beautiful blue eyes locked onto hers and he said, "Darling, I've been searching for you everywhere."

She felt a thump of dread. Had she loved him? Not this Perry. This one was like a Martian to her, strange and dangerous. She said, "I'm sorry you were shot. I didn't know about it until today."

Perry said, "It was Hoyt and his posse. They shut me down."

Isolde said again that she was sorry.

Perry said, "You disappeared." Isolde said she'd wanted to. Perry said, "Your mother told me she didn't know where you were."

Isolde said, "That's right." Isolde picked up a wine bottle she'd filled with cool water.

Perry frowned at it as if he didn't recognize it and said, "I lost everything."

Isolde said, "So did I." She carried the bottle of water past him and outside to Woody.

Woody took Chip aside and said that he was missing the last check from his checkbook. He told Chip to give it back. Chip said, "What?" He looked offended. He said, "What the fuck are you talking about?"

Woody said, "Don't bullshit me."

Perry came into the kitchen and said to Isolde, "Woody doesn't know who I am, does he?"

Isolde, chopping tomatoes for the pasta sauce, said, "He knows you're a junkie." A voice on the radio was saying, ". . . *now expected to come ashore between Palm Beach and the Florida Keys some time around 3 a.m.*"

"I mean to say, you haven't told him anything about us."

"There's nothing to tell," Isolde said.

Perry looked delighted. He said, "How delicious."

Isolde stepped to the door and shouted, "Woody! Perry's going to put the patio furniture into the pool!"

"Okay, honey!" Woody shouted.

Isolde pointed the knife at Perry. She said, "Put it all in the shallow end." Perry watched her chop tomatoes. She added, "That alligator hates junkies."

"Jolly old Mrs. McCracken?"

Isolde glanced up. "What does my mother have to do with it?"

Woody noticed that just about every time Perry went into the house, Isolde came out to check on how he, Woody, was doing, or to bring him water, give him encouragement and a kiss and the latest hurricane news. Like figures in a Swiss clock, Woody thought. One goes in, the other comes out.

* * *

Isolde served up pasta with vegetable sauce and salad on plastic plates. Chip and Perry took folding chairs out to the pool deck and ate and smoked and scratched themselves. Isolde and Woody ate in the living room, watching the hurricane news.

Woody said to her, "You knew Perry before, didn't you?"

She frowned down at her plate of pasta and nodded, and Woody waited. She was thinking, Now? Tell him now? But her nerve failed her. She panicked at the thought of telling him about Fiona. Isolde said, "He was famous in Jamaica."

Woody said, "Was he a junkie then?"

She said, "He used a lot of drugs, but he was different then. Everyone liked him. His bar was a success. The drug thing didn't seem so bad—" She paused, then said, "I guess it was bad. Really bad. But no one realized until it was too late."

Woody said, "That's all you have to tell me?"

Isolde felt herself beginning to shake. "I'll try to remember more," she said. She picked up their empty supper plates and carried them into the kitchen.

Woody went back to putting up the shutters. The sun had set, but there was light enough to see. It was very hot and humid. The others took turns helping him. Meanwhile, they cleared the yard of branches, coconuts, and other debris, brought plants and orchids into the garage, lowered patio furniture gingerly into the shallow end of the pool. Chip and Perry acted increasingly strung out and irritated. Woody tried to ignore them.

Perry and Chip came outside, and Isolde, who'd been helping Woody, went back into the kitchen. Chip lit up a cigarette. Perry signaled to Woody that he had something to say. Woody turned off the electric drill. Perry said, "You've got the words wrong, you know."

Woody said, "Words?" He asked what words Perry was talk-

ing about. The words, Perry said with irritation, to the Rolling
Stones song Woody was singing over and over and over.

"Song?" Woody said.

Chip said, "'You Can't Always Get What You Want.'"

Woody apologized. He'd been concentrating on what he was
doing.

"Well, I can tell you," Perry said, now very angry, "it's not 'I
was standing in line with Mr. Jitters.' The correct version is, 'I
was standing in line with Mr. Jimmy.'"

Woody said that he liked the other version. Perry said, "It's
wrong." He'd gone red in the face. He said with shocking force,
"And you're a bloody awful singer."

Chip said, "Hey, Perry, cool it."

Woody raised the electric drill to about an inch from Perry's
heart and clicked it on and off, saying, "Fuck you. I'll sing whatever I want. You keep singing 'Danke shon, darling, danke shon/
Thank you for all the joy and pain.' Now that's bloody awful."

Woody and Perry stared at each other, until Chip pulled
Perry away.

Lord Jitters, Woody thought. Fuck him.

It was almost dark when a battered white Lincoln turned into
Woody's driveway. The driver blew the horn. Chip trotted down
the drive, followed by Perry. Two large black men climbed from
the front seat of the Lincoln and stood behind their open doors,
looking bored while Chip chattered away. Then Chip and one of
the men walked into the street and out of sight, returning almost
immediately. The black men got into their Lincoln, shut the
doors, reversed down the drive, and were gone. Chip and Perry
sauntered past Woody, who called after Chip, "Found my check
yet?"

Some time later, Chip and Perry carried their two folding chairs
and a jar lid ashtray back out onto the pool deck. Woody found

them there, smoking and chatting, their air of tension gone. Perry was saying to Chip, "Oh, it was the usual, fraudulent trading, false pretences, fraud against a gaming casino, purchasing a Rolls-Royce with a worthless check. But I knew they were going to arrest me two days in advance. A detective came round and said that for fifty thousand pounds the case against me would be dropped. Because I believe in God and England, I told him to get stuffed. Then I packed my bag and hopped it to Brazil. I met Ronnie Biggs there—" He noticed Woody and paused.

Chip looked around, saw Woody, and jumped to his feet. He stepped over and dropped the cell phone into Woody's shirt pocket with an air of irritation, saying, "Take it. I've been carrying that damn thing around all afternoon."

"We're almost done with the shutters," Woody said. "Isolde's pretty pooped." He told them they could smoke in the guest room too, as long as they closed the door.

Perry thanked him, but said that the guest room was hot, so he'd smoke out here by the pool as long as he could. Woody could tell that Perry regretted his earlier outburst.

Isolde slipped into the master bedroom and opened her closet door. From the top shelf she brought down an old tin cash box. Inside were loose photos of her grandparents, father, mother. And five photos of Fiona: Isolde looked at them now, imagining herself coming from that shower wrapped in a towel and taking the rabbit-ear antennae out of Fiona's hands, saying, "No, little darling, those are not for you," and Fiona giving them up, grumbling a little . . . Isolde imagined this scene every day before she went to sleep, but sometimes it came to her when she was driving or in school or cooking. The scene was so real to her. Isolde kissed a photo of Fiona and said, "Sleep tight."

Woody found Isolde lying on the bed. She'd been remembering when she met Perry, at his bar. Those amazing blue eyes, that

English accent. She'd gone after him . . . Woody said he needed her help again outside. She told him she was too tired to move. He said that Chip and Perry were so relaxed now they were even less useful than when they'd been strung out. The good news was that only three shutters remained to be put up.

Isolde told Woody that they had to talk. Woody felt his heart skip. He said, "Talk now?" Isolde was silent, then told him it could wait until the storm was over. He saw ashes falling all around him like dead snow. She was going to leave him, just as his first wife had. Woody thought that when it came to the human heart, he was so blind, he was an idiot. He'd been astounded when his first wife left him for a middle-aged veterinarian.

The noise of the wind grew louder and rain gusted against the house, ceased, and gusted again. The weatherman said that the western edge of Hurricane Ernestine was coming ashore in the Miami area. Perry brought in the folding chairs from the pool deck and Woody closed all the doors. Isolde and Woody split a bottle of Cabernet and everybody watched a film on video, though Chip and Perry had to take regular cigarette breaks, going into the guest bedroom and shutting the door, so they missed a lot. The film was *La Nuit de Varennes*, with Hanna Schygulla and Marcello Mastroianni. The characters are passengers in a coach driving through the French countryside during the revolution. Mastroianni plays the aged Casanova. He's wonderfully gallant with Hanna Schygulla, but thinks, Too late. He has difficulty peeing and remarks afterwards to Hanna Schygulla that "God punishes us where we have sinned the most."

Suddenly, they heard an explosion nearby; the electricity went off. Isolde and Woody lit the lamps and passed one over to Chip and Perry, and for a moment the four of them sat in the flickering lamplight, unspeaking, Woody watching Perry, who was watching Isolde, who seemed to be listening to something special in the noise of the storm. Chip was wearing his dark glasses, so nobody could tell what he was looking at.

"I love boy-meets-girl stories," Perry said to Woody. "How did you and Isolde meet?"

"It's the old story." Woody, scenting danger, got to his feet. He picked up their lamp, saying in a bad Bogart imitation, "Of all the rooms in all the museums in the world, she had to walk into the room where I was standing."

"Waiting for me?" Isolde said, getting to her feet.

Woody nodded.

Chip slowly clapped his hands. It was, for Woody, an appalling sound. He noticed the dim smile on Perry's face as he looked from Woody to Isolde. Woody imagined braining his brother with the empty Cabernet bottle. Chip finally stopped clapping and Woody held out his hand for Isolde and said that now they were both too tired for words and needed to say goodnight. He led Isolde into their bedroom and shut the door. They lay on their bed, holding hands.

The hurricane moved over them. Water and debris pelted the house. The noise was big, and it was everywhere. It sounded to Isolde as if they were caught inside the engine of an insane machine. Then she felt the pressure change and saw the doors creak and strain against their fastenings. The house was breathing like a giant lung.

Around 4:00 in the morning, as the eye of the hurricane was passing and the other side of the storm approaching, Isolde got up to use the bathroom and felt damp air blowing through the house. She walked onto the back porch and saw that the door to the patio was open. She walked outside. The wind was rising. It was dark, dank, humid; there was a strong smell of earth and brine. Perry had brought a folding chair out to the pool deck and was sitting alone, smoking. She touched his shoulder.

The fresh, moist air awoke Woody too. He sat up, looked

around, then slipped out of bed. Wondering about Isolde, he walked onto the back porch. He heard voices outside, from the pool deck. Isolde was talking to Perry. Woody saw them and stepped back inside the dark open doorway, where he could listen and see, but not be seen.

Isolde was saying, "It's no joke." Her voice was raised against the noise of the wind. "You can't stay out here. The hurricane's coming back."

Perry got up and moved closer to her. He said, "I love you."

"I don't love you," she said.

Perry said, half-shouting, "Four bullets, Isolde. Not many people survive four bullets. What kept me alive in that Kingston hospital was the determination that we'd meet and I'd apologize for the terrible things that happened, and we'd live together again."

"Perry, I divorced you."

"I didn't divorce *you*."

"We are divorced. *This* is my life."

"I got four bullets. You got our Miami bank account. That's fair, is it?"

"I didn't know you'd been shot," Isolde said. "Anyway, it was a joint bank account."

"For emergencies only."

"I needed medical treatment, money to live on. I knew that money was all the settlement I'd get from you."

"Half this house belongs to me," Perry said. "Your paramour—husband, whatever you choose to call him—should know that. I will tell him."

"If it makes you happy, tell him."

"I'll do it. And I'll tell him that you are my wife."

"That's insane."

"I'm perfectly sane!" Perry shouted into the wind. He reached out and took her arm. She tried to jerk away, but he held on and leaned in closer, raising his voice to be heard, saying, "Please listen, darling, you've got to listen," but she wrinkled up her nose and shouted, "God, Perry, you stink, you're disgusting!" and she pushed him hard toward the pool, saying, "Go take a bath." Perry lost his balance, stepped back, and went feet first into the water, still holding onto her arm and pulling her into the pool with him.

Perry's feet, descending, landed on the alligator's back. The alligator had been asleep underwater and now it erupted off the bottom, all four hundred pounds of it, snapped its mouth shut around Perry's right foot, rolled over, and dragged him back down to the bottom of the pool. Isolde was dragged down too, and then Perry's hand, which had been gripping her forearm, was yanked away.

In its frenzy, the alligator tore off Perry's right foot, then fastened its jaws around Perry's left thigh and began twisting and banging its head with terrific force back and forth on the concrete pool bottom.

Isolde saw nothing, but as she was kicking upwards through the warm water, the alligator's tail thumped her right leg, and she thought, *Alligator*, and then she was clawing to the surface and a hand grabbed her arm and pulled her up onto the deck. She saw Woody.

"Oh my God," Isolde said, panting. "Oh my God." She got up onto one knee and then Woody helped her to her feet. They looked at the water, which was covered with leaves and coconuts and other debris. Something was happening down there that was roiling the surface. The wind was strong now, the trees around them bending and lashing the sky. A powerful gust almost unbalanced both of them and sent them into the pool.

"Come inside!" Woody shouted. Isolde was moaning and trembling; she looked at him and then back at the pool, where the water was still heaving.

"That's over with!" Woody shouted. He was filled with a fierce exultation, and he put his arm around Isolde and moved her toward their house.

A branch blew past them and clanged against the metal shutters of the porch. Over with? Isolde thought, as Woody pulled her inside. He slammed the door shut and slid the bolt home.

But Perry's in the pool, she thought. He'd always be down there, and what did that leave them with now?

PART III

Vices of Miami

THE TIMING OF UNFELT SMILES

BY JOHN DUFRESNE

Sunny Isles

At 9:15 on Thursday morning, June 4, while Jordan Delreese was bludgeoning his two young children to death, I was sitting in Dr. Hamburger's consulting room at the Sunny Isles Geriatric Clinic with my father, who was just then at a loss for words. He had been trying to explain to the doctor why he no longer felt comfortable being in the same room with his shadow. He'd said, If light can pass through the universe, why can't it pass through me? But now he could only manage to hum and to shake his head. I highlighted a speech in my script. Dad's contention, as near as I could figure it, was that light had a mind of its own and had taken to behaving arbitrarily and recklessly in the last six months or so. After Dr. Hamburger clicked off his desk lamp, Dad took off his eyeshade, blinked, rubbed his rheumy eyes, and asked me who I was. Dr. Hamburger tapped the side of his prescription pad on his desk blotter, leaned back in his squeaky Posturetech office chair, cast me a glance, raised his articulate brow, and lifted his upper eyelids. Lid-lifters tend to be a tad melodramatic.

Dr. Hamburger had diagnosed Dad with Alzheimer's. Dad said he was merely closing up shop. He hadn't lost his ability to make metaphor, not yet. And he did have his lucid moments. He was in and out, however, and he was hard to read. His expressions were often without nuance or blend. He was extremely angry, extremely happy, or extremely vacant. He could remember what he had for breakfast on June 15, 1944, in Guam (gumdrop candy, two cookies), but not that he just turned on the gas without lighting the pilot; which is why I had to move him into an all-electric, assisted-living facility.

Jordan Delreese walked down to the kitchen after slashing his wife's throat and changing out of his blood-soaked pajamas and into a maroon polo shirt and khaki chinos. He clapped his hands and told Davenport and Darchelle to finish up their Cap'n Crunch quick like bunnies. Darchelle said she thought she heard Mommy screaming before, but then it stopped.

Jordan said, You did, dumpling. Mommy and Daddy were playing Multiply and Replenish again.

In the morning? she said. That's silly.

Jordan asked the kids if they wanted to play a game too. They sure would. Okay, then you have to clean up your mess, put the bowls in the sink and the spoons in the dishwasher, handles up. Davenport wanted to know what the game was called. Just Rewards, Jordan said.

The kids giggled when Jordan blindfolded them. He told Darchelle to wait in her room and to count to two hundred. One Mississippi, she said. He locked her door and led Davenport to the children's bathroom. The tub was full. He asked Davenport to lie on his back on the floor. Yes, I know the tile is cold, but it won't be for long. Jordan took the hammer from the ledge of the tub, raised it above his shoulder, and brought it down on his son's right eye, and then the left eye, the mouth, the forehead, the forehead again. He wiped the slick face of the hammerhead on an aqua hand towel and walked to Darchelle's room. One hundred and eleven Mississippi, she said. Darchelle lay on the floor like her daddy asked her to. Jordan said, I saved you for last, dumpling, because you are my special angel. She did not get to say, Goody! or, Thank you, Daddy.

And then, to be extra certain that his buddy and his dumpling did not wake up in pain, Jordan laid the children face down in the bathtub. He washed his hands with antibacterial soap, singing "Happy Birthday" twice while he did. Dr. Sanjay Gupta on CNN said that's how long it takes to wash your hands properly. Jordan went downstairs and made himself breakfast. Scrambled eggs on a blueberry Pop-Tart, sausage links, a box of grape Juicy Juice. While he ate and read the *Sun-Sentinel*, he called his mother and asked her if she and Dad would be home this afternoon. He'd like to pay a visit. Do I have to have a reason? His mom told him she'd make gingerbread and whipped cream. Jordan said, I'll be there one-ish.

Jordan lifted the children out of the tub and dried them off. He noticed a small mole on Darchelle's left hip, examined it, touched it, figured it was probably nothing. He tucked them both into Davenport's bed, pulled the sheets to their chins, covered their faces with the lace doilies from Darchelle's vanity. He nestled cuddly toys next to their bodies and read them the Bible story about Abraham and Isaac. He sang their favorite lullaby. *Sweetest little baby, everybody knows. Don't know what to call her, but she's mighty like a rose.* He choked back tears. Jordan decided to drive to North Beach in Hollywood, stare at the ocean, clear his head. And then maybe surprise his parents by showing up early. He'd drive by Whole Foods and pick up lunch. Some of that tabouli he likes so much. And the grilled portobellos. He cleared the table, started the dishwasher, went up to the master bath, and hopped in the shower.

I told Dad I was still Wylie, the same old Wylie.

"Well, you look a little like my boy Winston."

"Winston was your bulldog."

"Like Cameron, I mean."

"Cameron's dead. I'm all you got."

"Where's Birute?"

"Mom's dead."

"I know she's dead. That's not what I asked you."

Dr. Hamburger had Dad take off his shirt—easier said than done—and climb up on the examining table. I turned my script toward the window light and read Willis's next speech. *It's like you're in ninth grade, and you die and go into high school. That's all death is.* I was playing Willis Harris in the Gold Coast Theatre's production of *Trailerville*. Willis is a true believer. I'm not. It was one week till dress rehearsal. *Or maybe you're humming along in a big rig, and you see a long straightaway up ahead and you shift gears and jam that pedal, and just like that the hum of the engine's an octave higher. Dying's like that, like shifting into a higher gear.* My cell phone vibrated. I excused myself and stepped out into the hall. Dr. Hamburger was trying to unknot Dad's T-shirt from around his neck.

The call was from my friend, Detective Carlos O'Brien of the Hollywood Police Department, requesting my immediate services. He had a situation in the Lakes. Three bodies, two weapons, one missing suspect, much blood. "I need you here, Coyote. Now."

"I'll have to take my dad."

"How's he doing?"

"He's not himself."

"Ten minutes."

I couldn't leave Dad in the car with the keys in the ignition, so I opened the windows and gave him a Fifteen Puzzle, told him to slide the numbers around until they were all in order.

"In order of importance?" he said.

"In numerical order."

I'm not a police officer. That morning I was a forensic consultant. Sometimes I work for lawyers who are trying to empanel the appropriate jury for their clients. Sometimes I sit in my office and help my own clients shape their lives into stories, so the lives finally make some sense. A lack of narrative structure, as you know, will cause anxiety. And that's when I call myself a therapist. And that's what it says on my business card: *Wylie Melville,*

MSW, Family and Individual Counseling. Carlos uses me, however, because I read minds, even if those minds aren't present. I say I read minds, but that's not it really. I read faces and furniture. I look at a person, at his expressions, his gestures, his clothing, his home, and his possessions, and I can tell you what he's thinking. I've always been able to do it. Carlos calls me an intuitionist. Dr. Cabrera at UM's Cognitive Thinking Lab tells me I have robust mirror neurons. I just look, I stare, I gaze, and I pay attention to what I see.

Carlos showed me the framed wedding photo they'd found on the slain wife's body. No, I said, I'd prefer not to see the victims. The photographer had posed the couple with Jordan's cheek on—"applied" might be a better word—with Jordan's cheek applied to Caroldean's temple, and he'd canted the shot at a thirty-degree angle. I wondered what he saw that suggested the pressure and the slant. Jordan's smile was thin, yet wide, as wide as he knew was appropriate to the occasion and pleasing to the photographer. Adequate but unfelt. His eyes were eager, yet slightly squinted. I guessed that the obvious accompanying brow lines had been Photoshopped out. You can't trust photos to tell you the truth anymore. Caroldean wore a diamond stud in her left ear and a thin silver necklace. She had a dimple on her right cheek, like she was used to smiling out one side of her face. This ingrained unevenness suggested a lifetime of feigned emotion.

Jordan River Delreese was a thirty-five-year-old graduate of FIU's College of Business Administration and the CEO of, and the creative force behind, Succeedingly Wealthy, Inc., a company that produced and sold motivational artwork. Like there's this photo of crashing waves on a rocky, forested coast, and beneath it, in case you think this is just an empty, if dramatic landscape, are Jordan's words: *Sometimes amidst the waves of change, we find our true direction.* Or maybe there's a lighthouse, its beacon shining above a roiling sea, and Jordan has printed: *The savage sea can pull our customers in many directions. Our duty is to light their way to safety—before the competition does.* Above his desk in his office at the back of the house hung his company's best-selling framed photo, a shot of a golf green in the brilliant light of early morning, dew still on the grass. The photo is titled *Success,* and beneath the photo, Jordan's inspiring words: *Some people only dream of success . . . other folks wake up early and work at it.*

You can lie with your possessions, of course. I suppose we all do this a bit, stash the Enya CDs in a drawer and leave the Chet Baker and the Louis Prima conspicuously on the coffee table. Jordan had lined his office bookshelf with the hundred-volume set from the Franklin Library of *The Collected Stories of the World's Greatest Writers, from Aesop to Thomas Wolfe.* Each book had gold decor on leather boards, gilt page edges, silky end pages, and a ribbon bookmark. None of the spines had been broken; none of the pages in those volumes I checked had been thumbed.

The neatness of the office, the precise arrangement of items on Jordan's desk—laptop computer, family photo, cherry wood and punched-black metal desk organizer, matching Rolodex and pencil cup, stapler, tape dispenser, wire mesh paper clip holder—told me that he was a man with a firm handshake, a pumper, not a wrist-grabber, a man who numbered his arguments, asked and answered his own questions, and was given to proverbial expression. Tucked into the side rail of his mocha desk pad, a note on pink "while-you-were-out" message paper, presumably to himself: *Stumbling isn't falling.* I took a business card from the leather card holder. The "S" in "Succeedingly" was a dollar sign.

In the family photo, our four Delreeses are posed casually, sitting on a white rug against a white backdrop. They wear white, long-sleeved oxford shirts, white casual slacks, and white socks. Jordan's in the middle, one hand on his leg, looking up at Darchelle, who smiles back at him. Caroldean—there's that dimple again—has her arm around Davenport. His is the smile of a child about to drift away to sleep. You can always tell a happy marriage. People in love begin to acquire each other's traits, each other's styles—they begin to look and act alike. They want to please. They admire each other and, naturally enough, want to become what they esteem and cherish. That had not happened with the Delreeses.

Carlos handed me a sheet of lime-green stationery. "He left a note."

Jordan's writing was half-print, half-cursive; his words began with a flourish and ended with a flat line.

I killed the children. Five minutes of pain for a lifetime of suffering. I know that Jehovah will take care of my little ones in the next life. And if Jehovah is willing, I would love to see them again in the resurrection, to have my second chance. I don't plan to live much longer myself, not on this earth. I have come to hate this life and this unreasonable system of things. I have come to have no hope. I give you my wife, Caroldean, my honey, my precious love. Please take care of her.

I told Carlos that no person who has ever tried to be honest for even one second of his life could think like this.

Carlos said, "He's a deacon in his church."

"Of course he is. And he's probably a scoutmaster."

"Soccer coach."

"There you go."

"So you think the volunteer work is pretense? You don't think he's sincere?"

I shook my head. "I think sincerity is his honesty. And I think you'd better find Mr. Delreese soon. He's not finished. The family was just the flourish. He'll kill again. My guess is he's killed before."

* * *

Back at the car, I nudged Dad awake, strapped him in his seat belt, closed the windows, cranked up the AC, and drove toward Federal Highway. I told Dad about the victims, omitting the gruesome details. He shrugged. "Life is nothing," he said.

"But it's all we've got."

"Nothing's plenty for me."

"Did you finish your puzzle?"

"The zero was missing."

"So what did you do?"

"Killed some time." He picked up my script, fanned the pages, found a highlighted speech, and fed me my cue. "*You want to lose her too?*"

"*A man belongs with his family, Arlis. Where we come from, the elderly are not discarded like old rags.*"

"Are you listening to yourself?"

"That's not in the script, Dad."

"What was her name?"

"Who?"

"Your ex-wife."

"Georgia. What about her?"

"On my mind is all. You lost her."

"She found someone else."

"So she's dead to you."

I dropped Dad at Clover House in North Miami, told him I'd pick him up on Sunday for the Marlins game.

On the way to rehearsal I took a chance. I checked Delreese's business card and called his cell. I told him who I was and said I was hoping he could design me a piece of art I could hang in my office. What I had in mind was one of those Hubble shots of distant space, maybe the one of the eagle nebula or some radiant spiral galaxy, and it'll say, *I love the light for it shows me the way. I endure the dark for it shows me the stars.* Something like that.

* * *

Jordan Delreese told his parents that the kids were swell, fit as fiddles, never been better. He asked his mother to pass the tabouli. She told him to leave room for dessert. Caroldean's busy with her scrapbook project, he said. He told them that when he was at the beach earlier he saw this cloud that looked like an angel. Did they see it too? Like Michael the archangel. They hadn't seen it. What do you think it means? he said.

Rain, his father said.

Jordan said, He makes the sun to rise on the evil and the good, and sendeth rain on the just and the unjust.

Amen, his mother said.

Jordan's BlackBerry played "You Are the Wind Beneath My Wings." He checked the number and punched *Ignore*.

Emotions don't lie, but you can lie about them. Of course, lying about them's not so easy. You're angry, but you say, I'm not angry, but then just for a moment, you draw your eyebrows down and together, flash those vertical wrinkles on your forehead, and press your lips together. Or maybe it's your body that leaks the truth. Your natural-born liar understands that everyone is watching his transpicuous face, and he knows that an easy smile is the cleverest mask. Gestures, however, may belie that smile. He brushes a nonexistent piece of lint from his slacks, drums his fingers, leans forward.

You can't command emotions to appear, but you can coax them, summon them. I learned that in acting class. Stanislavsky said if you move your hands in a tender way, you'll begin to experience tenderness. You move with the quality of tenderness, in other words, and the movement will evoke the sensation of tenderness, and that sensation will lead you to the true emotion, and now you're feeling it. No pretense. Change your expression and you change your nervous system. And you can use your own life experiences and your remembered feelings to help you understand your character. Work from an aroused emotion back to the source of it. In other words, to lie on stage, you need to be honest with yourself.

I was working on feeling Willis's exhilaration, his joy about life after death and the promise of eternal salvation. Easy enough to slap on the brilliant smile, brighten the bountiful eyes. I stood on my toes like I couldn't hold the good news inside, like I was bursting with beatific energy. I started hopping, pounding my fists in the air. Hiroshi, our director, asked me to take it down a notch, or several. "It's only life everlasting, Wylie; it's not a weekend with Madonna." I wondered if I had any exhilaration in my past to call on. When had I ever been so deliriously excited? Maybe on my wedding day, but the failure of that whole enterprise got me sad like it always does. When I was five or six I ran everywhere. I ran to school, ran to the kitchen. I couldn't wait to get to wherever I was going. And I was happy wherever I was. I ran down the stairs, over to the park. I ran to the swings. I ran to church. So what happened when I was seven? Hiroshi put his wrist to his forehead and told me he couldn't take another interruption. I said, "I'm ready," and then I saw Carlos backstage waving me over.

Jordan Delreese asked his father Calbert to tie him to the cyclone fence in the backyard. Calbert smiled and turned on the TV. *Let's Make a Deal* on the Game Show Network. Jordan said how that would be the best thing for all of us. Calbert told the contestant, a man in a hoop skirt and red baloney curls, to just take the cash and be happy with it. Cripes, he said, people don't know when they have it good. Calbert sucked on a sour ball. The contestant went with whatever was behind Door #3. Greed, Calbert said. Jordan said, I have no way to control my stress. Jordan's mother said she'd like to serve dessert out by the pool. Calbert said, Put on your sunscreen, Vernal. The contestant seemed delighted with his six-piece gray mica bedroom suite, complete with platform bed and Serta Perfect Sleeper mattress and box spring. Jordan said, That way I won't fly way. Calbert said, What way? Tied to the fence with baling wire, Jordan said. And you'd better do it now.

While they ate, Jordan brought up the time his father had caught him masturbating into a tube sock while he was watching *Bewitched*. His mother said now what she had said then. About Onan spilling his seed. *And the thing which he did displeased the Lord: wherefore He slew him also.* Calbert said he couldn't remember what happened after he'd caught Jordan abusing himself, so Jordan reminded him. You took the TV cord off the old Motorola, plug and all, wet it, ran it through the sandbox, and put it in the freezer. Bringing back any memories, Dad? Then Mom filled a tub with ice-cold water and had me sit in it. Then you had me stand naked in the kitchen; you took out the cord and whipped me with it. I've still got the scars. Calbert said he wasn't proud, but it had to be done. You were committing an abominable sin, son. You were no better than a viper. And look how you've turned out, Jordan. A success. A God-fearing, law-abiding man, a solid citizen, and a pillar of the community. You should thank me. Jordan poured his parents two glasses of sweet iced tea and proposed a toast to discipline. Calbert said, You might want to try a little tough love with your own kids, Jordan. That grandson of mine has a sassy mouth on him.

Jordan finished his gingerbread and then his mother's gingerbread and his father's. He talked while his parents nodded off. He'd dissolved six Ambien in their tea. Worked like a dream. He told them about how if you wanted to get away with killing someone, you should kill them in a pool. Not that he was trying to get away with anything, you understand. Too late for that. Drowning is a diagnosis of exclusion, he said. It cannot be proven in an autopsy, cannot be disproved. He told them about the actor who drives a spaceship through the universe, how he drowned his wife in Beverley Hills, and everyone knows he did, but they can't prove it. You could see this guy any week on his new TV show, and he behaves like butter wouldn't melt in his mouth. That's acting.

Jordan slapped his mother awake. He told her what he'd done this morning. Vernal blinked, looked at Calbert with his face in the bowl, and laughed. This is the strangest dream, she said. He told her how he'd carved Caroldean's throat with a serrated kitchen knife, how it felt like slicing through a mango when he hit the larynx. Oh dear, Vernal said. Whee! Jordan reached out his foot and rested it on the seat of Calbert's chair. He kicked the chair over. Calbert hit his head on the concrete skirt of the pool. A floret of blood bloomed on his teal Marlins cap. Jordan stripped his parents to their undies and slid them into the pool. He sat under the umbrella and watched, saw those brief spasms when the water first hit the lungs, and then the flutter as the body fought for air. He watched them float, knock against each other, sink to the bottom of the pool. He knew it would take a couple of days for the bodies to bloat with gas and rise again. He knew they'd be discovered long before that. He fetched his dad's Sony Handycam, sat at the edge of the pool, and taped the bodies, looking like the last two pickled eggs in a jar. Then he turned the camcorder on himself and told his story.

Jordan explained how he had a crew in his office tearing up the place. So could we meet at your place? he said. That way he could take some measurements, note the color scheme, kill two birds with one stone. I gave him my address. That's over by the Fetish Box, isn't it? Yes, it is. Twenty minutes.

He said, "Determination is often the first chapter in the book of excellence."

"Excuse me?"

"Maybe the photo's of a long-distance runner on her last leg, gritting it out to the finish line."

"Do you have one for honesty?"

"I can give you serenity."

"I wish you could."

"Will truth do?"

"Close enough."

"Okay. An old man, red jacket, floppy cap, walks through the autumn woods in New England. Glorious colors. Clear, crisp. We can see the steam of his breath. His head's down. Below that the word *truth*—all caps—and below that, *Purity is born of virtue*."

Jordan Delreese knocked shave-and-a-haircut-two-bits on my office door, pushed the door open with his shoulder, and poked his grinning face into the room. He held his BlackBerry to his ear, rolled his eyes, smiled at me, and told whomever he was speaking with or pretending to speak with that he'd get back to them with the figures a.s.a.p. He scratched his nose. Okeedoke. He nodded. Ciao!

He holstered the BlackBerry, clapped his hands, and stepped toward the desk where I sat. He said, "I pictured you bald, slight, with maybe a pitiful little mustache. Funny how a voice can fool you." He admired my autographed Marlins base-ball, gripped it like he was pitching a curve. "Well, here we are, Mr. Melville."

"Call me Wylie. All my friends do."

"I pegged you for a sociable guy."

"Except Carlos. He calls me Coyote."

"And you call him The Jackal, I suppose."

"Have a seat, Mr. Delreese."

He pointed to the wall above the sofa. "We'll hang it there." He put his fists on his hips, swivelled and looked left, then right, looked at me, and shrugged. "No photos of the wife and kiddies."

"No wife and kiddies, I'm afraid."

"Fag?"

"Excuse me?"

"Are you a fag?"

"That's an inappropriate question, Mr. Delreese."

"If you say so."

"But a revealing one."

He sat, crossed his legs, folded his hands behind his head, smiled, and I knew that he knew that I knew. "No kids." He clicked his tongue and shook his head. "Fruitless." He raised an eyebrow, stuck out his lower lip, and cocked his head. "No regrets, Coyote?"

"Plenty."

He picked up the photo of Dad and me squinting into the sun at the News Café. "They fuck you up, don't they?"

"Who?"

"Your mom and dad."

"They did their best."

He smiled and aligned my Post-it note dispenser with my saucer of paper clips. Ordering his thoughts. He turned my little ceramic flamingo so she was facing me. He leaned back in his chair. I leaned back in mine.

He said, "I see what you're doing."

"You're a perceptive man."

"Why didn't you call the cops?"

"Who says I didn't?"

"Your need makes you transparent." He steepled his fingers, brought them to his lips. "So what do we do now?"

"You tell me your story."

"And you process my behavior and feed it back to me."

"I listen."

"Why should I tell you my story?"

"Why did you kill your family?"

"Why not?"

"Because it's barbaric, illegal, immoral—"

"Insane?"

"Did you think you'd get away with it?"

"I already did, dipshit." He laughed. "They're dead." He put his face in his hands. "My parents had outlived their usefulness. They disgusted me. They smelled like rancid milk."

"How do you feel right now?"

"Like I'm wasting my time. If you're looking for credible motivation, Melville, you won't find it here."

"Every lie is a victory for you, isn't it?"

"You want to make sense of this so badly, you'll believe anything I tell you so long as there's an element of horror and remorse. Am I right? You want the world to make sense, but it doesn't."

"It does if you bother."

"Most times nobody knows why they do anything."

"Most times they don't want to know."

"Don't you go to the movies? This is the twenty-first century, Wylie, the Age of Unreason. Kill someone in the morning; go to the theater at night. No reason, no resistance. Action is its own motivation. It's kind of funny if you think about it." Delreese pulled a snub-nosed revolver out of a shoulder holster, said he bet I wasn't planning on this, and I told him he was right about that, and he told me he had nothing to lose, and I told him that I did. How on earth had I missed the signals? Had his lips narrowed while I blinked? Did the pitch of his voice rise, not in deceit, but in anger?

He said, "You know what's easy, Wylie? Lying to someone who wants to be lied to." He aimed the pistol at my heart and asked me if I was a religious man. I told him I was not. He said, "Too bad for you then. You don't get saved."

"There's no salvation for you either, Delreese. Every child knows that this is our only life. Every pig knows it. Every snake. Just people like you who don't."

"People like me."

"People who feel that the world has let them down, who

can't imagine existence without their own presence. Dishonest people."

"The only honesty is a lie well-acted."

I told him to put the gun away and let's talk. I said it like I was soothing a feisty dog.

Delreese picked up the Marlins baseball, lobbed it across the room, fired the pistol at it, and put a bullet through the window. "I suspect we don't have much time now." He pointed the gun at my face. I squeezed my eyes shut. I tried to breathe deeply to keep my heart from exploding out of my chest. I trembled and held onto my chair. I thought about my father waiting for me on Sunday, sitting with the cigarette-smoking attendants on the shady bench outside the Clover House lobby, tapping his foot, chewing his lip, trying to remember why the hell he was sitting there, and I understood that without me around to fight for him, the health-care system would swallow him up, strap him to a bed in some shadowy ward, and let him waste away. When they told him I was dead, would he know who they were talking about?

Delreese said, "Cat got your tongue?"

I thought if I could talk, maybe I could save my life, but in order to talk I'd have to think; only I couldn't think; I could only remember. I saw my brother Cameron and me, and we're six and on the floor in the den with Oreos and milk watching *The Lone Ranger*. Dad's snoring over on the couch, and Mom's out on the patio smoking up a storm and reading another Harlequin romance. This bad guy from the Cavendish gang has the drop on the Lone Ranger and tells him to nice-and-easy-like take off his mask, which looks like my father's eyeshade, and which, of course, he will never do, even though I kind of want him to myself, which is sort of a betrayal, I know, and the Lone Ranger pretends that someone's behind the bad guy by making these not-so-subtle head and eye gestures that arouse the desperado's suspicion, and then the Lone Ranger says, "Get 'em, Tonto," and when the bad guy turns and fires, the Lone Ranger jumps him, grabs the six-shooter, and knocks the bad guy out with a single punch.

Delreese said, "I call this game Meet Your Maker." He laughed. "Ten Mississippi," he said. "Nine . . ."

Cameron changed the channel and told me to stop crying. I told him I wasn't crying, but I could taste the tears on my lips. Bugs Bunny aimed a pistol at Elmer Fudd, pulled the trigger, and a flag popped out of the barrel of the gun, unfurled, and said *Bang!* Bugs gave Elmer a big wet kiss. I couldn't remember my mother's face, just the back of her head. I knew I wouldn't hear the gunshot, wouldn't feel a thing. Everything would be over before I knew it. What would be the last thought I thought, the last picture I saw?

"Five Mississippi."

What I did remember about Mom was her silence, her ratty chenille robe, and her pink Deerfoam slippers. When she thought I was lying, she'd tell me to stick out my tongue, said that if I was lying it would be black. It was always black, even those times I was sure I wasn't lying. She'd wash my mouth out with Lifebuoy soap or spoon horseradish on my tongue. Cameron called her The Beast. Cameron, my twin, who looked exactly like me, people said, but was somehow more handsome, who always knew what I was thinking and could make me laugh at the drop of a hat, who fell into a life of drug addiction and robbed my parents blind, died in room 201 at the Pirate's Inn in Dania, beaten to death by his playmates with a studded mace and a stone war club. He was twenty-four.

I realized that Delreese had stopped counting, and I waited and thought maybe I was dead already, that this dark stillness was life after life, that I'd already been shot, that I'd been wrong about death too, and Willis had been right after all; there is no pain, no past, no present, no future, just the everything all at once, just a floating toward a resplendent and cleansing light, so I opened my eyes to see it, to let it wash over me, and I saw

Delreese, who must have been waiting for this moment, with the black barrel of the gun in his mouth, saw him smile and wink. I reached for his arm, and he squeezed the trigger.

BOOZANNE, LEMME BE

BY VICKI HENDRICKS
Miami Beach

I never needed "stuff," so it was easy to live—till Boozanne come along. Most stuff is just to impress women, and I didn't need them either—till Boozanne. I had a cute face—like a puppy dog, I heard—but being 4'10", I was too short for normal chicks, too tall for a dwarf. I didn't try to fit in. I could afford a handjob now and then. Did me fine. Keep it simple was my motto. When Danny DeVito retired, maybe I'd head out to Hollywood, but for a young guy like myself, the deal I had going was almost as good—till Boozanne messed me up.

Ma had always told me, if you're gonna steal a VW, might as well steal a Cadillac. Well, Ma had that wrong. A VW would've been the right size for me. But when I got outta prison for stealing the Caddy, I gave up car theft altogether. My home was gone. Ma had passed on, bless her soul—Pop was never around. Being broke and alone, I hitched down to Florida, remembering how warm it was that winter when Ma and me took vacation, my best memory as a kid. I met Weasel in Miami, and he's the one told me about this gig. It fit me perfect, even better than a VW.

What you do is find a big old wood house, with two foot of crawling space underneath, and cut a hole in the floor under the bed. Easy, if you can look in and measure. Beds are never moved. Weasel burgled his way around the islands, so by the time each hole got discovered, he was long gone. With my carpenter experience, and considering I needed a home more than anything, I went him one better by saving the piece of floor, so I could latch it back in place underneath. Not many nice wood houses left in Miami, but one should've been enough. No mortgage, no taxes, and free food as long as you're not greedy. Nobody would notice, even if they ran a dust mop over the hardwood, a thing that—I'm telling you—most people never do.

My home with the Lamberts, Bob and Melodie, was walking-distance from the beach, came with *Sports Illustrated* and *Gourmet* subscriptions, cable, big-screen TV, and a cat. It had those wood Bahama shutters that hang down and cover the windows, so nobody passing by could see in. A carport instead of a garage was good for knowing if either car was home, and thick foliage around the perimeter made it easy to sneak to the back and go under, though I did most of my crawling in and out in the dark. I had plastic sheeting and a rug remnant from Goodwill under there, my clothes sealed up in black garbage bags to keep out the bugs, a flashlight, toss pillow, and a *Playboy* to pass the waiting time. I never needed toiletries like toothpaste, shampoo, or deodorant, cause the Lamberts were well supplied. Didn't shave, or I would've got my own razor. It was like living in a full-service motel, except I had to clean up after myself. I was set—till fuckin' Boozanne.

Bob and Melodie got home each night at 7 or later—depending if they ate out—so I'd drop down the hole around 6:30, crawl out at dark, and head to a cheap local bar, or out on a scrounge, then later to my chair on the beach to doze until it was getting toward dawn, time to head home. I'd picked 'em good—upper-middle-class workaholics, too distracted about their jobs to notice the house much, lotsa loose change and doggie-bag leftovers that they usually tossed into the bin within two days. Somebody might as well enjoy it all. Once in a while, I stuck a pepperoni down my pants at the grocery for extra meat. I didn't take big chances, didn't need much. Any violation would send me back to a cell.

I didn't have to be too careful at home, as long as I remembered to pick my long black hairs off the pillowcase, go easy on the tidbits and liquor, and wash my lunch dishes. Sometimes I got sick of looking at Bob's coffee cup that he'd leave on the bathroom sink, and I'd wash that too. I was kind of a dark male Goldilocks, only nicer. I grew attached to the Lamberts, seeing that I knew so much about their food tastes, possessions, and living habits. Melodie was like the sister I never had, little and dark-haired, big-eyed and innocent in her pictures. I felt protective toward her. Bob was like an older brother I could live without.

One day, Melodie came home early—I was lucky the lunch dishes were done—and I was in the living room to see the car pull in. I barely made it out the hole. She ran in and tossed herself on the bed and wailed. Her sobs broke my heart while I laid under there listening. I stuffed my face into my pillow not to make a whimper. I thought maybe her ma had died. After that, all signs of Melly disappeared for most of a week. Her black dresses were gone, and there were tons of used Kleenex left in the wastebasket in her bathroom. She must've had her monthly on top of it all, so I hoped no cramps. Eventually, from the sympathy cards, I figured out it was her pop that died.

Trying to be of help, I dusted, wiped out the refrigerator, vacuumed, and cleaned the toilets for her while she was gone. Bob didn't go to the funeral, and I knew he wouldn't take over the cleaning neither. I couldn't do anything obvious, but I just thought she'd feel better if the place somehow didn't seem to get dirty—and the refrigerator needed cleaning bad. Bob was your regular slob and never noticed nothin'.

Melly brought home some mementos from her father, his fishing license and a pin from the Marines, so I knew they were close. I admired the old fella, seeing he probably enjoyed life and had guts. I found some heavy dark-blue folders too, sitting in plain view on the desk. I thought they were books at first, but when I opened 'em up, they smelled musty and were filled with

U.S. silver dollars in little slots marked with the years, the real silver dollars that this country don't make no more. I could tell by the edges. I didn't know what they were worth, but there were close to four hundred of 'em, from the 1880s to the 1960s. I wondered if Melodie knew the value. I wished I could warn her to put 'em in a safety deposit box, in case of burglars, like Weasel.

I buddied up with their cat. He liked his water freshened a couple times a day, and he would have starved while Melodie was gone if I didn't refill his dry food. I really performed a service. He was smart, and I taught him to give paw and roll over for Whisker Lickin's tuna-flavored treats. I hid the packet in the empty cabinet above the refrigerator, and I had to laugh every time I pictured the Lamberts finding it and being downright stumped. I expect Bones thought I was his owner, considering all the quality time we spent together. I wished I knew his real name. I listened sometimes, waiting under the house, but the words were usually too muffled to make out anything, unless Bob and Melodie were having a fight. Bob could get pretty loud. I went through their address book, hoping for something like *Tiger's vet*, but no clues. He answered to Lazybones—or Bones— as much as any cat answers.

I generally took a long nap each day with Bones on my chest. It was like working the night shift, except no work! I sold off a lawn mower and weed eater—garage items from down the block—and got myself a gym membership so I could shower, swim, hot tub, and work out with the hardcore sissy fellas every evening if I wanted, and especially on weekends when I was stuck outside all day.

Things were going good. One night when I was still holding some cash, I thought I'd slug down a few shots at one of them outdoor South Beach bars, take in the fancy scenery, meaning women. It was just then, when I'd got my life all in order, I run into Boozanne. I come up to the bar and there she was, her back to me, lapping a little over the stool in the thigh area, a big girl with lots of curly orange hair and freckled white skin on her upper arms. She had on a thin nylon shirt that clung to every ripple of her—the handles of love and the lush flesh above the back of her brassiere. When she turned my way, there were those double-Ds staring at me, talcum still dry between 'em, and the smell of a baby wafting off her, even in eighty-five degrees and heavy humidity. Stars were winking in the black sky over her head, so I shoulda known the joke was on me.

A flamenco guitar strummed away in my left ear, traffic and ocean crashed together in the right. "Hi there!" I yelled. I pointed at the only empty seat, the one next to her, where she had parked her pocketbook.

"I'm Junior," I said. I was more often called Mouse, but I didn't like it.

"Name's Susanne," I thought she said.

I nodded. "Pleased to meet you, Susanne."

She scrunched up her little pig nose with the freckles on it, but I didn't know what the problem was. She had a puckered set of red lips to go with that nose. "Boooz-anne," she drawled.

That there was the killer. Her voice flowed out like syrup and I damn near choked. I wondered if she could be a Kentucky girl, hot and smooth as the bourbon I'd left behind those two years ago. I musta stared at her—I wasn't sure what was polite to say.

She picked up her beer can. "Booooz-anne!" she hollered. "Buy me one."

The bartender looked at me, and I put up two fingers.

Boozanne stared at my legs. "You need a hoist onto that stool, pal?"

I ignored her and used the step under the bar to give me the extra lift. Boozanne lit a cigarette. Her cheeks sucked in and her lashes kinda flickered in pleasure as she drew the smoke. When her chin tipped back on the exhale, I remembered how Ma used to aim her smoke at the ceiling by protruding her bottom lip like a funnel. Boozanne's white neck and the pattern of freckles spilling down resembled one of the girls' chests in Bob's porno video. The smoke hung in the air and the flamenco ripped to a finale as she focused on me.

"You're pretty cute for a shortie. Been working out?"

"Some," I said. It came to me that she might want to get naked, despite my body being two-thirds her size. I wasn't against it.

"You know how long a man's legs are supposed to be, don't you?"

I shook my head, getting ready for a joke about my height, figuring it was worth the ridicule to get laid.

"Long enough to reach the ground," she said. "Abraham Lincoln."

"Abraham Lincoln said that?" I scratched my head. "He had real long legs, didn't he?"

"Yeah, but that's not the point. Yours are long enough."

I smiled. "It all evens out horizontal, don't it?"

She laughed, and after that my memories are spotty. Sometime, Boozanne and me staggered across the street, holding hands and bumping together. We stumbled over the sand toward the water, to my favorite wooden lounge chair, chained behind a low dune of shore grass, far enough from the street to be dark. My mind wasn't working too good, but I recall taking off my pants, falling over once into the sand.

Next thing, there was Boozanne, buck-naked and white as whip cream, like an art model with all the rich layers of her unfolding, as she laid down on the lounge and opened her arms to me. I stopped trying to brush off and leaned over her and straddled one of her thighs. We did some tonguing, I think, but mostly I remember the feel of her, meaty and cool, as I pawed over her big tits and nuzzled her neck. When I scooted on down, that baby powder drowned out the fishy smell of the beach. I suckled her nipples and crawled onto her lap. She weren't my first woman, but there hadn't been many, and none of this size.

I poked into her soft gut and jelly thighs a few times, and then I located that sweet spot you don't never forget.

Over the next week things heated up even more, and I needed extra money to show her a good time. Besides sorting most of the quarters out of the change jar, I made some easy pickings from a tree service trailer, and took a chain saw to the South Dixie Pawn Shop. Boozanne—surprise, surprise—could put away the liquor. I convinced her to go to my usual local bar, where it was homey. Quantity was more important to her than scenery, so she didn't complain much.

Besides liking the sex, she was a woman who could tell a joke. I enjoyed her stories about idiots at the office, and the quick way she saw through her boss with his snooty manners. She had some schemes for easy money, and she promised to let me in. I'd started talking to Bones about her, and when I pictured her pretty face I felt something way stronger than the tightness in my balls.

One night when we were sitting on the lounge chair smoking some weed, I dropped the roach into my shirt pocket and the damn fabric flared right up. Boozanne was fast with her hand to pat it out. "Your heart's on fire for me," she said. She was laughing, but I couldn't deny it. I took that as a sign.

Course, the subject came up of going to my place instead of the sticky, sandy lounge chair, and I couldn't fend her off for long. She had an efficiency and a roommate, so it was up to me to make arrangements if I wanted to "continue enjoying her womanhood." Now, I was really working her pussy hard, and I had a suspicion that she liked the fucking as much as me, but I knew there were plenty more men where I come from—taller ones, with better income—whereas she was the only woman ever come on to me that didn't ask for money up front. The chair hurt her back, and she wouldn't get on top cause she was embarrassed about how she outweighed me. She kept harping on it until I let loose of the truth.

I thought it would be the end of us, but it turned out my living conditions were a real amusement. I'd lied that I was on disability, but now I gave out all my secrets, including my nickname Mouse—which she promised never to use—and my recent incarceration.

Before I had time to think, she'd took the day off work, and I was sneaking her in between the air conditioner and Bob's moldy garden hose. I had to bend some bushes to get her through, and they took some damage, but the Lamberts hardly went into the yard, far as I could tell.

I had a long sheet of plastic stretching to the edge under the house, so I could crawl on my stomach without getting dirty, and Boozanne surprised me with the ease she wormed on through. She weren't afraid of the spiders or nothing. I went first and moved the bed aside, and she stood and took my hand, and stepped up into the room like a lady. It was a big hole, but she pretty much filled it. I'd told her I could go inside and unlock the back door for her, but she said the porch was too visible, and that was true. She went wandering around the house, while I slid the wood to cover the hole, enough so Bones couldn't get out, and scooted the bed back in place so the room looked nice.

Boozanne came floating my way in the living room, with a cigarette, sipping from one of Melodie's good glasses filled with a clear gold liquid. I hoped it wasn't the scotch Bob was saving from his birthday. She'd stripped off her clothes and put on a see-through robe that left a gap in front, with pink nipples and red muff peeking out.

I grabbed her cigarette and flung it into the sink, even though the Lamberts wouldn't be home for hours.

She clucked her tongue at me. "Such a worrier." She held up her glass. "They've got all kinds of booze in the cabinet, Junior. I'm surprised you haven't polished it off."

"Now I shoulda told you—you got to be careful not to start suspicions. I hope that's the Cutty's."

She tossed her curls. "Why drink Cutty's when there's Glenlivet?"

"Okay, just take it easy. We'll add a little water. Don't open new bottles and don't drink more than a couple shots of any one thing."

"No problem. There's lots to try. I haven't had this much fun since I was twelve and broke into the neighbors'."

"Oh yeah? What'd you do?"

"Not much. Three of us girls—we just put a little hole in the screen door and got excited sneaking around, looking in the bedrooms. Adrenaline rush."

"There is something to that," I said.

"I don't know why we didn't check for money or take anything."

"Maybe you didn't need anything."

"Oh, Junior, you always need money," she said. She cuffed me on the chest.

"I don't. Not always."

"That's why you're special—besides this."

She bent down and undid my belt and zipper, dropping my pants, and pulled me against her big powdered tits for a long sloppy kiss. I was useless, barely able to waddle to the bed and kick my pants off my knees so I could climb on top of her. I got her breathing hard, grunting and cooing, and we were both sweating rivers. I thought for a second about messing the sheets, but I had plenty of time to run laundry.

After that, Boozanne got the fancy platter out of the china cabinet, and the cloth napkins, and we ate a snack—olives and crackers and imported cheeses, a small chunk of goat cheese, Parmesan, some Stilton. I wouldn't've touched the moldy stuff on my own, but the Lamberts had introduced me to lots of new food, and most of it was pretty damn tasty. Boozanne was still hungry so I made her a peanut butter and jelly, which was always safe, but she didn't much like it.

She left around 3, and I was exhausted, but there was plenty of cleaning to do. I panicked when I picked up a juice glass and saw a white ring on the coffee table. I found some furniture spray that didn't work, but while I stood there pulling out my hair, the ring started to lighten up, and it finally disappeared. I did the dishes and threw the napkins into the washer with the sheets. I hoped there was no ironing required.

Bones came out from somewhere to lay on me while I waited for the fabric softener cycle. He was purring and it felt good relaxing with him on my chest after the wild afternoon. "Bones," I said, "here's a woman who knows all about me and still likes me." I massaged behind his ears and his jaw went slack because it felt so good. "I'm pretty damned fond of her too." I couldn't say the word *love* out loud, not even to Bones.

He stared me in the face with his big green eyes, and I thought I saw sadness. Course, he always looked like that, and just because Boozanne came around, I wasn't gonna ditch him.

Soon Boozanne quit her job. It was understandable—all the typing they piled on her. She was consulting with a lawyer on some female issues too. I was glad to see more of her, but it was worrisome, her not having any money coming in. She had to turn in the car she had on lease, but luckily her apartment was on a bus route. We went on like that for a couple weeks, wild sex and a snack several afternoons. She passed some time looking through the Lamberts's closets and drawers. I'd seen it all already, so I sipped whiskey and watched her flesh move around in that skimpy robe. Lucky I had the place memorized, cause caution was not her strong feature, and I had to make sure everything got put back. As it was, a wine glass got broke. They had plenty, so it was no problem, but she scared me sometimes— yet I couldn't think of what I used to do without her.

I picked up bottles and cans for extra money, so I could pay for beer at night. A couple times I did dishes for cash. I wasn't really allowed out of Kentucky, so I couldn't take a job that checked records. I got into a neighbor's storage shed and found an old waffle iron and ice skates to pawn, and let my gym membership go. I could swim and shower at the beach, and let my clothes dry on me Saturday and Sunday. I didn't have much time to work out anyways with all the hours it took to scrounge. Boozanne got some kind of weekend job, just enough to keep up her rent until she could find something good. She wouldn't take no cash from me.

In early July, the Lamberts went to California for a week. It was blocked out on their calendar ahead of time and Boozanne and me couldn't wait. Boozanne moved right in and we took over the place. The first morning she cooked me biscuits and fluffy eggs like her grandma taught her, and we took our time eating, and left the dishes all day, and smoked a little of the weed that Boozanne found in Bob's chest of drawers. The only problem was that Bones was shipped off somewhere so we didn't have our pet. I wished I could have told Melly that I'd take care of him.

One day we were lazying around in the bedroom and I showed Boozanne Melodie's "secret" drawer. Big mistake. My plan was to slip one of the old rings on her finger to see what she'd say, but she spotted Melodie's gold heart right in front. It was a real delicate necklace that was usually missing, so I knew Melodie normally wore it a lot and must have left it home for safe keeping. Boozanne became instantly attached, but I didn't want to let her take it. It wasn't so much that I thought we'd get caught, but it was probably a present from Bob, or maybe even an heirloom. None of her other stuff was gold.

Boozanne put it around her neck and asked me to fasten it. "Please, baby?" She was stroking my bicep and I liked that.

"Just wear it while you're here, then put it back."

"My birthday's coming up and I know you don't have money to buy me a present."

"When's your birthday?"

"November, but you won't have any money then either."

It was true, and I had never bought her a gift.

"It'll be a nice memento of our vacation," she said. "Please, baby, please?"

I suggested a small silver heart that was far back in the drawer, but she was allergic to any metals except gold. I felt terrible about Melodie, but seeing how pretty the gold looked in Boozanne's freckled cleavage, and how much she wanted it, I let her take it. Maybe I didn't have a choice.

When the Lamberts got home, I checked for extra Kleenexes in Melodie's bathroom trash, and there weren't none, but over the weekend an extra lock was installed on each door, and that creeped me out. One more mistake and they'd start checking more carefully. I tried to get the heart back so I could plant it in a front pair of underwear in Melodie's drawer, like it fell there, but Boozanne wouldn't give it up. She didn't understand my feelings about Melly and how I enjoyed having a home.

Things went good for a few more weeks, and then Boozanne got tired of the job hunt and lack of cash. Safe pickings for the pawn shop were running slim in the neighborhood, and without a car, it was tough. Boozanne said she had a plan to make some real money, live high on the hog for a while, do some traveling, then get an apartment of our own, a used car. Sneaking around was exciting at first, but she was tired of it. I didn't want to leave the Lamberts, but my odds for getting caught were climbing, and I wanted Boozanne.

We were sitting on the couch, me petting Bones, when she told me the specifics.

"I'll handle it," she said. "We've got credit cards, Social Security numbers, birth certificates, checkbooks, bank statements, passports, and salable goods. You've heard of identity theft?"

"But they're nice people. Melodie is. I don't want to steal from them."

"What are you talking about? You've been stealing from them for months."

"Not enough to matter."

"That's what I'm saying. It's time to do something that matters. They've got almost $10,000 in their checking account."

"I can't," I said. "They're like relatives."

"And I'm not?"

When she put it like that, I had no argument. I'd only seen them at a distance and in pictures, but it still didn't feel right.

"You don't have to do anything," she said. She went to the desk and brought back some insurance papers. "Look, they're well-insured for their possessions—and the credit cards pay for fraudulent charges. I won't write checks if you don't want me to. It seems tricky anyway."

"I can cut a hole somewhere else for the burglaring."

"Too much trouble and you might not be as lucky. Besides, I already started." She pulled two credit cards out of her pocketbook and held them in front of my face. There was one card for Melodie and one for Robert.

It was all real then, and my guts were shot out. "Jesus," I said.

"We've got their spare cards, plus these new ones I applied for, $5,000 limit on each."

She dug back into her pocketbook and pulled out a small satin pouch. Gold and cut stones glittered inside. "Necklace and earring set—charged off the Internet. I've got more stuff coming. We can get cash for these, and I bet you can find somebody to buy the passports."

It was too late to stop her without calling in the law.

"I'll fly us anywhere you want in the fifty states. You deserve it, baby," she said.

I let her kiss me then, and when I felt those lips, my mind went into a haze, a vision of us sipping bourbon on the porch swing of a cozy cabin in the mountains of Kentucky, Boozanne exhaling smoke into the cool summer breeze.

Three weeks later was moving day. Boozanne had bought two suitcases on wheels, filled them with our new clothes and more high-end jewelry pieces she'd ordered. She was busy wrapping up old silver trays she'd found in a chest. I'd liquidated the necklace and earrings and some nice watches, and we had $6,000, airline tickets, and room reservations for someplace exotic—a surprise—and the new credit cards to charge whatever we needed when we got there. Visa and MasterCard had called about unusual activity, but Boozanne answered all their questions. We took the bills for those old cards out of the mailbox, so we had plenty of leeway before the Lamberts could notice anything wrong. She figured we could vacation for two weeks and still have resources to rent a place and get a cheap car after that. When we ran low on money, we'd start over, somewhere else. I was excited about traveling with Boozanne, but I still hated ripping off the Lamberts. They'd been good to me, in their way.

I finished wiping the furniture and appliances for fingerprints and closed the suitcases, and Boozanne was still poking around, wearing rubber gloves. Bones was sleeping on the couch and I gave him a goodbye pet, feeling real sad.

I went into the kitchen and looked at the clock. I couldn't believe it. "Damn!" I yelled. "It's a quarter to 7!"

I ran back into the living room. She was searching the bottom drawers of the desk.

"Boozanne! We gotta go. It's not like we're headed to a movie."

"Five minutes. I don't want to miss anything. Money goes fast on vacation."

"We're cutting it too close. I never stay this late."

"No worries." Just then she opened the drawer with the folders of silver dollars. I held my breath, hoping she'd pass them by again, thinking they were books.

She flipped open the first cover. "Oh, wow!" She lifted them out and carried them to the coffee table. She opened another and another.

"We don't have room for those old coins. They're too heavy," I told her.

She pulled out a dollar and studied it. "Mouse, these could be worth a fortune! They're antique silver dollars."

"Naw, put 'em down. You're allergic to silver. We gotta get out of here."

"No way. Open the suitcase."

"Boozanne, I won't take 'em. They're Melodie's inheritance. It's all she got."

"You're insane. Now open that suitcase, or I will. I'll leave you here with your fucking Melodie."

I didn't have time to let that sink in. There was the sound of a car pulling into the carport. "Jesus Christ," I whispered. I ducked and took a glance out the corner of the window. "It's her." I grabbed Boozanne's hand, but she didn't budge. "Come on!" I hollered. "We can make it out the hole."

"I'm not leaving without the coins."

I just stood there, unable to gather a thought. She was digging into her pocketbook.

"Stand next to the door," she said. "Grab her mouth from behind and hold her."

I did as I was told, and Boozanne ducked around the corner. In seconds, the key turned and poor Melly stepped inside. I yanked her from behind, clamping a hand over her mouth and kicking the door shut before she could scream. I pulled her down against me and fell half on top of her. She was more delicate than I thought, and her fine skin had wrinkles I never saw in the pictures, but she was beautiful. My eyes filled because I knew I hurt her. She whimpered and my heart broke. When I looked up, Boozanne was bent toward us, those freckled double-Ds spilling over her brassiere near my head, her purple shirt pulled up, covering her face and hair. The shirt was nylon, and she was stretching it so she could see through the thin mesh. A .25 in her other hand pointed straight into Melodie's ear.

"What the fuck?" I was so stunned I let go of Melodie's mouth, and she yanked her face sideways and screamed. I cut her off fast and pushed her head under my armpit, but she'd already seen my face. Bones was there, staring at me, his green eyes huge, not knowing whose side to be on.

"Move aside!" yelled Boozanne.

All I could think of was sweet Melodie's brains splattered on my shirt. None of it her fault. I grabbed the barrel of the gun and tilted it toward the ceiling. I couldn't risk any new ideas of Boozanne's that might get Melly shot. "Go!" I yelled at Boozanne. "You go! I'll hold her while you get away."

"You sure?" she said. She didn't sound too disappointed.

"Hurry up."

She blew me a kiss, opened a suitcase, threw out my new clothes, and dropped in the books of coins. I stayed on top of Melodie, my head sagging onto her neck. I smelled her hair, clean and flowery. I tried to sooth her by stroking it. Bones gave paw onto my cheek, but seeing no treats, climbed up and sat on my back. I laid still while the squeaky wheels of the suitcases rolled past my nose.

"We could've been great together," she said, "if one of us was a different person."

I looked up and thought I saw a glint of tears in her eye, as she shut the door. Boozanne was gone, taking our dreams with her.

It all hit me then—Melodie would have no idea I saved her life, and she was never gonna think of me like a brother. She'd have a fit when she found out I'd been living there, intimate-like, with her and Bob, even if I did keep the house nice and feed Bones. Some of her ribs were likely broken too. I'd never be able to explain. I was headed back to the slammer for a long, long time.

I thought about Boozanne. I didn't even know her real name and hadn't never seen those airplane tickets to ponder where she was headed. It could've been so perfect, if she hadn't got greedy. Our plan was to walk down to the bar, have a beer, call a taxi to the airport . . . She wouldn't do that now.

Bob's car pulled in, and I was still laying there, half on Melodie. My arm went limp, and Bones jumped off my back as I sat up. Melly rolled to her side wailing, her eyes glazed, flat as those silver dollars. I said, "Sorry, so sorry, Mel," but she didn't hear.

I leaned back against the wall and pictured Boozanne, down the block—big and bold as she was, in that purple shirt, sticking out her thumb—and a gold Cadillac stopping, its doors opening like wings, to fly her away.

THE RECIPE

BY CAROLINA GARCIA-AGUILERA

Downtown

L isten, you either find a home for your mutt by tomorrow, or I'll take it to the vet to put it to sleep." Rob was speaking so loudly that I had to hold the cell phone a foot away from my ear. "I mean it, Lily, no more excuses—either you find it a home, or I swear I'll do it for you."

I knew Rob was not yet finished threatening me. Sure enough, less than ten seconds later, he added, "Lily, you have until 5 o'clock tomorrow afternoon—I already called the vet, and they're open until 6." In spite of the loud noises from the traffic, I could hear his breathing.

"Rob, I know you're fed up with Royal. You've been so understanding, really—and I appreciate all you've put up with." Although my heart was beating so fast that I thought it would burst through the cotton shirt I was wearing, I could not let Rob know how upset I was. I knew it was best to approach my husband from a position of strength. "I'm sorry, honey, but I can't talk now—I'm late for an interview—can we please discuss it later, when I get home?"

"There's nothing to discuss—you have twenty-four hours, period." I flinched at the harsh sound the receiver made as Rob slammed the phone down. Although it was another unbearably hot steamy August day in Miami, I was ice cold.

I could feel my eyes begin to fill up with tears as I thought about what Rob had just said. I did not doubt for one second that he was capable of carrying out his threat. It was true that Royal, at his advanced age, would have accidents inside the house. Because he had problems with his digestion, he would pass gas often. In addition, it was easy for him to become disoriented: He would bark at odd hours and, every so often, wander outside and get lost. I had spent quite a few hours searching the neighborhood for him. In spite of those problems, though, Royal was in good health and, according to Dr. Roth, could last a few more years.

I had found Royal twelve years ago, late on a cold and wet night during the summer vacation after my freshman year in college. I had been gassing up my car when I heard a noise coming from the bushes next to the ladies' room door and had gone to investigate. I found a tiny puppy, a bundle of shivering flesh no bigger than my hand, cowering in the corner. I picked him up, without any hesitation, and took him home. I bottle fed him every few hours for the next month, until he was healthy enough to eat on his own. Even Dr. Roth had not been able to tell what breed of dog Royal was—all he could say was that his mother had had a "hell of a Saturday night."

Royal, who weighed over 140 pounds now, had wiry golden hair and enormous black eyes with lashes that curled up. One of his ears lay down and the other stood straight up. We had not spent a night apart since the day I had found him. I loved Royal with all my heart and could not imagine life without him.

Although it was clear that my relationship with Rob had been rocky for the past year, it was difficult for me to imagine how it had deteriorated to the point that Rob would actually threaten to put Royal down. As I sat there in my car, at the intersection of N.W. Twelfth Avenue and 12th Street, waiting for the traffic light to change, all I could do was ask myself: What happened to us? How could the relationship between two people who had been so in love, and so happy together, disintegrate in such a terrible way?

Rob and I had been married for five years. When we met, he had been a successful architect with a thriving practice, and I had been working as the in-house private investigator for one of Miami's best known criminal defense attorneys.

I came from a family of lawyers, so, naturally, it was assumed that I would follow in my relatives' footsteps and become an attorney, as they had. My parents, my brother, and a cousin, who all practiced criminal defense law, had offices located in a one-story, ramshackle building in Coconut Grove that they had purchased years before.

Due to the kind of law they practiced, they needed the services of a private investigator on a daily basis, so they always employed one in-house. During summer vacations, I would work in their offices, doing various clerical jobs. One summer, however, they had so many cases pending that I had to assist their in-house private investigator. After the first week of shadowing her as she went about, I knew what I wanted to do.

I loved everything about the job—from interviewing witnesses to conducting surveillances. As soon as I graduated from college—I studied business at the University of Miami—I set my sights on my goal. For two years I interned at the office of one of the most successful criminal defense attorneys in Miami. Once I had fulfilled the state of Florida's requirements to be issued a license, I began working.

Although I could have worked for my relatives, I did not think that was a good idea. I was fortunate in that the attorney at whose offices I had interned offered me a full-time job working for him, which I quickly accepted.

I met Rob while working a case that involved his architectural firm. When, a few days later, I bumped into him while shopping at my neighborhood deli, we struck up a conversation. It turned out we lived in the same neighborhood, had both studied at the University of Miami, and we went to the same church. As we were both unattached at the time, it seemed almost natural that we would begin dating. A year later we were engaged, and six months after that we were married.

The first four years of our marriage had been blissful—we lived in a town house in the Coconut Grove section of Miami that we had bought in a deplorable state but that with Rob's know how and many contacts, had renovated to the point where it tripled in price.

Life had been good, so much so that we had even talked about starting a family. Then, suddenly and without notice, the architectural firm where Rob worked was forced to close, and he lost his job. It really wasn't his fault: One of the senior partners had had a stroke and, as a result, had been unable to work, and the other partner then left his wife to marry his longtime mistress, something which was going to cost him plenty. Under such circumstances, the partners had decided to shut the office down, leaving twelve architects jobless.

Unfortunately, Rob had not been able to find another job— well, that was not exactly true. Other possibilities had materialized, but Rob insisted on holding out for a job with the same pay and status he had enjoyed at his old firm. Meanwhile, I became the sole supporter of the family.

Although I was making good money, it was not enough to pay our bills, so we had to take out a second mortgage, then, last month, a line of credit which enabled us to continue to live in the style we were used to. Our credit cards were maxed out and it was clear that we were in serious financial trouble. I was so worried that I actually began to listen to those credit counseling ads on television.

I had to sign all the loan documents as well—something which I strenuously objected to, but which Rob forced me to do. It was easier to give in than to fight him. Besides, at that point I was still in love with him, and believed in him and in what he told me. For a smart woman, sometimes I was pretty dumb.

Later, when the creditors were hounding us in full force, I found out that he had forged my signature on other loan applications. In spite of the fact that we were one step away from the poorhouse, Rob refused to cut down on our spending, proclaiming that we had to maintain our standard of living at all cost.

However, for the past few months, instead of going out and trying to find another job, Rob had been going to the gym, where he was now spending six to eight hours a day. As long as I had known him, he had never before shown any interest in working out, so I was a bit surprised that he threw himself into it so wholeheartedly.

At first I thought that he had begun seeing another woman, and was getting his body into shape for her, but after following him around for a few hours for a couple of days, I knew that I was mistaken. He actually did go to the gym to work out. In almost no time, he lost all kinds of weight, and his body became hard as a rock. Every night when I came home from work, he would show me his "six-pack" and tell me how low his body fat was. He had transformed himself from sedentary architect to full-fledged bodybuilder.

Exercising was normally considered beneficial for a person, but in Rob's case it was completely different. He became mean and abusive, and would wait for me to come home from work to berate me. Our relationship collapsed to the point that, had I been able to do so, I would have left him. Unfortunately, our financial situation was so dire that I would have been saddled with much of his debt; I would be paying it off for the rest of my life. And it wasn't just for financial reasons that I stayed with him. As a practicing Catholic, I took my marriage vows seriously and had married Rob for life. Evidently, we were now in the poorer part of the "for richer and for poorer" stage.

Now, with Rob's threats to euthanize Royal, the situation had reached the point of no return. I had to find a way of keeping my dog, no matter what it took. At that point in our relationship, if I'd had to choose between my husband and my dog, the dog would win, hands down.

Unfortunately, I could not formulate a plan for how to deal

with Rob and the Royal situation just then, as I was on my way to the Dade County Jail to interview a client represented by the criminal defense attorney for whom I worked. According to the preliminary notes that Adrian, my boss, had given me earlier that day, the client was charged with first degree murder.

It seems that Mr. Campos, our client, had plotted and planned to kill his next door neighbor, a young man he had come to loathe in such a way that living next to him had become unbearable. I had no idea what the circumstances surrounding the murder were, as Adrian had not given any details in his notes. We had been working together for so many years that he trusted me to get all the relevant information.

Once I arrived at the jail, I walked over to the far corner of the waiting room and handed my driver's license to a corrections officer seated behind the bullet proof glass, along with my private investigator's license and a letter from Adrian stating he was the attorney representing Mr. Lionel Campos.

Back at my office, I had skimmed the "A form"—the arrest affidavit—and learned that Mr. Campos had been born in Cuba, was sixty years of age, married, and lived in Hialeah, just like thousands of other Cubans who had come to Miami fleeing Fidel Castro. As I waited in the interview room, I decided to spend the time reading the rest of the A form. According to the report, Mr. Campos had killed his neighbor, a Mr. Kent Murphy, twenty-eight years old, Caucasian (or, as they were referred to in Miami demographics, a non-Hispanic white), single.

I was on my third reading of the A form when Mr. Campos walked in. I don't know what I had expected, but it sure as hell was not the slight, sallow-looking, white-haired individual with the twinkling blue eyes that came into the interview room.

I stood up and extended my right hand. "Mr. Campos? I'm Lily Ramos, the investigator from your attorney Mr. Langer's office."

Mr. Campos shook my hand, even as he checked me over

with a skeptical look on his face. I was not surprised at his reaction, as I knew I did not fit most individuals' preconceived idea of what a private investigator should look like. I was small—five feet tall if the wind was blowing right—and, although curvy, I only tipped the scales at one hundred pounds. I was olive-skinned, with straight, shoulder-length, light-brown hair and caramel-colored eyes. Although I carried a big, heavy gun—a Colt .45 (I had bad vision, so I wanted to make sure that if I had to shoot someone, I would not miss my mark)—I was not exactly intimidating.

"You have some kind of ID?" Mr. Campos was not the first client who doubted me, so I had come prepared. I took out one of my business cards from inside my notepad and handed it over to him. I waited while Mr. Campos carefully examined it, turning the small white card over as if there might be a secret message somewhere on it. "How old are you?"

"Twenty-nine," I answered. Then, thinking I was sounding just a bit too curt, I added, "I just had a birthday."

"You look very young—maybe twenty," Mr. Campos commented. It was not meant as a compliment and I did not take it as such. "Okay, we can start. What do you want to know?"

"Well, could you please tell me a bit about yourself, and then we'll talk about what happened—ending up with how and why you're here," I said. "Whatever you tell me will be kept in the strictest of confidence."

Mr. Campos, who had come over with his wife from Cuba thirty years before, had lived in the same house in Hialeah since then. He had worked as an automobile mechanic—he specialized in repairing air conditioners—at the same store since his arrival in Miami. His wife worked in a factory, as a seamstress. Although they had been very happy together, the couple had no children—"a great sadness," as he said.

Mr. Campos told me that he had retired from his job five years before, not by choice, but on his doctor's orders, due to a heart condition which was being aggravated by his work as an air conditioner repairman. His wife, who was ten years younger than him, continued to work. According to Mr. Campos, he did not like just hanging out with other old guys—all they did was drink cheap beer, play dominos, and tell lies about life back in Cuba—so he dedicated himself to improving their home, thinking that if he were to fix up the place nicely, he and his wife could sell it, and with the profits they were sure to make, move into an assisted-living community. He spent hours landscaping the garden, and took great pride in the results.

Mr. Campos also began to take an interest in cooking, and said he very much enjoyed surprising his wife with the meals he had prepared for her when she came home from work. He would try out new recipes, tweaking the ingredients here and there until he was satisfied. He even invented several recipes for marinating especially tough cuts of meat before barbequing them, some of which were so successful that his wife asked for a list of the ingredients. Life was good, and it seemed that it would only get better.

It had been two years ago, when the new neighbors moved in, that the "trouble" began. The owner of the house next door had died, and his children sold the home to a gay couple. At first, although he disapproved of gay people and the "gay lifestyle," Mr. Campos had tried to be a good neighbor, greeting them whenever he saw them, even talking to them on occasion. Yet neither the Campos nor the couple ever went into each others' homes, and it continued that way for the first year.

It was during the second year that the situation started to deteriorate. The gay couple began having trouble—first arguments, then shouting matches that escalated into physical attacks on each other, which became so violent that the police had to come on several occasions. Finally, much to everyone's relief, one of the men moved out, and peace was restored in the neighborhood.

All was going well until the day when the remaining neighbor decided to buy a dog to help himself get over his loneliness. Everything would have been fine except for the fact that he was not just a dog, but a mastiff, a huge animal which barked all day. When he wasn't barking, the dog was howling.

The neighbor, who worked as a personal trainer in one of the giant gyms located in a mall a few miles away from home, was away for hours at a time, which meant the dog was alone—and lonely—a condition that he let everyone know about.

Mr. Campos told me he liked dogs all right, but the neighbor's mastiff drove him crazy. Not only did he bark and howl, he also left enormous smelly poops all over the neighborhood. The dog was especially fond of defecating on Mr. Campos's front lawn, marring the landscaping he had so meticulously worked on. Mr. Campos told the neighbor on numerous occasions to pick up after his dog, but the neighbor did not pay any attention, and continued to let his dog run wild. Mr. Campos even put up a fence to keep the dog out, but the animal just jumped over it.

Mr. Campos went on to tell me that he began plotting how best to remedy the situation. He had become so consumed by his relationship with his neighbor and dog that he began thinking about it almost continuously. Things got so bad that his wife told him to get over it and deal with it, or, if he couldn't do it by himself, get professional help. The fact that his wife told him he needed to see a psychiatrist had been the last straw. He had to do something about the dog, and he had to act fast, while he still had his sanity.

As I listened to Mr. Campos run through the events which led to him killing his neighbor, it was not difficult to see how it had been almost inevitable. As the time passed, it became clear to Mr. Campos that it was either the dog or him.

The longer the interview went on, the more I tried not to think about the situation with Rob, Royal, and me, and I slowly began listening to Mr. Campos's story with more of a personal interest than a professional one.

Mr. Campos told me that he came to the conclusion that the only way to save his sanity—not to mention his property—was to kill the dog. It was after much contemplation that he decided that the best, most efficient, and least painful way to get rid of the animal was to poison him. That night, for the first time in months, instead of sitting by the window, lying in wait for the neighbor's dog to shit on his front lawn, he slept through until morning.

First, he went to the library, where he conducted research on poisons, and he didn't leave until he found one which would not only kill without leaving any trace, but which was so quick and effective that the victim would not suffer. Mr. Campos took a bus across town, to a neighborhood where he was not known, and purchased a bag of that same poison.

Then, Mr. Campos told me in a perfectly calm and detached manner, all he had to do was wait for the perfect opportunity. Not wanting to get caught, he knew he had to be patient and wait for the perfect time to carry out his plan. It was as if God was helping him, he said, when his wife announced that she was going away for a few days, to visit her sister in New Jersey. As soon as her taxi pulled out of their driveway, he set out to purchase a juicy steak at Publix.

Mr. Campos told me he returned home with a five-pound sirloin steak, red, plump, and marbled with just the right amount of fat. As he wanted to make sure that the dog would come over to eat the meat, Mr. Campos decided to light the barbeque in his backyard and let the smell of the meat on the grill waft over to his neighbor's house. He lit the barbeque and, while the charcoals were getting nice and hot, stuffed a handful of the poison inside the steak. Then he placed the steak on the sizzling grill and waited for the dog to jump the fence.

Less than one minute later, he saw the dog stick his head over the fence. Mr. Campos, pleased that his plan was working so well, decided that it was time for nature to take its course and went inside the house. He sat in his favorite chair in the living room and turned on the television.

From the research he had conducted on the Internet, he knew that the poison would act almost instantaneously, but even so, he decided he would wait thirty minutes before going outside to check on the dog. It was a working-class neighborhood, and Mr. Campos knew there would not be anyone about at that time of the morning, so he was not worried that any of the other neighbors would see him dragging the dog around to the back of his yard to properly dispose of the body.

Imagine his surprise, Mr. Campos told me, upon discovering not a dead dog next to the barbeque, but its owner. The neighbor, dressed in his usual workout clothes, was lying next to the gym bag he always carried. The dog kept circling around his master's body, whimpering softly.

The only explanation that Mr. Campos—in his near panicked state—could come up with was that the neighbor had arrived home unexpectedly, and had smelled the steak cooking on the Campos's grill. The entire neighborhood knew of Mr. Campos's predilection for barbequing—it was possible to smell from miles away the secret recipe he used to marinate the meat—so the fact that there had been something cooking on the grill was not unusual.

Seeing that there wasn't anyone around, the neighbor must have decided to steal the meat, which looked and smelled so very appetizing. He must not have been able to wait until he had gotten home to taste it, and bit into the meat right then and there.

Seeing his neighbor lying in his yard had almost brought on a stroke. Mr. Campos told me that as repulsive as it was, he bent over the neighbor and touched him, to see if he could find a pulse. As he leaned over, he saw red juice coming out of the neighbor's mouth, confirming his initial theory about how he had ended up there, lying dead next to the grill.

In spite of his shock at having killed the neighbor, Mr. Campos could not help being angry at him—the bastard had been stealing his steak!

Mr. Campos insisted that there was no way he was going to go to jail, especially as it had been a complete accident. Mr. Campos was no lawyer, but he knew that Florida had the death penalty, and he was determined to avoid that fate. After having successfully fled the giant prison that Castro had made of his beloved Cuba, he was not about to die in an American jail.

Mr. Campos told me that on that day he had been lucky that he had time on his hands—his wife was out of town, and for the next few hours there wouldn't be many people walking around the neighborhood—so he could think clearly about how to properly dispose of the body. After deliberating for awhile, he decided that he would follow the plan he had thought of initially, had it been the dog who had died: He would chop up the body and bury it in the backyard. He headed to the garage where he had set up his workshop, got out his electric saw, the powerful one he had bought after Hurricane Andrew hit Miami and he'd had to cut up the trees littering his property.

First, he had to enlarge the hole he had dug earlier in the back part of the yard so it could accommodate a larger body. He had dug the hole as far away from the street—and prying eyes— as possible, to give himself time to bury the dog. Even though it meant more work for him—he now had to drag a heavier body—he was grateful he'd had the foresight to choose that spot. Even so, he was surprised to find out how much the man's body weighed.

After placing the neighbor in the center of the hole, Mr. Campos got ready to cut it up. The first step was to put on his safety glasses—he certainly didn't want to hurt himself during the sawing process—and then he plugged the cord into the outside wall with an extension cord. His preparations complete, Mr. Campos began the task of slicing up his neighbor. He told me that throughout the process, the dog had just lay silently by the wall, watching the proceedings. I tried to block out a mental image of Royal, and how he would react if someone were to cut me up. Somehow—old, sick, and senile as he was—I don't think he would just sit quietly by and watch.

Mr. Campos told me that when he first began to cut up the body, he was a bit taken aback at how much effort it required. He figured that it had been so difficult because he'd had to slice through mostly bone and muscle. The neighbor had once told Mrs. Campos that he was not only a physical trainer, but a champion bodybuilder as well—and those types had no body fat at all.

I have to confess that it was difficult holding onto my composure as I listened to my client describe his actions on that horrific afternoon, especially when he spoke about the neighbor's dog. Private investigators are never supposed to show emotion, as that can result in the interviewee clamming up. Even though the client may have committed unspeakable acts, no one wants to be openly judged, especially by someone who is supposed to be helping him or her. If a client were to suspect that I thought he or she was disgusting, they would hold back information, and might even lie to show themselves in the best light possible.

Mr. Campos, clearly, had no such hesitations: He was giving me all the gruesome details of what he had done, speaking in a plain and straightforward manner, without any attempt to make himself look good. In his eyes, he had done what he had done to protect his sanity and his property: He had come up with a viable plan to kill the dog that had caused so many problems. The fact that his carefully thought out plan had gone awry was simply too bad.

"So then, Lily—I can call you that, or would you prefer that I address you as Miss Ramos?" Suddenly, and without notice, Mr. Campos broke off from his narration, frightening me. I would have much rather kept the interview on an impersonal note.

"Lily is fine, Mr. Campos," I replied. "So, after you cut up the neighbor's body, then what did you do?"

He took a deep breath before answering. "As I told you, when I was cutting him up, I saw how very, very hard his body was—all muscle, no fat—and I was afraid that if I buried it that way, the gases that get into bodies after a few days would cause the body to stink, and then blow up. You see, Lily, the dog was easier to get rid of—smaller and all that." He shook his head slowly, almost regretfully. "Now I had to think of a way of getting rid of a human body without leaving evidence."

Because Rob had become such a gym rat, I too was aware of the fact that many bodybuilders have almost no body fat. After spending almost all of his waking hours in the gym lifting weights, Rob had sculpted his body to such an extent that on the very few occasions I touched him lately, it felt like I was running my hand over a rock. I knew exactly what Mr. Campos meant when he described the neighbor's body.

"So what did you do?" It frightened me, but I had lost all pretense of asking for professional reasons.

"I marinated him," Mr. Campos replied. "And then, when he was soft enough, I barbequed him."

"You *what?*" I had to restrain myself from reaching across the interview table and shaking the answer out of him.

"Lily, remember that one of my specialties is creating marinades that break down the fibers of cheap, tough cuts of meat so they will be tender enough to barbeque."

I nodded.

"Well, I figured if my marinades—there was one in particular which breaks down the sinews of chuck-grade meat—worked on a tough cut of low-grade steak, why wouldn't it work on a human being?"

As much as I disliked admitting it, I could follow Mr. Campos's logic perfectly—worst of all, however, was that my mind had now gone into overdrive. "So you marinated him?"

Mr. Campos just looked straight ahead. I took that to be a yes.

"For how long?"

He kept staring at the opposite wall. I hoped he was not shutting down on me—I still needed to extract certain information.

"Mr. Campos, please answer my question: How long did you marinate the body before you felt he was ready to be barbequed?"

"Overnight," Mr. Campos finally answered. "I put him on the grill the next morning, after everyone in the neighborhood had left for work." He shrugged his shoulders and continued with his explanation. "I would have liked to marinate him longer, but my wife called to tell me she was cutting her trip short and would be coming home that night."

I sat back and thought about what he had just told me. "What happened to the dog?"

"Ah! The dog!" I could see the faint outlines of a sweet smile on Mr. Campos's face. "It was because of the dog that I got caught. That's why I'm here."

"Can you explain that to me, please?" I couldn't recall having read anything about the dog in the A form.

"Well, of course, after the death of the neighbor, the dog didn't have any place to live, so my wife, bless her, decided to take him in until the owner came back." Mr. Campos leaned over the interview table and shook his index finger at me to emphasize his point. "Remember, at that point no one knew what had happened to the owner. Everyone still figured he was coming back."

I thought for a minute about what he had just said. "So why is it the dog's fault you're here? I mean, you did him a kindness—you offered him a home."

"Ay, Lily—it was because one day he dug up his owner's bones, dug them up from where I buried them in the backyard. And not just that—he did it while the detectives were at our house, interviewing my wife and me, asking us questions about our neighbor's disappearance." Mr. Campos shook his head at the absurdity of it all.

I thought about the dog, and how he had remained faithful to his owner until the very end. Then I thought about Rob, and what he intended to do to Royal tomorrow if I didn't find him a home.

Suddenly, I shoved my notepad over to Mr. Campos. "Please write down the recipe for the marinade you used to break down the tough fibers in the neighbor's body."

Mr. Campos did not move—instead he just stared at me, a knowing look in his eyes. Then, just as I was about to lose hope, he picked up the pen and began to write.

T-BIRD

BY JOHN BOND

Miami River

Before poker I was an insurance claims investigator, a corporate private eye with a short-sleeved white shirt and skinny tie, sometimes catching scumbags but mostly helping big guys screw little guys out of benefits they were entitled to. I put ten years experience to work on my own disability claim—a psych claim, though you can't buy a decent psych policy anymore. Now I just open the mail for my check once a month and play poker. I'm never wearing a tie or watch again. The trick is to keep your head straight, not be sucked in, not to want too much.

I play at McKool's, a sweet two-table poker room in a Miami River warehouse, minutes from the Dolphin Expressway. Across the bridge from the downtown ramps to I-95, it has easy access, drawing players from Boca to Homestead. McKool runs six nights a week, says if you don't give players Saturdays with their wives, then the wives won't let 'em play. I wouldn't know from wives, and with any luck never will.

Texas Hold'em's hot, and I play it, but I prefer Omaha 8-or-better high-low split, which McKool spreads on Fridays. There's more to think about in high-low, and a lot of seductive starting hands, trap hands which suck people in. I scoop both sides in split-pot games more than anybody. That's why McKool calls me Bobby Two-ways. Everybody has a nickname: Rebel, Bumper, Luckbucket, Goombah. Everybody except McKool.

McKool's has a kitchen girl who knows how you take your

coffee, what you want on your sandwich, what snacks you like. I catch two meals every play, and sometimes hit the fridge for a takeout bag at the end of the night. There's a shower, for guys who play all night and then head straight to the office. McKool's got a smoking room in back with its own vent system, and another room with two computers so people can play online poker while waiting for a seat. Both rooms have queen-size beds—some guys take a little nap then get up to play more, or snooze for an hour before heading to work.

I met McKool when he first came back to Miami after twenty years in the army, before he opened up his room. We were playing in the big game at Black Jack's, down in Ocean Reef—$100-$200-limit Hold'em. We'd played all night and were down to the hard cores. Only four of us remained. Tommy Trash—he had the garbage contract for the Keys—had lost $20k-plus, and wanted to play a four-handed $25k freezeout, winner take all. McKool had gotten beat up pretty badly too, and didn't have the buy-in. I'd been the big winner. So I bought McKool's cherry-red 1962 Ford Thunderbird Sports Roadster convertible with a 390 V-8 300 hp engine for twenty-five grand—a steal. The four of us played for the hundred thousand. It only took a couple of hours for McKool and me to bust out Tommy and Jack and get heads up. We played and played and played. And played some more. Fourteen hours later McKool busted me. His mental toughness and physical conditioning for the long sit made the difference. He won the hundred grand, and offered me $30k to buy back the T-bird. But I liked it and said no.

McKool used that win to bankroll opening his place. He's offered me forty, then fifty, and recently sixty grand for the car. I'm not much into things, but I love that ragtop. Besides, it's good when The Man wants something he can't have from you.

I don't really have friends, but McKool and I know we can rely on each other. I think I'm the only player in the game who has his private cell. I do a lot for McKool: recruit from the pari-mutuels; deal when somebody calls in sick; give up my seat when he needs to fit a live one in. Mostly I show up for the afternoon gin game before start time and stay through the last hand. Starters and finishers are key to running a profitable house game, getting games off early and keeping them going late.

My trouble started at McKool's Thursday game, No Limit Hold'em night, five hundred minimum/a thousand maximum buy-in, five and ten blinds. Rebel—Rebecca Ellen O'Shaunessy—strolled in after her shift as bartender at a trendy South Beach club, as she did a couple of nights a week.

Rebel's easy on the eyes, all natural. To see her is to want her. She'd sweetly turned me down more than once. Mid-twenties, about 5'6", maybe 115 pounds, green eyes and auburn-almost-red hair, perfect spinner bod. The kind of girl men would leave their wives for in a heartbeat. McKool uses Rebel like he uses me, like he uses everybody—hustling here, cajoling there, pushing buttons, building up a stash of favors so butts are in seats and the cards are always in the air by 7:00, and the game goes on toward dawn and beyond. Knowing the hottie was coming kept early players hanging on late, and gave the late players reason to arrive early. We rarely broke before sunrise when Rebel played.

Poker's not a game where you have to be the best player in the world—just the best at the table. Winning players aren't welcome at most private games. We take cash from the game, use it to pay rent and buy groceries. A houseman wants action. Gambling fools. The suckers who look for any excuse to play a hand, who don't understand that more often than not the right play is to pass, not get involved. Live ones attract players, working pros drive them away. I've been barred from the weekly games at the Coconut Grove Yacht Club and Lauderdale Country Club. I help McKool not because I'm a nice guy, but so he'll let me play in his juicy lineup of fish.

Rebel did her grand-entrance thing, giving this one a wink, tousling that one's hair, stroking the other's arm. Escort Randy— he owns a low-rent Internet escort agency, buck-fifty-an-hour girls, mostly but not all skanks—asked her for the zillionth time if she'd work for him, and for the zillionth time she smacked him on the arm, then gave him a hug. I like Randy—he gives me a twenty-dollar discount on calls.

McKool had his usual crew on hand: three dealers, Lilith the kitchen girl, and Cartouche, the half-Senegalese half-Moroccan from Montreal McKool had hooked up with in some little jungle war. Cartouche didn't exactly have a job, though he sometimes dealt and even sometimes cooked. He just stood by McKool's side, a silent giant.

Rebel sat down and set off on a chip fry like she hated her money. No Limit's a dangerous game for people who play fast. In limit games, when you make a mistake, you lose a bet or maybe a pot. In No Limit, when you make a mistake, you lose everything. Rebel got herself stuck fifteen hundred in less than twenty minutes, and soon had McKool pinned in a corner, stroking his arm, giving him that damsel-in-distress look.

McKool sometimes gives regulars a nickel or dime's credit juice-free, but only until the next play, up to a week max. Having players on the book is a necessary evil of the business. Problem is, when they owe you money, the next time they have a few bucks they take that money someplace else to play, instead of paying you. McKool, after his twenty years in Special Forces, doesn't have a lot of collection problems. Plus he has Cartouche. McKool's rule is only lend to people who have money to pay you back right away. I knew Rebel wasn't getting a penny more out of McKool.

She looked around the room, caught me eying her. She stuck out her lower lip in a pouty way, and mouthed "please." I shook my head. She smiled and shrugged, then grabbed Skip Converse, one of Miami's slimiest shysters, and pulled him away from the table. A minute later he plopped his big butt back in his seat—Skip's a fish with no clue when to pass and hates to miss a hand. Reb sashayed over to the other table, draped her arms around Big Country's shoulders, and whispered something in his ear. He got up and they stepped into one of the back rooms.

"Chick already owes me five hundred," Skip said. "I told her the next nickel would require sex. Can't imagine why she passed."

Five minutes later they came out of the back, Big Country laughing like a schoolboy. He bought two racks of reds from McKool and handed them to Rebel. She gave him a full-contact hug, something more than affectionate, and a kiss on the cheek.

"Thanks, Country, you're a real gentleman," she said. "I'll crush these fuckers, but if for some reason they escape, I promise you'll have it back Sunday." Then she terrorized the game. One hand she came over the top on Big Country and moved him off a big pot. I knew from the way she stared him down she'd bluffed him off. Lending people money to play against you is a bad bet. If they lose, you won't see it anytime soon. If they win, you lose. But I understand not being able to say no to a pretty girl. What man doesn't? In a couple of hours Reb won back the fifteen hundred she'd lost, the dime she'd borrowed from Big Country, and seven hundred sugar. Then she did something she almost never does. She locked up her win.

While McKool counted her down, Rebel came over, rested her hand oh-so-lightly on my inside thigh, and blew gently on my neck, sending a shiver down my neck and making my dick hard. She whispered in my ear, "Two-ways, I need your help. Meet me upstairs at the Road in an hour?"

I hate being manipulated by anybody, especially women. "Make it an hour and a half," I said.

As she headed to the door, Skip called out to her: "Hey, Rebel, what about my five bills?"

She smiled sweetly. "Next week, Skip."

Cartouche gave Rebel a look; she understood that really meant next week.

Every eye in the room followed her as she walked out. If God had ever made a more perfect ass than Rebel's, he kept it for himself.

I cashed out then headed down South River, the full moon behind me. Downtown and Little Havana meet here in Riverside, not far from the Orange Bowl. I often play dominos with the old Cubanos at Marti Park before heading to afternoon gin at McKool's.

Miami had been born along the river. South River Drive, with all its banyans, ficus, and palms, runs southeast-to-northwest by the riverbank, cul-de-sacs and dead ends off it on the river side. This once was a working river, but the fishing boats on the east end had given way to condos and office towers, though piles of lobster pots and crab traps lay stacked here and there along the banks. Scattered small freighter terminals serviced seedy tramps running back and forth to the Bahamas, Haiti, and other islands. Most of South Florida's stolen bicycles and chopped-up car parts found their way into these cargo holds, and more than a little of the area's dope came through here.

I parked by a sand-yellow, two-story stucco building on the riverbank: Miami's oldest bar, Tobacco Road. During Prohibition, rum-runners out of Bimini had unloaded their wares from the river behind the building, under the protection of the local sheriff. The day Prohibition ended, the bar opened fully stocked and has never closed since. Most Miami bars close at 2, but the Road has a grandfathered late-night license. I arrived twenty minutes late, figured if Rebel wanted something then keeping her waiting a bit would establish negotiating control. I climbed the narrow staircase to the tiny upstairs bar, but she hadn't arrived. I sat at a cocktail table, ordered a mojito from Maidel, the-waitress-who-wrote-blues-lyrics-about-three-legged-dogs-and-lovelorn-artists, listened to a frumpy grad student reading incomprehensible poetry from the tiny stage, and waited.

She arrived ten minutes later, on her arm a handsome blond guy. I stood as they approached. She kissed me on the lips, almost but not quite tonguing me. "Bobby, this is my boyfriend Dmitri. Dima, this is Bobby Two-ways, the poker player who used to do insurance investigations."

Dmitri smiled, showing hillbilly teeth. "Rebecca tells me you are a man to be trusted," he said with a thick Russian accent. "That you do the right thing."

I shot a glance at Rebel. In an after-game bull session one night, I'd told her I could always be trusted to do the right thing. The right thing for me, that is. She'd laughed, and many times since had made sly comments about "the right thing" with a wink and a knowing smile. "What's this about, Reb?"

"How'd you like to fuck me, Bobby?"

"Fuck you out of what?"

She licked her lips. "Really."

"Really? Like in sex? How's Dmitri here feel about that?"

"It's his idea."

"I'm not big on audiences." I thought she was inviting me to do a three-way with them. "And he's cute, but definitely not my type."

Rebel shook her head. "No, no, nothing like that. I need money. Big money. Dima came up with a scam we can work. We need a third person. All you got to do is fuck me."

"It would have to be after 2. I don't do mornings."

"You'd fuck me on I-95 in the middle of morning rush hour with your mother watching."

She was right, of course. I'd drag my dick through a mile of broken glass for a chance at her. Anyplace, anytime. "Why do you need money so bad?"

She laughed, not an amused laugh but a sharp one. "Why

does anybody need money? And why do you care? We can score. Big money. Low risk. If this was a no-limit hand you'd shove your stack in. You get ten percent for a half hour's work." She pressed her breasts against my arm, rested her hand high on my thigh under the table, breathed on my neck, and said huskily, "If you call this work."

Dmitri leaned toward me, whispered the details—a lawsuit scam, like those teams that stage car accidents to rip off insurance companies. I'd sent my share of those scumbags to jail, back when. He'd cased the target well, had the timing down. Litigation potential hit seven figures, easy. A quick settlement was worth a half mill, minimum.

Poker players make fast decisions, always on incomplete information—hundreds, thousands of dollars won or lost in a blink. Good players make quality reads of situations. We get into our opponent's mind. What is he thinking? What does he think I'm thinking? What does he think I think he's thinking? Anticipate what he's going to do, what he wants you to do, make the play that uses his thoughts against him. Investigating this as a claim, what would I go after? As a scammer, how would I avoid what the investigator would look for? What would the investigator think a scammer would be thinking? How could I use those thoughts against him?

"It's probably a winner," I said. Solid poker players, like insurance companies, act on risk-reward ratio. But it's more than just the odds. If ninety-nine percent of the time you get a good result, but one percent of the time the result is horrendous, then even a 99-1 favorite can be a bad bet. Dmitri's scheme looked good, yet even a slim chance of winding up in the slam made this an easy fold for me. "But I like my life the way it is." I laid a twenty on the table for my drink and Maidel's tip, and stood up. "Sorry, I'm out."

Rebel grabbed my wrist and yanked me back into my seat.

"Twenty-five percent," Dmitri said.

I live well, but not fancy, in a nice one-bedroom a block from the beach in Surfside. I have my T-bird. I have $70k sitting in a box at Banque de Geneve in Nassau, $20k buried in coffee cans in the trees lining the seventh fairway at Doral, and my working bankroll of $10k stashed in a shoebox in my AC vent. If they hit for $1.5 mill, the lawyer took a third—$250k would make a gigantic difference in my life. Enough to bankroll me for a shot at the World Poker Tour, maybe the big one at Binion's. Maybe even buy a little condo. "No," I said.

Rebel moved her hand up under the table and unsnapped my pants, pulled down the zip of my jeans, and slipped her hand into my boxers.

"All right," Dmitri said. "Even split. One-third each."

Rebel gently ran her nails up and down my rock-hard dick. She came close and whispered in my ear with hot breath, "Please, Two-ways?"

I shook my head no. "Okay. A third."

Friday I got up early, around noon, and drove up the Palmetto to Alligator Alley and cruised across the Everglades to Fort Myers in my T-bird with the top down. I found a Super Wal-Mart and bought a black long-sleeved shirt, two pairs of black socks, a Yankees cap, wraparound shades, a pair of flared black jeans a couple of inches longer in the in-seam than usual, four dog leashes, a roll of duct tape, a box of flesh-colored latex gloves, a box of safety matches, a $12 Casio watch, a dark-blue bandanna, a showercap, a small plastic wastebin, a five-gallon gas can, a bottle of Astroglide, a package of three condoms, and a small backpack. Cash, of course. Then I went to Payless and purchased a pair of size-eleven shoes with four-inch cork platforms— told the nearly oblivious clerk they were a gift, to explain why a size-nine guy was buying elevens. I bought a roll of quarters at a beachfront arcade, then stopped into a Supercuts for a buzzcut.

I drove home across the Alley, the winter sun setting behind me. I headed to the never-ending traffic construction on Biscayne, found a job on a deserted side street, hopped out of the T-bird, grabbed two orange traffic cones and a barricade, threw them in my trunk, then drove across the bay. I cruised South Beach waiting for a suitable parking space to open up on Washington. One finally did right where I wanted, just south of Lincoln Road. I pulled up alongside it, set the cones and barricade in it, and headed home.

I filled the T-bird and the five-gallon gas can at the Mobil on Harding around the corner from my apartment, then put the gas can in the trunk. In my apartment-house parking lot I looked about, found a perfect pebble—about a quarter-inch, rounded, with no sharp edges—and pocketed it. I placed my purchases in the backpack in the order I'd need them, last items on the bottom, first on top, shoved in a big green trash bag, then set the radio alarm for 9:45 and settled in for a nap to catch up on my lost sleep.

Jimmy Buffet woke me singing "Margaritaville" on the classic rock station. I spent a half hour shaving every hair off my body from the eyes down. I trimmed my eyebrows, made sure I had no loose eyelashes, then showered, wiping every speck of hair off my body. I dressed in my usual blue jeans and tee, strapped on the Casio, grabbed the backpack, put the pebble, quarters, and a plastic hotel key card Dmitri had given me in my pocket and headed out. In the parking lot I unscrewed the little light bulb over my license tag, put the trash can from Wal-Mart in the trunk with the gas, and threw the backpack on the passenger seat. I checked the Casio—an hour forty to go.

I drove past the Jackie Gleason across Lincoln Road to Washington Avenue, with all its spiffed-up Deco buildings—pastel paint jobs and colored lights showing off the architectural accents. I pulled up to my space, threw the cones and barricade back in the trunk, and parallel parked. South Beach parking spaces on weekend nights are like gold. I filled the meter with four hours' worth of quarters, then ambled down to the 11th Street Diner. The 11th is famous for the best meatloaf sandwiches this side of your mom's kitchen and the best milkshakes anywhere. But it suited me this night because it's 24/7 and bustles with club-goers from around 10 p.m. to 6 a.m.

I made my way past the crowded booths to the john in back, stepped into a stall, and hung the backpack on the hook on the door. I pulled out the Wal-Mart black jeans, socks, and black shirt and changed into them. I put on the showercap, tied the bandanna around my head so that not a single hair showed, pulled the Yankees cap over it, and slipped on the wraparounds. I shoved the extra socks into the toes of the platforms and set the pebble carefully so it rested just under my arch, and put on the shoes. I pulled on a pair of the flesh-colored latex gloves, shoved my sneaks, jeans, and T-shirt into the backpack.

Then I sat on the pot for five minutes so nobody who'd been in the bathroom still lingered, stepped out of the stall, through the diner, and back onto Washington. The SoBe party crowd milled about, just starting to cook. Teenagers wanting to be older, boomers wanting to be younger, loads of twenty-somethings wanting to be seen. Glitz, glamour, and grunge, hip-hoppers in baggy shorts with legacy hoops jerseys and hooded sweatshirts, supermodel-wannabes in short, slinky dresses, random retros in Goth, buffed-up boys in muscle shirts, bikers and beachboys and babes. I blended right in.

Rap, industrial, and hip-hop boomed from a parade of tricked-out cars circling through the Deco District, bass throbbing from over-powered woofers. Lines formed outside the most popular clubs. I ambled amid the throng up and across to Collins Avenue, the platforms making me a six-foot-one guy, not five-nine, with a marked limp from the pebble in my shoe. Poker players not only observe body language as part of the art of reading tells, but notice what their opponents observe, and then try to use that knowledge to deceive them. Real winners make this observation a habit of their lives. I'd discovered over years of watching what people see that you always notice, at least subconsciously, how people walk. The limp disguised me as much as the shades and the platform shoes.

Two blocks up Collins stood the former Hotel Roosevelt, a streamlined, thirty-five-story Art Deco masterpiece, restored beyond its former glory, renamed the Delano and now owned by an over-the-hill rock diva struggling to stay cool. Right that moment I found myself in my own struggle to stay cool. My palms were sweating in the latex gloves, a sharp ache throbbed in my shoulders. I took a deep breath. Focus, I told myself. Think, don't react. Adjust as each card comes off the deck. I breathed deeply, put myself in game mode, all focus, focus, focus. Just keep on reading the situation and make the right play. One card after another, one hand then the next, one step after another, then the next, until I found myself walking past the valets and doormen into the Delano's ornate lobby. I checked the Casio—still running good.

Bodies ebbed and flowed through the lobby from the adjoining coffee shop and nightclub. Dmitri stood at the concierge's desk. As I made my way through the bustle to the elevators at the back, the concierge handed him a slip of paper and made some motions with his hands as if giving directions. Dmitri tipped the concierge and headed out the grand entrance I had just come through.

I rode the elevator alone to the fourth floor. Dmitri had scouted two cameras on every floor, each pointing toward the center, showing half the hallway to the elevator. If he'd done his job, the camera at the east end would be tilted upward, leaving a blind spot so that the doors to the last four rooms or so were out of view.

I turned west and stopped at the end of the hall, in clear camera view, and tried a random door with the Holiday Inn key card Dmitri had given me at the Road. It wouldn't open the door, of course, but I wanted the cameras to see. Then I tried another door. I slapped my forehead as if I'd screwed up and walked to the east end, and now out of camera view went through the fire-escape door and took the stairs down to the third floor.

The camera here should be tilted too, but ever so slightly, so just the last room was unwatched. I opened the fire-escape door a crack and peeked down the hall. A lone couple entangled in an embrace stood waiting for the elevator. I checked the room numbers on both sides of the fire escape door. On my left, 327, just as Dmitri had said. I pushed on the door and it gave way. The small piece of matchbook that Dmitri had stuck in the latch so it wouldn't catch fell to the floor. I shut the door quietly behind me, picked up the bit of matchbook, put it in my pocket, and slipped into the room.

Rebel didn't look up as the door latch clicked. She sat on the edge of the canopied, king-size bed wearing only her panties—pink bikini bottoms—sucking on a cigarette, clinking ice cubes in a cocktail glass. A half-empty bottle of Jack stood on the nightstand. The bedcovers had been tossed on the floor. She caressed the bed. "Never in my life have I slept on sheets this soft, Two-ways," she said. "But at five hundred a night, you should get nice sheets."

I couldn't think of anything to say, so I just nodded.

She stood and faced me. Near-naked she was as perfect as I'd imagined.

Rebel handed me a buck knife. "Dima said you should cut the panties off with this, then before you go, hold it against my throat hard enough to make a mark. And leave the knife when you're done. It leads someplace a million miles from any of us."

I took the knife from her, opened it, slipped the blade between the skin of her hip and the panties, and cut. They fell to the floor. Her pubes were shaved. Above her pussy, *DIMA* was tattooed in script, inside a heart. "You look nice."

"I don't look 'nice.' I'm fucking *hot*. So fucking hot that you lose all control and just fucking take me. So hot you can't think straight." She grabbed my crotch. "Jesus Christ. Here I am, the hottest woman you'll ever fuck as long as you live, standing buck-naked for you to take, and you don't even have a hard-on."

I'd wanted to bed Rebel since the first time I saw her. Here she stood naked in all her glory for me to have. I couldn't remember a less erotic moment with a beautiful girl in my life.

"Two-ways, let's do this. We're on a schedule."

I took the leashes, Astroglide, duct tape, and condoms from the backpack and set them on the bed.

"You're going to wear a condom? Rapists don't wear fucking condoms."

"It's the twenty-first century, Reb. Rapists worry about STDs as much as the next guy. And smart rapists don't leave a load of DNA inside you for some crime-lab geek to analyze. If I'm going to be a rapist, I'm going to be as smart a rapist as I can be."

"Dima won't like it."

"Screw Dima."

"No—screw me. Right fucking now! Get naked already."

I stripped clumsily, sure I looked foolish in the bandanna, platforms, and latex gloves.

"Jesus Christ, Bobby, you're still not hard." She grabbed my dick and squeezed. "Doesn't this thing work?" She pushed me onto the bed, deftly manipulated my dick until it finally stood at attention, then tore open a condom and slipped it on. She crawled on the bed and threw her arms and legs wide, spread-eagled.

I looped a dog leash around each of her wrists and ankles, then tied them to the feet of the bed, snapped the d-ring at the end of each into place.

She strained at the leashes. "Left arm's not tight enough," she said.

I adjusted the leash securing her left arm, then crawled atop her—and realized I had gone soft.

She laughed. "Do you have this problem often?"

"N-n-never."

"Jesus Christ, untie me."

I did as she said.

"You should have taken some Vitamin V." She pressed against me, kissed my neck while holding my dick, wrapped her legs around me, massaged my thigh with her pussy. My dick grew, this time with conviction. She went down on me, playing with my balls while she moved her mouth up and down my shaft, until I was about to come. She climbed up my body, whispered in my ear, "Hold that thought for five minutes."

I tied her again to the bed, opened another condom, pulled it on, climbed back atop her, and tried to slip myself into her. She was completely dry. I rolled off her and, rubbing my dick against her leg to keep my hard-on, began to massage her clit.

"That won't work," she said. "Use the Astroglide."

I squirted the lube on her pussy, massaged her insides with my fingers, filling her with wetness. I climbed on top again—but again I had gone soft.

"Listen, Two-ways, you don't have to come, but you do have to get it inside me. I know from experience the police rape kit will show whether or not you penetrated."

I untied her and she repeated her oral magic, bringing me once more to the edge of orgasm. This time I didn't tie her but let the animal in me take over—I threw her back on the bed and mounted her quickly, shoving and humping and grunting until I exploded. I rolled off her onto the bed and began to laugh, a little nervously—at myself.

"We're behind schedule," she said matter-of-factly. "Get me tied down."

I tied her to the bed for the third time, pulled the leashes tight as I could.

"Now hit me in the face. Hard."

I hesitated. "I've never hit a girl and I'm not going to start now."

"Goddamnit, Two-ways. The more I'm hurt, the more we can win. Hit me."

I shook my head no. "Sorry, Reb. I won't. Can't."

"Dima's going to be pissed."

"Screw Dima."

"You said that already. Don't ever say it to him. He's not one to be fucked with."

I dressed in my Wal-Mart outfit, shoved the used condoms and wrappers into the pockets of the jeans, and put the Astroglide in the backpack. I picked up the knife.

"At least hold the knife against my throat," Rebel said. "Cut me some."

I did as she said, leaning over her with the blade held tight against her throat, but away from her jugular.

"Harder," she said.

"Shit, Rebel, how the hell do I know how much is hard enough?"

"Just do it, Bobby. Harder!"

I pressed down harder, afraid that I might hurt her. I managed to break the skin without doing any more damage. A rivulet of blood trickled down her neck.

"Good," she said. "Now hit me, goddamnit, Bobby. Leave bruises."

"No, Reb."

"Don't be such a fucking wimp. There's big fucking money at stake here."

I cut a length of duct tape off the roll with the knife and slapped it across her mouth, perhaps the most satisfactory moment of the night so far. I stepped back and looked at her spread wide on the bed, helpless, her beauty almost perfect, her pussy glistening with the Astroglide. To see her was to want her.

Wanting is good. Even better than having.

I looked at the Casio. My bout of erectile dysfunction had put us behind schedule, even with the extra time Dmitri had built in for margin of error. He'd be coming up the elevator to discover his raped girlfriend any minute. I shoved the duct tape in the backpack, threw the knife on the bed. Fibers from generic Wal-Mart clothes, no prints or hairs, size-eleven footprints impressed on the lush carpet. I looked around the room to make sure I hadn't left anything incriminating behind. I'd done what I could to minimize risk.

I slipped into the hall and ran down the stairwell to the first floor, moseyed out into the lobby. The Delano's nightclub in full swing, even more people milled about the lobby than earlier. I saw Dmitri at the elevator. Then he saw me. He checked his watch, scowled. If looks could kill, I'd have been dead on the floor. The elevator dinged, the doors opened, and he stepped on. We'd cut it mighty close.

I walked briskly back to the 11th, changed back into my own clothes and sneaks, shoved the platforms and Wal-Mart clothes into the backpack, then again waited a few minutes before stepping out of the stall, through the diner, and onto the street. Less than ten minutes after leaving Rebel, I was driving west on 17th Street, feeling empty but relieved, glad that it was over. I drove across the MacArthur past the parade of cruise ships waiting at dock to sail off for temporary island fantasies, and got on I-95 north. I exited at State Road 84 twenty minutes later, turned down a small street, then into an alley between two warehouses.

I poured some gas into the Wal-Mart wastebin and dumped in everything I'd used and worn—only the knife, a piece of duct tape across Rebel's mouth, and the four leashes that tied her to the bed remained. In life, as in poker, you can't control all the variables, but you do what you can. I poured in some more gas, struck a safety match against the box, and flicked it in, then dropped in the rest of the box. Flame wooshed upward. I watched it burn and visualized Rebel spread-eagle on the canopied bed. My dick hardened at the vision. I had to laugh at myself; oh well, what can you do?

The blaze left a goo of plastic slag. After the fire died, I shoved the mess into the green garbage bag, tied it off tight, and drove to a complex I'd once lived in on Marina Mile, where they had Saturday-morning trash pickup. I threw the bag into a dumpster; in a few hours it would be lost in the daily refuse of a million people, with only the vultures circling overhead and the never-ending parade of garbage trucks for company. I set the cones and barricade at a construction site, then took I-95 to the Kennedy Causeway, home across the bay into the pink dawn.

I slept later than usual Saturday. I went to Miami Jai-Alai, yakked with the $2 poker players, ate a breakfast of hot dogs and beer, then headed to Gulfstream, where I relaxed in the cheap seats basking in the afternoon sun with the racing form. The hard work was now on Rebel—Monday she'd retain a lawyer. He'd file the suit for inadequate security resulting in Rebel's rape, and the settlement dance would begin. Most cases like this never went to trial, but rarely settled before the eve of trial. All I had to do now was live my life and wait for my payday.

I cashed a $220 ticket in the last race, then went to the Porterhouse up in Sunny Isles to have a nice steak and flirt with the waitresses. As I ate, my cell rang. I didn't recognize the number, and didn't answer. A few seconds later it rang again, from the same number. The third time, curious about who would be so persistent, I picked up.

"Bobby, thank God you answered. It's Rebel." She sounded as if she were crying. "I need your help." She started to babble— Dima had gone crazy, beaten her. She was afraid. Could I meet her someplace private? No, not my place in Surfside, he'd check there. Freighter terminal #9 on the river, a few blocks from McKool's. Just get there and we could decide together what to do. An hour, please hurry. She abruptly disconnected.

I didn't like it a bit, but I didn't see how I couldn't go. I took 163rd Street to the Spaghetti Bowl, then I-95 to downtown and across the river. As I drove under the halogen-tinted sky, I slammed my fist on the wheel, telling myself this was wrong, that I was an idiot. Whatever Rebel wanted from me, I wasn't going to want to do it. Why couldn't my mother have raised a less chivalrous son?

Just past the Miami River Inn, I turned onto the street that dead-ended at terminal #9. The gate to the pier was open, the streetlight next to it burned out. I edged the T-bird past pallets loaded with construction materials waiting for the next freighter out, turned the corner along the warehouse, and saw Rebel's car parked by the gantry crane. Lights from across the river cast oblong shadows. Rebel leaned on her car, smoking a cigarette. I climbed out of the T-bird and saw in the glow of the burning ash that her face was all mangled, bruised yellow and purple, one eye bandaged. "Holy shit, Rebel."

"It pissed Dima off that you didn't beat me," she said. "The rape didn't look real enough. So he added that touch himself." She sobbed. "He likes hurting me too much. I'm scared, Bobby. I can't go to the police. I don't know what to do." She stared into my eyes.

I stepped forward to take her in my arms. Something about that look.

"I'm sorry, Bobby," Rebel whispered softly. "If it makes you feel any better . . ."

It was the same way she stared when she was trying to run a bluff!

". . . Dima's next."

From behind me I heard the double-click of a revolver's hammer pulling back.

Oh shit, I thought. I grabbed Rebel by the shoulders, ducked, and twirled around, holding her in front of me. Then came the explosion of a shot, the acrid smell of cordite, the blinding muzzle flash. The bullet that had been intended for me took her square in the chest, knocked her into me, came out her back, and hit me in the belly, but its momentum spent, didn't penetrate. The slug clattered to the ground. Blood seeped out Rebel's back all over my clothes. Dmitri stood in front of me, not ten feet away, a shocked look on his face that quickly turned to rage. It happened in seconds, but took forever.

He lunged toward me, screaming in Russian, pointing the pistol at my head. I pushed Rebel's limp body at him, dropped, and threw my weight at his knees; the three of us rolled to the ground in a tangle of arms and legs. The gun went off again, near my ear, the explosion deafening me. I grabbed Dmitri's hair, wrapping my fingers in tight, and smashed his head into the parking lot pavement with all my strength, and again and again and again and again, until he stopped moving.

I lay there covered in blood, entangled in two bodies, with no clue what to do next, where to turn. My head throbbed. How would I explain this to the cops? How did I know these people who had just reported a brutal rape? Any investigator worth a damn would toast me. Focus, I told myself. Think, don't react. Breathe deep. What are your options? What's the best play here?

I called McKool on his private cell. "McKool. Two-ways," I said. "What's that Explorer you drive worth?"

McKool started to say something, then started over. "Maybe 25, 30k. Why?"

"The Explorer and 25 for the T-bird," I said.

McKool hesitated a second. "Twenty."

"Deal. But I need your help with something right now . . ."

Less than ten minutes later he was there, with Cartouche. They quickly surveyed the scene. "Fine mess, Bobby," McKool said, as he tossed me his keys.

I pulled the keys to the T-bird from my pocket, pulled off my apartment key, then handed them to McKool. "She set us both up."

"Chicks can be that way," McKool said.

Cartouche bent over, felt Rebel's neck for a pulse. *"Mort,"* he said. Then he checked Dmitri and shook his head. *"Il n'est pas tout a fait mort."*

"She's dead. He's not quite dead," McKool translated for me. "This costs me. Rebel filled some seats." He thought a moment, then made a small flick of his finger across his throat.

Cartouche took a handkerchief from his pocket and picked up the pistol, stuck the barrel in Dmitri's ear, and pulled the trigger, then handed McKool the gun.

"He was near-dead anyway, and now he can't mention your name before he goes," McKool said. He stuffed the gun in his pocket. "We'll dispose of the bodies. Go home and get rid of those clothes."

"Thanks."

"Come before gin tomorrow," McKool said. "We'll do the car titles and talk."

I got the gas from the T-bird's trunk, then drove the Explorer home. I disconnected my apartment's smoke detector, threw my clothes in the bathtub, poured in the last of the gas, and burned my bloody clothes to ash. After making sure not a speck of fabric remained, I washed the ash down the drain, then stood under the shower until the hot water ran out, and fell into bed without even bothering to dry. I missed my T-bird.

Sunday afternoon, after a fitful sleep, I knocked on McKool's door. The peephole darkened, and Cartouche let me in. Lilith stood at the stove making dinner for the crowd to come, and one of the dealers, Lefty Louie, sat at a poker table making up decks.

"Step into my office," McKool said, and we went into one of the back rooms. He handed me the local section of Sunday's *Herald,* opened to page five. A story halfway down the page read:

POLICE SUSPECT RUSSIAN MOB HIT
*Two dead bodies were found early Sunday on a bus bench
off Brickell Avenue, near S.W. 10th Street. Dmitri Ribikoff,
a Russian national in the U.S. on an expired visa, had been
brutally beaten and shot in the head, execution-style. The
victim was a distant cousin of Russian oil oligarch Sergei
Petrov, and a spokeswoman for Miami PD said Russian
organized crime might be responsible. Police are withholding
the name of the other victim, a woman in her twenties, shot
through the heart and also badly beaten, pending notification
of her family.*

"They won't find any family," McKool said. "She had
nobody." There was a gentle tapping on the door. "Come."
Lilith stuck her head in. "Luckbucket and Bumper are
here."
"We'll be right out," McKool said. He handed me a manila
envelope full of hundreds rolled in rubber bands. I didn't need to
count it, knew the twenty grand was there. "You understand you
owe me," he said. "And last night never happened." He signed
the title to the Explorer and handed it to me with the pen.
"Never happened."
"Make it out to Jean-Luc Cartouche."
I looked at him, puzzled. "Cartouche? Why?"
"He wants it. I'd rather he have it and me want it. Ready for
gin?"
I signed the title over to Cartouche. "Yeah." Who knew
wanting and having were so complicated?
We stepped into the main room, where Bumper and
Luckbucket sat leafing through back issues of *Card Player.*
Luckbucket's was opened to an article by Roy Cooke headlined:
Some Hands You Just Don't Play!
Life is like the game, I thought. It's supposed to be the fish
who play the trap hands.

PART IV

CHASING THE CITY

SWAP OUT

BY PRESTON L. ALLEN

Miami-Dade Correctional Center

How'd the phone call go?

She ain't much of a wife no more. Tha's for sure.

You're inna joint. Whaddaya expect?

I'm inna joint one day. Less than one day.

One day, one hundred days, it's all the same ta them out there.

It ain't like I'm in prison.

It's all the same ta them out there. Out there is Miami. Here is here.

It ain't like I'm even guilty.

What you ain't is, you ain't out there. Tha's all that matters ta them.

We been married eighteen years. I was her firs.

Her firs what?

Firs, ya know, firs lover.

Oh. A virgin. Tha's nice. I didn know they made them anymore.

I doubt she even hadda boyfriend before me.

Well, aleast tha's what she told ya.

Whaddaya talking about? She was pure.

I'm not gonna argue with ya. You say she wuzz pure, then she's pure in my book. All I'm sayin is ya never really know with women.

Well I know, I can tellya that. My Merly was pure.

Merly. Tha's a nice name. Kinda like my wife's name. Kerly.

Your wife's name is Kerly?

My wife's name *wuzz* Kerly. She's dead now.

I'm sorry.

Yeah, me too. She wuzz a beaut. She woulda been a old lady now, but she wuzz the greatest gal in the world.

Wuzz she pure when ya married her?

Ya want me ta smack ya?

Want me ta smack ya back?

The trustee said, Ya got in a cheap shot this mornin, don't forget that. Had I been looking, I woulda nailed ya.

You wuzz sayin about Kerly.

Greatest gal in the world. It's becausa her that I'm inna joint these las fifteen, what, sixteen yearsa my life. They gave me life for it, but I got good behavior and extenuating circumstances, believe it or not, and they knocked a bunch of em off. So I got only six more ta do if I keep my nose clean and help out the guards, and I'm doin em here in the county instead of up at state where I was for ten, what, eleven of em. Up at state wuzz tough, I'm not kiddin ya. You don't wanna go there.

Nah. I don't wanna go there. Kerly. Some coincident. Ya killt her, huh?

Nah. I killt the guy what killt her.

Hoo. Hoo. Tough.

You don't know tough. He wuzz my best friend.

Hoo. Tough. What happened?

See, there wuzz these two beautiful girls we met at the fair.

Hoo! The fair. How corny can ya get? Hoo!

It wuzz the fair. Tha's where we met em. Kerly and her sista Pearly.

Hoo! Hoo! Go on, finish it. Hoo!

I'm tryin hard not ta smack you.

Hoo! Hoo! Go on, finish it before my lawyer gets here. I wanna hear this. Hoo! Kerly. Pearly. Hoo!

Then shut up and listen. We met em at the fair, me and my best friend Jasper. Don't laugh. Don't laugh.

Jasper. Hoo! Hoo!

For me and Pearly it wuzz love at first sight. She wuzz the most beautiful girl I had ever met. We started a talk, and we hit it off, we had so much in common.

Pearly? But didn't ya say—?

Yeah. Pearly. And Jasper, well he kinda got stuck with Kerly, who was cute in her own way, but nothing like her sister. Pearly had the long legs, blond hair, bluest eyes, perky breasts. The whole package. The other one, Kerly, she wuzz short, first of all, and her eyes wuzz dark, her eyebrows kinda thick, and she had more of a, how do you say, boyish body. Okay, she wuzz flat-chested. But still, she was pretty, and it seemed to me she wuzz a nice match for Jasper, who was not the tallest guy in the world and what with this nose that was kinda like a chopped-off carrot and these permanently red cheeks like they paint on a doll. Me, I wuzz the jock. Played baseball. I wuzz in good shape back then. Girls said I wuzz a hunk, though I didn pay it no mind, you know how it is. So there we wuzz at the fair, don't laugh, and I'm thinkin I've jus met the woman I'm gonna spend the rest of my life with, and Jasper comes over to me and he whispers to me, It ain't working, man. This girl I got is a dud. She's not my type. Let's swap. I want the tall one. And I sezz to him, I sezz, I kinda like the tall one. I'm not swappin. But I wuzz the jock, and his old man owned the bank, and my old man worked for his old man, so you know how it is.

Nah. I don't know how it is.

Well, I'm kinda shamed ta say it. He paid me twenny bucks ta swap out with him.

Twenny bucks?

That wuzz a lot. It usually cost him five to swap out with me. See, the best girl always went for me, and then he'd have to pay ta get her. It's terrible, I know, but tha's how it wuzz. I dunno whether he wuzz usin me or I wuzz usin him, but tha's how it wuzz. So anyway, it took some working on em, but finally we made the girls agree to the swap, and I got stuck with Kerly, the short dark one, who I had wanted all along.

You sly dog!

What can I say, I like girls who are dark and boyish-looking. The blond, voluptuous thing is way overrated. Plus, now I had twenny bucks and I could show her a good time. What a night we had. I fell in love with her on the spot and aksed her to marry me that night. God I loved that girl. God I loved her. And it worked out for Jasper and Pearly too. Pearly kinda fell in love with his money, and with him too I guess. A few weeks after Kerly and me got hitched, Pearly and Jasper did the same thing. It was great. I wuzz his best man. He wuzz mine. I nevah made it big as a baseball player, but the scholarship money got me and Kerly through school, and then we came back to town and worked at the bank, which Jasper was in charge of because his dad had retired to play golf and chase young girls, you know how it is. We wuzz married like ten years before the trouble started, but it had been brewing so long I feel stupid I didn notice. Me and Kerly, well, she got pregnant seems like ever'year. We ended up with four kids. Three girls anna boy. They's all grown up and got they own kids now. I love ever'one of em. Jasper and Pearly? Well, she was like the Holy Bible says, barren. She couldn have babies. Now that I've been inna joint so long and so many cons have told me they stories, I realize that most crimes is committed because of either ya hate someone too much or ya love someone too much.

So, because this fella Jasper couldn have babies, he killt your wife? Sounds ta me like he's crazy.

Well, crazy is the other reason people commit crimes. People commit crimes because they hate too much, they love too much, or because they crazy. But Jasper was not crazy. See, at one point he called me into his office and aksed if he could sleep with Kerly—

Hoo! Welcome to the crazy nut house.

Well, tha's what I thought too, but there wuzz a method to

his madness. See, this wuzz like ten years into our marriages, and the trouble had been brewing but I wuzz jus beginnin to notice. He was my boss, so I was careful how I answered him, but he wuzz also my best friend and my brother-in-law, so I figured I could have a little bit of slack with him. I aksed him if he wuzz outta his mind wantin a sleep with my wife. What the fuck, right? He explained that lots of people did it. Especially when they wuzz friends, and practically family, like we wuzz. Plus, he said, that I would get to sleep with Pearly. A swap out like inna old days. But jus for sex—no lovey dovey allowed. This is how he explained it.

Is that when you killt him?

Nah. That came later. I said to him, I sezz, Come on, Jasper, wha's the real deal here? Level with me. Jasper said, It's like this, you must know by now that Pearly can't have babies. I'm sure Kerly told you. Women talk and they're sisters, so I know that you know. There's no point in lying about it. What I want is for you to lay offa Kerly's sweet, fertile puss for a while and let me take a stab at it. She'll get pregnant, and you guys'll arrange for me and Pearly to adopt the baby. I wuzz stunned. Stunned. I wanted a smack him, but I wuzz jus stunned. I said, No! He said, Think about it. I said, Hell no. We ain't kids no more. This ain't no swap out. He said, Think about it. Think about all that I do for you. Think about Pearly's puss, which I know you do. You gotta wonder what it woulda been like ta be with the pretty one. I'm a fair guy, I'm giving you a crack at the pretty one. This way it'll be good for both of us. I said, No! He said, The girls have already talked about it and Kerly agrees. I said, No! And when I get home I'm gonna talk with Kerly and straighten her out on this here thing, talkin about this kinda crap behind my back. There's a goddamned sanctity in marriage, and this goes way beyond it. She oughtta know betta. He said, I'll pay you. I'll pay you lots of money. I said, Hell no! And then I smacked him. Twice.

Hoo. Hoo. Did he fire you? I bet he fired you.

I quit. And me and Kerly sold our house and moved upstate to another bank, where we got jobs. After a while, things calmed down between us. I mean, we had been best friends. I mean, he hadda know that what he had aksed me was too offensive for even friends. To sleep with my wife? To get my wife pregnant? And the way he had said it, *Lay offa that sweet, fertile puss.* Who wuzz he to be getting so familiar with the goings on between a husband anna wife? There's a sanctity to marriage. He hadda know that I had good reason to be upset. To be outraged. But eventually we started a talk again, sorta like the old days. Of course, it would never really be like the old days again. Then three years later he and Pearly adopted a set of twins, a boy anna girl, and aksed us to be godparents. Fool that I am, I thought all wuzz forgive and forgot. So when Kerly got sick . . . and she needed that kidney, and her sister offered, offered she did, to give hers, I didn think nothin of it. Kerly and Pearly had a unique blood condition. The doctor said there wuzz only one in a hundred million could donate a kidney to Kerly. With odds like that, how lucky she was that her sister was making the offer. And then the offer wuzz withdrawn. We got word that Pearly's doctor had detected a condition she had, a form a arthritis that attacked kidneys. In other words, the odds were pretty good that in a few years one of her kidneys would become sick and she would be dependent on the remaining one. In other words, it wuzz against the law for someone who is at risk for a future kidney disease to give up one of her kidneys that she may come to need later. So Pearly did not give up her kidney. Kerly got onna waiting lis for the one-in-a-hundred-million donor. Kerly died waiting on that kidney to come.

Hoo. Hoo. Sad.

Yeah. We had the funeral. Jasper came up to me and hugged me like a best friend should. And Pearly came up afterward and said, I shoulda give her that kidney. I shoulda give it. She wuzz my sister. I shouldna listened to Jasper. Jasper? I said. What does he got to do with this? She said, Don't tell him I told ya, but he loved me so much, he forbid me to give the kidney. He wuzz afraid somethin would happen to me on the operating table. He wuzz too afraid to lose me. Jasper? But nah. I had that letter from the doctor. I ran home and got out the letter Pearly's doctor had sent us. I read it and I reread it. When you know someone, you know someone. There wuzz one line in it that went somethin like the kidney being a *fertile ground for disease*. I kept lookin at that word *fertile* and I knew what Jasper had done and why . . .

Hoo. Hoo. You awright?

Nah. I'm not awright.

What he done to you wuzz wrong.

Maybe I wuzz wrong. Maybe I shoulda let him sleep with her. He wuzz my friend and he wanted kids and couldn have em. Maybe because I loved her so much my mind was closed on this point.

Hoo. Hoo.

So I aksed him to go fishing a month later. Jus me and him, like inna old days. I took him down to the Keys. It wuzz night. I pulled into a dark spot along the road where I'd left a marker pointin out the place where I had dug his grave. I took out the gun and stuck it in his ribs and I took outta flashlight and showed him his grave. He started a cry. Said he wuzz sorry. Real sorry. Said he'd pay me a lot a money if I didn kill him. I told him ta get outta the van. He said, No. I shot him in the shoulda and told him ta get outta the van or I'd shoot him like that a little piece ata time. He wuzz howlin and howlin, he didn like pain, tha's why he had nevah played sports, but he didn get outta the van neither. I shot him again in the other shoulda this time. He howled and finally got outta the van. He wuzz beggin me and pleadin as I pointed him to the hole with the flashlight and the gun. He said, You know you're not gonna get away with this. Too much blood in the van. They'll check the van. You can never get all the blood out. You gotta know that. I said, I don't expect ta get away with it. I figure Pearly will send the cops afta me when I get back and you ain't with me. But they ain't nevah gonna find your body. I want you gone forever like Kerly's gone forever. He pleaded one more time. Got down on his knees. Said he'd give me a blowjob if I promise to let him live. I shot him in the face, and he tumbled into the hole. I shot him again to make sure he wuzz dead. He wuzz my best friend. I didn want him to suffer. It took me like a hour to cover up the hole. Then I got back inna van and drove to the hotel room we had rented in the Keys and lived there for a week.

And then?

Then I went home. The police came. There wuzz court, and I told em what I had done and why. Then I got life in prison, but now I'm here cause of my good behavior.

Hoo. Hoo. Tough.

Shit yeah. Tough.

Wuzz it worth it?

Shit yeah. I'd kill him again if he rose from the dead.

Hoo. Hoo.

THE NOIR BOUDOIR

BY LYNNE BARRETT

Upper Eastside

On a warm Tuesday morning in late October, the tail end of the hurricane season, I sit in my car outside the Delphi and pretend I'm on stakeout: a honed tedium. Eight years retired, but you never stop being a cop. I sip coffee and look at the grand old apartment building, long ago converted to condos, recently rehabbed. The pressure-cleaned Sphinxes at the entrance cast sharp Sphinxy shadows, and fresh green awnings ripple up the front in the eastern ocean light as they must have in the Delphi's heyday. I think of all the stories the place could tell.

At least it's survived. On the next block I can see some foundation work and the signage for a new tower touting luxury living: *Buy your piece of sky.* The boom has reached this area north of downtown Miami. Deco buildings less cared for than the Delphi get condemned, knocked down, and replaced by glass towers that can't emulate their cool lines and glamour.

I'm parked behind Alex Sterling's white SUV, which was here when I arrived. Alex is young, gay, smart, a North Carolina boy with excellent manners and a work ethic. In three years he has built up quite a business: Sterling Estate Clearance. Old people die alone here in Miami and their children, living far away, often estranged or resentful, come in to take what they want, and then Alex appraises, bids for, and disposes of the rest. With his respectful tone and open face, his name that rings true, they trust him. As do I, as much as I trust anyone.

Right now, I know, he is inside going through the late Mrs. Dorsett's pockets. Alex deals in fine china and what we call "smalls": jewelry, silver, personal doodads which he sells at high-end shows around the southeast. He tells me that he learned the hard way that people hide their smalls, so now he combs through a place before we see it: He's found mine-cut diamonds in a denture case and a Rolex under the insole of a running shoe. To the finder go the spoils.

Which might be the motto for our team. When Alex has identified what he'll take, he brings us in for our specialities— depending on what the estate offers—and we give him a price for what we want.

Hank Kussrow & Son, Jeff, double-park beside me in their furniture truck. Jeff Kussrow is the one with the knowledge about furniture, his dad the muscle. Hank's up in his seventies but still a big guy with thick gray hair. I've seen many a sideboard go downstairs on his back. He had a moving business, but his son was more into refinishing than lugging, Hank says, and per-suaded him that's where the money is. We get out and make idle conversation about the weather and what Alex has told us so far: The estate is small but choice.

I hear from a block away a chug and backfire. "The old guy," says Hank, with a grin. The old guy's van comes into view with his little white dog barking out the passenger window. Others of us may be variously old, but none as decrepit as him. Alex calls him Cash, which may be his name or the way he operates. He helps Alex, and then at the end Alex lets him take all the dreck. He sells the least likely things—rusty tools, old pots and pans, broken cameras—at the flea market in Fort Lauderdale, passing them on to other old guys like himself. He gets out, leaving the van running; it can take him a good six or seven tries to restart it.

In his usual faded tropical shirt and disreputable shorts, longish white hair under a baseball cap, feet sockless in sneakers, he comes over just as Guillermo Reyes pulls up in his peach-colored panel truck inscribed, *The Gizmo Man.* Guillermo fixes clocks and radios and toasters. His shop on the beach sells a lot of mid-century kitchen stuff, from jelly glasses to Streamline Moderne blenders. Guillermo is a year or two older than me, in good shape, small, bald, and dapper. "Nice place," he says, as he joins us.

"We did a condo here last month," says Hank.

I say, "I wasn't called for that one." Guillermo shakes his head—him neither.

"Mostly crap," says Jeff. "The family took everything. All that was left was the bedroom set."

"Alex said it was good to get us in with the building," says the old guy, his voice frayed and shy. "And look, already they've called us for another."

Sharon Lawler parks across the street. She waves, but doesn't get out. Sharon, as we all know, runs hot and must blast her air-conditioning. She drives a wagon like mine but with purple-tinted windows to prevent fading of the vintage clothes she sells on eBay.

These are my fellow members of the species Magpie. We are smalltime antique dealers, which is to say we are collectors who sell to support our habit. We glean old things and send some on their journey up in price, which lets us make a buck and keep the treasures we cannot bear to part with. We'd be mere hoarders if we didn't sell.

Me? I'm Ray Strout. Old, but not that old: sixty-three, retired cop, good pension, bad arteries, but I keep going. I'm into paper ephemera. Books, magazines, letters, photos, bills, matchbooks—anything like that interests me. There's history in paper. The card for a boxing match, a punched train ticket, the menu of a dinner in honor of a later-indicted honcho—these fascinate me. I take apart vintage magazines for the ads, back them with cardboard, wrap them in plastic, and sell them on Lincoln Road on Sundays in the season. One old *House Beautiful* from the '40s can yield two dozen sales at ten to fifteen bucks each.

Alex comes out and waves and hops in with the Kussrows, who drive around the left side of the building, past the bougainvillea-draped stucco wall that hides the service entrance. We parade behind. Back here the balconies look out on Biscayne Bay. I gaze up at the building: twelve stories of curves and niches to break up the wind and survive a hurricane. When the glass towers collapse, the Delphi will weather on.

The truck backs up against the loading dock, while the rest of us park in its shade. I get out one of the old suitcases I use for hauling off my finds. My stuff, thank God, is light. The old guy leaves the dog in the van with the windows rolled down. From the back he takes out the first of many much-used liquor-store cartons in which he'll pack up smalls for Alex.

There's not enough room in the freight elevator for all of us at once, so Alex takes me, Guillermo, and Sharon up first. Guillermo has his satchel full of flannel sheets—he likes to swaddle his gizmos lovingly. Sharon—her hair tinted the color of Cherry Coke and her chest draped with lots of amber beads—carries her capacious purse. Most clothes she'll take right on their hangers.

Alex sends the freight elevator back down, and we follow him along the eighth floor hallway which smells of last night's dinners—you'll never catch me living in a condo—to Mrs. Dorsett's place. Alex unlocks the door and we're in 8-G.

"Nice," says the Gizmo Man. He's looking at the Grundig Majestic stereo hi-fi/radio in its Moderne cabinet.

But I echo, "Nice." The living room is '50s Louis Quinze, with pale blue sofa and chairs grouped around a coffee table. Alex shows us an elaborate silver lighter/cigarette dispenser: You lift the top and cigarettes rise like petals of a flower. Alex has marked it and the crystal ashtray with his red stickies: He's into tobacciana. Sheers cover the French doors to the balcony so the bay is just a pale blue suggestion out beyond there. There's a small kitchen to our left off the living room and, opening from both it and the living room, a dining area where the hutch flutters with Alex's stickers. To the right there's a hall, down which Alex leads us. He opens the bedroom door with a flourish.

Light slants through actual Venetian blinds, striping the pure Deco circle of the mirrored dressing table. The slipper chair. The ivory satin-padded curving headboard of the bed. Sherry breathes, "My God, the noir boudoir," and so it is.

"Great, isn't it?" says Alex.

The Kussrows come in behind him with the old guy peeking between their shoulders.

"A veritable time capsule," says Alex. "Listen, there's a lot in here for Sherry and Ray. You folks," he says to the Kussrows, "do the big pieces in the living room first. Cash, I need you to pack up all the stuff from the hutch and then Hank and Jeff can get the dining room set. We'll get the furniture from in here last."

Sharon dives into the closet while I move around, scanning for what I'll take. Books fill the lower shelves of both bedside tables. In a nook between bedroom and bath there's a lady's bill-paying desk. I glance at a picture on top of it in an etched Lucite frame. Alex hasn't marked it, so maybe the frame doesn't interest him, but I'll have to check. Lucite has value these days. I can always use frames and I like the picture. I assume it's the dead lady in her youth: white skin, full lips, beautiful curve of nostril and brow, the eyes pale under curved eyelashes. She's a babe. Her hair lifts from a side part and cascades. She's vaguely familiar, like a minor movie star.

I get a queen-sized sheet from the linen closet and spread it out to protect the bedspread; the satin looks glamorous with the matching pillowcases propped against the headboard. I open my suitcase on top of the sheet and lay the picture down next to it. I check the bedside table drawers. Spot a great little notepad holder, embossed leather. Mechanical pencil. Several match-boxes from restaurants. A double set of playing cards for bridge, shagreen boxed. I'm making a mental tally of what I'll offer Alex. I put things in my case but it stays open for his inspection. I toss a hankie over to the other side of the bed, for Sharon's pile.

Guillermo comes in to get the bedside clock radio: '60s tortoise plastic.

"Hubba hubba," he says, looking at the picture. "Nice frame too."

Sharon comes out of the closet with an armful of suits and asks, "That her?" and looks and says, "Oh." She lays the suits down on her side of the bed. "Alex," she calls, "what did you say her name was?"

"Dorsett," he says, coming in. "Helena Dorsett."

"The lovely Helena Dorsett," says Sharon. "What do you know. I didn't see an obit."

I ask, "Was she an actress?"

"Femme fatale," says Sharon, enjoying the effect. I notice that the others have come to the door to see what's going on.

"Well, tell us," Alex says.

"She was a singer, for a while, I believe," says Sharon, "but then she married. Twice. It was when the second husband got killed that she became notorious."

"Both husbands?" I ask.

Sharon nods. "I was in the ninth grade, so it was 1962. They lived in the Gables. They were society people. Dorsett—husband number two—was trampled to death by a horse he owned, in the stables at Hialeah. And then it came out that her first was run down when he was crossing Collins, a few years before."

"A theme," I say. "Death by transportation." They nod at me. They know I was a cop up north. Mine was a small dying New Jersey city, troubled, but not a patch on what Miami has to offer.

"Well, the first was just an accident, as far as I recall. But in the second husband's case, they found he had been murdered. Not by her. She was nowhere near the stables."

"Stable boy?" says Guillermo. "Jockey?"

"Another horse owner?" I say.

"No," she says. "The vet."

"Aah," I say. "Did something to the horse?"

"It had to do with drugging the horse, yes. This was so long ago, I'm surprised I remember it at all. I know I read a lot of stories about her in the newspaper. They as good as implied that she caused it or it was done because of her."

"Was she tried?" I ask.

"No. But she was smeared in all the papers. You know how it is when there's a good-looking woman. It has to be her fault, right?"

Guillermo and I look at each other and laugh.

"You guys," Sharon says.

"What about the vet?" I say.

"That was one reason there was so much coverage of the trial—everyone was waiting for him to implicate her, but he maintained it was an accident. I remember lots of reporting about her crowd, her house in the Gables, and then they went back into her past, because I saw this same picture and I think it's from when she was younger and singing."

"Well, everyone," says Alex, "however much this adds to the price of anything, we still need to pack up." Which is his polite way of getting us back to work. The others back out, and Guillermo takes the clock radio and goes.

I point at the picture. "You want it?" I ask Alex casually, meaning may I have it. I keep my tone cool, because if I express desire he'll think it's worth something and keep it.

Alex hesitates, but then says, "Hey, it's yours."

I wrap a towel from the linen closet around the picture and put it in my case.

Sharon says, "Her clothes, I'll tell you, are first rate. All these St. John suits cost something, and they're well cared for." She lays more on her side of the bed. I cart my case over by the desk and seat myself to go through it. With her story in mind, I take a little extra care. She's kept things tidy, and, as Sharon says, she liked quality. The desktop blotter holder is pale blue leather and a matching stationery case holds Crane's paper for notes and thank-yous. In the top drawer I find various business cards, but no address book. I'm always careful not to take financial info the estate might need, but I don't see any of it. In a folder labeled *Auto* there are expired insurance cards for a series of midsize sedans, and a prior driver's license from the '80s, but not the current one, if she was still driving. *Helena Dorsett, d.o.b. April 17, 1928.* A handsome older lady with gray hair—you can see the bone structure from the early portrait—and then my mind makes a shift and I recognize her. "Hey," I say, surprised. "I met her."

"Where?" calls Sharon. I hear her opening dresser drawers, her beads clicking. I lean back in the desk chair and I can see her bending over the bottom drawer. Her hair has fallen around her face and I try to picture what she looked like in ninth grade: a kid with a flip. In 1962 I was in the navy and skinny as a rail.

"On Lincoln Road a few times on Sunday mornings. She'd be well dressed, as you say, in a suit. And pleasant. She bought some crossword puzzle books I had, and then she'd ask for them each time she saw me. Said she liked to do them before she went to sleep. A well-preserved old lady, I'd have said. A femme fatale? You never know."

"Look at this," Sharon says. "Longline elegance." She holds up a beige foundation garment—bra to girdle, all in one.

I look away. This business is disgusting sometimes. We settle back to work. Sharon takes a load down and returns, complaining about how hot it's getting, and Alex kicks up the air-conditioning for her. I lug my first case down and bring back a stronger one to take the books. I poke my head in the kitchen where the old guy is wrapping the barware, and I ask him to save me any cookbooks. He points to a stack. I grab a *Joy of Cooking,* an *Esquire Book of Cocktails*, a few recipe brochures put out by companies. One, *Chafing Dish Cookery*, is '60s, I'd say, from the illustrations. People collect these, believe it or not.

The sofa is gone and the Kussrows are carting out the dining room table, murmuring to each other as they always do, "Left, a little left. More. Now, right, now." Guillermo is taking albums out of the stereo cabinet and fitting them into vintage carrying cases he has for them. "Put some tunes on," I suggest. He pulls out a middle-period Sinatra, and Frank fills the apartment with regret.

Alex sits on the remaining upholstered chair, boxing up ashtrays he's collected from around the apartment, most of them Wedgwood, and the cigarette lighter/dispenser. "Let me have a few smokes," I say, and he dumps them beside me. He likes tobacciana, not tobacco. I put them in a sterling case I carry. This is not an affectation, it's a deterrent; it helps to have to open it and consciously take one out. I've got myself down to three cigarettes a day. I can maintain like that forever, but if I try to quit, I'll swing back with a binge. Better this way.

"There were no other pictures?" I say. Again, casually.

"There were some family photos, but the daughter took those. Not sure why she left that one."

"She had a daughter?" I don't know why I'm surprised. A lot of femmes fatales have daughters. Marlene Dietrich did, for instance.

"She came down from Connecticut and handled things. She had dealt with all the business papers before she called me. All clean and organized."

"Did she die here?" I ask quietly.

He nods.

"How?"

"She didn't come down one morning to get her paper, so the manager checked. He says he's always alert to any changes in pattern, with so many older people here. She died sometime the day before—she was dressed but she'd lain down to rest, maybe felt ill. Anyway, peaceful."

His fair face is flushed. Alex, whose business depends on death, doesn't like it mentioned. I take my suitcase to the bedroom. Sharon has folded up the coverlet and stripped the pillowcases off the pillows and is stowing them into one of the trash bags she uses for loose linens. The headboard—padded satin—leans against the wall with the bed pulled away from it. When the Kussrows lift off the mattress, we can see, through the box spring, a pair of high-heeled pumps. She took them off and died, I think, but I don't say it.

Sharon adds them to her sack of footwear. "Nearly all the shoes were in shoe bags, dustless, perfect," she says. "Everything just so."

I squat down to pull the books out of the bedside tables, since they'll want to take those soon. I load them into the suitcase. They are mostly current hardcovers, only one or two vintage.

Hank comes back in and edges the vanity out from the wall. "Comes apart," he says. "Piece of cake."

Sharon says she'll have it empty shortly. He stands there for a minute, adjusting his weightlifting belt, then says, "Wife died three years ago."

Sharon looks up at him.

He tugs his iron-gray forelock. "Got my own hair and"— he clacks—"all my teeth. How'd you like to go to dinner sometime? I'll buy you a steak."

Sharon says, "Oh, I don't think so, Hank."

"No harm in asking," he says, and goes out with the bed frame.

There's a pause. I say: "What is he? Seventy-five?"

Sharon says, "In Miami, once a woman is over fifty, she's supposed to go out with eighty-year-olds. It's a tough market."

I shake my head, but it's true. She is—in ninth grade in 1962—I figure, fifty-seven. I'm sixty-three and I never looked at her that way. But I haven't been looking at anyone much of late except pretty gals forever young on paper. Last week I was smitten with an actress from the '20s and then I realized she would be 105 if she weren't already dead.

"My ex-husband has a thirty-eight-year-old girlfriend," she says.

"Does he have all his teeth and hair, though?"

She laughs. "No."

Mainly to change the subject, I say, "You know, what you said before, that would be a good name for a business: *The Noir Boudoir.* That stuff is big on Lincoln Road, things from that period: satin nightgowns and marabou slippers and dresser sets."

She says, "I do handle some old cosmetics and compacts and so on, which you can't get so much for on-line. People need to touch them to buy."

"Cast some glamour on them and you can get more. Anyway, it's a memorable name."

"You want it?" she says casually.

"No," I answer. "Not at all. Your idea." Punctilious as always, we go back to work.

When I'm done I stop by Alex in the living room, now cleared of furniture other than his chair. I tell him what I think my haul is worth to me and write him a check. He doesn't dicker; he knows I know he's seen everything I have. I cart my stuff out and then come back up to do a trip for Sharon, carrying down some garment bags and hat boxes to her car. When I leave, the old guy is filling a carton with partially used cleaning products from under the sink, and Hank and Jeff are moving the dressing table base, murmuring to each other. I ride down after them. It's hot outside, well up in the eighties. I take a moment to check on the dog, but he looks fine. There's a bowl of water on the floor of the passenger side in the shade. He's got short white hair, a barrel chest, and thin bare legs. I put him down for some sad mix of terrier and Chihuahua.

* * *

Somewhere, the newspapers that reported on the death of William Dorsett may be intact. Everything is still on paper some-where, that's my theory. But not where it's supposed to be, at the library or the newspaper's own morgue. Microfilm and scanning keep the text but not the context. The juxtapositions of facing pages, the ads, the color process, the smell of the paper itself, are gone, and with them a lot of the meaning. Still, I put in some time at the library on Wednesday, getting a headache from the smell of the microfiche baking as I read what I can find.

In February 1962, William Dorsett's horse, Panama Sailor, had been ailing, putting in poor times at practice. On a Saturday at Hialeah Park, Dorsett went to the stables to check whether he'd have to scratch him from a race that afternoon. Or, at least, so he'd said to several people in the clubhouse, where he left the missus in full view of many.

In the stables, running to where they heard sounds of dis-tress, a pair of stable boys found him, bleeding from his stomped-on head and chest, the horse over him, the vet there trying to calm the animal. The vet said he had been treating the horse at Dorsett's behest, and when the owner came into the stall, it had gone loco. The horse's right foreleg was badly smashed, and they had to put him down.

Between editions the cops must have sweated the vet, Dr. Lucas M. Pryor, because soon he told a different story.

On Dorsett's orders he'd been doping the horse. Panama Sailor's "ailment" was just one more ploy to help the odds. The horse was fit and then some. He was supposed to "recover" and win—but the scheme backfired on Dorsett. This was a crime, but the death itself, Pryor insisted, was accidental.

There it sat till the trial. In the interim the newspapers dug into Mrs. D.'s first husband, also a William, this one called Billy Hogarth. The Hogarths were down for the winter in 1953, from Pittsburgh. Dorsett was from Ligonier, horse country, not right next door to Pittsburgh but both in western Pennsylvania. So Mr. and Mrs. Billy Hogarth could have known Dorsett, but that was unconfirmed. On March 2, 1953, Billy Hogarth, having had some cocktails, was walking back to his hotel, crossing Collins Avenue mid-block, when he was struck and killed by a 1950 Studebaker belonging to one Roy Robineau. Robineau got out after he hit Hogarth and readily admitted he was drunk. Being drunk was its own excuse then, not a crime the way it is today. The 1950 Studebaker had the distinctive "bullet nose" front end which hit Billy Hogarth just right—or just wrong. Young Mrs. Hogarth was having her hair done at the hotel salon, in honor of a party they were going to that night.

By the trial's opening, reporters had gotten Helena's original name, Helen Immerton. A songbird from Kentucky—some implication of trashiness about Kentucky can be picked up even on microfiche—right across from Cincinnati. She'd sung with a band in Cinci and on live Ohio radio in the '40s under the name Helena Mar, or possibly Marr—it was printed both ways in different editions. She married Billy Hogarth in 1948 and had a daughter, and all was well till Billy Hogarth intersected with Robineau's front end. Dorsett married the pretty widow in 1954. She was twenty-six. Thirty-four in 1962 when she was tragically— the papers invariably appended "tragically"—widowed again. Nothing much was said about the daughter. She'd been away at school. Age twelve, but the rich ship them off young, and she was a stepdaughter. One columnist mentioned Roy Robineau not being locatable, rumored to have moved out west.

Between the lines, I imagine how hard the cops worked to find a connection between Dr. Pryor the vet and the lovely Helena Dorsett, whose photos from various social do's were reproduced: jaunty in sports clothes and shapely, but never vulgarly so, in evening wear. There were frequent references to their house on Leucadendra Drive, which clearly meant something about class and money. Dorsett looked handsome and strong-jawed, like an ad for aristocracy, and Dr. P. had the heavy glasses of the period and a crew cut, and that's about all you could tell about them from the microfiche. Everyone looked middle-aged in 1962.

The vet never implicated her. She testified that she had no idea of anything untoward in Mr. Dorsett's horse breeding and racing "hobby." But some dirt on her husband came out, a complaint the defense had found about a misrepresented horse he sold someone in Ligonier and a settlement, which tended to support the doctor's story, but that didn't mean there hadn't been a falling out between them. So Dr. P. got second degree murder. He went away to state prison for fifteen to twenty years—maybe a lot for second degree, but they'd loaded on some other charges about tampering and prescriptions. Took away his vet's license, of course.

And Helen(a), née Immerton, a.k.a., Mar(r), Hogarth Dorsett, twice widowed, presumably sold the house on Leucadendra Drive, and moved, perhaps straight into the Delphi. Who knows? On her inheritance she lived long and wore fine clothes and tried out drinks from the *Esquire Book of Cocktails* and played cards and did crosswords and died on her satin bedspread at seventy-seven. What's so tragic about that?

When I get home, I tell myself I need to buckle down to work. In the dining room, which is my workroom (I usually eat in the living room in front of the TV), I have stacked boxes full of papers I've picked up: billing records from long-gone businesses and vintage department store ads and menus and greeting cards and falling-apart old children's books and what have you. Take them apart and shuffle them up and chuck an assortment into a Ziploc and there you go: Ephemera Samplers. Very popular with scrapbookers who come by my booth on Lincoln Road on Sundays. This scrapbooking fad has raised interest in everything with old typeface or illustration. My samplers let me get rid of things of little value, though I find I go too slow because I get interested, wondering when they served broiled grapefruit as an appetizer at the Senator Hotel and setting that menu aside to keep, which is defeating my purpose.

This is tedium without much edge. I've got the lovely Helena's picture on my work table where I can see her. The photo has that strong line between light and shadow they liked in the '40s. Call it noir or chiaroscuro, it's dramatic. She seems a hard, lovely woman. But this isn't getting me anywhere. I assign myself to sit back down and make at least two dozen Ephemera Samplers.

I jump at the phone when it rings.

It's Alex Sterling, asking if I can come meet him at Café Nublado—right by his house and not that far from mine—to discuss something. "Sounds serious," I say, and he says it is, and so I allow as how I'll tear myself away from work and drive down to see him.

Café Nublado is Spanish for coffee with clouds. They do the usual Cuban coffee and guava pastries, but to compete with the high-end espresso chains, the walls are painted with idealized piles of cumulonimbus and the house specialty has a soft puffy topping you have to suck through to get any caffeine. *Whatever happened to Sanka?* I like to grumble, but the girl knows me and gives me a decaf skim Nublado.

Alex Sterling is in one of the big wicker planter's chairs out back, wearing chinos and a well-cut yellow shirt. I see he's looking worried, so I forego small talk. "What gives?"

"Somebody has burgled Sharon," he says. "She called me."

"Is she all right?"

"She's upset, naturally. I told her I'd ask you to go there. The police came and took a report, but I thought you might advise her on security. And then . . ."

I wait. It seems convoluted to meet here, so he must have something in mind.

"Do you think," he says, "I overlooked something yesterday?"

"At the Delphi?"

"She says the stuff they took was all from there. And I'm wondering if someone knows there was something of great value and got it."

"But you'd looked it all over—"

"Meticulously. You know me. It all seemed clean and organized. I didn't find anything hidden. But I didn't search every square molecule of space."

"I think you're as thorough as anyone could be. Did you go through the flour and sugar?"

He grins. "She didn't have any flour. I doubt she ever baked. And her sugar was lump."

"Really," I say, admiringly. "You never see that anymore, lump sugar. But you obviously looked. How 'bout the salt shaker?"

He shakes his head. "What would be in there?"

"Diamonds?"

"You're teasing me, Ray."

"Somewhat," I say. "Anyway, everything Sharon had was from the bedroom. And you'd been through that."

"Yes, and then Sharon handled it all, and she says she didn't find anything concealed. Did you?"

"Well, I haven't gone through every page of every book. She could have used a thousand-dollar bill as a bookmark. I'll be sure to check."

"If I overlooked something, you know," he shrugs, "that's the way it is. What I don't like is the idea that it could be one of the people who was there yesterday, who spotted something and then burgled Sharon to get it."

"Wouldn't be me. I was in the bedroom alone enough, I could have taken anything then."

"I know," he says. "And you were a policeman." Alex always says *policeman*, as in, *Say hi to the nice policeman.* "Couldn't you maybe figure out what it was and who took it? If it was someone on our team?"

"Tall order." I finish my Nublado. I want a cigarette but I had one an hour ago.

"Yes," he says. "But you could try, Ray, couldn't you?"

"Well, let's go see," I say.

He pulls out his cell phone and calls her to tell her we're on our way.

So I drive us over to Sharon's place, also not far from Café Nublado. We people with a taste for old things are clustered in the neighborhoods of Miami's Upper Eastside, where the houses were built in the '30s of cinderblock and stucco, in styles they're now calling Mediterranean Revival and Masonry Vernacular. I'm in Belle Meade, Sharon in Bayside, which is an historic district. Alex used to live there, but recently he cashed in and moved into a fixer-upper in Palm Grove, west of Biscayne Boulevard, for a long time the western frontier on realtors' maps. Lately, people good at restoration like Alex—that is to say, the gay guys—have hopped the line in search of fun and profit there.

On the way he tells me he keeps nothing of value in his house. He has safe deposit boxes at several banks. He adds that Mrs. Dorsett's daughter made it clear that her mother's real jewelry had been in *her* safe deposit box. All that remained was costume, and even that the daughter had gone through carefully. I ask what the daughter was like.

"Like a respectable woman from Connecticut," he says. "She was organized and I think she knew the status of her mother's estate in advance. No nonsense. I just don't see what it could be," he muses.

Sharon is out the back door to meet us as we pull up. Unadorned, wearing a white T-shirt and leggings, with her hair pulled back, she is a smaller woman than I'd thought. Perhaps she puffs herself up and puts on beads when she's working with us guys to hold her own.

She shows us where they came in. They simply bashed in window glass by the back door to the Florida room, reached in, and twisted the lock—no deadbolt. The alarm went off, of course, as soon as the door opened, but—as I'm telling her—there's a limit to alarm systems.

"The noise is useless. Neighbors won't stir to take a look. The important factor is the signal through your phone line to the alarm company, who then call your house in case you set it off yourself and can give them the secret code to revoke the alarm. If you don't answer, *then* they call the cops. And then the cops have to get here, so altogether your thief has a good ten to fifteen minutes. A real pro will take out your phone line, do a thorough job. What you have here is someone looking to smash and grab and run, usually kids wanting something to hock for drugs."

"Right," says Sharon. "But if so, why didn't they take the portable TV right here in the Florida room, six feet from the door?"

She leads us through folding doors to her dining room and down a hall to the back bedroom she runs her business from. He definitely went out of his way to get to this room.

"Forgive the mess in here," she says.

Of course, it looks far better than my place on a good day. Garments fill a chrome clothing rack, each hanger tagged with notes. Along the opposite wall, a long table holds a computer, scanner, postal scale, packing materials, and a piece of blue velvet with a desk lamp aimed at it, set up for photographing smaller objects. The open trash bags piled on and around an old couch under the windows are the only disorderly note. Heavy shades darken the room. I look behind them—jalousie windows, old thick glass, hard to break.

"Did you have your digital camera here?" says Alex.

"I'd been using it to shoot clothes outside, in sunlight—I hang them from my grapefruit tree. Afterward, I put it in the bedroom. It's still there."

"So what did they take?" I ask. Like Sharon, I say "they,"

even though I'm assuming it's a "he." It helps to keep it less vivid, I figure.

"I've been making a list. The police want one and my insurance will too, but I don't think it's going to be enough for my deductible." She picks up a pad. "Shoes, clothes, linens."

"Which?" asks Alex.

"Not the nicest ones, really." She opens the closet's pocket door and reveals shoe racks. "I'd put the best away in here. I guess they never opened this. So they just got a couple of pairs of day shoes, some blouses that were here on the arm of the couch—things I was setting aside to take to the women's shelter. The women always need clothes, especially for job interviews, work. Well, they took that whole pile. Oddly, they took the satin pillowcases but not the bedspread. I think some of the makeup and perfume is gone. They spilled some powder, see?"

"Young transvestites in the neighborhood?" I say.

Alex gives me an amused look. "Yes, probably."

I say, "They most likely used the pillowcases to carry the other items. That's common."

"Well, it breaks up the set," Sharon says, pointing to the spread, which looks much less glamourous in here, I notice.

"Had you gone through everything from the estate before the break-in?" I ask.

"Not really. I hung up all the finest clothes when I got home—that was the most important thing, to keep them nice. And then I was tired and my daughter and her family took me out for sushi. In the morning, I went out to the post office to ship things—I try to go early every Monday, Wednesday, Friday, so I don't get behind."

"Someone seeing you leave with packages would probably assume you'd be gone awhile."

"I suppose. I was gone about forty-five minutes. When I came back the police were here, and I turned the alarm off."

"Wasn't there some costume jewelry?" asks Alex.

"Yes. I put it in here." Sharon pulls out a vanity case from the closet floor. "It's mainly brooches. Substantial ones that look good on her suits." She opens a jewelry roll on the blue velvet piece and snaps on the light and they shine: fake pinwheels and starbursts.

"She wore the pearl one on Sundays," I say.

"That's the best," says Sharon. "Miriam Haskell."

"There was a decent coral one," says Alex, "set in fourteen-carat gold, which I have. The rest was costume, which is Sharon's territory."

"Any missing?"

They both shake their heads.

"Well," I say, "first thing to do is fix the window. And I think you need a deadbolt on that door—no reason to make things easy for them. I can do that for you, if you'd like."

"Thank you," she says, and gives me a big smile. She takes us into the living room, a quiet space in greens and beiges. One end is nearly empty. A low table holds candles and a mat is unrolled in front of it on the pickled pine floor. She sees my glance. "I do meditation," she says, "to calm down."

"Does it help?" I ask.

"Yes. You should try it sometime. It's good for your blood pressure. You tune in to yourself and just notice what there is: the light and little sounds."

"I think I've done it," I say. "On stakeout." I'm looking at her, recognizing that after—what, three years?—I don't know her at all. We're all such strangers.

Driving home, I tell Alex it's impossible to say what the burglary was all about. It might be something to do with the Dorsett estate or completely random. I drop him at his house in Palm Grove and tell him I'll stay in touch with Sharon, in case she notices anything else. And otherwise keep my eyes open.

And for the next few days I do, with no particular idea what

I'm getting at. I go back to help Sharon out, but she hasn't made any further discoveries. At home, I work through all of Helena Dorsett's books and papers. The only thing of real interest is a vintage book on how to dress, from 1939; she was still a girl, if she got it new. There are pencilled tick marks next to various tips. *A strawberry blonde should not wear orange-reds, but blue-reds and true violets.* There is a chapter about shopping that tells what kind of coat to have if you can only afford one, and then what to buy when you can purchase a second.

I have many pictures of Hialeah Park, postcards, programs. I went to closing day, back in 2001, and bought up a few future collectibles. It was a sad occasion. Even the pink flamingoes on their little island looked faded. I take a drive over there on Friday and circle around behind to see the area of extensive decaying stables where people used to board horses for the season. I forget what I last read about plans to reopen the track.

Then I drive on down to Coral Gables and tour Leucadendra Drive and spot the house. It's certainly worth a million now. But whatever it was worth in 1962 was plenty.

I think I hear someone scrabbling outside my sun porch, late Friday night, but I've had problems with possums there, getting in under the house, and anyway it might just have been palmettos chipping at the window as they do. You have to prune here constantly. I get up, turn on some lights, patrol, see nothing, and go back to bed. I take out the phone book and look her up: an *H. Dorsett* is listed at the right address.

Now I'm fully awake, so I go into my linen closet which is full of reference books. I have a half dozen assorted Social Registers I've picked up. In the one for Greater Miami 1955, I find, *DORSETT, MR. AND MRS. WILLIAM ELSFORD (Helena M.H.)*, listed at the address on Leucadendra Drive, Coral Gables. Then:

Summer: Little Chestnut Farm, Ligonier, PA
Miss Diana Hogarth
*Clubs: Riviera (CG); Princeton (Miami); Rod and Reel
(MB); Jockey. Clubs, Mrs.: Opera Guild.
Coll., Mr:. Princeton
Yacht:* Sea Lark

I note that she chose the initial of her stage name, and then
Hogarth's—which was needed to indicate where Miss Diana
came from. No *Coll.* for the Mrs. was not all that unusual in
those days. I presume the Opera Guild interested her due to her
musical background.

I look up Dr. Pryor, but I don't suppose veterinarians were
society people. Nor is there any Roy Robineau. I don't have a
register from the early '50s, but I know the Hogarths wouldn't be
in there—they were staying at a hotel, not a home or a club. I've
put Mr. Billy Hogarth down as a young guy with a little family
money, not in Mr. William Dorsett's league.

I think about money and Florida. When I first came down
here, years ago, after I got divorced, looking to have some fun
and cheer up, I was amazed to see how much money was here,
filtering in from all over America as people cashed in their piles.
I cannot completely explain the fascination of discovering where
they all went. In my old town when I was growing up, there were
some rich people. You knew who they were; you worked for
them. Then they deserted, and a lot of the people in the middle
left. After they made me chief, I put in a few years at my best
salary and then deserted too. I bought myself a little house down
here in a neighborhood that was turning around and added my
bit to the comeback. Here, I got interested in life's cast-off paper,
and started to buy and sell and learn the worth of the worthless.

Sunday morning early, I'm at the Lincoln Road Antiques &
Collectibles Market. The humidity has lifted and it's cool, in the

fifties at 8 a.m., though it promises to warm up later. I'm in my usual spot on Drexel just off Lincoln near the community church—the side street gets morning shade. I have set up my tent with plastic side flaps. Rain—even a stiff breeze—can do a lot of damage to my stuff. But it doesn't look a bit like bad weather today, so I leave them rolled up. I get to work, unpacking the rubberized tubs of pages organized by subject, and the display rack for the intact magazines. I never dismantle anything that's perfect. Boxes of books go on the ground, and my best stuff under glass on the back table.

Other dealers pass by, circulating—we check out each other's stuff early. Sometimes an item has changed hands twice before the average buyer comes out looking. There's interest in my 1934 *Vanity Fair* with the Albert Einstein paper doll page: mint. I have the whole thing encased in plastic, but dealers know better than to touch. No one buys. I don't expect it; I've set the price high because I don't really want to let it go. When I have things laid out, I stand and stretch and look around. The Kussrows, as usual, have the corner of Drexel and Lincoln, across from where the SPCA has its table and pen of dogs up for adoption. Jeff and Hank are angling their stuff to best advantage: a bunch of Heywood-Wakefield chairs, a dresser, and there's Helena's dressing table with the circular mirror, catching and reflecting the morning sun like a fat full moon.

Sharon arrives, as promised, bringing me coffee, the Starbucks version of Nublado decaf skim, lacking the Cuban depth. While I was putting in her deadbolt on Thursday she said she'd take me up on sharing my space and see how she did selling some things, as a start on the Noir Boudoir idea. She covers one side table with a vintage cloth and lays out an assortment of compacts, old lipstick cases, evening bags, and so on. I have the other side table and the back table—a U so the customer can walk in and browse. We'll sit at the outer ends in lawnchairs I brought. She's not only got on all her amber, which I now think of as her chest guard, she is wearing some heavy tortoiseshell vintage shades. "You look invincible," I tell her, but she shakes her head.

The old guy comes by with his doggie on a leash. The pooch is wearing an argyle vest this morning, though the old guy himself is his usual shambles. He nods at us and heads for the Kussrows.

I ask Sharon to watch my stuff while I go chew the fat.

The old guy is running his hand across the dresser top. "What is this, Jeff," he asks, "mahogany?"

"Veneer," says Jeff. "In great shape. No label, but it's got the look and the lines."

The dog jumps up on the vanity bench and peers inquiringly at himself in the mirror.

"Gorgeous day," I say to all and sundry.

"Finally some fresh air," Hank says, and takes a deep breath to show off his chest expansion. I think he's looking in Sharon's direction.

I say, "You guys hear Sharon got burgled?"

Jeff nods. "Alex mentioned it. They get anything valuable?"

I shrug. "Just some assorted duds from that estate we did. She's mostly upset that anyone came in. Probably someone who saw her unloading."

"That's what you get when you run your business from your home," Hank says.

I say, "I've always counted on no one thinking I've got anything. House doesn't look like much, you know. Probably the least improved property in Belle Meade at this point. You guys have a warehouse, right? Design district?"

"Right above there, Buena Vista," says Hank.

"It's a fortress," Jeff adds. "We all move in when there's a hurricane. Where I live on the beach, they evacuated twice this fall, for nothing, really."

Hank says, "But if a big one came, we'd be safe in there. Got a generator and everything."

"Well, looks like we're through with that this year. Weather's changed." I stretch. "I'm going down to Islamorada and fish a bit, I think. I'll head down this afternoon against the traffic coming back from the Keys, take a few days."

"You got a boat?" asks Hank.

"Just a small one. Boston Whaler. Sixteen feet. How long have you lived down here?" I ask Hank, now that we're talking.

"I grew up here," he answers. "But I lived in Southern California for a while—used to surf, loved the beaches. Then got married, had a family, brought them back here." He nods at Jeff. "Got Jeff and two more you haven't met, not in the business."

Customers are talking to Jeff, who has them around behind the dressing table to show how the mirror connects. The little pooch apparently has an overblown sense of himself from his time with the mirror, because he jumps off and yanks the leash from the old guy's hand and runs across to the SPCA gang, an assortment of biggish dogs who look like they could eat him for brunch. He growls at them from his side of their not-very-secure-looking pen. I go over and pick him up. His little body is vibrating with indignation or machismo or whatever it is.

"You've got guts," I say. I hand him back to the old guy, who takes the leash with a shaky old hand.

"Archie, say thank you," he instructs, and the dog yaps at me in what doesn't sound like gratitude.

"You should get a dog, Ray," he tells me, nodding at the orphans up for adoption.

"I probably could use a watchdog, at that," I say to the old guy, and he walks with me back to my booth. The dog sniffs around Sharon's ankles and the old guy peruses our goods while Guillermo comes up with some kind of heavy bundle he sets down by my chair.

Guillermo unwraps his find, a vintage interest-calculating machine with Bakelite keys. "In operating condition," he boasts.

"Seriously outmoded," I say.

"But," he says, "the guys who have outmoded it love these. I had three manual typewriters in my shop and last month they all sold to high-tech guys who like to decorate their offices with them."

"You never know," I say. "Business been good, then?"

He says, cautiously, "It runs hot and cold. I'm going over there to open up now."

"I could never stand being stuck in a shop all day myself," I say. And I tell him, too, that I'm going fishing, but he just shakes his head at my laziness. I let him leave a stack of cards for his shop on my table.

The little dog is nosing through my bin of Ephemera Samplers. I pull him away. "You looking for anything special this morning?" I say to the old guy. "I've got more at home, things that came from that estate. Nice stuff."

"Just giving the dog some exercise," he says, and shuffles off.

"How old is he?" whispers Sharon.

"Too old to ask even you out," I say. She gives me a look through her shades.

And so the morning passes pleasantly. Beautiful girls come by and Sharon and I sell them things. One buys a powderbox, another an old *Vogue*, several select the brooches and hankies and hats of Helena Dorsett, fragments of another woman's beauty, now theirs. We see a couple buy the dressing table, the fellow writing a check while the young lady sits on the bench, laughing up at him.

"I wonder if she kept it because it was a magic mirror," Sharon muses. "Maybe it showed her always beautiful and young."

"I think to her it stood for class," I say. "Some idea she'd formed of what she'd have, and when she got it she never let it go. Why did she keep that whole room like that?"

Sharon shrugs.

A collector comes back twice before finally buying my

Albert Einstein. "That's how it works," I say to Sharon. "If you want something too much, you'll pay any price."

She says we are all poisoned by desire and tells me some more about meditation. We discuss mindfulness and the radiance of things. It gets warm by noon, and Sharon breaks out a mini-battery-operated fan and fusses that the heat will ruin the perfumes. I agree with her by 1:00 that it's time to pack it in.

Late in the afternoon I get the Whaler out: *Paper Boat*, I named it. Hook the trailer to my car, drive it over to the marina on the Little River just north of Belle Meade Island, and leave the boat and trailer there, for a fee. Driving back through my neighborhood, I take a different route and park a few blocks down beyond my house. I stroll back, enjoying the air, and think how I really have to walk more.

Home, I settle down for a night of meditation. It's after 1 a.m. when I see the flashlight flicker by the dining room window. For God's sake, break in by the back door, I think. That window frame is rotting from the rainy season and needs to be replaced. I left the bolt off.

He works his way back there. A quick smash of glass, and he's in: sun porch, kitchen. He must be thanking his stars there's no alarm. He slows down. In the dining room, his flashlight circles the piles on the table, and then he sends a beam into the living room. And there I'm waiting. I turn on the standing lamp by my chair.

I say, "Where'd you leave the dog?"

"Home," Cash says. He sighs.

"What are you looking for?"

He tries to shrug, the big robber: "Anything of value."

"No," I say. "You're looking for something about you—or you and her. Which one are you? Robineau or the vet?"

"I'm . . ." He sits in the other armchair across from me. "Cash Pryor. As you say, the vet."

"Lucas turned into Cash?"

"No one ever called me Lucas much," he says. "Newspapers always use your formal name. I got the nickname as a boy because other kids were always hitting me up for small loans and I was generous. You wouldn't think it now, I realize."

"You killed the second husband," I say.

Sadly, he says, "And I killed the horse."

"Well, then you served your time," I say. "Can't be tried twice. So it wasn't that she had evidence. It was—"

He pulls out a gun.

"Oh jeez," I say. "I've got one too." And I show him my Glock. "Yours looks rusty." It's a Jennings J25, dregs of the gun world, and the finish is gone on it. "Ever shot it?"

He shakes his head and lowers the gun, some. His hand is trembling so much I'm afraid he's going to shoot me accidentally. Those pistols jam a lot, but every once in a while one manages to emit a bullet.

I say, "Put it down and let's talk."

He sets it on the broad arm of the chair. I lay mine on my thigh, where I can get to it if needed.

He says, "You were expecting me."

I nod. Though to be honest, I'd also worked out a theory where Hank Kussrow was Robineau.

I say, "I figure you killed her. Are you looking for something you touched when you were there before? Something that might have your fingerprints that you couldn't explain? Maybe this?" I point to the picture in the Lucite frame, on the table beside me. "Did you expect Sharon to have it?"

"You don't understand," he says.

"I probably don't. Let's go back. What was it all for? You killed Dorsett for her?"

"She needed him dead."

"Oh," I say. "Did she ask you?"

"She . . . implied it."

"Why'd she need him dead?"

"Dorsett was a bully. And a killer. Let me explain how it was. She told me that he'd seen her when she and her first husband came to Miami Beach. And he wanted her, naturally. But she was married with a child. And then someone ran her husband down and she was a widow, so when Dorsett courted her, she married him. It was only later—years later—that she found out he'd hired the man who hit her husband. This is what she told me, you understand?"

"Dorsett hired Robineau?"

"She said that when she expressed a desire to leave Dorsett, he told her so and frightened her."

"And Robineau, what happened to him?"

"She said Dorsett took him out on his yacht and drowned him, in the Bahamas somewhere. And let it be thought he'd moved away, west. This was right after Hogarth was killed, she said."

"More death by transportation," I say.

"It's not funny."

"So she told you all this, and you decided you could take him on, this brute?"

"I was thinking about it."

"She was worth killing for?"

"You should have seen her. At the racetrack, in blue linen. She was a dream. Then Dorsett asked me whether I could make it seem that the horse was having problems, to jigger the odds. So I did that, God help me. He was, as she said, a bully—he bullied me, never knowing what I was thinking. I stopped doping Panama Sailor in time for him to run. That was the plan. But on the day I gave the horse a little something else, Dorsett handled him rough and the horse knocked him down and I . . . helped."

"And then you didn't tell."

"I kept my mouth shut for her," he says.

"Did she ask you to?"

"We only had a moment," he says. "At the stables. She came in after he was dead. They didn't let her see his body, but then she asked to see the horse, and I was in with Panama Sailor, trying to fix his leg, but it was no good. She said, 'Thank you, Cash,' and it might have been thank you for the horse, but . . . And after that, we couldn't speak again because the cops had me."

"You hadn't slept with her?"

"Oh," he says. "I had. Twice. She was a dream, I told you. Your loveliest, dirtiest dream."

I'm thinking that's a quote from somewhere, but I'm not sure.

"Did you figure if you killed him, you'd keep her?"

"I didn't think that much. I felt she was a creature in trouble and I would get her out.

"The police took me in right after I put the horse away, and all I could do was try to keep her out of the story."

"You're an idealist," I say. "You could have cut a deal and given her to the law."

"I *was* an idealist," he says. "Certainly so."

"And when you got out of prison, you didn't look her up?"

"No," he says, "I stayed away."

"Why?"

He shakes his head. "Well, prison . . . broke me, I suppose you'd say. I didn't do well there. I loathe violence." He clears his throat, his sandy old voice wearing thin. "When I got out, I hated that I'd killed and I didn't want to see her or for her to see me. I didn't try to find her, I didn't want to know where she was. I couldn't earn a living as a vet, just did odd jobs and picked up money and lived close to the ground and tried to . . . recuperate. You could live cheaply here then. I've been over ten years in Palm Grove. I'm just down the street from Alex. It cost very little, till lately. I live in a building they're about to redo now, but for years it was full of poor folks. Nobody bothered us, Archie and me, because we didn't have anything worth taking, as you said this morning about your house. When you were implying you had something I'd want."

I ignore that. "Okay, so you steered clear of her. Then?"

"About a month ago, we did a job at the Delphi, a small estate. You weren't there. Just Jeff and Hank. I was lugging stuff out for Alex. And she saw me. She caught me outside when I was alone putting things in my van and . . . asked me to come see her."

"Did you recognize her?"

"She hadn't changed nearly as much as I had. And she recognized me." He clears his throat. "Like I say, prison broke me. But I did learn to think more—what would be the word—more *cunningly*. And I had thought about her story." He gives a dry smile. "Often. As you can imagine. It was too . . ."

"What?"

"I kept seeing patterns. I killed the second husband, somebody killed the first. The guy who killed the first got killed—at least that's what she'd said. It couldn't be simpler, I felt. I did it for her. So maybe the others did it for her."

"Wait. Robineau killed Hogarth for her?"

"Could have been. Could have been just because Dorsett paid him, but I looked up what I could find and he hadn't been a bad guy, just a silly rich drunk. So I think he may have done it for her, yes sir."

"And Dorsett killed Robineau?"

"So she said. For her, I think. I mean, at her behest. Possibly."

"And you killed Dorsett."

"Indisputably. So, if you pay attention to the pattern, someone ought to kill me. I'm the loose end. She could have been looking for me, but I would have been hard to find. I'd entered the cash economy. I have no phone. And maybe she just didn't have a man to sic on me."

"Well, maybe," I say.

"I don't have a lot of evidence. But she said she was happy to see me. Now, should she have been happy?"

"Well, you'd been a stand-up guy and gone to jail without ratting on her. You might have been her idea of a hero," I say, though I know he's right.

He shakes his head. "But I could still have sent her to prison. Now."

"Let me get this straight: She knew you were going to kill the husband ahead of time?"

"She asked me to do it . . . in the clearest way one could, without saying it right out."

"In bed, was it?"

"In bed. Her bed. I have no evidence for that. But if I were to say she had done so, even now, would the police not at least speak to her?"

"Cops aren't that eager to open settled cases from 1962."

"But there was scandal and she'd become respectable again. And she might think the police would care. My impression was that she was scared that I'd appeared in her building."

"Okay. Let's say you're right. She should've avoided you. Instead, what did she do?"

"She wanted to get together, she said. I agreed to see her, but said I had a lot of work." He laughs his dry laugh. "So we made the date for a week from then. I was to come to her place, have a drink, then maybe we'd go out to dinner. I wanted a week to think. What would she do with the loose end? She'd be looking for a way to kill me, I felt. She had to. I considered running, but she would be able to find me now. People can't disappear as easily they used to. So I put on my jacket and tie, and left my dog with plenty of food and water and the door ajar in case I didn't come back, and went to see her."

"Did you take your gun?" I gesture at it.

"No, I didn't own it then. When I got there I was scared. She offered me a cigarette, but I don't smoke. Offered me a drink, a martini, which I accepted, but didn't drink, just lifted it to my lips and put it down. My dog, Archie, has quite a few ailments. I had a dog tranquilizer with me to put in her drink, but I didn't get a chance. Her eyes were on me all the time. Intent." He sighs. "I was raised to think of women as emotional creatures."

"Creatures?"

"Weren't you? Soft, dependent, lacking calculation. Of course, that's a mistake we make about many other creatures too, underestimating them. In any case, believe me, she was rational, detached, watchful. She said she'd thought about me, a lot. That she'd been alone a long time. And she invited me into the bedroom. Perhaps I was supposed to be woozy. I know I was shaky, anyway, following her in."

"My God," I say. "That bedroom."

"She lay back on the bed the same way she had when—" He pauses, clears his throat. "And I sat beside her and leaned forward and I put the pillow over her face."

"That's why you stole the pillowcase."

He nods. "She died unexpectedly fast. I was thinking I would give her an empty injection, just put some air into her vein and cause an embolism."

"You had a hypodermic on you?"

"I have a whole kit. You know, you can buy anything in Miami. But she just stopped breathing. She must have had a heart attack—perhaps the shock?"

"She was old."

"And she smoked," he says. "She may have had heart disease. I figured nobody pays attention to the death of an old lady in her own bed. I took off her shoes, and wiped them, and set them under the bed. I wanted it to look like she'd felt ill and had to lie down and then died. I cleaned up the glasses, dried them, put them away. I have them now—I got them from the kitchen. I believe I have washed them half a dozen times. Interestingly, among her liquor there was a bottle with a dropper, hand-labelled *Bitters*. I don't know what was in it. Maybe it was bitters, maybe something else. I moved it to the kitchen cabinet, and later threw it out, then realized I should have kept it, had it tested if I needed to prove self-defense. I left her one cigarette butt in the ashtray. I wiped whatever I thought I'd touched. But I was fairly sure we'd be in there to do the estate clean-up and I'd handle a lot of things and so my fingerprints wouldn't mean anything. I'm not going back to jail!" He shrieks this last.

"I understand," I say, soothingly. "How did you know Alex would get the estate job?"

"Oh," he says, "Alex left cards when we were there before—at the desk and by the mailboxes and so on. So I didn't think anyone would find it odd that Helena had picked one up and had it in her desk, where she had other business cards. The daughter saw it and called. It was a gamble, but a good one. I left feeling fairly confident and calm. It was only afterwards that I started to doubt myself and worry about little things. I couldn't have taken the pillowcase. That would have drawn attention. But later I kept thinking about it—forensics people can pick up tiny fibers, hairs. That day we were there, I never could get into the bedroom alone till after Jeff and Hank carted off the furniture, and by then Sharon had packed up the bedclothes. I am sorry I had to steal from her."

"What'd you do with the pillowcases?"

"I burned them both. I didn't know which one was which."

"And the rest of the stuff you took?"

"In my van. I was going to put it in a dumpster, but I kept worrying it would be found."

"Sharon was going to give it to abused women."

He looks somewhat ashamed.

"Did you touch the dressing table?" I ask.

"I don't think so. But afterwards I wasn't sure."

"So on Lincoln Road you touched it and you let the dog hop up there?" He nods. "Did you touch the portrait?"

"I don't recall. There were a number of pictures in the living room that she showed me—her daughter and her grandchildren. I think it was there. I don't think I touched it. Did I?"

I say, "Lucite does hold prints. But I had already cleaned it myself when I got it home. Here—look at it. You're safe."

He takes it, holding it between both palms, and I lift his pistol off the chair arm and put it on the floor beside me.

"So there's no evidence," he says.

"Just what's in your head."

"What are you going to do?"

I shake my head. "Don't know."

"I wouldn't have hurt you, Ray," he says. "Tonight, I didn't even think you'd be here."

"But you brought the gun. Where'd you get it?"

"In my neighborhood. I bought it from a sad woman, a . . . prostitute. I said I wanted it to defend myself. I just thought if the police were to surprise me—if I had no warning—I could use it on myself. Or wave it at them and they'd shoot me. I'm not going back to jail." He says it calmly this time.

"Miami," I say. "This place is full of killers. Guys who work on your car may have been in death squads in Peru, dictators own steak houses, drug kingpins become developers. I can't fix every little thing. Go home. I know you did it, and you know I know, but there's not a bit of evidence left, I promise you. She's ash and her things are scattered, and scattering further every day."

He uses his shirttails to wipe off the picture frame and hands it back to me. I clasp it. Her eyes smile at me in the lamplight.

"Is that how she looked when you knew her?"

"She's a little younger, but yes."

"It's driving you nuts," I say, "isn't it?"

"What is?" he says, but he knows.

"The shred of a shadow of a glimpse of a chance that she might have been innocent. That the first story was true, the one she told, with Dorsett the killer and bully and you the rescuer. The one you went to jail on."

He says, "I'm sure as one can be."

"It's just too bad you have a conscience."

He blinks at me. "She didn't," he says. And sighs. He picks up his flashlight and nods to me and leaves. I bolt the door after him. On close inspection, his gun's in even worse shape than I thought. I put it into a bag. I'll drop it out to sea. I listen to the sound the palmettos make chattering against my windows and treat myself to a cigarette.

Three weeks later, on a Friday, I'm getting spruced up to go out. Two days after our long discussion, Cash was found dead in his apartment He had a needle beside him containing nothing but air. In a note he left his worldly goods to Alex and asked that I take care of his dog Archie. He left no explanation for his suicide other than to say, *I'm very tired.*

Our team cleared out his place. He had many old books, those of most interest with illustrated plates of birds and animals. He owned a complete medical bag and a collection of antique vet instruments that Guillermo says might be worth something. He's researching it. These things might possibly realize enough to repay Alex for the cremation. None of us could start the van, but Alex located some of Cash's buddies from the flea market in Fort Lauderdale and they came down and towed it away. The Kussrows declared his furniture of no resale value and we put it all out on the street for pickers to take. The building itself will soon be gutted.

Alex is looking for another trustworthy clean-up man. I haven't told him about Cash. The morning after my talk with him, Sharon found the stolen clothing tossed behind her hibiscus bushes. Alex and Sharon like the theory that the burglar was a boy seeking women's clothes who found them too dowdy.

Archie came to me with a list of what he eats and his ailments and a wardrobe of waistcoats and sweaters. I think Cash underestimated him. There's a nip in the November air this evening, but I'm making Archie tough it out. We'll walk down to Sharon's to pick her up and have dinner at a new restaurant on Biscayne that Alex recommends. We'll go on afterward to Café Nublado, and beyond that, who knows? She's a warm woman, as I'm coming to appreciate.

On my way out I stop in the dining room—as I often do—to look at the portrait of Helena Dorsett. What was it she had? Beauty enough to kill for, any way you look at it. I strain to recapture the woman I met. Quite a lady, I remember thinking. Her face is a pattern of shadow and light. Now, just paper.

MACHETE

BY BARBARA PARKER

Biscayne Bay

The Miami PD had beaten us to the scene. Yellow tape already circled the yard from one royal palm tree to the next. An officer in a rain poncho held up a hand and I waited, wipers flapping, while the fire-rescue truck pulled out of the driveway. No emergency lights, no siren. The bodies would be taken out later in the ME's unmarked van.

I drove past the police vehicles and parked at the end of the block. The house was in Coconut Grove in a wealthy enclave of narrow streets that deadended at Biscayne Bay. Confined by the downpour, neighbors watched from their porches or second-floor windows.

The only thing I could find to keep myself dry was a plastic bag from Target in the backseat. I dumped out the jeans to be returned, grabbed my camera bag, and shoved the door open just as a silver BMW sedan lurched around me and skidded on wet leaves. Its brake lights went off, and through the misted rear window I could see Charlene on her cell phone. She disconnected and struggled out of the car with an umbrella as thunder rattled the sky.

I called out, "Did you reach her?"

"No. Doesn't matter, we're here. Come on, let's go." I could hear Brooklyn in her voice, though she'd practiced law in Miami longer than I'd been alive.

Charlene held the umbrella for both of us, but I told her to go ahead, and she clattered along beside me in her high heels and tight skirt. An officer stopped us at the end of the driveway.

"I'm Charlene Marks, Mrs. Zaden's attorney. Would you kindly tell the lead investigator I want to see my client? Who's in charge, by the way?"

Ignoring the question, the officer lifted a radio to his lips. Water dripped off the hood of his poncho. I looked at the house from under my white plastic bag. Standard South Florida mansion: red barrel-tile roof, a portico over the circular driveway, double doors with beveled glass, a chandelier in the foyer. The builder had probably bulldozed the little three-bedroom-with-carport that used to sit on this lot. What can I say? I don't like bling.

My name is Sara Morales. I do private investigations, and Charlene's firm is one of my accounts. I used to work for the Miami Police Department until I slid down some stairs while chasing a supposedly docile suspect and broke two vertebrae. I've recovered from the injury; I run five miles a day, when the weather isn't so hot it melts my shoes to the asphalt, but I won't go back to police work. I've come to enjoy my freedom.

I rent a two-room office in a commercial strip on South Dixie Highway, walking distance to my apartment if I had to. My parents still live in Little Havana in the first house they bought after coming to the U.S. on a raft. Literally a raft: inner tubes and a wooden platform that broke up halfway across the straits. Three of the people who started out, including my grandfather, didn't make it. Till the day she died, my nena claimed she could talk to him in the other world. Of course she could. She was into *Santería* big time. I moved out after high school, a sacrilege for a Cuban girl.

Twenty minutes ago I'd been at my desk writing invoices when the phone rang. I picked up and heard tires screaming down the ramp of a parking garage. Charlene had told me whatever the hell I was doing, drop it and meet her at Kathy Zaden's house. She said a woman had come in and slashed Dr.

Zaden with a machete. Kathy heard him yelling for help, and ran downstairs with a pistol. She killed the woman, but not soon enough.

"The idiot called 911 before she called me. Damn it!" Charlene wanted to get there before her client said anything stupid to the cops. She told me to bring my camera.

I was out the door in less than thirty seconds.

The uniformed officer lifted the tape. "You want to speak to Sergeant Bill Nance."

"Thanks." Charlene headed up the driveway. Water sheeted over the interlocking pavers.

Bill Nance. He'd been my supervisor in the detective bureau. I'd been promoted to homicide after only five years on the force, so to him I was a minority cutting in line. When I left, he didn't send me a goodbye card.

We ran under the portico, where the mist was blowing in sideways. One of the front doors was wide open, and Nance stood there, feet spread, leaning back a little to balance his gut. Short white hair, gray slacks, gun on hip, silver shield clipped to the holster. He dismissed me with a glance and nodded at Charlene. They go back to her days at the prosecutor's office. They'd been close, but damned if I can see why.

She propped her folded umbrella against a poured-concrete lion, one of a set flanking the entrance. The humidity had frizzed her curly gray hair. "Hello, Bill. Crummy day for this, isn't it?"

"It'll blow over."

"What have you got so far?"

"Two dead downstairs in the study. Dr. Howard Zaden and a black female, early fifties. Mrs. Zaden ID'd her as Carmen Sánchez. She's from the Dominican Republic. It appears she attacked Dr. Zaden with a machete, and Mrs. Zaden shot her. I'd like a few more details, but your client won't talk to me."

"It's my fault. When she called, I told her to sit tight. Where is she?"

"Sitting tight." Nance looked at me, at my camera. "No photos, Morales."

"Nonsense," Charlene said. "We have a right to record the scene, and if you make me call a judge, he'll tell you so. You've got the gun, and Kathy Zaden admitted firing it. How could we possibly impede your investigation?"

There was an argument, which Charlene won by dangling the possibility that she'd let Kathy Zaden talk to him. I don't think Nance bought it, but he took us inside.

My wet sneakers chirped on the marble floor and fell silent on the Oriental rug. A crowd at a door on the opposite side of the living room meant I'd find Dr. Zaden and his guest over there, but Charlene said to come with her.

Nance led us through a dining room overlooking the canal where the Zadens's boat was docked, then to a kitchen done in stainless steel, cherry wood, and black granite. Either nobody cooked in here, or they had a better staff than I did.

Kathy Zaden was sitting at the counter with her head in her hands and a wad of tissue in her fist. She saw us and stood up, and her crop pants and sleeveless yellow top showed splashes of red. Her knees were bloody, and her forearms, like she'd crawled in it.

"Oh . . . Charlene!"

Making shushing noises, Charlene patted her on the shoulder. She didn't bother setting down her purse. She wasn't staying long enough to chat. "You need to put something else on, darling. We're leaving. Pack your jammies and a toothbrush."

"Will they let me go?"

"They will unless you have confessed to something extremely naughty."

"I didn't! I had to . . . oh. Oh—" She sobbed. "He's dead. Oh, God. The blood. It was so terrible. I was sick. I threw up."

"Let's just run upstairs and get you into some clean clothes, shall we?"

"The detective said to give him these."

"Oh, really." Charlene looked darkly in toward the door, where Sergeant Nance lingered. "Well, if and when a warrant is issued, he can have them."

"Why are they acting like I did something wrong? They swabbed my hands like I was a criminal. Why?"

"It's routine. Come on, let's go."

Kathy blew her nose. A weak smile came my way. "Hi, Sara."

I put an arm around her. "Don't worry. It's going to be all right."

She lowered her head to mine and made another little sob.

Kathy Zaden and I are the same age, thirty-three. That's as far as the similarity extends. I'm short and dark, thanks to my mulatta grandmother. Kathy Zaden is a sexy blonde with long, tanned legs. She had a realtor's license, and she'd met Dr. Zaden four years ago showing him an apartment on South Beach. He had just dumped his first wife and was looking for something more exciting—in both real estate and women, I suppose. Howard had made a fortune doing plastic surgery. He had a good build, an easy smile, a Mercedes CL500 coupe, a forty-two-foot Bertram sport fisher, a condo in Vail, and a tax attorney who showed him how to shelter his assets. For her birthday, he'd done Kathy's boobs.

You want to hate men like Howard Zaden. I'd wanted to hate Kathy, but I couldn't. She'd been born poor in Valdosta, Georgia, and fought her way out. She sent money home; she organized charity events; she took in stray cats. But she finally got it: She believed Howard when he said that two kids from his previous marriage were enough. She believed that one day he would dump her too.

Kathy had gone to Charlene to see about breaking the twenty-page prenuptial agreement he'd made her sign. Needless to say, Charlene had not been Kathy's lawyer for the prenup. I'd been shadowing Dr. Zaden for a couple of weeks to see if we could find anything useful, and I was getting nowhere. Now it didn't matter.

We went upstairs. When I was finished taking shots of Kathy Zaden and the blood stains, Charlene shooed her into the bathroom, and I found my way to the study.

The cool stares I got from the crime scene technicians meant that Bill Nance had told them who I was. He gave me a pair of blue paper booties and said, "Don't touch anything, and don't get in the way. You've got five minutes."

It was more a media room than a study, with a huge flatscreen television facing a leather sofa, rows of DVDs on the mahogany built-ins, and audio equipment behind glass doors. Hitting the shutter of my digital SLR, I maneuvered toward the other side of the room, where a desk and a clot of detectives hid my view. When they moved I saw two bodies in a puddle of dark red seeping into the ivory-colored carpet.

Howard Zaden lay on his back in a blue dress shirt, arms out like he was soaring, gold on his cuffs. A heavyset woman in black pants and a white knit top lay facedown across his lower legs. I barely saw her; my eyes were on Dr. Zaden.

His head had rolled to the side, and his neck looked like a piece of fresh steak. I could see something paler red protruding: bone, cartilage. His tie was gone just below the knot. Sweat prickled my scalp. This had not been the first cut; he'd survived long enough to scream and hold up his hands. Half his left hand was missing, and a long gash had opened his shoulder. More cuts went through his left bicep, his chest, his abdomen, as though she'd kept chopping after he hit the floor.

I forced myself to concentrate on what I saw through the viewfinder. Carmen Sánchez was black, or Afro-Cuban or Afro-something. Her hair was medium length, processed straight. I squatted to see her face, but her hair covered it. There were two red holes in her back, another in her neck. One shoe had come off, and I saw a brown foot, a tan sole. It reminded me of Nena's feet, the calluses, her cheap plastic sandals. I didn't see a purse.

If Kathy Zaden had said Carmen Sánchez was stalking her husband, then Charlene had to know about it. Charlene hadn't told me, but then, I hadn't been hired for that.

The machete lay near the bodies, a shiny curve about three feet long. Wood handle, blood drying to brown on the steel. I waited for a female officer to walk by, then zoomed in for a closeup. The edge had been honed till it shimmered. Something odd on the trailing edge: black smudges, like soot. Like she'd tried to burn it.

Why had Howard let her in? Most sane people would have slammed the door on a woman carrying a machete. Then I noticed a raincoat on the floor and pressed the shutter.

Sergeant Nance stood beside me. "What did she want with Dr. Zaden?"

"I have no idea." My viewfinder showed the desk, the stuff on it. A checkbook lying open, the big kind with a leather-bound cover.

He said, "She doesn't look like a disgruntled plastic surgery patient."

"No, she's a poor black Dominicana."

"Take it easy, Morales."

I shot images of the blood spatter up the side of the desk, over the bookshelves behind it, across the ceiling.

He asked, "Who was it answered the door? Mrs. Zaden?"

"I don't know."

"Somebody let this woman in."

I looked at him. "You think?"

Nance made a little smile, showing his teeth. He was still smoking, I noticed. "This lady came to do harm to Dr. Zaden, and we don't know why. His wife could shed some light. We're not out to get her. We just want to clear things up."

"Okay. I'll be sure to tell her."

"You're done here," Nance said. "Put it away."

I shot one more for the principle of it. At the door I took off the booties and balled them into my pants pocket.

Nance leaned closer. "Lucky thing you tripped down those steps, Morales. Know why?"

I turned away, but his voice followed me.

"Because they gave you disability instead of firing your ass. You weren't cutting it."

I kept my reply to myself. You don't get anywhere arguing with a cop.

The clouds had rumbled off, dragging the heat with them, leaving a gray overcast and a few stray drops of rain. Beyond the crime tape, the crowd of onlookers had grown. Two local satellite news trucks had set up operations on the street, and another was moving into position. The murder of a prominent Miami plastic surgeon would be breaking news at 6 o'clock.

Among the assorted police vehicles in the driveway, I spotted a red Toyota with a missing hubcap and a cracked side window. A Florida tag. I went over and took a picture of it, then the vehicle ID through the windshield. Whoever owned it would know Carmen Sánchez.

Nance would do the same thing. This case would be all over the front page, and Nance would work it. Somebody—hair stylist, personal trainer—would eventually tell him that Kathy had wanted out, and that she'd get more from a dead husband than an ex-husband. Nance knew that Carmen Sánchez had been stalking Dr. Zaden. He was wondering who let her in. Had Kathy waited until her husband was dead to fire the pistol into Mrs. Sánchez's back?

A movement on the street caught my eye. A monster Hummer painted bright yellow turned into the front yard, tires digging into the wet grass, chrome snout pressing on the crime scene tape. The door opened, and a guy slid off the seat. Short brown hair, average build, a Hawaiian shirt. He shouted something to a uniformed officer and ran full speed toward the house.

I'd seen him before: Richard Zaden, age thirty-one. He owned an overpriced pizza restaurant in the Grove that his father had bought for him. People came and went that I thought the DEA would've liked to interview.

Maybe I still look like a cop. Rick Zaden saw me and veered in my direction. He said he was Dr. Zaden's son, and a neighbor had called him. What the hell was going on here? Where was his father?

I should have turned him toward the door and suggested he find Sergeant Nance, but instead I told him the truth as gently as I could, then said I was sorry. I told him he probably didn't want to go in there right now.

He broke down, hands over his face, wailing. Then he looked at me with tortured eyes and whispered, "My father. He's gone? Oh my God, no. Dad."

Call me hard-hearted, but it seemed overdone. I knew that Rick and his father had been at odds. But this didn't mean anything. Lose your father, feelings can change.

He sagged against the front fender of the Toyota. "She shot the bitch. Jesus Christ. I can't believe it. Kathy shot her. Where is she? I want to talk to her."

"Not now. She's on her way out. Her lawyer won't let her talk to anyone."

That got me a blank stare. "Her lawyer?"

"When the police get involved, people call lawyers."

"Is she . . . under suspicion?"

"Not that I know of."

He took a long, slow breath. "I want to go in."

"Just a second." I held onto his arm. "Who was Carmen Sánchez?"

"She wanted money from my father. It was a lawsuit or something. An accident when he was on vacation in the Dominican Republic. Some guy—her son—walked right in front of his car. It wasn't Dad's fault, but she wouldn't leave him alone.

He said he was going to pay her off." Rick wiped his hands down his face. "What am I supposed to do now?"

"Somebody will be out to speak to you. Excuse me, but did this person, Mrs. Sánchez's son, did he die?" Rick nodded. "And then what? She came here on a tourist visa?"

"Yeah. That's what they do, then they don't leave." Rick Zaden gave me a closer inspection. "Are you a police officer or what?"

I had to tell him. "I'm a private investigator. I work for Kathy Zaden's attorney."

He stared at me, turned his back, and walked under the portico, leaving me with the answer to at least one of Sergeant Nance's questions: Carmen Sánchez had come here to collect money from the man who had killed her son. Had Dr. Zaden planned to write her a check? If the death had been an accident, why would he pay her? And if she'd thought he would, why did she want him dead?

I scanned the faces across the street, wondering if anybody had seen a middle-aged Latina getting out of her car in a raincoat. I noticed the house next door. It wasn't much of a house, but it had a terrace on the roof, and a man leaned on the metal railing with a long-neck beer. A chickee hut with a palm-frond roof had been built up there, and the flag of Great Britain hung from one end of it like a curtain.

My pant legs got soaked as I cut through his overgrown yard. He was around forty, with bright blue eyes and spiked, sandy hair. He wore old khaki shorts and a sleeveless T-shirt that revealed a pair of nicely muscled arms. I asked if I could talk to him. He said to come up.

Circular metal stairs took me to a teak deck on the roof. He had a view of the houses along the canal, sailboats and sport fishers at the docks, and a slice of Biscayne Bay at the end of the canal. The water repeated the dull gray of the sky. He'd installed a bar, a hot tub, and a sunning area. The reed privacy screen made me think he liked an all-over tan.

His name was Ian Morris. After I'd told him what had happened, he asked if Kathy was all right. "Is she, really? Poor baby. She must be in shock."

"Are you English?"

"Born in Newcastle. That's on the North Sea. I came here ten years ago. Love the weather, most of the time." He finished his beer, went to a small fridge under the chickee hut, and took out another, lifting it toward me inquiringly. I sat on a stool and he opened a bottle for each of us.

He told me he was a metal sculptor, which explained the big arms. I asked if he'd made the piece on the sea wall, a rusted oval that swung and groaned from an arch of polished aluminum.

"Not your style, is it?" He grinned. "I sold one similar for twenty thousand dollars to a collector in Mexico. Oh, but Howard told me it sucked, and he wanted it gone. That and my little roof garden too. He promised to sue me into the ground, and I said fine, give it a go. Horrible man. Am I speaking ill of the dead?" He took a swallow of beer.

I asked him if he'd seen Carmen Sánchez arrive.

Ian Morris said that at about 4 o'clock he'd been taking down his umbrella before the storm broke, and he'd noticed a little red car pull into the Zadens's driveway, a black woman at the wheel. Then the car went out of sight.

"I didn't know who she was. I certainly didn't see her get out with a machete. Howard had come home early, so I thought she might be his voodoo lady making a house call."

"His . . . ?"

"Psychic. Spiritual advisor? Tarot card reader?"

"No. Dr. Zaden had a psychic?"

With a grin, Ian said, "This is Miami, love. With a name like Morales, you must have an altar to Chango or Eleggua in your bedroom."

I smiled and shook my head. "Most of us are smarter than that."

"Well, Howard went for his reading at least once a month. He said his voodoo lady guaranteed the code-enforcement people would be on my ass. I told him I was shaking in my boots."

I nudged him back to the point. "What about Carmen Sánchez?"

"Yes. Kathy told me about her, although, as I said, I didn't recognize her." Ian Morris shuddered. "My God. What a hideous thing to do! Even to Howard. And poor Kathy. I have to call her. Would that be all right?"

"She'll be with friends for a few days."

"I have her mobile number."

Did he, now?

From the roof I could see the windows of the Zadens's master suite. Their balcony overlooked the pool. Kathy had said she knew it was time to leave Howard when she started watching him do his hundred laps every morning and think about heart attacks. I could also imagine that Ian Morris had watched Kathy standing on the balcony in her nightie.

I said, "I met Rick Zaden a little while ago. I told him his father had been murdered and he seemed . . . like he had to convince me he cared."

Ian laughed. "He doesn't care. He's probably ecstatic. You see, Rickie had borrowed, or conned, his father out of so much money that Howard finally decided to shut him down. Howard had a mortgage on a restaurant Rick owned, and he was going to collect."

I sipped my beer. "How did you know this? From Kathy?"

"Howard was yelling about it right down there on the dock. He was hosing off his boat, must've been a weekend, and Rick came over. I don't know how it started, but Howard told him he wasn't getting another effing cent, and furthermore, he'd be calling his attorney and taking the effing restaurant. He finally told Rick to get off his property or he'd have him arrested for trespassing."

"When was this?"

Ian's eyes focused upward. "I'm going to say . . . three months."

Plenty of time for them to get over it. "Anything more recent?"

"Couldn't say. Rick hasn't been around." Ian shrugged. "Kathy tried to be a peacemaker. I kept telling her, why bother? Can I get you another beer?"

"No, thanks." Ian Morris liked to talk, so I asked him if he knew anything about the car accident in the Dominican Republic.

He gazed past me at the Zadens's house. "I don't think Kathy would mind. It's no secret. She and Howard were visiting friends over there. They rented a car and went sightseeing. It happened outside some wretched little village. Mrs. Sánchez's son, her only son, was walking along the road, and Howard hit the poor sod and killed him."

"Was he drunk?"

"He'd been drinking, but he wasn't drunk. No, he was yelling at Kathy just before the impact. She doesn't remember what about. Something petty. Howard was a shameless verbal abuser. He didn't strike her, at least she said not, or I'd have been forced to beat the crap out of him."

Ian crossed his arms on the bar. I could see little scars from metal cuts or torch burns. "Anyway, the accident. The *policía* investigated, but Howard's friends were wealthy, quite connected, and so forth. Howard felt he'd done nothing wrong, but he paid the man's burial expenses and returned to the States. That would've been the end of it, except that Mrs. Sánchez turned up. She wanted compensation, and Howard basically told her to bugger off."

"How much was she asking for?"

"Ten thousand dollars for every year of her son's life, and he was twenty-five. Oh, Howard could've paid, he just didn't like to be told to. Carmen Sánchez came here to torment him. The staff at the clinic would find things at the entrance—a doll with pins in it, or a dead chicken—and it was driving Howard crazy. The police wouldn't do anything because they couldn't catch her at it. Howard filed a report with Immigration and maybe they'd have gotten around to deporting her in a year or two. Meanwhile, the bones kept appearing on his doorstep. Bad for business. A lot of Howard's patients were Cubans, and Cubans know *Santería* when they see it, don't they? He had no choice but to pay her."

I let these facts settle, then said, "But why did she kill him?"

"Ha. Now there's a question." Ian Morris lifted his beer in a salute.

As night closed in, Charlene Marks put Kathy Zaden in the passenger seat of her BMW and eased through the pack of reporters shoving cameras at the windows. I followed on her bumper. At Bayshore, the BMW put on its left-turn signal, then squealed right as I blocked the street. I saw the brake lights go on at Seventeenth Avenue, and the car disappeared behind thick foliage.

I hooked up with them a couple of minutes later on U.S. 1 heading downtown. Charlene would deliver Kathy Zaden to a friend's condo on Brickell Key, a posh private island overlooking the city. If you aren't invited, you don't get in. I called Charlene on my cell phone and gave her a quick summary of my conversations with Dr. Zaden's son and the next-door neighbor. I was curious whether either of them had known Carmen Sánchez. Ian Morris had told me no, but I've been lied to before.

I asked Charlene to pull over and let me talk to Kathy.

"Make it quick," Charlene said. "Somebody's about to pass out on me."

She parked a block off Brickell Avenue on a side street overhung with oaks and air plants. Glass towers haven't completely taken over, not yet. A street light at the corner sent a weak yellow glow through the branches.

I opened the rear door and got in. Kathy rolled her head on the seat back to focus on me. Whatever she'd found in her medicine cabinet, it was kicking in. "Hey. What a mess, huh?"

"Kathy, I talked to Ian Morris. He told me about the accident in the Dominican Republic. Did you ever give him Mrs. Sánchez's phone number?"

"Ian? No. Why would I?"

"You're sure?"

"I'm sure."

"Who let Mrs. Sánchez into the house?"

"I did."

The lack of reaction from the driver's seat told me that Charlene had already learned this much from her client. "I talked to Rick too. He thought she had come to collect money from his father." Kathy nodded. "Did you know she was coming over?"

"Yes. I asked her to."

Charlene sat up straighter.

Kathy sighed. "I'm sorry, Charlene. I didn't want to lie to you, but . . . I don't know. It sounds so bad. The truth is . . . I arranged the meeting."

Charlene said, "Well, well."

"It was Ian's idea. He said we should offer her less money. She wanted $250,000! He said offer her $100,000."

"Why was Ian being so helpful?" I asked. "He hated Howard."

"He cares about me."

"Is he in love with you?"

"I suppose he is. He knew things were bad between me and Howard. I was depressed, and I wasn't sleeping." Kathy frowned. "Maybe Ian did have her number. The first time I called her, it was from his house."

"Kathy." I shifted between the seats to see her more clearly. "Did Mrs. Sánchez say she would accept $100,000?"

"She said she'd think about it. I told Howard, and when he finished screaming at me, he said he would ask his tarot card reader. I'm serious. He had to get permission. She said yes, but he wouldn't pay more than fifty, so I called Mrs. Sánchez back and told her. She said she'd come at 4 o'clock today and pick up a check."

Kathy hugged her arms around herself and stared through the windshield. "Howard told me to get the door. It was raining, and . . . she was standing there in this long black raincoat. I didn't want to let her in. I mean, I had this, like, premonition. She was going to kill him. I could see it. She was . . . death, and she'd come for him.

"I tried to close the door, but she held it open. Howard took her into the study. I heard them arguing. She started yelling and cursing, and I went to get Howard's pistol out of the bedroom. I ran downstairs and opened the door, and she was killing him, swinging the machete up and down. I shot her. I kept on shooting till I just heard clicks."

Tears were sliding down Kathy's face. "It was my fault."

"How can you think that?" Charlene pulled her close. "You didn't know what she would do. She was out of her mind."

"Yeah, she's not the only one." Laughing, Kathy opened her purse and found a tissue. "Can we go? I'm so tired. I want dinner. I have to sleep."

"One more thing," I said quickly. "This psychic that Howard used. Who is she?"

"Rosario . . ." Kathy closed her eyes, then said, "Cardona."

"Did Ian know her?"

"I think he met her once. It was like two years ago. The grand opening of Ponte Vecchio—that's Rick's restaurant. Next to Señor Frog's. Rick hired her to read palms. A marketing gimmick, you know? She read Howard's palm and said he'd win his lawsuit with his partner. He did. The next week the judge ruled in his favor, so after that, he believed anything Rosario Cardona said."

"She could have learned about the lawsuit from Rick," I said. "Have there been any fights lately between Rick and his father? Ian said they had a big one a few months back."

Shaking her head, Kathy said, "Rick was pretending to be very good. I don't know if Howard believed him or not. I don't care. Please. Can we go? I'm so tired."

Charlene turned the key. "Sara, you ride over there with us. I'll bring you back." Headlights made a brilliant wash of white on the street. It was raining again, and the wipers moved silently across the glass. Charlene turned onto Brickell, a leafy canyon of bank buildings and million-dollar apartments. Banyan trees and royal palms divided the street. A short bridge took us onto Brickell Key, and out of habit I studied the cars behind us as we waited in line at the visitors' gate.

"Howard didn't kill her son. It was me."

Charlene and I looked simultaneously at Kathy Zaden.

Her lips barely moved. "He wasn't driving. I was."

A horn sounded, and Charlene moved forward. Kathy twisted her tissue into a rope and started tearing pieces off the end of it. "We were having an argument. I wasn't watching the road, and then I heard this loud . . . *thump*. I stopped the car and we got out. Howard was a doctor. I was screaming for him to do something. He grabbed my shoulders and shook me. 'He's dead. Can't you see he's dead?'"

Charlene pulled her eyes off Kathy long enough to give the guard the name of her friend in the condo.

"A truck came along with workers in the back. Howard told them he'd been driving and the man walked right in front of him. I didn't say anything. I went back to our car and just sat there. I didn't open my mouth."

The gate arm rose, and Charlene moved at a slow speed toward the entrance of the Atlantica. She idled in the driveway.

"I had nightmares. I could hear the body hitting the car, then flying up and shattering the windshield, and the blood everywhere. Howard gave me some antidepressants, and I was okay, until Carmen Sánchez showed up."

A uniformed valet waited under the bright lights of the portico.

Kathy said, "We're here."

Charlene pulled to the curb and pressed the trunk release. The valet opened the passenger side door, then hurried to get Kathy's suitcase. I stood by the car. Charlene took Kathy into the lobby. Through the glass doors I saw them embrace.

When Charlene came back, she got in the passenger side. "You drive. I want a drink. I want a drink bad."

We went to a quiet Cuban bar on West Flagler where for under $10 you could get a draft beer and a pretty good grouper sandwich. You could also smoke without getting cursed at. We found a booth in the back, and I gave Charlene one of my cigarettes when she held up two fingers.

She was on her third scotch and soda before either of us said anything about Howard Zaden's murder. I told her I wanted to find Rosario Cardona.

"What for? You need your tarot cards read?"

"No, I'd like to know why she advised Dr. Zaden to let Carmen Sánchez come to his house. The woman was obviously unstable. It was like letting a rabid dog in the house."

"Rosario Cardona was wrong."

"Wrong? Oh, come on, Charlene. She's a fraud. She rents out by the hour to read palms at parties. They're all frauds."

"No, they aren't. I've had my palm read. She said I'd have a younger lover within the year, and I did." Charlene set her elbow on the table and dragged in some smoke. She let it out slowly through an O of red lipstick. "You think someone paid her to set Dr. Zaden up? That's far-fetched."

"Probably."

"Let's just hope it wasn't Kathy."

* * *

The Yellow Pages listed two dozen psychics in the Miami area, but only one called Rosario. No address, but the phone number indicated an area about four miles west of Dr. Zaden's clinic in Coral Gables, convenient enough. The flowery border of the ad encompassed a sketch of a woman's hand holding a crystal ball and the name *Rosario* floating above it. Underneath she listed her specialties: *Horoscope forecast. Crystal energy. Healing. Specialist in auras. Palm and tarot card readings. Call today for a better tomorrow. Private and confidential. Over 15 yrs. exper.* At the bottom, a pair of scissors and dotted lines made a coupon: *$25 off first visit.*

When I called, I heard wooden flute music, then a female voice telling me, in English then in Spanish, that Rosario regretted not being available, but if I would leave my number . . .

I requested an appointment as soon as possible, and she called back an hour later and agreed to see me at 10 o'clock the next morning. It would cost me a hundred dollars.

I Xeroxed the page and clipped out the coupon.

Rosario Cardona's studio was in a tree-lined warehouse district with rows of small shops and tree-shaded parking. I drove past open bays of unpainted wooden furniture, racks of clothing, and bright pottery, the sort of stuff that comes from China or Mexico in containers, to be grabbed by Miami Latinas hunting for a bargain.

She had told me to enter through number 8750-B. I parked and went into La Couture Shoes, specializing in knockoffs of $500 designer names with skinny straps, five-inch heels, and polka-dots, the kind of footwear that requires a professional pedicure. When a saleslady approached, I pointed at the stairs going up the left side of the shop.

Rosario rented the second floor. She didn't have a sign on the street, so I assumed the landlord didn't know. The stairs led to a door painted dark green. On the wall somebody had hung a framed print of a naked angel with long blond hair and golden wings, flying through pink clouds with a crystal ball in her hand. The door opened, revealing a petite, dark-eyed woman in jeans, high-heeled boots, and a silky white shirt. Her hair was in a ponytail, and gold circles hung from her ears. She looked to be about thirty-five, younger than I'd expected. She had all the sexuality of a porcelain doll, but I could see how a man of fifty might keep coming back.

"Ms. Morales?" Bracelets tinkled softly as she took my hand. "Come in."

My eyes had to adjust to the dim light. The room was about twenty feet square, with a painted concrete floor and area rugs. Candles flickered from wall sconces, shelves, and low tables. A brass chandelier with a dimmer on low hung from the midnight-blue ceiling. Wind chimes turned in front of the air vents, and water splashed in a rock fountain. There were display cases with crystals, oils, candleholders, and packaged sticks of incense; a revolving rack of greeting cards with angels, unicorns, and Native Americans; shelves of CDs and books.

A glance to my left revealed a fringed curtain, behind which the spiritual advising took place. The whole setup reminded me of La Botánica Lukumí, around the corner from my parents' house, which I swear my grandmother had single-handedly kept in business.

Rosario Cardona's eyes rested on mine, unblinking. "You didn't come for a reading, did you?"

I took a business card out of my shoulder bag. "I'm working for Kathy Zaden. I don't know if you heard the news yesterday about her husband, Dr. Howard Zaden. He was one of your clients."

"Yes, I heard about it." Rosario set my card on the low table that held the fountain. "What a terrible tragedy. I am so sorry for Mrs. Zaden."

"We're trying to understand what happened. You knew him. If I could just ask you a few questions—"

"You know, I could have taken another appointment, but I made room for you." She shook her head when I went for my wallet. "No. You should have told me, that's all I'm saying."

"Please take it." I put five twenties on the table next to my card. "I should have told you." And if you were for real, I said silently to myself, you'd have known. "Can we sit down?"

She was still giving me a look you couldn't get through with an ice pick. "I'm sorry. I don't discuss my clients."

"Dr. Zaden is dead."

A couple of seconds ticked by. She said, "Transformed." Her voice was as soft as the glass wind chimes tinkling overhead. "We use the word 'dead,' but the dead are still with us."

I started over. "His wife blames herself for letting Carmen Sánchez into their house. Carmen Sánchez is the woman—"

"Yes, the story was in the *Herald* this morning."

"Kathy just needs to understand what happened. You advised Dr. Zaden to let Carmen Sánchez come pick up a check to settle her claims. Could you tell me why?"

I listened to the splash of water until Rosario took a breath, let it out. "All right. I'll talk to you."

She led me farther into the room, to an overstuffed sofa with wine-colored cushions and a cat curled up on one of them. I saw a woman in the corner. Candles flickered on her pale face, her red lips, her stiff hands. In the next instant I saw a mannequin dressed like a Spanish dancer in a black-lace mantilla.

"Jesus," I muttered.

Rosario smiled up at me from the sofa. "Her name is Fátima. She's my gypsy. She isn't real, in the ordinary sense of the word, but she guides me. Please, have a seat."

The cat wasn't real either. It was one of those stuffed things made out of rabbit fur. Rosario set it on the coffee table. At least she didn't pet it.

"Dr. Zaden came to me and asked what he should do about Carmen Sánchez. I said that he needed to free himself, and if he had to pay, so be it. We did some cleansing rituals, and I gave him some oils for protection." She lowered her lashes. "I make no claim to perfect vision. I don't always see the outcome. Tell his wife . . . Tell her that I am sorry."

I'm usually pretty good at reading people, but I didn't know if Rosario Cardona was real or as phony as her friend Fátima. "Did Dr. Zaden ever talk about his next-door neighbor, Ian Morris?"

"Yes. They had some problems. He and I tried to resolve them." Rosario cocked her head as if puzzled. "Why do you ask?"

"Did Dr. Zaden ever say that Mr. Morris had talked to Carmen Sánchez, or that Mr. Morris knew how to reach her?"

"No. I can't remember Dr. Zaden saying anything about that. Why?"

"You know Rick Zaden, Dr. Zaden's son."

"Yes, of course. I did a reading for him once, but that was before his father became my steady client. I don't read for people in the same family. There could be conflicts."

"Did Rick ever mention Carmen Sánchez to you?"

"No. I haven't seen Rick in a long time." Rosario Cardona lifted her brows. "These are strange questions. What is it you're looking for, Sara?"

I had the sensation of walking on a moving sidewalk going the wrong way, losing ground. The sofa faced a long table piled with the implements of a *Santera*: strands of colored beads, a vase of feathers, a drum. Tall glass candleholders for San Lazaro, Santa Barbara, San Antonio. I saw a flat can of lighter fluid and a long butane lighter, and I remembered my grandmother dancing around a circle of flames. I'd been in the middle of the circle on my knees.

As the air conditioner cycled on, the wind chimes tinkled softly and the candles flickered at the gypsy's feet.

I said, "I'd like to know why Dr. Zaden died. I don't think it's as simple as it appears."

She nodded slowly, not that she agreed with me, but that she understood. "Why does it have to be complicated? Most things aren't. A woman was grieving for her son. She wanted justice. She wanted the blood of the man who killed him—"

"Howard Zaden didn't kill him," I said without thinking, then added, "I suppose he told you."

"Yes. Kathy is responsible. And now she suffers. Carmen Sánchez got her justice. You see? It's simple. The universe knows what it's doing."

I stood up, wanting to get out of there. "Thank you for your time."

Rosario said, "Please take your money back. I haven't earned it."

"Keep it."

As we walked to the door, she lifted her hand and held it close to my neck, not touching my skin, but I could feel the heat. "You're very tense. Wait." She went over to the display case and returned with a small brown glass bottle. "This is lavender oil, very good for tension, for headaches and sleeplessness. Take it with my compliments."

She held onto my hand and came closer. Her eyes were huge, outlined in black. "I see . . . I see loss. I see grief."

"What?"

"Was it a child?"

"Not mine. I never had any children."

"But I do feel something, Sara. A death. There was a child, and it's gone. You suffered from this loss."

I dropped the little bottle into my purse. "That's news to me."

"Well, all I can tell you is what I feel. Someone died. A girl, I think. Maybe a young relative? The child of a friend?"

"You're fishing, Ms. Cardona."

With a smile, she crossed to the door and opened it. "Goodbye, Sara. If you would ever like me to do a reading for you, please call."

I held on tightly to the railing on the way down, a habit I'd developed since my fall. Or maybe it was that my legs were trembling. I got halfway and leaned against the wall to catch my breath.

Rosario Cardona talked to a mannequin named Fátima. She had a stuffed cat and she believed in spirits. Bullshit. Total bullshit. So how had she known? When I'd fallen down the stairs chasing the suspect, I'd been two months pregnant and trying to decide what to do about it. I lost the baby. Nobody knew. No one, not even my mother.

The idea that Rosario Cardona knew made me queasy.

She hadn't known, she'd guessed. She'd read my body language, picked up a clue in my reaction.

Simple.

As simple as the reason for Howard Zaden's murder. He was dead because Carmen Sánchez had decided on her own to seek justice.

But I had no faith that Bill Nance would see it that way.

It took me the rest of the day to track down the owner of the red Toyota. He was a cook at a Nicaraguan restaurant in East Little Havana. The police had already been there. They had his car. He didn't know Carmen Sánchez, except from the restaurant. The food was cheap, and she came in a lot. She had given him $50 to use his car for a few hours. She had seemed very nice, but she had murdered a man. *¡Qué barbaridad!* The cook didn't know her, not at all, no. He'd only loaned her his car, and he wanted it back. The police were thieves. He thought that Señora Sánchez had lived in the pink apartments on Southwest 1st Street.

It was a two-story, stucco-over-frame building, twelve studio units built in the 1920s, when Miami was growing past the river. A ranchero tune came through open glass jalousies. I took the concrete steps to a door with a security screen. It wasn't locked. The dim hallway went straight through, and stairs turned toward the second floor.

I asked an old man coming out of apartment four if a lady named Carmen Sánchez had lived here. In Spanish accented with Portuguese, he told me the police had just left. They had searched an apartment upstairs, the one right over his head, *el número diez*. Was it true she had killed two people with a machete? Was it true that she herself was dead? Thanks be to God. He'd thought something was funny with her, the way she never spoke to anybody, the things he'd heard through the ceiling. *Candomble, Palo Mayombe,* who knew what? He'd been afraid to complain. A woman like that. No, he'd never seen anyone come to her apartment.

I thanked him and took the stairs and walked to the middle door on the left side. It was open, leading to a small room with a vinyl tile floor, burglar bars at the windows, a single bed, and a kitchen area to one side. A big woman with her hair in pink rollers was cleaning out the refrigerator.

She saw me and asked if I was a reporter. She had already thrown reporters from four TV stations out of the building. I gave her my card and said I worked for the murdered doctor's wife, and I had seen the dead bodies.

The woman closed the refrigerator and peeled off her rubber gloves. For the price of a few details about the murder scene, she agreed to talk to me.

She hadn't seen any American men visiting Señora Sánchez. No men of any kind, or women. And no big yellow trucks had ever parked in the lot. She would have known. She kept her eyes open. Carmen Sánchez was crazy, no doubt about that. Just look. Look at all this.

She didn't mean the ordinary clothes in the small closet, the shoes side by side on the floor, or the cans of beans and bag of rice in the kitchen cabinet. She meant the heavy purple curtains that made it dark as a cave in here if you closed them. She meant the things on that table over there in the corner. What kind of a crazy person would have such things in her house?

I'd seen the like in homes of Cuban believers in *Santería*, but this made Nena's simple collection look almost Puritan. Mrs. Sánchez's altar had a three-foot-tall statue of St. Michael the protector, about to slash a demon with his sword. There were drums, conch shells, cowrie shells, beads, feathers, and carved gourds. There were candles in glass holders, dozens of them. Little bottles of perfumed oil. I saw a box of kitchen matches, four butane lighters, and a quart bottle of Ronrico rum. I lifted the lid of a wooden box and saw a pile of small charred bones.

"Did she burn these in the backyard?"

The landlady gave a shake of her head that bounced her pink rollers. No, that wasn't allowed, burning bones. Such things were not permitted.

I thanked her for her time.

Before I went away to the police academy, my grandmother stopped crying long enough to make me promise to come over for a sacred fire circle. I'd seen her do one before, when my cousin joined the army, and he came back from Iraq in one piece. So I said okay. If it would make you happy, Nena, okay.

It's best to do this under a full moon. You need a flat concrete surface, like a driveway. Or a back porch.

Mami was there, and my Aunt Josefa. I can't say they believed, but they didn't want to tempt fate, so they agreed to help. Nena made me kneel, then she used two entire cans of lighter fluid to make a circle around me. She clicked a lighter, and orange flames shot up in a whoosh of heat. I coughed on the smoke. Meanwhile, Aunt Josefa poured rum over the blade of a machete. I believe she got it from my Uncle Raul, who had been clearing weeds in their backyard.

Blue flames poured off the steel and dripped to join the orange circle. Nena took the machete and sliced through the flames. *"Olodumare, rey del universo, protégela. Protege a esta niña. Cuídela."* She was praying to the gods for my protection in the line of duty, but I remember looking side to side and hoping none of the neighbors were seeing this insane little white-haired lady dancing around the fire.

The women passed the bottle around and filled their mouths. They pressed the trigger of a butane lighter and sprayed out the rum, which turned to a fiery blue mist. I was afraid my clothes would catch on fire, but miraculously all I felt was a cool rush of air. The orange flames sputtered and went out.

For years I thought Nena had invented this ritual, and that she and her friends used it as an excuse to get drunk. She had put her own touches on it, but she hadn't made it up.

When I broke my back, Nena came every day to the hospital and reminded me I was alive. She said it was a sign: I should get out of police work and take a normal job like other women.

If Nena is looking on, I don't know if she's happy with what I do. It may not be a normal job, but it's a job, and I'm pretty good at it.

For the second time that day, I went through the shoe shop and up the stairs to Rosario Cardona's place. It was a few minutes past 6 o'clock, and her last client had just left. Heavy clouds were moving in, bringing an early twilight.

I knocked. Rosario Cardona frowned when she saw who was there. "I'm sorry, but I can't see you now. If you could call tomorrow—"

"I only have one more question. I promise it won't take long."

I slid past her. The sound of New Age flutes and a harp came through hidden speakers.

Rosario pushed the door shut. "All right. What's your question?" Her perfect little mouth was in a polite smile, but her body language said something else. Arms crossed, weight on one hip. The sharp heels of her boots cut into the rug.

"Has Rick Zaden been here lately?"

She waited for me to explain this. When I didn't, she said patiently, "No. I told you, I haven't seen Rick for a long time."

"At his restaurant in the Grove."

"Correct."

"Then why—and I guess this makes two questions—why did the lady who owns the shop tell me she'd seen a yellow Hummer in the parking lot two days ago?"

Rosario Cardona shrugged, a slight lift of one shoulder. "There's more than one yellow Hummer in Miami."

"And last week, and sometimes at night—"

"It wasn't Rick," she said. "I don't know whose car it was, but it wasn't Rick's. Excuse me, but I have work to do." She went to the door and swung it open for me.

From my purse I took a small plastic bag and held it up to let her see the brown glass bottle inside it. "Do you remember this?"

"Yes. I just gave it to you."

"No. You gave it to Carmen Sánchez. I found it in her apartment."

There was the first flicker of dark anger in her eyes, like distant lightning. "Everyone sells that."

"I called seven *botánicas*, and they never heard of Nature's Meadow."

"I don't know what your little game is, but I want you to leave. Right now."

I pivoted and crossed the room to the table in the far corner. The gypsy smiled blankly at me. Rosario's boots thudded across the floor. "I'm calling the police."

"Go for it." I tipped a basket to see what was inside. "Bones. Mrs. Sánchez had these in her apartment too."

"Get out."

"How did you meet her? Did you bump into her by accident at Sedano's Supermarket on Calle Ocho? At the Nicaraguan restaurant where she ate? No, not there. Someone might've remembered you. What did you say to her? *I see loss. I see grief. A young man who died.* Is that what you said? Rick knew she was nuts, but he couldn't play her like you could. But you wouldn't have used your own name. You couldn't bring her here. Did you open a studio in Little Havana? Turns out, you didn't have to worry. Kathy Zaden shot her."

"I said get out!"

"I can't decide if you're sleeping with Rick Zaden or he's paying you. It must be tough working over a discount shoe store."

She leaped for the first thing in reach, a wrought-iron candleholder about waist high. The candle flew off the top, leaving a bare black iron spike that came straight for me. She was a small woman, and I wrenched it out of her hands, put a hip in her side, and threw her to the painted concrete floor.

She lay there wheezing, no wind in her lungs. I picked up the stuff that had fallen out of my purse, including the bottle of oil. Maybe her fingerprints were on it, maybe not.

When I looked back at the shoe shop in my rearview mirror, they were turning off the lights, closing up.

I dialed a direct line to Miami homicide and listened to the rings on the other end.

What would Rosario Cardona do next? Make her own phone call. And then she and Rick Zaden would run around trying to figure out what to do, and they would trip over themselves. Rick wasn't that smart.

I didn't have all the answers, but I had a few.

A man's voice said, "Nance here."

Nena used to tell me that a psychic couldn't read her own

cards, couldn't see into her own future. That must be right, because Rosario Cardona didn't have the least idea what was coming for her.

THE SWIMMERS

BY JEFFREY WEHR

South Beach

J acques first saw the other three Haitians through the darkness as he stepped into the go-fast boat at the dock in Freeport, Bahamas. They were sitting huddled together on the deck, leaning back against the side. Paul had nodded to Jacques in greeting as soon as he saw him, and Jacques returned the nod. Though sitting, Paul looked short, had a well-groomed mustache, and was bald. His wife, Bahy, looked even shorter, had thickset stubby hair, and was overweight. Bahy's head rested on Paul's shoulder and she looked at Jacques with suspicion, and then pressed her face against Paul so hard that Jacques could see her neck straining. He thought the third passenger, Emania, was beautiful—stick-thin legs, bulbous knees, high cheekbones, and night-black, shiny skin that glowed in the dim light from the wharves. The unblemished white of her eyes flickered when she blinked, and when Jacques looked for too long, she fixed them to the floor between her knees.

There were two Bahamians taking them; one was the driver and the other was to make sure the cargo didn't try to take the boat. Jacques was told to sit low next to the other three, and not to talk or raise his head to look around. He sat then, listened to the lapping water and the few murmurs between the Bahamians. He leaned his head back against the fiberglass and noticed there were no visible stars or moon that night, or evident wind. The other three were looking back and forth at each other in distress and Jacques wanted to tell them not too worry, that it was a good night to cross.

There was intermittent laughter from the beginnings of a party a few piers down, where none of the Haitians could see, and the smugglers looked from their map. The second smuggler then told the four Haitians to go underneath through the hatch between the two front seats, and so the four crawled through the small opening. Inside there was one dim overhead light that flickered occasionally, a fiberglass counter to the side of the entrance (with a hole where a small sink had been removed), an empty fiberglass floor space that sloped up the sides, and a two-foot-high plywood platform (stained with the quilted pattern of a mattress) that occupied the front half of the cabin, contouring the long V-shaped bow to a point. It smelled strongly like mold, vomit, and gasoline, and Bahy made a whimper noise as they sat on the curved floor against the walls.

"It is not that bad," Paul told her. He looked at Jacques, who sat next to Emania across from him. "I am Paul."

Jacques introduced himself and they began talking in Kreyol. Jacques learned Bahy had a wealthy cousin in Weston who had sent them $6,000 in the Bahamas to pay the smugglers. Once they reached Florida, they were to use a pay phone to call him collect and let him know where to pick them up. They had never been to the United States before but were excited for their new lives. Paul was planning on becoming an immigration attorney (he was an attorney in Cap-Haitian) to help other Haitians that arrived, and Bahy wanted to finish high school and then study to be a nurse.

Before Jacques could talk to Emania, the second smuggler poked through the hatchway and said, "We are leaving now." Then he closed the door. They heard the engine start, then rumble and spit as they pushed from the slip. The overhead light flickered, then shut off, and they drifted into the darkness where they hoped the United States was.

For the next three hours they bounced on the sloped floor as the boat smacked one wave after another at high speed.

Jacques watched young Emania's shadow as she carefully moved from her spot next to him to the top of the platform where she had enough room to kneel on all fours, hoping she could adjust her body to absorb the shocks more effectively. Baby rubbed Emania's leg as they bounced, and the plywood snapped against the platform with each rebound from her weight, making it sound like there were firecrackers exploding inside. Jacques knew she must be sick and waited for her to vomit.

After an hour, the second smuggler opened the hatch and flashed a light in, then directed it on her. "Is she cool?" he yelled over the sound of the motor.

"Yes," Paul said back.

"She better not retch, mon."

Paul stared at the silhouette of the man. The man stayed a few more moments, then backed out and closed the door.

Jacques began to fear that if she vomited they would try to throw her over, and tried to prepare himself for it. He created the scene in his mind while watching Emania: the driver grabbing her from under her arms while the other grabbed her legs, avoiding her kicks. Jacques dug for the courage then, so when they tried to take her he would not freeze in dismay, and would step forward to defend her. Emania never vomited though, or at least not that Jacques could tell.

They reached the coast of Florida in early-morning darkness. The four felt the driver slow the boat and their bodies began to relax some after hours of impacting the waves. Then they heard the sound of sand scraping the bottom and the boat jerked to a stop, sending their torsos forward in unison.

"We must be on the beach," Paul said. The engine was shut off and the hatch opened. The second smuggler, talking above the cursing of the driver, told the four to come up top. Once there, Jacques saw they were not on the beach, but had run aground on a sandbar a hundred yards offshore.

"Get in the water," the man said.

Paul's eyes widened. Bahy put her trembling hand to her heart and shaped her mouth like she was going to make a noise, but nothing came.

"We are not on land yet," Jacques said. "We paid for you to take us to the shore."

"We need you to lighten the weight and help shove the boat off. We're stuck."

"We will not do it," Paul said.

"Didn't you hear me, we're stuck! We're all going to get caught!"

"You get out then too," Paul said.

The driver turned around, shoved the second man out of his way, then rushed up to Paul and seized his arm. He put a pistol to Paul's forehead, moving his wet face and fierce eyes closer, his gun hand shaking. "Get the fuck off the boat," he said, tapping the barrel on Paul's head six times, one for each word that had strained through his clenched teeth.

Paul stared to the man's side, unable to make eye contact. Jacques looked on, pressing his lips together tight in anger. The man breathed hard through his nose, then stepped back from Paul and waved with the gun for all of them to go in the water. Jacques put his legs over the side and hopped in first, finding the sandbar was about two feet below the surface. He helped Emania into the waves carefully, then helped ease Bahy in while Paul held her by her arms from the boat and whispered encouragement. She was so scared she claimed she couldn't use her legs.

"I cannot feel them, Paul. What's holding me up?"

Paul hopped in and the two Haitian men were able to shove the boat afloat again. As it drifted, Jacques jumped to it and clung onto the side to keep it from moving too far, but the second man kicked his fingers off and pointed the pistol at him as the driver started the engine.

They were left alone waist deep in the darkness, listening to the motor grow quieter behind the sound of the crashing surf. They turned and could see the lights of the hotels along the beach across the expanse, and the sky beginning its first shade of dark blue, then hugged themselves and shook from the cold.

"My wife, she cannot swim," Paul said to Jacques.

"You don't know that," Bahy said. "I've never tried."

Paul kept his eyes on Jacques. Jacques met his glance, but didn't know what Paul wanted him to do. He looked at the distant beach.

"We shouldn't try now anyway. I see someone running," Jacques said.

"What?" Bahy was panicked, and pulled Emania close. "They are running to get the police!"

"No, no. They are running for exercise," Jacques said.

"What? Who runs for exercise? Paul, what kind of place are you taking me to?"

"Hush up."

"Do not tell me to hush up."

"We should go on after that runner, before too many people are on the beach," Jacques said.

"She cannot swim," Paul said. His eyes were wide now. He tried to keep his balance against the waves.

Jacques looked at Paul for a few moments. "After I go, please give me at least a half hour before you yell for help."

"No!" Bahy said. "I am not going back to Haiti."

"Hush up." Jacques's and Paul's eyes stayed on each other. Then Paul looked at the water. "We will."

Jacques nodded. Bahy held on to Paul's arm, darting her eyes between them.

Emania swayed with the water a few feet behind. She pointed to the beach and said, "Look!"

Jacques distinguished a man driving an ATV and scanning the water a few feet offshore with a spotlight. They all dropped to their knees, so that the waves frequently covered their backs or knocked them over. Then they heard the sound of a helicopter, but didn't see anything.

"Maybe they are looking for us," Paul said.

Jacques stared at the ATV. He wanted to swim to the beach right then, to get it over with before the sun came. Everybody would see them on the sandbar during the day, the lifeguard, the helicopter, the beachgoers. But the ATV wouldn't leave. The driver finally parked next to a small dark structure on stilts fifty yards down the shore. He would see Jacques cross the beach no problem now, and might have a radio in there. Jacques supposed he could swim, then crawl across the beach. Or even run—they can't catch him with a radio. The water looked dark and wild. He was scared of it. He stayed on the sandbar. They all fought the waves in silence, each trying to figure out their circumstances.

Bahy began protesting again and Paul moved her slowly through the crashing waves to the other side of the sandbar to talk things out, which frustrated Jacques. He wasn't sure he wanted to wait for them, but he couldn't leave while they were away. It would be rude. He cursed once, then remembered Emania was close. She held her crossed arms against her stomach and Jacques knew she must still feel sick.

"Can you swim?" he asked her.

"I think so."

"You'd better know. You might drown."

She was offended. "I can make it. Can you?"

"Yes, but I can't carry you."

She was silent. Then she said, "You don't have to carry me. You don't have to do anything for me." She glanced at the beach and rung out a portion of her T-shirt.

Jacques looked at the water. "Your mother can't swim. Your parents might have to call for help."

"She's not my mother. They are friends of mine."

Jacques didn't respond. He was curious, but didn't want to waste time.

"I am going to swim no matter what they do," she said, then looked at Jacques. "And if I can't make it, you will carry me on your back like a boat." She smiled. Then she seemed to shrug off her nausea and Jacques couldn't get her to stop talking.

She told Jacques that she was the citizen of no country; her parents had emigrated from Haiti to Marsh Harbour, Bahamas before she was born, and then conceived her there. She was not a Haitian citizen, in fact had never been to Haiti, and was refused Bahamian citizenship because her parents were Haitians. She had lived her whole life with her mother and father in a one-room plywood shelter in a crowded ghetto west of Marsh Harbour called Pigeon Pea, until eight months earlier when her parents had died from cholera within a week of each other.

Emania told Jacques that over the seventeen years her father was in the Bahamas, he had worked as a gardener for a large vacation estate, and after nine years had saved enough money to get all three of them to the U.S., but was swindled by smugglers who left him with nothing. He found out later that the three men who cheated him were brothers who never even owned a boat, and who used the money to travel to Las Vegas in the U.S. Her father started over and began saving again, but became paranoid. He kept all their savings in their shelter and wouldn't let his wife and Emania have any friends, scared if anyone found out about the money they would be killed for it. He kept the savings in a steel padlocked box buried three feet deep in the ground beneath the ant-infested carpet, and would dig it up and rebury it every Friday when he was paid. To save money on dinner, he often collected shellfish from the shallow reef on the vacation estate's property for himself and Emania's mother, though Emania refused to eat them. For her, he would buy ramen noodle packages at the convenience store on the way home from the estate and she would boil them and eat separately. It was those shellfish that gave her father cholera, and he died before he could again make enough for all three to be smuggled, refusing to pay even a dollar for simple medical treatments that would have saved him, and with his haggard last words told Emania and her mother not to pay for a funeral.

Afterward, there was enough money for Emania and her mother to hire smugglers, but her mother had become paranoid too without her husband and was afraid to approach a smuggler. She fell sick to cholera (spread either from the shellfish or her husband's vomit) and died before she could arrange anything. The bodies were taken and disposed of by the Bahamian government, and Emania was cleared of having the disease. They wanted to burn her shelter, along with others nearby, but her neighbors had gathered into a mob that wouldn't let the police near. The Bahamians compromised and posted a sign at the entrance to the settlement warning of cholera. No one else there ever caught it.

Then she was alone and had seven thousand dollars, but was too scared to let anyone know. She kept it buried like her father had, and for eight months would occasionally dig it up in the middle of the night and take only small amounts for ramen noodles and wedding-planning magazines. She spent her nights praying like she had with her mother. During the day, she looked in the magazines at cakes, dresses, flowers, and planned for her day; she was to be married within the rose bush–bordered vineyards of the Ledson Winery in Sonoma Valley on a cloudless day—the groom (as of now, a nameless man who better behave himself) arriving on horseback and situating himself under the arch. Then Emania would appear from the winery's castle, striding elegantly to his side, escorted by no one. She had the dress narrowed down to six choices and was going to wait to try them on before a decision, but most likely it would be the Alvina Valenta style #AV3159, the pink one with the side slit and deep cowl back.

"The Avrils said they would find me work somewhere," she told Jacques. "They would help me find a place too. They were able to transfer the rest of my money to Bahy's cousin in the United States."

"You don't know anybody else here?"

"No, do you?"

"No."

"We should stay together then," Emania said. She looked at Jacques firmly, then pulled herself to him so that they held each other. Their faces were close enough that Jacques saw her white eyes through the darkness, saw how desperate she was for someone, anyone, to know and to know her. He saw hope in her eyes too; she could see the Unites States now, it wasn't a myth, and she had a man by her side. He knew she thought the Lord was answering her, affirming she had been right to faithfully wait in solitude. He wanted to pull her close and press her head against his chest and tell her she was right. He wanted to give her a place and a life where she belonged, and could afford the dress. But he couldn't give that. He had been enduring for a long time too, and now it was the only thing he knew how to do; instinct wouldn't let him give, no matter how much he wanted to. He wasn't there yet.

The Avrils were arguing when they drew closer. Bahy still claimed she could swim, but in their twenty years of marriage Paul had never seen her do so.

"It is dumb, Bahy, to drown just because you do not want to go back to Haiti," Paul said.

"I can swim."

"Then swim now. Let's see you swim."

"Where am I going to swim? If I swim, it's going to be to the beach." She sounded angry, but Jacques could see she was crying. Paul took Jacques aside and gave him the contact information card for Bahy's cousin in Weston. It was wet, but still intact, and Jacques put it in his back pocket.

"Let him know we did not make it," Paul said. "Please."

* * *

Before the top of the sun could glimpse over the water, Jacques and Emania began the swim together, and to Jacques's disillusion, were followed by the Avrils.

Once Paul and Bahy jumped into the depths from where they could stand, Bahy had begun swatting the water in hysteria while Paul treaded at her side, trying to calm her and keep her afloat in the current. They both became exhausted, and Paul used all of his remaining energy to hold her in his arms. Bahy responded by halting her frenzy to hold him. She held him so tight that it forced all his air out, but he didn't let go. They sank until they were standing on the sand and coral, and in the darkness she gave him a quick peck on the lips while the surface heaved only four feet above. Their bodies were found still together two days later by a fisherman about a mile north, so bloated that they at first looked like the body of a single strange sea creature being carried in by the tide.

Jacques reached the beach first and ran to the shadows beside a hotel to wait for Emania, and to put on the tennis shoes he had wrapped around his neck for the swim. Five minutes passed and she didn't show. He leaned his face as close to the shadow's edge as he dared and squinted, but couldn't see past the unlit beach to the water. The sound of squeaking wheels echoed off the wall, and he ducked behind a large shrub against the building in time to avoid a cleaning woman pushing her cart. The woman's cell phone rang and she stopped the cart on the concrete path in front of him to spend valuable minutes scolding what must have been her child or husband.

After she moved on, Jacques came out from behind the shrub and saw Emania face down in the sand about thirty feet up the beach, toward the small building on stilts. He began to move in her direction through the knee-high grass along a low fence marking the upper border of the beach, then saw the headlight of the ATV turn on and heard the engine fire. Within seconds, the machine was roaring and bouncing at full speed toward her. Jacques stepped into the darker shadows, then leaned against the hotel building behind him. As he watched, he beat his palms against the concrete until his wrists hurt.

At last he decided there was nothing he could do. He cut through the hotel property and ran west as fast as he could— only stopping while crossing the deserted width of A1A to snatch off his sloshing tennis shoes and throw them into a cluster of shrubs beside a bank. He crossed a canal bridge and found cover in the semidarkness of a strip mall parking lot where the bridge reached the mainland, then keeled over and vomited.

After heaving a few minutes, he walked behind the strip mall and found a faucet on the building in the alley. He drank until he was full, and then washed his face to flush the sea salt taste that was migrating to his mouth from his face and hair. A light wind funneled through the alley and chilled his body under the wet clothes. Part of the sun appeared and poured through the hotels and across the canal. Jacques looked to the direction of the beach.

He tried to conjure the image Emania must have glimpsed as she struggled against the waves with her throbbing lungs and tight heart, choking on saltwater and tears: the silhouette of Jacques reaching land, then springing from all fours and running across the beach in panic. Then the hardness of the dry, dark beach after she had crawled from the waves and waited in exhaustion for Jacques to reappear and take her numb arm into his grip. She had told him she could make it, and she had. She had done her part, and now he was to come forth and carry her on his back, not like a boat then, but like a car or that ATV, all the way to Sonoma Valley. But she did not feel his grip, and not trusting her sense of touch, kept her eyes open slightly to see if she was being carried or dragged. And when she heard the ATV fire up, she must have realized he was truly gone, that he had already begun in America, perhaps had already made his fortune and was happily married. And again she was alone, and so this time gave up. Her face showed no indication, nor did she make a sound—she merely tucked her arms under her head like a pillow and fell asleep, oblivious to the dry sand pasted to the wet on her lips.

Jacques couldn't know what happened after she was found; that she was given a bed in a clean hospital where she slept and was hydrated. That she was questioned days later and admitted to the officials that the middle-aged couple found drowned had been on the sandbar with her, but no one else. That she was transferred to Krome Detention Center outside Miami to be incarcerated for over a year and raped twice before being repatriated to Haiti, where she had never been and knew no one. He couldn't have known all this, but still he dropped his gaze to the tangle of shadows on the concrete behind the strip mall, and began crying.

The ink had bled on the contact card Paul had given him, but the penmanship was still clear. He had seven American dollar bills, folded together and pasty. He washed his face one more time under the faucet, then shook the drops from his fingers and began to walk.

ABOUT THE CONTRIBUTORS

Jill Drumm

KEVIN ALLEN has been a newspaper reporter, and is currently completing his MFA degree at Florida International University, where he also teaches. He is the fiction editor of *Gulf Stream* magazine and has lived in Florida since 1982.

Roland Joynes

PRESTON L. ALLEN, recipient of the State of Florida Individual Artist Fellowship, has authored the novels *Jesus Boy*, *All or Nothing*, and *Hoochie Mama*, as well as the Sonja H. Stone Prize–winning collection *Churchboys and Other Sinners*. He teaches English and creative writing in Miami.

Michele Baker

LYNNE BARRETT, recipient of the Edgar Award for Best Short Story, is the author of *The Secret Names of Women* and *The Land of Go*. Her stories have been anthologized in *A Dixie Christmas*, *Mondo Barbie*, and *Simply the Best Mysteries*. She is coeditor of the anthologies *Birth: A Literary Companion* and *The James M. Cain Cookbook*, *Guide to Home Singing*, *Physical Fitness and Animals (Especially Cats)*.

DAVID BEATY graduated from Columbia College and received his MFA in creative writing from Florida International University. His story "Ghosts" appeared in *The Best American Mystery Stories 2000*.

Jon Deininger

JOHN BOND has written articles and books about poker, real estate, travel, and scuba, and is coauthor of 2005's *Cooke's Rules of Real Poker*. He is a freelance writer, attorney, scuba instructor, boat captain, adjunct professor, realtor, poker player, and raconteur, living in Dania Beach, Florida with his wife Jeannie and their two Shi Tzus.

TOM CORCORAN is the author of five Alex Rutledge mysteries set in the Keys and South Florida. His most recent novel is *Air Dance Iguana*.

JOHN DUFRESNE is the author of three novels, two story collections, and a book on writing fiction. His most recent collection is *Johnny Too Bad*.

ANTHONY DALE GAGLIANO is a personal trainer and part-time English teacher who lives on Miami Beach. He is the author of the novel *Straits of Fortune*.

CAROLINA GARCIA-AGUILERA is the author of eight books, the first six of which are in a series featuring Lupe Solano, a Cuban-American private investigator who lives and works in Miami. Garcia-Aguilera, who is a private investigator herself, has been the recipient of many awards, including the Shamus and the Flamingo.

JAMES W. HALL is the author of fourteen novels, including his most recent, *Magic City*.

Brian Sullivan

VICKI HENDRICKS is the author of the noir novels *Miami Purity, Iguana Love, Voluntary Madness,* and *Sky Blues,* as well as many short stories. She lives in Hollywood, Florida, and teaches writing at Broward Community College. Her latest novel of murder and obsession is *Cruel Poetry.*

Jim Norman

CHRISTINE KLING is the author of the suspense series featuring tugboat captain Seychelle Sullivan. She lives aboard her thirty-three-foot sailboat in Fort Lauderdale.

Alan Weissman

PAUL LEVINE is the author of *Solomon vs. Lord, The Deep Blue Alibi,* and the Jake Lassiter series. He is a former trial lawyer and winner of the John D. MacDonald Fiction Award.

Laura Parker

BARBARA PARKER, best known for her *Suspicion of . . .* series set in Miami, left her legal practice to become a writer. With an MFA in creative writing from Florida International University, she has written twelve novels. Parker lives near the beach in Lauderdale by the Sea.

Chris John

LES STANDIFORD is the author of ten novels, including the John Deal series, and two works of nonfiction, including *Meet You in Hell.* He wrote a chapter of *Naked Came the Manatee,* and edited *The Putt at the End of the World,* a collective novel of golf.

Meredith Baum Tucker

GEORGE TUCKER grew up in the Ozarks of Arkansas, where he hunted for arrowheads in creek beds and cow fields. He received his MFA in creative writing from Florida International University. He is currently at work on his second novel.

Nathalie Targete

JEFFREY WEHR lives and works in South Florida. He is currently working on his first novel.